The Three Miss Margarets

The Three Miss Margarets

A NOVEL

LOUISE SHAFFER

Random House New York

Library of Congress Cataloging-in-Publication Data
Shaffer, Louise.
The three Miss Margarets: a novel / Louise Shaffer.
p.   cm.
ISBN 0-375-50852-X
1. Women—Georgia—Fiction.   2. Female friendship—Fiction.   3. Secrecy—Fiction.
4. Georgia—Fiction.   I. Title.
PS3569.H3112 T48 2003   813'.54—dc21   2002069769

Random House website address: www.atrandom.com

Printed in the United States of America on acid-free paper

98765432

First Edition

For Clara's oldest son,
who provided the faith, the music,
the sounding board, and the love.

And for Mama,
because everything always is.

Acknowledgments

Sometimes you find yourself surrounded by blessings because of the people in your life. That's how it is for me with this book.

Among the miracle folk: first and always, Eric Simonoff, who is not only a savvy, incredible agent, but a caring friend who believed for seven long years that I could write this story. Heartfelt thanks to and for him. And amazing Lee Boudreaux. Whether it's giving the book the perfect edit, or shepherding it to publication with enthusiasm, smarts, and charm that awe me, I'm still waiting to find something this woman doesn't do right. Plus, it's just plain fun to talk to her on the phone.

Then there's a whole new world of people at Random House I am getting to know and be grateful for: Alexa Cassanos, Kate Blum, Tom Perry, Laura Ford, Carol Schneider, Dennis Ambrose, Ivan Held, Libby McGuire, Robbin Schiff, Steven Wallace, Toni Hetzel, Kevin Haberl, Jonathan Schwartz, Eileen Becker, and Dan Rembert. When I tell writers who are more experienced than I that my publisher is Random House, I am greeted with wistful sighs and looks of envy. I now understand why.

Thanks to Cecile Barendsma for getting my book out into the world.

For their patience in educating me, thanks to Cathy Collins, Bee Crews, Marie Shaffer, Brad Shaffer, Susan Varlamaff, Ellie Quester,

Ricky Tyler, Margarett Garret, Kali Lightfoot, Glenn Gordon, Robert Stoney (who spent hours on the phone with a total stranger making Barnsley Gardens bloom long-distance), and Charles Duck, who is watching from somewhere and feels, I hope, that I "done good."

And a special thank you to the ones without whom I can never do anything: Ellen, who is always there; Charlie, who keeps the magic feather aloft; Jefferey; Gerry; my beloved godmother, Aunt Ginny; Cynthia, who stays up all night arguing points of honor, logistics, and grammar; and Christopher and Colin who keep my transplanted southern roots firmly in the ground. By all of these I am truly blessed.

The

Three

Miss

Margarets

Chapter One

S HE'D GONE TO BED with her shoes on, and not by accident. She'd deliberately climbed under the covers fully clothed and pushed her shod feet down between the clean sheets. Because she felt like it. Because she was mad at the world at large and whatever force passed for God in particular. Because it was the kind of thing an icon didn't do. And Margaret Elizabeth Banning, otherwise known as Miss Li'l Bit, definitely qualified as an icon in her little part of the world. Which just went to show that if you lived long enough, any old damn thing could happen to you. At least it could in a place as lacking in a sense of humor as Charles Valley. Humor and memory. There probably weren't five people left in town who remembered that in her youth, at six feet tall, with far more nose than chin and a father who was, to put it politely, different, she had been considered a disaster. Then she was the homely-as-a-mud-fence daughter of the local lunatic who couldn't get herself a man if her life depended on it. Now she was an icon.

"That Miss Li'l Bit," the locals would say, to visitors who'd come to Charles Valley to soak up its southern charm and visit its world-famous horticultural center, "she's the real thing—Old South to her toes. She's a Banning on her daddy's side. They've been here since before the War of Northern Aggression, which is what we like to call it." Pause to allow the listener to chuckle at adorable southern humor. "She still lives in that big old white house that's been in the Banning family since her great-granddaddy bought it in eighteen sixty-eight. Runs it herself, does Miss Li'l Bit, just has that girl Cora come in to do for her twice a week. And she keeps up the Old Justine Gardens too. Well, they're not the originals, you understand, but she redid them close to. The Justine family is famous in these parts. They owned a plantation that covered all of Lawson County until the family lost it during Reconstruction. Miss Li'l Bit's great-granddaddy bought the big house and the gardens around it to keep it from going for taxes. The Justines were his wife's people, cousins a couple of times removed. And Miss Li'l Bit, she keeps the gardens like they were back in the olden days. Why, she's even got some magnolia trees that were put in a hundred years ago." Pause for inevitable tourist response to quaint local eccentricities. "Yes, ma'am, I guess we Southerners do take our history real serious. And Miss Li'l Bit—like I said, she's the real thing."

Well, the "real thing" was lying like a lump under her blankets, wearing the skirt and blouse she'd put on yesterday morning, her support hose, and her second-best pair of Natural Bridge oxfords. Her admirers would be shocked. And if they knew what else she'd done in her time. . . . But she wasn't going to think about that.

She hoisted herself up in bed so she could read the clock on her nightstand. The numbers were insultingly large, meant for eyes that were starting to fail, although of course the salesgirl who suggested it had not said so. Her nap had lasted forty-four minutes. Pleased, she turned off the vanquished alarm. She prided herself on waking before the thing went off, because no clock was going to tell her when it was time to stop sleeping. Especially not tonight. She was in control tonight. She had to be.

Slowly, she pulled herself out of bed, her knees giving her the hard time she'd come to expect. But she wasn't going to coddle them. Tonight there was no such thing as aching joints. Tonight her body would have to perform.

The phone rang. "Yes, Peggy," she said, too quickly to give the caller time to identify herself. Proving she was still in control. Staying a step ahead of the music.

"We're here," said Peggy. Her voice sounded tired, not too young for her age as it usually did. "Maggie's in the cabin. I came out to call you from the car phone."

"I assumed as much." It was indulgent and needlessly showy to have rented a car with a telephone in it, and she'd told Peggy so when she got the foolish thing.

"Do you need me to come get you?" Peggy asked.

"No, I'll be fine on my own."

"It's real cold out, Li'l Bit. Couldn't you please drive?"

"I'll have my flashlight, and I'll take the shortcut over the ridge." Impossible to explain how much she needed the short walk alone in the dark to collect her thoughts.

There was a weary laugh on the other end of the phone.

"What's so funny?" she demanded.

"Maggie said you'd want to walk through the woods. She says when you're alone in the woods that's when you pray."

That was total nonsense. She did not pray—not in the mealy-mouthed way most people meant—she never had and she never would. She left the praying to Maggie, who insisted in believing in her saints and Madonnas in spite of having a first-class mind and an excellent education.

Peggy continued. "That's what we've been doing, Li'l Bit. We've been praying. Maggie gave me her rosary beads and we've been saying that prayer to Jesus' mother. I never thought I could do it tonight, but somehow having those beads in your hands really helps. And it's much easier praying to a woman; at least that's how it feels to me. Maybe I should convert to Catholicism after all these years. What do you think?" She laughed again, and sounded close to tears. Too close.

"Peggy, how much have you been drinking?"

Pause. "Not more than usual. And Maggie's sharp as a tack. She's remembering everything. So if you'll just change your clothes, the three Miss Margarets will be fine."

"I wish you wouldn't use that ridiculous phrase. It makes us sound like a Gilbert and Sullivan trio." No need to address the issue of changing her clothes. Maggie and Peggy knew her too well.

"Li'l Bit, stop stalling. It's not as bad as you're afraid it's gonna be." There were times when Peggy could be unpleasantly clear-sighted. "Just get yourself over here now," she said, and hung up.

Peggy was right. It was time to get on with it. Li'l Bit took a moment to steady herself, then marched into her bathroom, where she'd already laid out her clean clothes. Her freshly ironed clothes, thank you very much.

As she entered the bathroom, a dog the size and color of Gentle Ben heaved herself up from her resting place on top of the heating vent and came over, her long brush of a tail wagging happily. Automatically Li'l Bit reached out in time to save a box of tissues that was perched on the vanity before it went flying.

"Petula's lights are usually on dim," Peggy had said, when she conned Li'l Bit into adopting the half-starved mongrel, "but she'll be a true and believing acolyte. You two need each other." Peggy was ruthless when it came to finding homes for strays that were left at the shelter she had founded; she'd talked poor Maggie into taking three. Peggy named her dogs after performers she had admired over the years. Giving them a little pizzazz, was the way she put it.

"Not now," Li'l Bit said to the dog. "I can't take you for a walk. Go back to sleep." Petula sighed and plopped back down on the vent. Li'l Bit picked up her comb and began to drag it painfully through hair she hadn't touched in days.

It was so like Peggy to turn to the sloppy comfort of Maggie's religion. Well, let them chant over their beads and confess their sins and beg for God's mercy. Li'l Bit would not be joining them. She did not need mercy. And as for praying to God, she sincerely hoped she'd been right all her life and no such being existed. If one did, he or she had much to answer for.

Suddenly the comb became too heavy. She put it down and turned away from the mirror. Petula was still watching her. Li'l Bit lowered herself to the floor, ignoring the grumbling of her knees, and wrapped her arms around the dog's neck, burying her face in thick black fur. But she was not crying. On this night she would not shed one tear.

PEGGY GOT OUT OF THE CAR and looked at the cabin in front of her. In spite of her brave words to Li'l Bit, she needed a minute before going back inside. She leaned back against the car and looked up at the stars. She shouldn't have teased Li'l Bit by bringing up the three Miss Margarets. They'd been called that for as long as anyone could remember, but Li'l Bit hated it. It was the idea of being lumped together that made her so mad. Li'l Bit's fascination with her own uniqueness had always been a pain in the butt. Lately, some of the things she'd been doing were downright weird, like that trick of hers of going to sleep in her clothes. Maggie said it was a form of depression. Well, they were all depressed, and mad, and desperately sad too, but Peggy couldn't see the point in letting yourself go. If anything, she'd been even more careful to keep herself together. She'd had her hair done early that morning before she and Maggie drove to Atlanta. But then she'd always been one for keeping up appearances. So often they were all you had. In her mid-sixties, she was still the perfect size six she'd been when being a size six meant something. She favored the cotton-candy shade of blond that had done so much for Marilyn Monroe's career, fringed her china-blue eyes with black mascara, and accented her still-curvy mouth with a coral lipstick that was specially formulated not to settle into the cracks. No one had ever seen her wearing flats.

She forced herself to look at the cabin again. In the dark, the little house almost looked cozy. You couldn't see the peeling paint and the weeds climbing up onto the porch. The old peach tree dying of neglect in the backyard wasn't visible at night.

The cabin nestled at the foot of a curved ridge that separated Maggie's thirty acres, the eighty-odd acres Li'l Bit owned, and the two hundred and sixty acres Peggy had inherited when she became the widow Garrison. Peggy, Li'l Bit, and Maggie split, not evenly, a pie-shaped piece of land that sat awkwardly in the middle of Highway 22. A dirt road connected the cabin at the center of the wedge with the highway. As was explained in the informative brochure provided to tourists by the Charles Valley Visitors Bureau, all this land had originally been the rolling lawns surrounding the Justine Great House. Back then the might of the family had been such that the road had been split to go around it. The configuration was kept when Highway 22 was put in decades later.

The lawns were long gone, as were the Justines. Over the years Maggie's family had bought the piece she now owned, Li'l Bit's people had acquired the chunk her house sat on, and the rest had been swallowed up by the Garrisons—as had just about everything else in the area. Much of the land between the houses was now a forest of wild pines and kudzu mixed with the remnants of old peach and pear orchards. All that remained of Justine grandeur besides Li'l Bit's house were four huge live oaks, the last of a line of trees that once grew along the top of the ridge. Peggy looked up at them, ancient, silent witnesses to what she—what they all—would be doing that night. She shivered and scanned the ridge instead.

But there was no sign of Li'l Bit's large frame emerging from the darkness. Why did she have to pick this night to go scampering through the forest like some outsized nymph? She had a perfectly good car; she could have driven like a sane person. The last thing they needed on this night was Li'l Bit with a broken leg. Peggy leaned back against the car, lit a cigarette, and tried not to want a drink. She'd deliberately left her engraved thermos (somehow it made being a lush better if your accessories were attractive) back at her house.

Maggie had had the electricity turned on in the cabin so a faint glow was coming from the shuttered windows, and the smell of the wood fire she and Maggie had laid in the fireplace was starting to perfume the air. Had the chimney been cleaned for this night or had Maggie been keeping it up all along? Even though she no longer owned it, Maggie still took care of the cabin. Peggy wished someone would tear the stupid thing down. She wished Li'l Bit would show up. She wished she could have a damn drink.

In the distance a dog started to bark. After a second, several more joined in. She sighed; they were probably hers. She had twelve dogs in residence at the moment. The Historical Society crowd was very upset with the way she let her darlings run free in the house, which was a Garrison home and therefore a shrine.

Once in the early eighties there had been talk about having the place turned into some kind of landmark, on the grounds that it was the largest log house in the nation, but the whole thing came to nothing when it was discovered that a country singer in Nashville had built a bigger one. So her babies continued to run the hallowed halls, scratching up the foyer with doggy toenails and periodically peeing on sacred heart-pine floors. A large wooden sign outside her home proclaimed it to be GARRISON COTTAGE, a form of old-money understatement she had once found enchanting. Presidents and prime ministers had slept under that eight-thousand-square-foot tin roof; there were brass plaques on the doors of the bedrooms to prove it. Sonny and Cher, her two pit bull–husky mixes, slept in the room some ambassador from France had used when he stayed with the Garrisons in the fifties. The three-legged black Lab puppy she'd named Elvis swam in the pool where FDR had taken his daily exercise.

Peggy stubbed out her cigarette carefully in the dirt driveway. All they needed was a fire tonight. Funny to think that as ambivalent as she was about her home now—and there were days when she really hated it—there had been a time when she had wanted it enough to pay any price for it. Be careful what you wish for, children.

The barking trailed off. The cabin still loomed in front of her. And the night still stretched out ahead of them. It wasn't right to leave Maggie on her own this long. She took a deep breath and started toward the cabin, then stopped. Just a few minutes more, she told herself. She lit another cigarette and looked up at the stars again.

INSIDE THE CABIN, Maggie closed the bedroom door behind her and moved into the living room. The important thing was to keep focused, she told herself. Just think about one thing at a time. And stay in the present. No wandering back to the past and getting lost in days long gone. There would be no escaping tonight, though normally she believed in it with all her heart. Escapism, denial, and the occasional lie were the Holy Trinity of survival as far as she was concerned. To hell with the psychiatrists. Let them live to be eighty-six, then they could talk to her. The fact was, she'd always been tougher than she looked. When you were not quite five feet tall, had never weighed more than ninety-seven pounds, and had a face that had once been described as doll-like, people tended to underestimate you—which was a big mistake.

She looked around the room, checking to see if she'd missed a dust ball or a spiderweb when she'd cleaned it. It was spotless. But it was all wrong, because it was empty. If she closed her eyes for just a minute, Maggie could see it the way it should be, with the things that belonged there. There were four kitchen chairs and a wooden table with a red linoleum top in one corner, a sagging bed that served as both a sofa and place to sleep rammed against the wall. Tossed over it, a hand-stitched quilt pieced together from scraps of denim, blue jeans, and overalls that had become too frayed to mend, and backed with old flour sacks; the antiques dealers who descended on Charles Valley every weekend would pay a fortune for that quilt today. A rag rug—also handmade—protected the precious wood floor, and dominating the center of the back wall was an old Philco cabinet radio purchased secondhand after electricity was installed in the cabin. Those were the things that belonged in this room. She could see it all clear as day, and she could hear the voices laughing. But she mustn't let herself. Not now. Later would be time enough to escape. Now she had to be clear.

She moved to the window and looked out at Peggy standing next to the car. The poor thing still hadn't gotten up the nerve to come back in. Well, it was only natural. She was the youngest of the three of them, and she hadn't had as much time to toughen. Besides, Peggy never had been as strong as she and Li'l Bit were.

Maggie was feeling very strong tonight. She was a little light-headed, and her heart was fluttering. But given the fact that it had been broken, it was doing well to beat at all.

She pulled away from the window and looked back at the bedroom. It wasn't empty. It was fully equipped.

When she first joined the Roman Catholic Church it was the Agnus Dei that attracted her, a mantra of forgiveness that seemed to her to be the heart of her new faith. The priests said it in Latin then, the majesty of the language giving it a power that was reassuring in those years when she had been so young and needy. The words floated through her mind now.

Agnus Dei, qui tollis peccata mundi, miserere nobis.

"Lamb of God, You take away the sins of the world, have mercy upon us."

But would He? Or had they finally gone too far? The fluttering in her chest pushed up to her throat; the light-headedness became a roaring in her ears. Palpitations, she diagnosed, good doctor that she was. A reduction of stress was what she would prescribe. Her mind made a frantic dash for safety, away from this empty room back to the time when it had been the center of a home. Back to the time when two young girls rolled back the rag rug and danced the Charleston on the wood floor.

That was when it had all begun for her. That was the time that had made her different. Because she and Peggy and Li'l Bit were all different. That was why they had been able to do what they had done. And it was why, after so many years, they were able to do what they were going to do now. Maggie sighed and closed her eyes. It had all come full circle, and it was right to have it happen here in this cabin, where they had made decisions and changed lives. For the better, she prayed. *Agnus Dei, qui tollis peccata mundi, miserere nobis.*

And now the circle was complete. Except for the one loose end they'd never been able to fix. Except for the girl.

"Maggie?" Peggy's gentle voice yanked Maggie back from her thoughts. She blinked and saw Li'l Bit and Peggy standing in the doorway of the cabin. Peggy was looking like she'd love to run. Behind her, Li'l Bit was trying to be stoic and succeeding except for her eyes.

"Are you okay, Maggie?" Peggy asked.

She nodded. Of course she was. Now that they were together she was fine. "I was just thinking," she said.

Chapter Two

THE NIGHTLY SHIFT OF GEARS at the Sportsman's Grill was starting. The family-dinner crowd was going home to their regular dose of domestic boredom or bliss, and the serious drinkers were moving to the bar. Denny and his band were setting up to start playing. And Laurel Selene was nicely, though not excessively, drunk.

She hadn't planned it that way. She'd gone home after work, decided she was too tired to rustle up anything for herself, and gone out to grab a quick bite—a burger and fries and one beer. But just when she was about to order a cup of after-dinner coffee, Ed had walked in. Sheriff Ed Hood, her ex-lover: he of the glinting eyes, the slow-moving smile, and the still admirable butt of a high school jock who had not yet totally gone to seed. Also he of the fourteen-year marriage to Cathy Sue, mother of his sons, who were the reason why he couldn't ever make an honest woman—his words, not hers—of Laurel. So he had dumped her six weeks ago, even though he loved her dearly and would rather cut off his right hand than hurt her.

Which, if she was honest about it, he really hadn't. The main reason she had stayed with him for six years, besides the semi-tight butt, was the fact that Cathy Sue had her pink acrylic claws in him for life. The thought of Ed suddenly divorced and available was enough to make Laurel break out in hives. Let Cathy Sue fetch his Saturday-afternoon beers and raise his gargantuan sons while holding down a full-time job running her gift shop and smiling gamely throughout it all. At least when Laurel got him for long lunches at the Breezy Pines Motel, he brought the sandwiches.

So it wasn't the fact that Ed had come into the Sportsman's Grill with Cathy Sue and the kids that set her off. Laurel had been watching that pretty picture for years and figuring that there but for the grace of God went she. It wasn't the way he delicately put his arm around his wife and guided her into the booth like she was made of glass. It wasn't the way he smiled his magic smile at Cathy Sue or the sparkle in her eyes, even after all these years, when she smiled back. Ed would use that smile on anything female that moved, and Cathy Sue had been sparkling publicly since the days when she was head cheerleader for Charles Valley High.

No, what made Laurel cancel the coffee and go for another Bud was the wink he sent her over his wife's shoulder as Cathy Sue checked her lip gloss in her little hand mirror. It said he figured he could get Laurel back anytime he wanted. And given the way she'd messed up her life, plus the slim pickings testosterone-wise in Charles Valley, he was right. It depressed the shit out of her.

So she had a second beer at the bar, which soon became a third, and by the time the Husband of the Year had called for his check she was working up to a half dozen, and little bubbles of pissed-off were rising inside her like yeast working its way through bread dough. Soon she was gonna have a big explosion of ugly, as her ma used to say. And Christ, if she was thinking of Sara Jayne she really was in trouble.

Mitch, the college kid who tended bar on weekends, broke into her internal riff. "Who the hell is that?" He did a little nodding thing with his chin that indicated something behind her. She turned and focused, after a second, on the front door. A stranger had entered. A man in his late forties was her guess. He was obviously out of his element, but he didn't seem bothered by it. He scanned the room calmly, then headed for the bar.

Strangers were not a novelty in Charles Valley. The town was home to a world-famous botanical garden called, naturally enough, Garrison Gardens. It boasted, in addition to the Garrison Center for Horticultural Research, a thirty-thousand-acre forest called the Garrison Nature Preserve. Over the years the Garrison nurseries had developed over forty new hybrids of azaleas. For this and other achievements it had received a variety of awards from university agricultural departments and environmental groups that covered two walls of the Garrison Gardens Visitors Center.

On a less exalted and more lucrative note, Garrison Gardens also offered its guests the Garrison Golf Course, Garrison Lake for swimming and boating, the Garrison Country Store, the Garrison Patio Restaurant, the Garrison Recreational Vehicle Campground, weekly rental units in the Garrison Chateaux, and a sprawling hotel built out of heart-pine logs called the Garrison Lodge. The entire enterprise was known to the locals simply as "the resort." Attaching themselves to the resort and feeding off its leavings like pilot fish surrounding a great white shark were an army of gift shops, art galleries, antiques marts, crafts stores, restaurants, bed-and-breakfasts, and motels, which the trustees of Garrison Gardens allowed to stay in existence as long as they did not offer serious competition to the mother operation.

So Laurel and Mitch were used to visitors in sherbet-colored leisure wear wandering around their town asking stupid questions. Strangers were accepted by the locals as a necessary evil, to be smiled at during peak months, courted during down months, and silently cursed when the roads were clogged with traffic during azalea season.

But this man was not the usual resort visitor. For starters, he had wandered off the reservation. The Sportsman's Grill was strictly a hangout for locals. The beer was American, the only water served came from the tap, and there was no low-fat vegetarian entrée. Resort guests usually took one look at the menu and ran.

Then there was the matter of the stranger's clothes. The golfers, hikers, and wildlife aficionados who came to the resort prided themselves on their casual vacation attire. Shorts and rubber flip-flops appeared regularly in the four-star Patio Restaurant at the Lodge. But the mystery man was wearing a jacket, a long-sleeved shirt, and the kind of soft leather loafers that appeared on the pages of men's magazines.

"Sign on the door says dinner's from six to nine. Is it too late for me to get something to eat?" he asked, in the accent all America knew from television. Mitch shot Laurel a look. They had themselves an honest-to-God New York City boy.

"Waal, Ah thank we got some frahs 'n' wangs left, yew wunt summun to looknsee?" Mitch slurred his words, slow and dumb, the way they all did when talking to Yankees, so as not to disappoint them. The man smiled. Not a slow heart-melting smile, it was quick and knowing, as if somehow he could tell Mitch had a four-point grade average and the redneck routine was a crock.

"Sounds good," he said. "And I'll have a Johnnie Walker Red." Mitch sent a waitress off for the wings while he got the drink, and the New Yorker calmly continued to survey his surroundings. Through her mist Laurel eyed him. He had the wiry build of a jogger, which was not a good sign. It could mean he was one of the tribe of lunatics who puffed along the side of Highway 22 breathing in truck fumes every Sunday morning. On the other hand, he didn't have one of those fake tans some of them got in their fancy gyms. His face was on the bony side, with strong features, a nose that was a little too large to let him be really handsome, and a full mouth. His hair, which was mostly gray, was cut short enough to be either practical or fashionable. His eyes were the most compelling thing about him. Deep-set, under dark lashes, they were a pale blue-gray, like the eyes of a dog that has wolf blood in it. She wondered what he'd be like in bed, which didn't mean anything; she wondered what every man would be like in bed. Although, when she had enough beer on board she was more likely to try to find out. She was getting to the point of no return now, so this would be a fine time to pay her bill and get her butt out of here. Except that Ed was heading out the door with his family. And as he went he frowned at her, in a way that said he had caught her checking out the stranger and was not amused. That was more than enough reason to have another beer and hang around. She ordered it.

Mitch set a huge platter of wings in front of Wolf Eyes, who looked a little dismayed at the pile, but gamely started to eat. Laurel checked herself out in the mirror over the bar. She was wearing her standard Friday-night eating-out ensemble, a scoop-neck T-shirt tucked into jeans, with a wide belt, and her red cowboy boots. It was a look that suited her; it showed off her small waist, good boobs, and long legs. She liked her body, although she never did anything to keep it in shape, so someday it would probably go lumpy and soft like her ma's had. But for now it was still good enough to get looks when she walked into a room. She might have gotten more if she'd been willing to fool around with makeup and hot rollers, but she didn't have the patience. She usually pulled her red hair back with a rubber band, although she had been known to use a barrette if she was feeling the need to be dressy. Her face was composed mostly of circles: round cheeks, round mouth, round brown eyes, and a rounded nose. It was an old-fashioned country face, the kind people never could quite remember. Which was okay. She had ways of being memorable when she wanted to be.

Wolf Eyes had pushed his food away. The grease factor in the Grill's cuisine quickly separated the men from the boys. Laurel watched him. He had good hands, and that full mouth had a firmness that would be real fine for kissing. But she needed him to turn around and take notice of her so she could gauge what was going on in those pale eyes.

As if on cue, he did. The look he gave her was steady, and he didn't duck when she returned it. A few seconds passed, or maybe it was a year or two, it was hard to say. And then there it was, that little jolt of electricity that went through her when she knew a man was on the loose and he knew she was and possibility was suddenly in the air. The night was definitely looking up. On the other hand, it was also early. She was sober enough that a voice inside her head was saying that proving a point to Ed might not be worth whatever else she'd be getting herself into. But there was that mouth. And that jolt. She picked up her beer and headed to where Denny and the boys were playing. She could feel the New Yorker's pale eyes following her as she went.

Mitch had turned out the lights over the restaurant tables so the band was in the only bright spot in the room. She stood on the edge of the pool of light and hummed along for a couple of moments as they wandered through a popular anthem to love gone wrong.

"Hey, Denny, you trying to put these good folks to sleep?" She raised her voice so it cut over the music. Denny rocked in time to his own guitar and asked mildly, "You got a problem, girl?" The regulars in the room started perking up. Laurel ragging on Denny was a favorite Friday night routine.

"Yeah, it's you and this crossover shit. You forget how to play God's music?" There was a pause; then Denny swung out of Garth Brooks's latest and pulled the band into Hank Williams's old foot-stomping celebration of party time on the bayou. Laurel stayed out of the light and began to sing in the husky alto that was her next best feature, right after her boobs and legs. Then Denny eased over to her and she eased over to him, and finally they were sharing the mike.

"Jambalaya, crawfish pie, filé gumbo." She sassed out the words as Denny's guitar did a good imitation of fiddle riffs, and Ricky on the drums set up the beat of an old-time Cajun two-step. "Son of a gun, we'll have big fun on the bayou." Denny's hoarse tenor came in on the harmony under her, driving her and carrying her; then she took the top over his melody and drove him, and Lord, it was like really good sex. The crowd was feeling the heat, a couple started dancing, and the New Yorker was watching her in the darkness.

Denny went into bridge of the song and she quit singing to give the band some space to stretch out. Now she was dancing, her feet and hips moving inside the beat and on top of it. She was drinking and dancing and Wolf Eyes was watching and they were gonna have big fun, son of a gun, and then she felt the wetness as she accidentally dumped her whole damn mug of beer down her front. The cold shocked her stock-still, and she looked down at the sopping T-shirt plastered to her breasts. She had started to step out of the light when something came flying at her from the darkness and landed at her feet. It was Wolf Eyes's pricey sports jacket. She looked out and saw he had moved to the front of the crowd and was standing in front of her in his shirtsleeves wearing a shit-eating grin. So without taking her eyes off him she began to peel off the wet T-shirt. He stopped grinning and started watching hard. She didn't know how far she would have gone, but then there were whistles from the crowd and Ricky started doing a stripper roll on the rim of the drum, so of course she had to make a joke out of it. She did a few bumps and grinds, which got her a round of applause. Denny pulled himself back from whatever planet it was that music took him and she heard rather than saw him pick up the jacket from the floor just in case she was drunker than he thought she was and he had to throw it around her fast. Wolf Eyes kept on watching, daring her, as she finally pulled off her shirt and tossed it into the crowd, and Denny slid the jacket on her before half the people in the place realized they were out of luck because she was wearing a bra that night. It was just her little black lace half bra, to be sure, but it wasn't what a certain element had been hoping for. Catcalls and boos and more laughter from the crowd as somebody rushed up to hand her another beer, and Denny started to play again, and as if nothing had happened she picked up singing where she'd left off.

After that, things got kind of blurry. With the band behind them, she and Denny sang all the good old songs they'd learned from listening to records with his gran when they were kids. They went from Hank Williams to Loretta Lynn to Tanya Tucker to Mother Maybelle Carter and Johnny Cash. Then Mitch left, the band packed up and split, and the crowd thinned out till only the hardcore Friday night regulars were left. Wolf Eyes hung in, still watching her. She and Denny were alone on the stage. Denny handed her a guitar and started playing soft and sweet "Just a Closer Walk with Thee." He was singing and murmuring the key changes so she could chord with him. She found the harmony and everyone joined in on the chorus. Then the whole room sang "Amazing Grace" and "I Saw the Light" and "How Great Thou Art," with a few hitting the high note on *art* and the rest cutting out like they did in church on Sunday. Even Wolf Eyes tried to sing along, going lah-lah-lah when he didn't know the words, which was most of the time. And she knew tomorrow it would be all over town that she'd been singing hymns in the Sportsman's Grill, drunk as a skunk, with her titties hanging out of some strange man's jacket. But at that moment it was worth it to be flying so high and feeling so good.

When she got to the parking lot after Denny finally closed down the bar, Wolf Eyes was waiting for her.

"Thought I'd drive you home," he said, as if it was already arranged between them that he was going with her, which in a way it was. And she damn sure wasn't going to whatever hotel he was staying at because there wasn't one in town where some member of the staff hadn't gone to grammar school with her, and there was just so much gossip she wanted to generate in one night. On the other hand, her place was way outside of town, which meant she'd have to keep him around long enough in the morning to get her back to her car. And the long drive out there would mean they'd have to talk and that would spoil everything. She didn't want to know he was a dentist back home, or an insurance salesman, didn't want to know why he'd decided to come slumming in a local joint tonight. She didn't want to start guessing how many kids he had or why his wife didn't come with him. Mostly she didn't want to hear the lies he'd tell her or the ones she'd tell him. Tonight she was in a hot-air balloon floating high above everything, and if this nice stranger would just stay a stranger she could make it through the night without coming down.

So she nodded without saying a word, hoping that would give him a hint how the night should go, and followed him to his rented SUV. "Pussy-whipped trucks," Denny called them. But it was better than a convertible. Yankees usually rented convertibles when they came to Georgia, even in November. As soon as they got south of Pennsylvania they thought they were in the tropics.

"I'm Josh," he said, as he helped her climb into his wannabe truck.

"Laurel Selene," she said. It was the first time they'd actually spoken to each other all night.

She told him to turn left out of the parking lot and warned him that her house was twenty minutes away in the middle of a forest. He said fine and they drove in silence for several minutes and it looked like they were gonna be quiet all the way, for which she offered up a quick thank-you-Jesus. Her balloon was nicely in place. He really wasn't her type, but for tonight he was Lancelot and

Romeo and Sir Walter Raleigh offering her his sports coat. She'd love him forever if he'd just keep his mouth shut now and not be perky in the morning.

Then he ruined everything by saying, "You're good, you know. You and that guy you were singing with."

"We just fool around." She tried to shrug him off.

"You sounded pretty smooth to me. Ever think about turning pro?"

"Once—a million years ago. But we dropped it."

"Why?"

Her balloon was sinking fast. "You always ask so many questions?"

For some reason that seemed to amuse him. "Sometimes," he said. "So why did you drop it?"

What was he trying to do, turn this into prom night? I'm a girl you picked up in a white-trash bar, she told him silently. You don't need to know my life story.

But out loud she said, "We were gonna go to Nashville once. Be big stars. Some guy who was staying at the resort heard us and said he wanted us to come and try out for this club he owned."

"What happened?"

"We never got there."

"Why?"

Didn't he know how to talk without asking questions? What was it about him that made her keep answering them?

"We were scared shitless. So Denny got stoned and drove our pickup into an embankment on I-Eighty-five. We were lucky we weren't killed. The good news was, that time when his family put Denny into rehab, it took. He's been clean ever since." The bad news was, the newly careful twelve-step-alumnus Denny never talked about leaving town again. Now he did his music in the Sportsman's Grill, which happened to be his daddy's bar.

Josh threw her a glance. "Where did that leave you?"

"Here."

"You couldn't go to Nashville without him?"

"Music was Denny's dream, not mine."

"What's yours?"

"I don't dream. I just wanted to get the hell out of town."

She leaned back and closed her eyes to show him the conversation was over. The SUV drove smooth. Not like her ancient Camaro, which registered every bump in the road. This was like riding in a steel womb. She was starting to drift. Maybe if he'd just keep his mouth shut she could get her balloon back in the air before they got to her place.

"Before you pass out on me, where are we going?" asked the irritating voice next to her.

"I'm not gonna pass out. I was resting my eyes."

"Uh-huh. Where are we going?"

"Stay on this road. It'll split down either side of a chunk of land that's shaped like a piece of pie." For a second, she thought he gave her a strange look. But he didn't say anything, so she figured she imagined it. "There will be a sign saying GARRISON NATURE PRE-SERVE with arrows pointing to the left and right. The piece of pie sits in the middle of the nature preserve. When you see the sign, bear right. You with me so far?"

"Yeah. I got a wedge of land shaped like a piece of pie on my left and whole lot of nature on my right. What does a nature pre-serve look like, by the way?"

"Trees. And there's lots of wildlife. You'll pass two houses on your left. The first one will be behind a big stone fence and the gate will say GARRISON COTTAGE big enough for you to see it in the dark. The second one will look like Scarlett O'Hara should come running down the front steps, and there will be a lot of magnolias in front of it."

"You live in Tara?"

"I live across the highway from Tara. In the nature preserve."

"With the wildlife."

"I find it soothing."

"Okay."

"About five hundred feet past Tara, you'll see a dirt road that crosses the highway. Turn right and go into the Nature Preserve. My house is in there. There will now be a short quiz."

"Pass Tara, turn on the opposite side of the highway."

"Just make sure you don't turn on the Tara side and go into the wedge."

"Got it. Why are you living in a nature preserve? Isn't the whole point to preserve the place for nature?"

She sighed. The world was full of men who didn't want to communicate. Why the hell did she have to wind up with one who did? "It's a long story."

"We seem to have a lot of time."

"Not long enough. This is the South. You need a map, a score-card, and a family Bible to follow one of our stories."

He seemed to be satisfied with that. So just to prove she could rest her eyes for a few minutes and not fall asleep, she closed them again. This time Josh Wolf Eyes didn't disturb her.

PEGGY LEANED AGAINST THE WALL and watched Maggie and Li'l Bit move around the cabin bedroom. They looked oddly graceful, like dancers in a sad ballet. For a month the room had been equipped as a makeshift hospital room, waiting for the moment when it would be needed. That moment had come, and they had done what they promised they would do. Now her two friends seemed beautiful and almost otherworldly as each brought the night to a close in her own way. Maggie finished the last prayer of her rosary, crossed herself, and bent over the figure on the bed. "Rest now, dear one," she murmured, so softly it made Peggy's heart ache. Li'l Bit reached across the bed to pull the sheet up, but she couldn't make herself cover the face. Instead, she folded the sheet gently, as if she was tucking in a child. She bent over to kiss the cheek and Peggy thought she heard her whisper, "I'm sorry." They turned to Peggy and it was her turn. She moved to the bed and said the only thing she could: "Good-bye."

LAUREL AWAKENED BECAUSE THE CAR had started bumping. Which had to mean they'd turned onto the dirt road that led to her place. She shook herself and looked out the window for familiar landmarks. There was an oak with a broken branch that should be coming up, and then a hole in the dirt road that could bust your shocks. But there was no oak branch. And the ground never cut out from under them.

"Josh," she said, "this isn't the way to my place; you turned wrong."

He kept on driving.

"Did you hear me? We're going the wrong way. You turned next to Tara instead of across from it." He slowed down but kept going. Ahead of them she could see the Justine Oaks clearly silhouetted against the sky. Suddenly he stopped the car, cut off the lights, and sat staring ahead.

"What are you doing?"

"Look there." She followed his gaze, and there it was: the cabin. "There's someone inside," he said.

"You're crazy. That old wreck has been deserted for ye—" she started to say, then trailed off because she saw what couldn't be, but was—a faint gleam coming from the windows. Someone had turned on the lights.

It had to be kids who had broken in, or maybe tramps. Either way they'd have to report it. Which meant by noon the whole damn town would know she'd been wandering around the woods with the stranger from New York. Just in case there were two or three people left by that time who weren't talking about her performance in the bar.

The lights went out in the cabin, and a flashlight beam passed by one of the windows, moving from the back of the cabin to the front. A second beam joined it and then a third. Three people came out and stood on the porch. And even though it was too far away and too dark to see their faces, she recognized the figures that were silhouetted by the flashlights. One was tiny and ramrod straight, one was mid-sized, and one was so tall she'd had to duck her head going through the door. The three Miss Margarets were hanging out in the cabin in the middle of the night! At least she wouldn't have to report them to the cops. The three Miss Margarets went anywhere they wanted to. And besides, Dr. Maggie took care of the cabin. But there was a car in the drive in front of it, which meant the ladies would get in it, come down the drive, and find them.

"Josh—" she started, but before she could tell him they had to go, he had turned the SUV around much more neatly than she would have thought possible without switching on the lights, and they made their way back to the highway in darkness.

FOR A MOMENT PEGGY THOUGHT she heard a car pull away, but there were no headlights so she decided her mind was playing tricks on her. Neither Maggie nor Li'l Bit seemed to hear it, but then there were many things they didn't hear these days. She looked at their weary faces. Maggie had held up beautifully all night, but now she looked so frail a puff of wind could blow her away. Li'l Bit seemed to have gotten bigger and heavier, as if grief had swelled her like a sponge. Impulsively Peggy reached out to hug her, and Li'l Bit held on for dear life. Then they each hugged Maggie, and it was partly for comfort and partly because no one could bear to leave. Peggy wanted to say something that would help, something that would be wise and important. But when she opened her mouth, all she could get out was, "It's late; why don't you let me drive you home?" And she wondered when the hell she'd become the practical one.

Li'l Bit shook her head, and Maggie said softly, "I think we both need to walk," and Peggy knew there was no talking either of them out of it. So she and Maggie watched as Li'l Bit trudged back up the ridge with the light from her flashlight flickering in front of her. Then Maggie reached up to pat Peggy's cheek and say, with a whisper of a smile, "It'll be all right, Peggy dear, you'll see." And then she was gone too, picking her way through the remains of the pecan grove that had once surrounded her house, the beam from her flashlight lighting the way ahead of her. Peggy waited again until the light vanished; then she made herself leave the porch and walk to the car. But she couldn't go just yet. She leaned against the car and stared up at the Justine Oaks without seeing them.

JOSH DROVE IN SILENCE, and except for telling him when to turn, Laurel kept her mouth shut. Seeing the old cabin had driven away the last wisps of her lovely high. Standing on its porch tonight were three of the four remaining heavy hitters on her ma's hate list. Add old Lottie, and you'd have all the ones who were still alive, right there at the cabin where it all began.

According to some stories, Lottie's family had lived in it since they were slaves on the Justine plantation. But Laurel never put much stock in that. More likely they'd moved in when Lottie's mama and daddy started working for Dr. Maggie's family. Now the cabin belonged to Lottie. Dr. Maggie had given it to her shortly after her own parents died. And Miss Li'l Bit had put in the dirt road that ran from the cabin to the highway. Laurel was on top of this history, because when she was a kid, her ma would get tanked and go on and on about it, for reasons Laurel didn't understand.

Lottie had raised her daughter, Nella, in that cabin. Then Nella and her husband came back to live with Lottie and raise their daughter—until all hell broke loose and Nella's husband died and Nella left town with the child. Then Lottie lived in the cabin on the side of the ridge alone. And now Lottie was in an advanced-care facility that was much too PC to call itself a nursing home, and the cabin was empty. At least it had been until tonight.

Chapter Three

WALKING HOME FROM THE CABIN might not have been such a good idea, Maggie realized, as she began to shiver. She hadn't dressed warmly enough, or maybe it was shock setting in. She should have let Peggy drive her. But just as she was starting to get nervous, her house was in front of her, looming up out of the darkness with the magnolia trees on either side and crowding too close. It was a disgrace the way she'd let the pruning go.

"You can make it," she told herself. "You'll be fine." There was one more pecan tree ahead of her, the big one she always thought of as Lottie's tree. Once she was past it, she'd be in the backyard. She walked under the tree, her feet crunching the rotten nuts that had fallen on the ground because she never thought of harvesting them anymore.

IN THE OLD DAYS when the pecans were ready to fall, Lottie's daddy, Ralph, who was the caretaker on the farm, would hire a couple of workmen for the day. They'd spread soft old white sheets on the ground under the trees and shake the branches with poles while the nuts fell to the ground. It was Lottie's job to climb up to the limbs the men couldn't reach and bounce on them until the rest of the nuts came down.

One autumn when Lottie was up in the big tree working, Maggie waited until no one was watching and climbed up to help her. At first she was scared being up so high, but Lottie showed her how to brace herself against the tree trunk and she was fine.

"Look, Maggie," Lottie said, and pointed down at the world below them. There were the sweet-potato fields, her mama's kitchen garden, and the rest of the pecan grove, all spread out at her feet. This was glory indeed. Up until that moment it had belonged to Lottie alone, but now Maggie was sharing it. Life, she felt, didn't get much better than that.

They began bouncing on the branches, and soon the pecans fell like large green hailstones. They were getting the job done in half the time it usually took Lottie, and Maggie was feeling terribly proud, when a scream cut through the still morning air. Mama had seen Maggie in the tree and came running from the house, yelling that it wasn't safe. Ralph, seeing his home and his family's only source of income disappearing before his eyes, began a frantic climb up the tree to get Maggie. Because he looked so scared, she came down to where he could reach her, and soon she was in her weeping mama's arms. No one seemed to notice that there was another little girl in the tree.

Years later, Maggie realized Ralph had never said it wasn't safe for his own daughter to shake the pecans down because he was afraid to, and she wondered what had gone through Lottie's mind while she was up in the tree, alone and ignored. But at the time, Maggie looked up at Lottie still high in her perch and took it as a token of her friend's total superiority to her humble self. Lottie was the leader in all their games, bigger, stronger, and smarter than she, so it made sense that Lottie was allowed to stay up in the sky, mistress of all she surveyed, while Maggie was brought back to the ground.

After the nuts were gathered, the men took them to the kitchen where Lottie's mama, Charlie Mae, set Maggie and Lottie to the task of hulling them and picking out the meat.

To Maggie the kitchen was a place of alchemy where Charlie Mae took raw ingredients and turned them into high rich cakes and pies oozing with fruit and spice. "That child should have been born a darky," Mama said, when talking about Maggie's fascination with all things culinary. But that wasn't the only reason Maggie helped. The more work she did, the sooner Lottie would be finished with her chores and they could ramble off on their endless rounds of the farm and the forests that surrounded it.

Lottie hated kitchen chores. Worst of all she hated hulling pecans, because it was fussy work, and her hands were too big for it. But the results were worth it because when the nuts lay in a mound on the wooden counter, Charlie Mae would use them in the fruitcakes Maggie's mama gave as Christmas presents every year. The recipe had been in Mama's family for generations, and something must have gotten left out, because the cakes were nasty. But Mama handed them out like crown jewels.

The finished fruitcakes might be awful, but the raw batter was ambrosia to Lottie, who loved sweets. The girls had an elaborate system worked out for stealing it. They waited until Charlie Mae had beaten the butter, sugar, and eggs into a pale yellow fluff. Then Maggie would find the sharpest knife in the drawer and say, "Charlie Mae, let me chop the fruit." While Charlie Mae dropped everything to grab the knife away from her, Lottie would stick a cup into the bowl, scoop out a heaping mound of the rich mess, and hide it in the pantry. Later they would retrieve it and share the sugary goo. Maggie was never sure whether it was the crime they pulled off or the booty itself that pleased Lottie so much. They both knew Lottie never could have done it on her own. Maggie was Lottie's protection against Charlie Mae's belt. If Charlie Mae had caught Lottie messing up Miss Carolyn's Christmas cakes she would have beaten her, but if Maggie was in on it they'd get off with a tongue lashing.

So it had started way back then, Lottie using Maggie to get what she couldn't get on her own, and Maggie accepting it because, for reasons that were impossible to understand, the world was set up so Lottie needed her.

THE PECAN TREE was behind Maggie. It wouldn't be long now. A minute later she reached the six steps that led up to the back porch of the house. Using the railing more than she usually had to, she climbed them and let herself in.

She went through the kitchen into the living room, where she turned on the gas logs she'd had installed in her fireplace. A real fire might be romantic, but at her age she wasn't about to mess with kindling and ashes. She collapsed gratefully into her old wingback chair. From her bed on the floor her dog, an aged sheepdog and chow mix, got up and moved over to lie down on Maggie's feet. Laverne's litter mates, Patty and Maxine, had gone on to the great front lawn in the sky, and for the first time Peggy wasn't trying to con her into taking in any more strays. She was probably afraid a young dog would outlive Maggie. The good Lord knew Maggie felt old right now, old and aching with tears she didn't have the energy to cry. But it was all right. Because she'd seen everything through as Lottie would have wanted her to. Over the years she had failed Lottie, because there were things she couldn't control. But she hadn't failed tonight. There was comfort in that.

JOSH TURNED THE SUV into Laurel's drive. They passed under the hanging oak branch and he swerved neatly to avoid the huge hole, while Laurel tried to make her mind a blank. A lost cause; it was now full of the cabin and memories of old Lottie.

IN THE BEGINNING, she had liked Lottie. When her ma was on a bender, lying on her bed too drunk to work, Lottie always seemed to know it. And just about the time that the groceries were running low and Laurel was getting really scared, there would be a knock on the door and Lottie would be standing there with a sack of sweet corn and beans from her garden so there would be something to fix for supper. Sometimes when Sara Jayne took off for a week or two, there would be tomato sandwiches dripping with mayonnaise or biscuits and cornbread wrapped up in a clean napkin.

"Thought you could use this," Lottie would say, without smiling, and turn and leave as Laurel called out *thank you* to her back. Many times the woman just left the food on the back stoop, but Laurel always knew who it was from. She would bring the sack into the house and tear into the sandwiches or the cornbread like a starving thing, which by then she usually was. Even more comforting than the food was the idea that someone had thought to feed her.

Eventually her ma found out about Lottie's missions of mercy, and she went crazy. She ranted and raved that she didn't want Laurel taking anything from that nigger, and if Laurel did it again Sara Jayne would take a switch to her. There wasn't anything unusual about Sara Jayne exploding like that; her mother's moods were unpredictable at best. But the intensity of her fury was strange. Sara Jayne was usually a tearful, self-pitying drunk, stroking her misfortunes like pets.

The mystery was cleared up when Laurel was six. By then she was old enough to understand what it meant to be a bastard and why the other kids called her one. So Sara Jayne told her what had happened at the cabin and why Lottie was to be hated.

The next time an offering appeared on the back stoop, Laurel carried it back across the highway and up the long dirt road to Lottie's cabin. Lottie came out and stood in front of her. She was a big woman, with long arms and legs and strong hands. Her dark eyes were impassive as Laurel handed her a basket of newly picked peaches and said, "We don't need food from you. Don't bring it again," and fled.

🌿

That wasn't the only time she turned down help. Her ma had told her the three Miss Margarets were the enemy, too. So when Miss Peggy offered Laurel a job at the resort she refused. When Miss Li'l Bit said she could help get her a scholarship for college, she said no, thank you. And when Sara Jayne was racking up astronomical medical bills in the long months it took her to finally die, Laurel never let Dr. Maggie treat her for free. Which meant that in addition to being badly educated and without any options for the future she was up to her ass in debt. But she'd been a loyal daughter, her ma's second-in-command in the dumb, sad war their adversaries hadn't even known they were fighting.

THEY PULLED UP in front of her house. Josh looked out his window at the surrounding trees.

"This it?" he asked.

"Welcome to my ancestral home," she said.

"WHY DO YOU KEEP ON LIVING HERE? You hate this place," Denny had said once, right after he got sober. He was seeing a therapist in his rehab program, and "confronting issues" was part of the cure. Fortunately, he'd gotten over it.

"I own it, remember?"

"You could sell it for a fortune to some rich jerk from Atlanta."

"I've gotten kinda partial to it."

That wasn't true; she disliked everything about the house. A small rainstorm could wipe out her driveway, making it an impassable trail of red clay muck. A medium-sized rainstorm could knock a tree branch down on her one power line and wipe out essentials like the lights, the well pump, the television, and—God help her in summertime—her precious AC. Squirrels got themselves trapped in the crawl space under her roof and died horribly; mice fried themselves chewing electrical wires, and one day they'd probably burn the place down. And then there were the memories of Sara Jayne, drunk and living or finally sober but dying.

In spite of all that, she stayed. Because the place was a reminder that being a loser was not necessarily in her DNA. It was a symbol of the one battle her family had won. And living in it was her way of giving the finger to Garrison Gardens, the trust that now ran them, and to the town that sucked up to them.

JOSH GOT OUT OF THE CAR and looked around at the surrounding trees. "Jesus, it's quiet!" he said.

"That's the point of living in the bosom of Mother Nature."

"Don't you go out of your mind?"

"I'm a simple country girl. I love it."

He shot her a look that said *bullshit*. Obviously, in spite of all her attempts to put him off, he'd spent at least a few seconds wondering who she was. She wasn't sure how she felt about that. The light sexy mood of the night had long since shattered. She probably should hand back his expensive sports jacket, which now smelled of beer, get rid of him, and find some other way to go to work in the morning. It certainly would be the smart thing to do. So she said, "Why don't you come on in?"

BACK IN HER BEDROOM AT LAST, Li'l Bit pulled on a freshly washed nightgown and buttoned it all the way to the neck. Her discarded clothes were in the hamper. Her shoes were on the rack in her closet. The sink in the bathroom had been rinsed, and she'd lined up her toothpaste next to the brush. She walked out of the bathroom and got into bed. It was over. There was nothing more to be done. She closed her eyes and tried to will herself to sleep.

But she couldn't because she heard the sound of someone sobbing. And when she reached up and felt the wetness on her cheek, she realized she was crying.

WITH A BOURBON BOTTLE in her hand and a bag of dog biscuits tucked under her arm, Peggy went from room to room turning on all the lights. The dogs followed her in a pack, silent for once, all twenty-four eyes fixed on the treats. Finally, the house was as bright as she could make it. She moved into the den, selected a CD from her stack of golden oldies, and popped it in the player. The sound of Frank Sinatra filled the air. She turned to the dogs. "We're gonna celebrate," she told them fiercely. "We're gonna have a goddamn celebration."

THE FIRE WAS HOT, but Maggie wasn't aware of being warm at last. She was back in a world when the pecans fell like green hailstones so the men below could harvest them, and Mama's magnolias were always cut back to manicured perfection. Back to the time when Lottie was slender and strong and they were young.

WHEN IT CAME TO SEX, it was a good rule, Laurel decided, not to put yourself in the position where you had to follow through. Even though the TV talk shows all said a girl had the right to change her mind right up to the last moment, she felt there was a point at which it seemed like bad sportsmanship to back off. Unfortunately, defining this point had always been dicey for her. Tonight she had missed it. Because at the moment when Josh Wolf Eyes began kissing her, her thoughts had been elsewhere—about twenty-five years back in the past, to be precise. Not that Josh was lacking in the kissing department. Her early assessment of that mouth had been right. And when they finally got naked, he definitely knew how to use his hands. On a scale of one to ten Josh got a nine and a half.

The half he didn't get was for not realizing that at that very moment, even as he was suspended over her getting ready to hump his way to glory, she was wishing he was in the next country. And then suddenly it seemed she was going to get her wish. Before she could murmur, "What's going on, sugar?" Josh had rolled his nice tight body off and was lying next to her.

"So were those women who freaked you out the three Miss Margarets?" he whispered cozily.

It took her a second to get her bearings. When she did, she sat bolt upright, a move she would have sworn never happened except in fiction until she did it.

"Yeah, I thought that would get your attention," he said smugly.

"How the . . . how do you know about the three Miss Margarets?"

"Actually it was a lucky guess. But I'll take that as a yes."

"Who *are* you?"

For an answer he swung out of bed and padded across the room to get his blue jeans. She got out of bed, started to follow him, and stubbed her toe. He watched for a few seconds as she hopped around in pain, bare boobs bouncing.

"My, this is romantic," he remarked.

"You're the one who cut off the romance," she panted. "Damn, shit, damn!"

"Maybe some ice?" he offered sympathetically.

"How do you know about the three Miss Margarets?"

"Could I have a cup of coffee?"

"You didn't make a mistake when you turned the wrong way, did you?"

"Not exactly."

He finished putting on his jeans and went into the living room. She pulled on her robe and limped after him.

"That's got to smart."

"Shut up about my damn toe!"

"Okay. You want to know how I know about the three Miss Margarets." He paused. "I'm a writer."

For a moment she thought he was putting her on. Her job description at the town newspaper was *reporter*. Her real work was that of handmaiden and periodically just plain maid, but she was foolishly protective of her title. She was about to inform him that she was a writer too when he said, "Most of the time I write celebrity profiles." And she had the presence of mind to ask, "Where?" before spouting off about the *Charles Valley Gazette*.

"For the past few years I've been a regular contributor at *Vanity Fair*. I was on staff at *People* before that, and I worked for *Entertainment Weekly, Us*—the usual stuff."

And she'd been getting beer smell on the inside of his jacket all night. She sent up a silent thank-you to God for not letting her mention the *Gazette* and make a total horse's ass of herself.

"What are you doing here?" she asked.

"I've been working on a story about Vashti Johnson," he said.

That was when she decided to go put some ice on her foot. Because she needed time to get herself together. The night had just officially gotten too strange.

Chapter Four

IN A WAY IT MADE SENSE that a writer from New York was writing a story about Vashti Johnson. Vashti was the Valley's golden girl—golden woman by now. She did something no one could pronounce that had to do with scientific research. Something massively important and esoteric in the field of genetics that only two or three people in the world understood. But that was just the beginning of her accomplishments. She was an advocate for children's education in the sciences. She had testified in front of Congress twice. There were rumors in Charles Valley that she had missed getting the Nobel Prize by inches. She had written a book, and there was a scholarship fund for minority kids that had her name on it. So even though no one was clear on exactly what it was she did in her laboratory out in northern California, she was as close to a celebrity as the town had. Not that she had ever claimed the town as her own. Not since she and her mother ran from it years ago.

Vashti was Lottie's granddaughter. She was also the daughter of the woman who, when the booze was flowing and the listener was sympathetic, Laurel's ma had cursed in bars up and down most of the major highways of southwest Georgia. Every tragedy that had occurred in Sara Jayne's life, from the death of her ancient pickup in the parking lot by the Winn Dixie to the time Laurel's appendix burst, could be laid at the feet of Vashti's mother, Nella. Any blame Ma had left over went straight to the three Miss Margarets.

Not that Laurel was planning to mention any of that to Josh Wolf Eyes. She took a deep breath and said, "I'm out of coffee. Do you like tea?"

"Let me make it. You keep that ice on your toe. Just point me in the right direction for the tea bags."

"First shelf, cabinet over the sink." He began rummaging around. She sat at the kitchen table, trying to seem a lot more together than she felt.

"So that wrong turn . . . ?"

"When I was interviewing Vashti, she said something about living on a pie-shaped piece of land in the middle of a forest."

"And you thought you'd check it out."

"Since I was there, it seemed like a good idea."

"And Vashti told you about the three Miss Margarets?"

"Once. She described them enough so I thought I recognized them tonight. Did I?"

"Yeah, that was them." But she wasn't ready to talk about the three Miss Margarets. "What gave you the idea to write about Vashti?"

For the first time he didn't want to answer her. "Do you have any sugar?"

"Canister next to the stove. Where'd you get the idea?" Two could play the question game.

Finally he plunged in. "There was this woman. Smart and angry. At me."

"Why?"

"We had a difference of opinion. She thought I was a cheap commercial sellout, I thought I was being responsible and paying the bills. Anyway, one day she asked me if I was going to waste the rest of my life writing about airhead actresses and models or if I had the balls to do a story on a woman who was working on something worthwhile. Vashti had just been elected a member of the National Academy of Sciences. She—the woman, not Vashti—dared me to do the story."

"And the woman is?"

"My wife. At the time. Actually, my second wife. Ex-wife."

It made her really mad at herself that for a second Laurel calculated the likelihood of the existence of a third Mrs. Wolf Eyes.

He went on. "The more I got to know about Vashti, the more I wanted to write about her. She was just a kid when she was elected to the Academy, relatively speaking. She did her post-doc with a team that was working on the Human Genome Project back in the days when it was totally a boys' club—well, it still is to a great extent. You can count on the fingers of one hand the number of women who are doing research at her level, to say nothing of African Americans." He paused, then added, "I did some digging and found out what happened here with her mother when she was a kid. How the hell do you get past something like that?"

Some of us didn't get past it, Laurel thought. "So you're writing about Vashti for *Vanity Fair?*"

"No. I couldn't get my editor to go for the piece, and *People* would only take a thousand words. I wanted to do a lot more on her than that. So I'm taking a year off to write a book. Only now I can't find her."

"What?"

He started pacing. He had a slight dusting of curly hairs on his back.

"About six months ago we were supposed to talk on the phone. She'd agreed to answer some questions. But when I called she'd disappeared. She'd closed down her lab, canceled all her speaking engagements, rented out her house, and dropped out of sight. No one knew where she was." He stopped pacing. "Water's boiling."

He found the milk under her direction, handed her a steaming mug, and slouched into the chair across from her. Even in that slumped position he didn't have any love handles. No question about it, he worked out somewhere.

"Then about two weeks ago the guy who was renting her house in California got a letter from a lawyer in Atlanta. Vashti was offering to sell the house. The lawyer told me he didn't know where Vashti was, but he'd been dealing with a Dr. Margaret Harris of Charles Valley. So I caught the next flight to Atlanta and came here." He smiled at her and she smiled back, but small alarms were going off inside her. In spite of herself, she wanted to like him. And not just because he was the closest thing to a star she'd ever met or was likely to meet, she told herself firmly.

But he'd done some digging. He knew enough about the three Miss Margarets to identify them with a lucky guess. She couldn't help wondering what else he knew about the three Miss Margarets, and Vashti and Nella. And especially her own mother, Sara Jayne. And if any of that stuff had been on his mind when he tossed his jacket to Sara Jayne's baby girl in the Sportsman's Grill.

"What do you think the three Miss Margarets were doing at that cabin?" he asked.

"Don't have a clue."

"Why don't you want to talk about them?"

"I didn't say I didn't want to talk about them—"

"You didn't have to. Reading people is what I do for a living."

"You read me wrong."

There was nothing in his face, nothing in his manner, to say he knew anything about her history with the three Miss Margarets. Laurel's every instinct told her he was genuinely looking for information. Of course, her instincts usually stank. But just to show him he was wrong, she said, "Dr. Maggie is in her eighties somewhere; Miss Li'l Bit, whose real name is Margaret Banning, is in her seventies; and Miss Peggy is the baby—she's just in her sixties. Miss Li'l Bit and Dr. Maggie come from fine old families that have been in Charles Valley since before you Yankees came down here to violate our states' rights with your Civil War. Miss Peggy married into the Garrison family, which around here puts her at the right hand of God."

"Tell me why you don't like them." If he knew anything about her connection to them, he wouldn't ask that. Or would he?

"They're from the right side of the tracks. I'm poor white trash."

"I thought poor white trash was fashionable these days."

"Not to women like the three Miss Margarets."

"In that case I can see why you'd resent them."

"No resenting to it. I just see them clear."

"Tell me." He thought she was funny and he was enjoying her. She could swear he wasn't trying to play her. She could almost swear it.

"When the three Miss Margarets were younger they got a reputation for being a lot better than they were because they did a lot of good deeds that never inconvenienced them," she said. "Now that they're old, mostly they just hang out on Miss Li'l Bit's front porch and believe their own press."

He leaned back, tilting his chair, and hooked a bare foot on the rung of the one in front of him for balance. He had slim feet with straight toes and high arches. "So it's an honesty thing with you?"

She had a quick flash of her ma yelling, "Those old bitches lied. I know they lied!"

"What did they do to you?" he asked. If he knew, he was the greatest actor on the planet.

"They never did anything to me. We were talking generally. Is this interrogation over?"

"Nah. Tell me about the Garrison family."

"You're staying at the lodge at Garrison Gardens, right? Well, there's a brochure under the Bible on your nightstand with a picture of Miss Lucy Garrison's chapel on the front. It'll tell you all about the family."

"But I want to hear it from you," he said, smiling, like he was settling in for a really good show and knew he wasn't going to be disappointed.

She wondered if he knew how sexy all that attention was and

decided yes indeed, any man who strutted his stuff the way Josh did knew exactly how sexy he was. Which didn't diminish his sexiness. So what with one thing and another, she decided to hell with her warning bells. It was probably just a coincidence that he had picked her up, and she wasn't going to ask him about it. It wouldn't be the first time she'd decided to trust a man for reasons that had little to do with her better judgment.

"OKAY," LAUREL BEGAN, "this is the version of the Garrison legend you won't get from the tour guides at the Gardens. Your big hotel started out in the twenties as a private lodge for the Garrisons to entertain their friends—many of whom were the financial barons who brought us the Great Depression, incidentally, but we don't mention that around here. The original lodge was a rustic retreat where the Garrisons entertained in simple style and demonstrated to the world what humble Christian folk they were. Then the Depression hit and local farmers started going belly-up. The Garrisons sent out their agents to buy up the farmers' land for a fraction of what it was worth, business being business after all, and to hell with all that subversive Commie stuff in the Bible about being your brother's keeper."

It was a soapbox she'd been on before, but no man had ever looked quite so fascinated while she was on it.

"By the time the Depression was over, the Garrison family had collected thirty thousand acres that used to be homes and farms. Somebody got the idea that the private lodge could turn a profit if it became a resort. For reasons having to do with the government's unreasonable application of the income tax, the Garrison accountants tucked most of the newly acquired land into a charitable trust that was to be used in a manner loosely described as being for the public good. Several golf courses were put in, and facilities were built to house an annual steeplechase that put Charles Valley on the map worldwide. How this benefited the public was never made clear; the golf courses were kept private, and tickets for the steeple-chase cost as much as the average family earned in six months. But these goodies made the resort into one hell of a draw for the exclusive clientele the Garrisons wanted. Are you with me so far?" Josh's pale eyes were warm; by now Ed's would have glazed over.

"Oh, yeah, you're very clear," Josh said softly. "You deliver this riff often?"

"Only to total strangers who will soon be leaving town."

"Smart move. Go on."

"The land that was not developed reverted back to forest and became hunting grounds for resort guests and Garrison family and friends. The farmers watched the rich people play on what had once been their cotton and sweet-potato fields and tried to tell themselves they were grateful for the resort because without it to provide jobs they would have starved—all but one drunken old cuss, who didn't like progress and refused to sell, mostly because he enjoyed watching the Garrison agents go nuts trying to con him. And he never had given a damn if his kids were hungry."

"And this old cuss would be?"

"Don't get ahead of the story. Right now all you need to know is there *was* one.

"It wasn't until the fifties that the real bonanza kicked in. That was when Dalton Garrison took over and decided to make a contribution to mankind—while expanding the family's assets, of course. He hired horticulturists from universities around the country to plant gardens here. Azaleas were the specialty; they put in every species there was, including several new hybrids they developed. Mr. Dalt was the one who built that greenhouse in the Gardens and stocked it with orchids and all those other exotic plants. If you haven't seen it yet, you really should before you leave."

"I'm not much of an exotic-plant person."

"Pity. We have some of the best. He also put in that huge vegetable garden that's been on TV, he had a lake built, and he put in the hiking and biking trails that go through the forest.

"He named the whole thing Garrison Gardens, and in a gesture that was as noble as it was shocking he opened it to the public."

He smiled as he fed her her cue. "Shocking because?"

"He let the peasants in. For the price of a quarter, a family could park in the public parking lots, picnic on the lawns, swim in the lake, and visit the nurseries where the botanists grew the Garrison Azalea and the Charles Valley Rose. Children got lectures on how flowers are cross-pollinated. New techniques for growing corn and tomatoes were demonstrated at the vegetable garden. Schools sent their kids to the Gardens on field trips. Educators applauded. The lodge became the big pissy hotel you're staying at. Less expensive A-frame cottages were built for guests who couldn't afford the hotel. A campground was set up for those who couldn't afford the cottages. It was democratic as hell. And profitable?"

She let out a little laugh. He laughed along with her.

"Money was rolling in. And Charles Valley, no matter how it felt at first, wound up being grateful. Most country folks were watching their kids run to cities in the North as soon as they graduated from high school, but parents here could tell the young 'uns to stay home and go work for the Gardens. So even if Mr. Dalt rigged the occasional election and made the zoning board keep out new businesses, at least a man would get to know his grandbabies and they wouldn't grow up talking like Yankees. And because of that, people were willing to forget they had never been anything but waiters and bellboys. Except the family of the old cuss."

"Good. I was hoping we'd get back to him."

"Actually, he died in a bar fight that was such a Willie Nelson cliché it's embarrassing to talk about it. But he left his land—two acres, including a right of way to the road—to his son, who left it to *his* son, and so on down the line."

"The end of that line being . . . ?"

"Me."

"And the land?"

"You're sitting on it. Right smack in the middle of the beautiful Garrison Nature Preserve, where it sticks in their craw and screws up the bucolic landscape. Over the years, my people have sold junk on this land and turned it into an unauthorized trailer park and a used-car lot. I'm a better neighbor than the others, I just have a habit of shining bright lights into the woods and banging pots and pans to alert the deer during hunting season. The Garrison Trust has tried to buy this place time and again, they even offered fair market value for it, but no matter how broke or desperate or drunk we might be, we have never ever considered selling. Praise Jesus and Amen."

She resisted an impulse to bow. Josh stood up. Somehow she wound up much closer to that bare chest than she intended to be. She told herself.

"Are you still mad at me for not . . . ?" He trailed off.

"Finishing what you started? I never said I was mad."

"Yeah, you did. Sort of." He grinned at her, but there was something sad in it. "I always know when smart, angry girls are mad. They're a specialty of mine." She noticed she hadn't moved away from that chest. He hadn't moved either.

"The thing is," he said softly, "I like to have the woman's undivided attention. You know?"

She was now sober and it was late. But he did have that body. And it would be good to have her bed smelling of a man again. She nodded and reached up to him at exactly the same moment that he bent down to her. And the kissing really was good when she put her mind to it. And he knew exactly where to put his hands. And what to do with them when he got them there. And this time she didn't have anything else on her mind. And as far as she could tell, neither did he.

Somewhere close to morning, Laurel woke up. She opened her eyes just enough to see that the room was still inky dark. Josh had tossed one arm over her chest and was pulling her to him, squashing her breasts. His other arm was bent so his hand was under her shoulder, and his body was curled around her. It seemed the big New York writer liked to sleep spoon style.

Her leg was getting stiff. As gently as she could, so as not to disturb him, she turned onto her back. Without waking he shifted with her. Sleep choreography was obviously a skill of his. Suddenly, for absolutely no reason she wanted to cry. She had to get out of the bed. But then, again without waking, he sighed and did something that could only be described as nuzzling her neck, so she closed her eyes and concentrated on not letting the tears well up. And eventually she went back to sleep.

Chapter Five

THE ELECTRIC MIXER WAS WHIRRING smoothly through the cake batter. Maggie added a teaspoon of vinegar, watched it blend into the red-brown mixture, and turned off the motor. It didn't do to overmix. It had been years since she made a red velvet cake, but she'd awakened before dawn with a need to do something useful. She did that a lot now, but there had been a time when sleeping was one of her major pleasures. She could stretch her body out under cool clean sheets, and give herself over to oblivion for ten or twelve hours. Now she got scratchy as a cat after half that time, and often spent the rest of the night wandering through the house or reading books she'd already read, waiting for seven o'clock so she could phone Li'l Bit and begin her day. Peggy, on the other hand, was not to be disturbed before noon.

Maggie checked her watch and glanced at the phone. There were still hours to go before she could call the sheriff's department. She could try Li'l Bit, who was usually up early too; it was tempting, but she could wait. They had a long day ahead of them. Long and sad. Which she wasn't going to think about. Finish the cake, she told herself.

Fortunately she had some cream cheese in the fridge for the icing; butter frosting was out of the question for red velvet cake.

She was orthodox about her baking. Perhaps because doing it the old way brought back the early days with Lottie.

IN THE BEGINNING it had been about idolatry, plain and simple. Lottie could run faster, climb higher, and jump farther than anyone else. She was the author of the endless sagas they played out day after day, serial dramas based on *Grimm's Fairy Tales, Little Lord Fauntleroy,* and a gloomy little tearjerker called *Nobody's Boy.* These were the stories Maggie's mother read to her every afternoon as a reward for memorizing the alphabet and learning to read. Mama had trained to be a teacher before she got married, and she wasn't about to let her smart little Maggie idle away her days just because she was too young for formal schooling. And anything Maggie learned, she passed on to Lottie, who picked it up secondhand as fast as Mama could teach it.

Soon Maggie and Lottie had devoured every book on the shelves in Maggie's playroom. Maggie smuggled Mama's magazines out of the house, and they spent hours under the magnolia trees, puzzling over household hints and stories about ladies who weren't acceptable in something called polite society because they had Sinned.

They were polar opposites, she and Lottie. She was a steady child, smart but not brilliant and not given to quick emotions. Lottie was all speed and fire. She learned fast, got bored easily, and reacted viscerally.

When an early hurricane uprooted an old Douglas fir tree and knocked it across the driveway, the workmen who were clearing it up found a nest of orphaned baby squirrels in the trunk. Pink-skinned, hairless, with eyes still closed, they were too young to survive without a mother. Ralph was going to take them to the spring and drown them, but Lottie couldn't bear it. She wept so hard, begging him to let her have them, swearing that she and Maggie could take care of them, that he finally gave in. Maggie looked on, knowing the enterprise was doomed. But she helped Lottie wrap the little creatures in towels to simulate the nest they had come from and heated milk to feed them from an eyedropper. For three terrible days they tried to force milk and sugar water down the throats of the baby squirrels. Maggie watched Lottie stroke the little bodies, fighting to keep them alive through sheer force of will. There was something almost cruel in Lottie's determination, and it was a relief when one by one the poor little things died. As they buried the last one, Lottie whispered, "All I wanted to do was save them. Why couldn't we?" Maggie started to say, Because they were too little, and we never should have tried. But Lottie's eyes looked so tragic that she said, "We didn't know enough. Next time we'll know more, and we'll do it right."

The next day Lottie said, as if they had just been talking about it, "That'd be the best thing in the world, wouldn't it? Knowing how to make something keep on living."

And for the first time since they buried the baby squirrels, Lottie smiled the big joyful smile that lit up her face. Sometimes Maggie thought everything that happened afterward had stemmed from that moment. And moments like it.

THE CAKE PANS WERE GREASED AND FLOURED. Maggie grasped the bowl of cake batter and began pouring it into the pans, dividing the batter evenly without having to measure it. These days, because of her arthritis, she used an aluminum bowl; the old ceramic ones she loved were too heavy for her to lift off the shelf. So she was stuck with this metal thing that reminded her of the sick pans in hospitals. She finished pouring, tapped the pans gently to get rid of the air, and put them in the oven.

HER LIFE HAD BEEN SO SIMPLE when she was growing up. She was the only child of two doting middle-aged parents. Except for

Lottie, the only other youngster around was Harrison Banning's daughter, who was ten years younger. Lottie's older brother and two sisters were already out of the house and working when Lottie was born. So Maggie and Lottie ran free on the farm, playing their games untroubled by outsiders. Sometimes it seemed to her that it had been unfair of God to make it all so easy back then. Those days had not prepared her for what lay ahead.

In the early years, Maggie's mama hadn't worried about the friendship between her daughter and her cook's child. She assumed it would end when Maggie started school. It often happened that way: A white child would befriend a Negro playmate, particularly when they lived in an isolated area without any other families nearby. It all sorted itself out when the white child went off to school with her own kind. So Mama waited patiently for Maggie to drop Lottie and start making some real friends. When she didn't, Mama finally felt she had to say something.

"Don't you see how unkind you're being, Doodlebug?" she asked gently. "Lottie doesn't even talk like a colored girl."

It was true. She and Lottie did sound alike, although she hadn't realized until that moment that Lottie spoke the way she did. The idea pleased her.

But not Mama. "All you're doing is encouraging poor Lottie to get above herself. It's not fair to her."

Maggie thought about giving Mama a list of all the things Lottie could do better than she did, but it would only make Mama lecture even more. So she smiled her sweetest, which could be very sweet indeed, and she and Lottie went on as they always had.

Until Mama lost all patience. "Maggie, I told you to stop this," she said. "I won't have people talking about my daughter and saying she's strange."

"It's nobody's business what I do."

"Of course it is. Your family has a reputation in this town. People watch us, don't you forget that. And for a young lady your age to have no friends but one little colored girl doesn't look good. If you don't stop, I'll have a talk with Charlie Mae, and you know what she'll do to Lottie."

So Lottie and Maggie took their friendship underground. On a thirty-acre farm with numerous outbuildings it wasn't hard to duck the adults. And every once in a while, to appease her mama, Maggie brought schoolmates home to play. She thought she and Lottie could go on forever with their life.

But they were growing up. Their bodies were racing toward a maturity she wanted no part of. In the course of one summer, Maggie developed a porcelain prettiness that caused Mama's friends to cluck and say she was going to be a regular little heartbreaker. And Lottie became beautiful. Years later Maggie would still remember with an ache Lottie's transformation from a skinny girl into a tall slender creature with high cheekbones, brown satin skin, and huge dark eyes. Maggie stayed childishly petite, but Lottie blossomed into a classic hourglass. She carried herself proudly, even when Charlie Mae punished her for being vain.

Lottie had a dream. She was going to be a doctor. The boldness of it awed Maggie. They had never heard of a Negro, male or female, being a doctor. But there was a supervisor who visited Lottie's school, a young Negro woman sent around by the state, who took a special interest in Lottie. Miss Monross told her there were colored colleges she could go to, and schools where Negroes learned to be doctors. Miss Monross threw around names like Spelman and Bethune-Cookman—names Lottie wrote in the diary she kept under her mattress. When the time came, Miss Monross said, if Lottie worked hard at her studies and prepared herself, she, Miss Monross, would see to it that Lottie got to one of these schools. But she warned Lottie that she would have to study on her own. The education she was getting was not adequate for a future college student.

This was not a surprise to Maggie and Lottie. It hadn't taken them long to figure out that the Negro school was inferior to the one Maggie went to. Lottie's school was held in the church; the children sat in pews and worked on their laps. There were subjects the Negroes weren't taught, because they didn't have books or supplies. While Maggie was learning fractions and the capitals of Europe, the kids in Lottie's school were struggling with basic reading and writing. By the time they were in high school, most of the Negro children had already left school to work.

So Maggie and Lottie began studying together, as they had done before when they learned to read. There was an old barn on the property that no one ever used that had become a storage place for unused junk. It was perfect for them. At night they waited until everyone was asleep; then they put on coats over their nightgowns and sneaked out. Lottie brought an oil lamp from the cabin, which they lit and put on the floor so they could see enough to read, and Maggie brought her school textbooks and spread her worksheets on a blanket on the floor. Lottie worked her way through the books, asking questions when she didn't understand something, and Maggie would have to remember what she had learned in class and explain it. Later, she realized she got as much as Lottie did out of those nights. Knowing she would have to answer Lottie's questions, she became a much better student than she ever would have been. Her ability to absorb information quickly would last for the rest of her life. But back in those days, it was all about Lottie. The memories of those nights in the old barn, huddled in her coat against the chill of winter, working by the light of the oil lamp, were some of her happiest.

MAGGIE SET HER LITTLE KITCHEN TIMER for thirty-five minutes and took the thing back into the living room to wait. Laverne, whose arthritis had been bothering her, had to scramble to follow. Maggie sat in her chair, and the dog settled next to her on the floor, muttering canine curses under her breath. "I know," Maggie said sympathetically. "Getting old is just plain nasty." She leaned back in the chair, her head finding the dent she'd made in the upholstery over the years.

WHEN HAD IT STARTED TO CHANGE for her? It was hard to remember so far back. Maybe it was when she saw Lottie walking home with three girls from her school. Maggie was in her room watching them from the window as they stopped at the end of the driveway to talk. It only took two or three minutes before they went on their way and Lottie ran up the drive to the cabin. But it was the first time Maggie realized that Lottie was making new friends. And what was worse, they were her own kind, as Mama would say. Suddenly Maggie was angry, in a scary kind of way she had never been before. Thoughts of getting even raced through her brain. She would refuse to talk to Lottie. She would not go to the barn that night; let Lottie wait and wonder what had happened. But when night came she couldn't stay away from the barn, and once she was there she couldn't stay mad at Lottie.

Or maybe it started when Lottie was crying over some hurt Maggie had now forgotten. But she could remember how she had wanted to put her arms around Lottie and hug her tight. But for reasons she couldn't put into words, she didn't.

Sometimes it seemed to her that she had always known she was different. Certainly by the time the girls in her school were giggling at boys and trotting out their early attempts at flirting, she knew she was. She understood their feelings, the giddiness, and the misty half-formed urges that drove them. But also she knew, by some deep instinct, that there would never be a boy who would inspire those feelings in her. If it had been important to her to fit in, she might have been horrified. But her life happened in the barn, after the rest of the world was asleep and she was alone with Lottie.

Loving Lottie was such a habit that it felt like the most natural thing in the world when she realized her feelings had changed to the kind that made other girls blush when they talked about boys. She watched the shadows on Lottie's face as the oil lamp flickered, watched Lottie close her eyes to concentrate on a tricky math problem, and she was full of achy longings she could not describe. She waited for something wonderful to happen, something bigger than she had ever known before. Sometimes she drifted as she waited; sometimes she felt she would explode with all the things she was waiting for.

They had always stayed to talk after they were through studying, but Maggie found she had less and less to say. And Lottie seemed to be pulling into herself too. Now there was pain in being with Lottie; there was a distance between them that she wanted to smash through, but she was afraid. Because, for the first time in all the years she and Lottie had known each other, she wasn't sure how Lottie felt.

A boy named James who went to Lottie's school had walked her home twice after the Saturday-afternoon movies. Maggie had looked up at the colored section of the balcony and watched him maneuver so that he was next to Lottie when they got to the stairs. The second time he brought Lottie home he asked if he could sit with her on the porch. Lottie dismissed him. "I have better things to do with my time," she told Maggie. "I'm not gonna end up like Momma, having a baby before I'm twenty and with no work I can do but cooking."

But Maggie could see Lottie was pleased, because she liked the attention from a boy. Maggie wanted to cry out, What about me? but she was too afraid. She became irritable and moody, snapping at Lottie for no reason and then apologizing. She had always been a rational, confident child, but now she was full of doubts. Mama wanted to take her to the doctor, but Maggie knew what she needed. She had to find the courage somewhere to tell Lottie how she felt.

There were several nights when she came close to saying it. There were nights when she thought Lottie knew. Once, when she had been staring at Lottie, she found Lottie looking back at her. Their eyes met and she almost blurted it out; Lottie looked away quickly and she lost her nerve. But she had to say something because time was running out. They'd be graduating in a year, and they had to work out a way to be together when they went to college.

Then the county school board announced they'd be closing the colored high school in Charles Valley. Negro students who wanted to continue their education would have to get themselves to Ashtabula, twenty miles away.

Lottie was beside herself. There was no way she could make the daily round-trip. Maggie was heartbroken for her, but there was nothing she could do to help. Even if she kept on tutoring Lottie every day, it wouldn't get Lottie the diploma she needed. Charlie Mae said it was just as well. Lottie's Aunt Grace had started working as a maid at the new resort the Garrisons had just opened, and she thought she could get Lottie a job there too. Times were still bad in Charles Valley, work for pay was hard to come by, and Lottie's family could use the money. Desperate, Lottie spilled all this to Miss Monross, who came up with a solution.

"She says there's a family I can live with in Ashtabula," Lottie reported to Maggie. "They have a girl my age who's going to high school. Miss Monross is gonna talk to Momma and Daddy and see if they'll let me stay with those people and finish high school."

It was like a physical blow. "You want to . . . to go away?" Maggie stammered.

"I don't want to, I've got to, Maggie. I have to get my diploma."

"But what about me?" The words were tumbling out now. "What will I do?"

"I'll be back sometimes. . . ."

"We've always been together. . . ."

"I know. . . ."

"You can't go." As she said it, Lottie's eyes met hers the way they had before. Only this time there was something in her look. As if Lottie sensed what she'd been trying to tell her. And then she could tell that Lottie knew. For a moment she was just plain happy. Lottie knew. It was out in the open. They could say it. But then Lottie turned away again.

"You can't leave," Maggie repeated, determined now.

"Maggie—"

"You can't leave me."

Lottie wouldn't look at her. But it was too late. They had to have it out now. She was starting to cry.

"Lottie, please!" she begged, as she reached out to take Lottie's hand.

She never knew what happened next, whether she knocked the oil lamp over or Lottie did when she jerked her hand away. The hot oil spilled on the papers they had been working with and the burning wick fell into it. The papers blazed into flame, and the dry straw on the floor of the barn began to burn. Lottie and Maggie froze, watching as the fire started spreading across the floor to the junk piled up on the sides of the barn. Then together they went into crazed action. Lottie grabbed the algebra book they'd been studying from and began beating at the burning floor until the book caught fire in her hands. Maggie grabbed the blanket and threw it on the flames, stomping on top of it in a crazy dance. They managed to put out the fire, and she didn't even realize the ruffle at the hem of her nightgown had caught until Lottie started screaming.

Both sets of parents heard the commotion and came running. They found the girls outside the barn. Lottie had bundled a coat around the burning nightgown and was helping Maggie roll on the ground. Maggie was screaming now in agony as together they smothered the flames against her bare legs. When it was over, Lottie's hands were burned and the doctor said Maggie's left leg would be scarred.

Later, after the doctor had wrapped her leg in gauze and ointment and given her something to help her sleep, Mama demanded to know what happened. Maybe the drug loosened her tongue. Or the pain. Or maybe she thought her mother would help Lottie if she understood. Whatever the reason, Maggie told her mother about teaching Lottie. She explained about the colored school being so terrible, and Lottie needing help because she was going to college to be a doctor. She stopped short of telling her mother that she planned to pick her own college to be with Lottie. She wasn't that far gone.

She never knew exactly what Mama told Charlie Mae, but Lottie never went to live with the family in Ashtabula. Her schooling ended that night. Miss Monross called at the cabin to protest to Charlie Mae and Ralph and was politely told to stop filling Lottie's head with foolishness. As soon as Lottie's hands were healed she went to work at the new Garrison Lodge, cleaning bedrooms.

If Maggie had hoped to keep Lottie home, she had won. But in another, much more painful way, she'd lost. Because Lottie was staying away from her. And Maggie knew it wasn't just because Charlie Mae had ordered it, or because Lottie was angry that Maggie had spilled their secrets to her mother. It was because of what Maggie had started to say in the barn. In the dark days that followed the fire, Maggie got the answer to the question she had never been able to ask. Lottie understood what Maggie felt and it disgusted her.

The months that followed were bleak. In all her charmed life, Maggie had never been seriously unhappy. Now she felt swamped by waves of despair. Everything that had happened was her fault. She hated herself. And worst of all there was no one to confide in. Lottie was as far away as if she had left Charles Valley. Maggie was alone. The doctor told Mama her low spirits were to be expected, after the shock she'd had, and to give her time to get over it. Maggie was afraid she never would.

But then, because she was young and resilient, she began to fight her way back. She learned to live with Lottie's rejection because she had to. And she learned not to think about the guilt she felt for the disaster she'd set in motion. Above all, she knew she had to get away from home. With nothing else to distract her, she focused on her books and finished high school a year ahead of schedule. She was accepted at Emory in Atlanta and started making her plans to leave in the fall.

James got himself a job as a waiter at the resort. He stood behind the buffet tables wearing a uniform and white gloves while he served the guests boiled shrimp and baked chicken. He walked Lottie home from work every day; Maggie watched from the window in her bedroom, where she now did her studying.

The night before Maggie left for Atlanta, she walked down to the old barn. She hadn't been there since the night of the fire. As she passed the cabin where Lottie's family lived she thought she saw someone at the window watching her. Then she heard what might have been the back door of the cabin opening. She didn't look back to check, but as she walked she prayed.

A faint smell of burnt wood still hung around the barn, and one wall was charred. She stood in the middle of the floor, in the place where she and Lottie used to spread the old blanket and set out the schoolbooks. She heard footsteps behind her. She turned and Lottie was there.

"Momma never would have let me go away to high school," Lottie said.

Maggie felt tears start to sting at her eyes. She blinked them back, terrified of scaring Lottie again. "Maybe we could have convinced her."

Lottie shook her head. "She doesn't understand. She can't."

"Maybe you don't have to have a diploma to go to college. Maybe there's some kind of test you could take. You're so smart—"

But Lottie was shaking her head. "Maggie, I've got something to tell you. I'm going to marry James."

The words were out before Maggie could stop them. "You can't. You're only sixteen."

"I'm going to have a baby."

There was no way to stop the tears now. But Lottie smiled at her.

"It's okay, Maggie. I won't turn out like Momma. Work hard in college." Then she ran off into the night.

THE SWEET SMELLS OF BAKING—cocoa, sugar, and butter—filled the house. Trusting her nose more than the kitchen timer, which still had minutes to go, Maggie went into the kitchen and opened the stove. The cake layers had risen nicely, with no cracks; the sides had pulled away from the pans. She knew they were done, but just to be sure she stuck them with a broom straw, which came out clean. She pulled the pans out and put them on cake racks to cool. Later she'd make the frosting, take a piece to Lottie at the nursing home, and tell her what had happened last night. Lottie wasn't going to hear about it from anyone but her.

Chapter Six

WHEN SHE WOKE UP, it took Laurel about thirty seconds to realize that the pillow next to hers was empty. And it took another two or three seconds to tell herself that that was just fine. In fact, it was the way she wanted it. One reason why she gladly worked the weekend shift at the *Gazette* was because she had a built-in excuse for getting rid of the occasional Friday night date who wanted to hang around on Saturday morning. Clearly, today that was not going to be a problem.

Still, as she looked at the blanket pulled up neatly on the empty side of the bed, she remembered a morning when she was a kid and had awakened to find her mother had taken off with the latest man who was going to rescue them. Laurel had known by the time she was five or six that none of them ever would.

She banished the memory instantly. No need to start thinking about abandonment because a guy who was passing through town and would never see her again had laughed at her jokes. Even if he was a hotshot writer who worked for magazines she inhaled when she could get her hands on them. And even if he had wrapped his body around hers when he slept.

She hauled herself out of bed and padded barefoot toward the bathroom. She was moving slow, but that was to be expected after the amount of beer she'd put away. If she drank about a gallon of water and swallowed an aspirin or two along with some caffeine pills, she could probably fend off the headache that threatened to take over the top part of her head. She was firmly convinced it was the caffeine that did the trick. She looked down and saw that her toenail was turning blue. But it didn't hurt, so all in all she was in better shape than she deserved to be.

Then she swore loudly. Because she remembered that her car was still in the Sportsman's Grill parking lot. Josh Wolf Eyes had left her high and dry without a way to get to work. Cursing all men, not for the first time in her life, she went into the bathroom.

She was in the shower when she heard the police siren. It was a shocking sound in Charles Valley; she could count on one hand the number of times she'd heard it before. Ed and the boys must have something really big going on. It was followed a few seconds later by what had to be a voice talking on a bullhorn. She couldn't make out the words, but it was definitely coming from the direction of the highway. She couldn't imagine an accident big enough to warrant such commotion on a peaceful Saturday morning. She'd pulled on her clothes and was heading out the door when Josh appeared in front of her with two white Styrofoam coffee cups in his hands. He thrust one at her.

"Come on. All hell's breaking loose, and you can get more from the cops than I can," he said.

"You came back." She tried not to sound impressed. Or pleased.

"I went out for coffee. You can drink it in the car." He turned and started for the SUV.

"Good morning to you too."

"Hurry!" he said. She got in next to him.

"What's going on? Is it an accident?"

"I think something happened at that cabin," he said, as he turned on the engine and peeled off.

They reached the highway in time to see an ambulance come down the road from the cabin. Four squad cars, half the Charles Valley highway patrol, were parked haphazardly by the side of the highway. Several yards away, men in uniforms were standing in a circle around Ed. She couldn't hear what her ex was saying, but he seemed to be in high cop mode.

"Which one of the boys in blue do you know?" Josh murmured in her ear.

"All of them."

"Who's most likely to talk to you?"

"Mike Murray's got the loose lips."

"Wait till they break up, then grab him fast."

As if on cue, the little group dispersed and Laurel moved quickly to Mike, reaching him just as he was about to get into his car. Josh did his best to melt invisibly behind her.

"Hey Mike," she said. He eyed her warily. "What's going on?"

"Now, Laurel, you know I can't talk to you."

"Off the record." She held up her hands. "See? No notes, no tape recorder." She could feel the look of surprise she was getting from Josh. "Come on, Mike," she said. "You know whatever it is will be all over town by noon. I could hear the ruckus you boys are making all the way to my house."

"All I can tell you is we just found Vashti Johnson in her grandma's cabin."

Behind her she heard Josh's sharp intake of breath.

"Vashti?" she asked. "What's she doing there?"

"She wasn't doing anything. Not anymore. We found her body. The boys're taking her off to the coroner's office."

She thought she'd heard it wrong.

Josh said, "Oh, my God!" in a stunned voice.

"Vashti's dead?" she repeated stupidly. "Vashti Johnson? I didn't even know she was home."

"No one did," said Mike.

It was unthinkable. Vashti, daughter of the archenemy Nella, was dead.

"How?" Josh demanded. "What happened?"

Which of course made Mike clam up instantly. Then Ed appeared.

"Morning, Laurel," he said, smiling pleasantly, but his eyes narrowed when he saw who was standing behind her. Clearly he remembered Josh from the bar. Or maybe the rumors of her exploits had already started traveling.

Ed dismissed Mike, who got dutifully into his car and roared off. She knew Josh was wanting to ask a million questions, but he wasn't going to risk it. She gave Ed her best pretty-girl smile.

"What's going on, Ed?"

"Sorry if we woke you," he said, and turned away, blowing her off the way he used to when he was canceling a date and not about to give her an explanation. She did a little dance step that put her directly in his path and stopped him. "You found Vashti Johnson dead in the cabin?"

Ed's face flushed. Mike would get the riot act read to him later.

"Is that true?" she urged.

"You know I'm not gonna talk about this now. Tell Hank to come over to the station in a couple of hours and I'll have some information for him." Hank was her boss at the *Gazette*, and they both knew he would see to it that he wrote this one.

"Who found her? How'd you know to go to the cabin?" she asked.

"I told you, Laurel, not now." He started to turn again, but she did another dance step.

"Thing is, we might be able to help," she said, turning back to include Josh. Ed shot him a quick look of dislike. Ed might not want her himself but he sure as hell didn't want anyone else to have her.

"We got in very late last night," she went on. "We might have seen something."

"Who's he?" Ed growled, indicating Josh without making eye contact.

"A friend—from New York." She gave it a second to sink in. "Anyhow, last night—actually, it was this morning—we were at the cabin. We were on the way to my house, but we took a wrong turn." That would clinch it, just in case his imagination wasn't fleshing out the details. "I don't know what time it was, but it must have been after two o'clock."

"You saw something?" Ed demanded.

"Someone was there. Inside the cabin."

"Vashti." He didn't add *obviously*, but she could feel it hanging in the air. "You were probably the last one to see her alive."

"No, it was someone else." She could hear Josh clearing his throat behind her, warning her to keep her mouth shut. But she knew Ed better than he did. "The Miss Margarets were there, all three of them."

"You've lost your mind," Ed said. "Dr. Maggie phoned in the report this morning. She saw lights on and was afraid someone broke in. She asked us to check." As soon as he said it, he realized he had slipped. "But I don't want to see that in the *Gazette*. You tell Hank."

"Sure." She turned to Josh. "Let's go."

She started off, but Ed called out, "Wait!" She'd never noticed how really slow he could be when you got him rattled. She turned.

"You sure you saw the three Miss Margarets?"

Josh stepped in. "Actually, we were kind of drunk, officer."

"Sheriff," Ed corrected. "You saw them at the cabin around two A.M., Laurel Selene?"

She couldn't resist it. "Yes. Of course, we were a little preoccupied."

Ed turned a satisfactory shade of brick red under his tan. "I'll talk to you later, Laurel," he said pointedly, and he turned on his heel and walked away.

Josh said, "Let's get out of here, now that you've blown it."

"I blew it? I just found out who called in the report."

"You gave away something more valuable." He strode back to his car and got in, leaving her to climb up into the big stupid thing on her own. "We had information no one else does. You don't give up an edge like that."

"I got information for that information."

"Bull. You just wanted to send your boyfriend Billy Joe Bob on a testosterone high." He drove back across the highway and started down the dirt road to her driveway, going fast.

"His name is Ed, and he is not my boyfriend."

"If he's not, then worry about being stalked. If that guy got any more territorial he was going to start pissing a circle around you."

"Look, I was going to have to tell the police or my boss what we saw."

"I assume 'boss' refers to the mysterious Hank. He's your boss at what job?"

"I work for the local newspaper. As a reporter."

"You didn't think to mention that you're a writer when I was giving you my résumé last night?"

"While you were dropping names like *Vanity Fair* and *People*?"

"I do not drop names."

"It's a little tiny paper called the *Charles Valley Gazette*. And my job, when I'm not busy watering the plants, involves covering the bake sale at the First Baptist Church." That seemed to appease him. He nodded and sped on in silence, hitting the hole in her road full force. Thank God the lids were still on the coffees.

Finally they jerked to a stop in front of her place.

"That was bracing," she said.

He wasn't listening. "Jesus Christ, what happened to her?" he asked.

"You mean Vashti?"

He nodded. "If she was sick, I didn't know it. But what else could it have been? Those three women were there. . . ."

"Trust me, the three Miss Margarets didn't kill her, if that's what you were thinking."

"I don't know what to think. Vashti Johnson's dead." He seemed genuinely dismayed.

"Does this mean the end of your book?" she asked.

"Hell, no. I want to tell it even more now."

He sat for a moment in silence. Then he turned to look at her, and there was something thoughtful in it. Like he was calculating something in his head. He kept looking at her until she was about to ask him what the hell was wrong. Then, suddenly, whatever he'd been debating seemed to have been resolved. He smiled at her.

"We never drank our coffee," he said. "How about it?"

She'd probably be late for work if she said yes, but something was up with him and she wanted to know what it was.

"Just a few minutes," she said.

"Great." He got out and headed for the house. She grabbed the two Styrofoam cups and followed him.

He was in the middle of her living room looking at the shelves of books that covered one of her walls. He was back to calculating again. About what?

"You read all these?" he asked.

"Not the encyclopedia or the almanac." She stuck his coffee in the microwave and turned on the timer, hoping as she always did that the chemicals in the Styrofoam wouldn't somehow melt into the hot liquid.

She moved to the doorway between the kitchen and the living room and watched him take down a frayed hardcover book with a disintegrating binding titled *The Complete Shakespeare*. He opened it. On the front page, right under the name of the professor who had written the foreword, the words *Baby Merrick* had been scrawled in pencil. The handwriting was large and round like a child's. Beneath it, in ink, in a tidy prim hand was written *Laurel Selene McCready*, with *Merrick* added in parentheses. She watched him take down the rest of her hardcover books; three *Reader's Digest* Best of the Year anthologies, a copy of *Valley of the Dolls* with the original jacket, and a volume of Emily Dickinson's poetry. He checked the front pages.

"The names are in all of them," she said. "My father wrote the one in pencil before I was born. He didn't know if I was gonna be a boy or a girl, so he put down *baby*. I wrote my name in ink when I was eight." Josh put the book back on the shelf. He gave her a smile and another nod. She couldn't lose the feeling that he was after something. The microwave dinged and she brought him his coffee.

"Interesting collection you have here," he said at last. "Lot of range."

"I didn't pick them. My father left them to me." He left the books and a whole lot of heartache, but Josh didn't need to know that.

"He was an eclectic reader." He was eyeing the paperbacks now, taking in the jumble of titles, murder mysteries, thirty-year-old how-to manuals, romance novels, and dog-eared copies of the classics.

"He never read them. He bought them at a garage sale for me when he heard my mother was pregnant. I guess he thought it would give me class." She went into the kitchen to zap the second cup of coffee. He followed her.

"Nice thing to do for your kid."

Nicer would have been if he hadn't ruined her mother's life. And hers. She shrugged.

"You never knew your father?" Josh asked. But he was a little too casual about it. The microwave made its dinging sound. And suddenly, in the way that the brain puts things together when you're not expecting it to, she got it. She'd been suspicious of him since the first moment he mentioned the three Miss Margarets, but she'd pushed the thoughts aside. Now she knew she'd been had.

"You son of a bitch!"

"What?"

"You knew who I was, didn't you?"

"What are you talking about?"

"You've been working on that damn story about Vashti forever. You've done your homework."

"Some," he hedged, suddenly wary.

"You know why Vashti and Nella left town."

"Yes. What does that have to—"

"When you picked me up last night, you knew whose daughter I was."

"Of course not."

"Don't lie!"

"For Christ's sake, how could I—"

"My father is part of your story."

"How the hell would I know you were John Merrick's daughter?"

"So you do know about John Merrick!"

"Yes. But I didn't know he was your father last night when I came here with you. That's the truth."

But it wasn't the whole truth. There was something else . . . then she had it. She looked at the bookshelves. "This morning you weren't planning on coming back, were you? You were just gonna take off. But then you went poking around my books and read my father's name in the front." He didn't say anything, but he didn't have to. She remembered how happy—no, how flattered—she'd been that he'd come back with his goddamn coffee.

"Okay, I did look at your books," he said. "I look in people's medicine cabinets too. I read the mail upside down on my doctor's desk—"

"Where did you go for coffee?"

"A place called McGee's."

"Did you ask Sammy McGee about me, or was his wife the one waiting tables?"

"Look—"

"Her name is Faith. She wears a red handkerchief fixed like a flower in her breast pocket."

"I didn't—"

"Never mind. I'll get it from her."

"I asked a couple of questions. It's what I do. I ask questions."

"You were going to use me." She wanted to kill him. She couldn't believe she'd been such a fool.

"And last night you were using me," he said. "My guess would be to get back at Sheriff Billy Joe Bob—"

"Don't change the subject. You came back here to get the dirt on my father—"

"I came back because I remembered you didn't have a fucking car!" he shouted. He paused. "And because I wanted to ask you about your father."

"Thank you! Now get out."

"Look, I still have to drive you back to the bar."

"I'll get there on my own."

"You're a million miles from nowhere."

"I'll manage." She hadn't a clue how. But the idea of a twenty-minute drive with him was impossible. She snatched up her purse and stalked out. He came racing after her and grabbed her arm.

"Where are you going?"

She tried to back away; he held her even tighter. "Leave me the fuck alone!" she shouted.

They stood so close she could see the vein on the side of his temple beating. For a crazy minute she thought he might pull her down on the ground and start making love to her right there. Or she might pull him down. Or she might twist out of his grip and slap him hard. Or they might both laugh. They teetered on possibilities.

Then he dropped her arm and said, "To hell with it. Walk to town, I don't give a shit." And he got into his SUV and took off so fast he literally left her standing in a cloud of red clay dust. Which was another one of those things she thought only happened in bad fiction.

By the time she had walked halfway down the dirt road, Laurel was already regretting her grand gesture. It was a chilly morning, and she had the hike from hell ahead of her unless some kind soul picked her up. Which would be embarrassing, given the number of people who knew she'd left the Grill with the guy from New York. Furthermore, Hank would kill her if she was late for work again. Or, worse, fire her. Bad as her job was, she didn't want to lose it. She tried to walk faster, but she'd forgotten to take her caffeine pills, so the headache that had been threatening all morning was beginning to kick in.

When she got to the highway, all the cop cars had cleared away. Ed and his troops had moved operations elsewhere. Josh was probably trying to find them so he could get all the gory details for his story. Well, lots of luck on that.

The highway traffic hadn't started yet; it was too early. The good news was she wasn't likely to run into anyone who knew her. The bad news was, she wasn't likely to run into anyone who knew her and might offer her a lift. Damn Josh.

She heard a horn. Surprised, she looked up. No one used their horns in Charles Valley except the tourists. Denny was approaching in his old green pickup. He waved, drove past her, made a U-turn, and pulled up alongside her.

She climbed into the front seat gratefully. "Bless you. What are you doing out this way so early?"

"I went over to the bar to get a delivery and saw your car in the lot. Figured your date, not being a well-brought-up son of the South, might have left you stranded this morning."

"You don't know the half of it."

Chapter Seven

*L*I'L BIT WALKED ONTO HER PORCH and looked out at the empty highway. She watched as Denny Larsen's green pickup drove past her house, made a U-turn, and stopped. A girl had been walking along the side of the road, partially hidden from Li'l Bit's view by the magnolias. Li'l Bit thought it was Laurel McCready, although that could have been her imagination. Laurel had been on her mind a lot lately, not that she would ever admit that to Maggie. The truck picked up the girl and drove off. The highway was deserted again.

Li'l Bit lowered herself into the old wooden rocker that had been built for her father and was strong enough to take her weight. The medical examiner had taken away his black-plastic-covered gurney. Soon he would be discovering answers she already knew, to questions she and Peggy and Maggie had agonized over months before. Then it would all be over. She looked at the porch swing Maggie still used every afternoon when she came over, even though she had to hoist herself up into it and her feet dangled above the floor. Peggy's wicker chair was next to it, the seat padded and upholstered with a fabric of pink cabbage roses, the frame so fancy with Victorian curlicues it looked more like the work of a mad pastry chef than a chair.

How many times had she sat on this porch with people she loved sharing hot or cold beverages with, depending on the weather, and talking? Talk was her hobby, her sport of choice, her lifeline. Talk was what made her what she was.

"Different," Maggie had said once. "We're different."

"Actually, we're weird," Peggy said.

Li'l Bit herself used the word *outsider.*

But however you said it, it added up to the same thing. They were not like most people they knew.

THE SHAPING OF HER CHARACTER had started here on the porch with her father, Harrison Banning III. She sat at his feet, absorbing his maverick's passion for radical ideas and his loneliness. She had always been his girl. Mama was a great beauty, but highly strung and given to "moods." At times, the mere sight of her oversized daughter could drive her to a frenzy. "Get out of my sight, you big clumsy thing!" she would scream. Then she would sob, "My baby, my poor little baby!" until Millie, the housekeeper, managed to coax her upstairs to bed and soothe her to sleep.

And Daddy would take Li'l Bit out on the porch and try to make it better by explaining that Mama didn't mean to be hurtful, it was just that she'd never gotten over the loss of Li'l Bit's older brother, who died before she was born. And Li'l Bit would try to believe him, even when she overheard Mama laughing with her friends and calling her "my child, the horse," or "the Giantess." Or when she moaned, "Why can't you at least develop a sense of humor? A homely girl can be popular if she can make people laugh." But Li'l Bit remained solemn and shy and unpopular—especially with kids her own age. Daddy said not to worry. "They're ordinary and you're special," he said. "Wear their rejection as your red badge of courage, Li'l Bit."

Mama rolled her eyes in exasperation and said, "Will you stop calling her that? Do you want to make her even more ridiculous than she is already?" But Li'l Bit understood that the pet name was her father's way of trying to make her life right and she clung to it. Then Millie started calling her Miss Li'l Bit, others in town soon picked up on the name, and there was no going back.

Eventually she understood that her daddy was wrong. Mama *did* mean to be hurtful. Beth Banning was the kind of woman who didn't like other females. The only way her daughter could have pleased her would have been by paying her the compliment of being exactly like her, which shy and clumsy Li'l Bit couldn't do. Instead, she became her daddy's lieutenant in the ever-escalating war that was her parents' marriage.

When she got older, she realized her father had not played fair with her mother. When Harrison met Beth, she was an Atlanta girl. She had a substantial pedigree and an active social life her daddy could no longer afford, because he'd been a cotton broker and the market had crashed.

Young Beth agreed to marry the hayseed from Charles Valley because he was small-town royalty and, more important, thanks to the first Harrison Banning's having invested heavily in Coca-Cola decades earlier, the family was still rich. She decided it was better to lord it over the yokels in a rural backwater than to continue dwindling in the city she loved. It came as an ugly surprise when she realized she had married not the town's prince but its rebel.

Li'l Bit never knew exactly what it was that made her father cast himself in that role. It could have been the brutality of his own father, a pillar of the Church of God who spoke in tongues, parented through pain, and was an enthusiastic behind-the-scenes supporter of the Klan. It could have been the years Harrison spent in New York getting his law degree at Columbia. Whatever the reasons, Harrison Banning developed a lifelong antipathy to all forms of organized religion and became a member of the NAACP. Both stands were undertaken from heartfelt conviction. An added bonus in later life was the fact that they drove his wife crazy.

Li'l Bit's mama threw temper tantrums and had sick headaches. She invoked her most powerful mantra: What-will-people-think-of-us? It didn't even touch Harrison. Sunday mornings, while God-fearing people were in church, he sat on his porch reading the newspaper. And his sizable donations to the NAACP went out four times a year like clockwork.

Her father's sympathies were well known in the Negro community, and to the extent that any white man was ever going to be trusted there, he probably was.

Negroes who were forced to deal with the white legal system went to Harrison as a matter of course. He kept their cases out of court, where they would have lost, and pulled strings when he could to get sentences reduced and fines rescinded. His greatest source of pride was his role in the battle to reopen the colored high school in Charles Valley. It took the elders of three Negro churches seven long years to get it reinstated. During that time, when they needed legal advice it was Harrison they called.

None of this made him popular in the white community. The men continued to do business with him because he was too rich and too good a lawyer to be ignored. But he was not welcomed as a dinner guest by their wives. Beth grew shrill and shrewish as she was forced into social limbo at his side. Harrison shrugged it off.

At night he sat on his front porch with his young daughter at his feet and talked about hearing Paul Robeson sing, the writings of Ida B. Wells, and William H. Hastie being appointed the first Negro federal judge. Li'l Bit learned to revere the NAACP and the Harlem Renaissance. She could recite Claude McKay's poem "If We Must Die" by heart. Her heroes were W.E.B. Du Bois and James Russell Lowell. And her daddy. With all her heart, she believed her daddy was the bravest man on earth. And as she grew into her teenage years, his courage made it easier to bear being the Giantess.

Then everything changed. It started on a bright Sunday morn-

ing when Millie's oldest son, George, cut his arm almost to the
bone mowing hay. He was bleeding so badly, there wasn't time to
go over to the next town, where the doctor was young and good
and willing to treat colored folks. So Millie's cousin Lottie ran to
get old Doc Brewster, who everyone agreed was so prejudiced it
was embarrassing. While Lottie banged on the back door of his
house and screamed that a child was dying, the doctor told her to
go home and come back on Monday. He wasn't going to disrupt
his Sunday dinner because some little jiggerboo had scratched himself. George bled to death while Millie and Lottie were trying to
get a car to drive him to the next town. Later, Doc Brewster would
explain he hadn't taken the situation seriously because Negroes always got hysterical and gibbered over nothing.

The story was so ugly no one wanted to think about it. Folks
liked Millie; she was hardworking and churchgoing and had a cross
to bear putting up with Beth Banning. But old Doc was set in his
ways, and it was unlikely that he would have had the skill to save
Millie's boy even if he had been willing to try. So people said it was
too bad and forgot it.

Li'l Bit wanted to scream. A terrible thing had happened and
they couldn't just go on as if it hadn't. She couldn't make it better
for Millie, but she wanted to make a statement, loud and clear, that
not all whites were like Doc Brewster. She came up with an idea
that was simple but bold. Mama would hate it, but she hadn't cared
for years what Mama thought. Daddy would see the rightness of it.
They had talked for so long about equality for Negroes and human
dignity, now there was something they could do.

Heart pounding, she broached the subject.

"You want to do what?" Mama screamed as predicted. Li'l Bit
tuned her out like radio static and turned her attention on her father, knowing this was going to be their finest hour.

"Daddy, after the funeral for Millie's George, I want to have the
reception here at our house."

"Have you lost your mind?" Mama yelled.

Li'l Bit kept her eyes on her father. "We'll ask Millie and her family and all her friends to come here for lunch."

"In my house? You want me to entertain Negroes in my house?" Mama's voice was heading toward the stratosphere. Li'l Bit ignored her.

"We'll make it pretty for them, Daddy. We'll use the china and the silver, and I'll put flowers on the table." Mama was making inarticulate sounds of rage now, but Daddy was silent. "We have to show that we care, Daddy. We have to say to Millie and her family that what happened was wrong."

Mama found speech again. "If you care about Millie, young lady, you won't say a word about this to her. You won't be that cruel."

There was no way to ignore her anymore. She faced her mother.

"It's not being cruel to want to do something for her."

"You think she'd want your *reception*? You think she'd want any part of doing that to me?"

"This has nothing to do with you."

"Millie would be mortified if she knew you were even thinking like this. She isn't one of those uppity niggers you and your father are always talking about."

Daddy never let anyone use that word in his house. Li'l Bit waited for him say something. But he stared blankly, as if he was in a dream, as Mama ranted on.

"I know what you're up to. You want to drag poor Millie over here so you can prove a point. You want to show her how smart you are."

"No!" But there was just enough truth in the words that tears started stinging her eyes.

"Because you're a selfish mean girl and you always have been."

The tears were spilling over now, running down her cheeks.

"You and your father giving yourself airs, thinking you're better than everybody else. You're nothing but a homely girl who can't get a beau!"

Finally Daddy seemed to wake up. "Beth—" he began, but she drowned him out.

"This is what you've done to her!" she screamed at him. "You've turned her into a freak. Are you happy? This is the only child I've got left, and you've made her into a freak!" And she ran out, slamming the door behind her.

Minutes seemed to go by. Daddy was very still, staring at the closed door. Li'l Bit swallowed back her tears and went to him.

"She's wrong," she said. "I just wanted to do something—"

"I know, honey."

"She's wrong about Millie too."

"No, honey, that's where *you're* wrong. Millie doesn't need us to have a reception for her. She needs to grieve with her own kind."

It was the first time she'd heard him say anything like that.

"Why don't we ask her? At least she'd know we thought of it."

"She'd think she had to come."

"We'd tell her she didn't."

"Li'l Bit, leave it alone."

"But if you just told her—"

"No."

And then she realized. "You're afraid she might say yes."

"I don't want to put her in an awkward position."

"You don't want to do it any more than Mama—"

"It's not that simple."

"Then why don't we ask her, Daddy?"

"It would be a strain on her. She needs comfort now."

"Let *her* tell us that."

"I told you to leave it alone! Millie and her family wouldn't know what to do if they were guests in our house." He took a long pause, and then he said quietly, "And I wouldn't know what to do either."

He looked beaten. She wanted to throw her arms around him

and tell him it was all right, she was sorry she ever had the idea, and he was still a brave good man. But then he said something that made it impossible.

"Your mother's right," he said.

That was what she couldn't forgive.

In one way it wasn't very significant. Life went on. Millie came back to work with an ache in her eyes that was hard to look at. But she still cooked and cleaned. She was still the only one who could soothe Mama when an evil spell hit. And Mama and Daddy continued their war.

But in another way everything changed. Li'l Bit and her father still sat on the porch and talked, but never again about Negro rights. Gone were the stories about Robeson and Ida B. Wells. Daddy tried to find other topics, she could see him racking his brain, but she didn't want to tell him about the misery that was her school day. And the weather was good for only a few minutes. Soon, he began going inside early because it was too chilly, or too dark, or just because. Finally he stopped coming out on the porch altogether. So Li'l Bit, not knowing what else to do, sat out there alone.

She felt she'd lost everything. The feeling stayed in the core of her until the night so many decades later, in a situation that was so different and totally the same, when she had finally taken action the way she had wanted to when she was young and still believed all wrongs could be righted. When her daddy was her knight in shining armor.

LI'L BIT SHIFTED IN HER CHAIR. The mass of magnolia trees down by the highway had gotten so blurry she could barely make them out. She wiped her eyes angrily. She was old and silly, getting all watery-eyed about something that happened a million years ago. But of course she knew the tears weren't just for old losses.

Inside the house Petula began the frantic barking that signaled that the phone was ringing. Li'l Bit hadn't even heard it. Her hearing was not what it used to be, which was not always a bad thing. It could be a wonderful excuse when she didn't want to answer her phone. Like now. She heaved herself out of her chair and walked slowly inside. By the time she reached the kitchen, Petula had stopped barking. But the red light on her answering machine was flashing. Now there was no escape. With a shaky hand she reached out and pushed the button on the machine.

"Li'l Bit?" Maggie's soft low voice came at her and waited for an answer. "Li'l Bit, are you there? I do wish you'd get the loud ring put on your phone. Or at least get one of those cordless things to carry out to the porch." There was another pause. Then Maggie, sounding painfully weary, said, "I've just had a call from Ed, Li'l Bit. He wants to come by and see all of us later today. I told him to meet us at your place. He seems to know we were at the cabin last night."

Chapter Eight

DENNY DROVE IN SILENCE, waiting for Laurel to talk. He was giving her her "space," or some such garbage he'd picked up in a twelve-step meeting. It drove her nuts when he did stuff like that.

"Don't you have any normal curiosity at all?" she finally demanded.

"You suggesting I should pry into the intimate details of your life?"

"I would, in a heartbeat."

"I'm a better person than you are. Besides, I know you're gonna tell me all about it."

"See, that's why no one likes you."

"Because I'm a better person than you are?"

"Because you're a know-it-all."

"Only when it comes to you, sugar."

He drove on in silence. Finally she couldn't stand it anymore.

"He's a writer. Works on big magazines like *Vanity Fair* and *People*," she said.

If Denny was impressed he didn't show it. "Sounds like he should be right up your alley."

"Oh, yeah. Want to know why he took me home last night?

He's writing a story about Vashti Johnson, and he knew who I was."

Denny smiled. "Didn't look like that was what was on his mind at the Grill. Sure you're not just being paranoid?"

"Okay, he says he didn't know then. But he recognized my name from those damn books at my house. He's done research on Vashti and her mom and why they left town. He knows about my daddy."

Denny stayed silent, which was smart. When they were small she used to beat up any kid who mentioned her father.

The little strip mall where McGee's Restaurant was located was coming up. "Stop and let me get some coffee," she said.

Denny drove into the mall parking lot, but he wasn't happy about it. "You sure you want to do this?" he asked. "Lotta cars in front of the place this morning."

Of course, as soon as he said that it became a matter of pride to go in. "You afraid they'll be talking about me?"

"You were . . . having fun last night."

"It won't be the first time I've gone somewhere and stopped the conversation."

"You'll be late to work."

"Hank'll live."

"Looking for a fight this morning, sugar?" he asked softly. Then, when she didn't answer, "Your New Yorker isn't coming back?"

"I hope not."

"I see."

"No, you don't." And that made her want to scream. "Don't you ever get tired of living in a town with people who've known you since you were drooling?"

"Laurel Selene, suppose you tell me what's really got you going this morning."

And because she desperately wanted to talk about it, and be-

cause he was Denny who came to get her after a Friday night fling
had left her stranded, she told him about Vashti dying. And as soon
as he recovered from that piece of news she told him about seeing
the three Miss Margarets.

"They were there at the cabin? You sure?"

"I was too far away to see their faces—but it was them."

"What the hell were they doing there?"

"I don't know. But I'd sure like to find out."

He watched her for a moment. "Lotta old shit will get stirred
up, won't it, Laurel?"

She shrugged. "Ma's gone. No one will even care."

He gave her a look that said he knew better, but he left it alone.
"You still want that coffee?"

"What the hell, I'll make a pot at work."

"Good idea." He drove back to the highway and took her to her
car. As she started to get out he stopped her. "You gonna tell Hank
about seeing the three Miss Margarets?"

"Ed knows about it. I'll see what he does with it."

"Let it lie, Laurel."

"I can handle whatever comes up. I'm not Ma."

"I wasn't thinking about you. They're old ladies, sugar."

ED HAD SOUNDED SERIOUS on the phone, Maggie decided, as
she headed for her morning shower. But Ed always thought he was
more important than he was. She had never liked him much even
when he was a child. Back then, he'd been an unpleasant little boy
who liked to bully the younger children, but screamed like a ban-
shee whenever she had to give him a shot. He'd married that twit
Cathy Sue, who was tough enough to be the perfect wife for him,
and then he'd cheated on her with Laurel—who wasn't tough at all,
no matter how hard the poor thing tried to be. Maggie sighed the
way she always did when she thought of Laurel McCready. Let Li'l

Bit say all she wanted that the girl wasn't their responsibility; they all knew better. But when they could have done something, they'd been too scared.

Maggie got into the shower and let the hot water beat against her tight muscles, loosening them enough so she could turn her head to the right. Mobility on her left side was a thing of the past. She had gotten so much older than she ever dreamed of being. If anyone had told her when she was young that she would be this person, she wouldn't have believed it.

WHEN MAGGIE LEFT HOME for college she was convinced she'd never forget Lottie or be happy again. She was right and wrong. She didn't forget Lottie, or the guilt she felt for what had happened. But eventually, because it wasn't in her not to be, she was happy again. It just took a while.

In the beginning she was in too much pain to even think about being in love. But finally she started to heal and had a couple of intense crushes she didn't dare act on. In her senior year there was a girl named Jessie, who wanted Maggie to room with her in Paris after graduation. Maggie thought she was getting other signals too, but she didn't have the courage to find out. Later on, when she was in medical school, she heard via a discreet grapevine about places to go where she might meet other young women like herself, but the risks still seemed too high. Or perhaps the timing wasn't right.

When she went home for visits, she caught glimpses of Lottie, who now lived in her own place with James, but their paths never crossed. Lottie's father had died, and Charlie Mae had gone to live with Lottie to take care of the baby while Lottie worked. The little cabin at the bottom of the ridge was empty. Maggie's mother wrote to her at school when Lottie had a son and named him after James. Later she wrote again when Lottie had twins who were lost at birth. Maggie wrote her parents an angry letter blaming Dr.

Brewster for not giving Lottie proper prenatal care, but she didn't try to get in touch with Lottie herself.

Then Lottie wrote to her. In the painstaking Palmer handwriting she and Maggie had learned together, she wrote about her son and working at the resort and the vegetable garden she'd put in behind her house. And Maggie understood that Lottie was reaching out because their friendship had mattered to her too. And Maggie was grateful. She wrote back a chatty letter in handwriting that had deteriorated in school to a fashionable scrawl.

After college, Maggie announced that she was going to become a doctor. Her mama was dismayed, and her daddy was bewildered. But she was their darling Doodlebug, so they got together the money to pay her way through the Woman's Medical College in Philadelphia and breathed a big sigh of relief when she came back south to practice in Atlanta. She was lucky enough to find a young male doctor who was willing to let her work with him, so she actually had a few patients. And if there were times when she thought that loneliness would swamp her, she usually managed to get busy and the feelings went away.

Until she met Catherine. It happened at a Christmas party thrown by some interns from Emory. She fell for brooding Mediterranean looks, smart brown eyes, thick hair that curled uncontrollably in the heat of summer or passion, a quick temper, and an even quicker laugh. Catherine introduced her to Catholicism and ravioli. And she reintroduced Maggie to fun. They never had a dime—Catherine was a nurse and made even less than Maggie—but no one else they knew had money either.

They moved in together and found a circle of friends, other young women who had come to the city to get away from small towns and families that would never accept a lesbian neighbor or daughter. "We've got our tribe," Catherine said. They still lived an underground life. Even in Atlanta, the threat to careers and reputations if they were discovered was an unspoken reality. But for the majority of the "tribe," the sense of freedom was exhilarating. And they would have agreed with Catherine when she said their lives were perfect. Most of the time Maggie believed it. But sometimes late at night, when she couldn't sleep, she knew there was another shoe waiting to drop.

Then one evening, the phone call came from Lottie. In a voice as dry as dead autumn leaves, she told Maggie how Millie's little boy George had died.

"We need a doctor here, Maggie," she said. "We need a real one who will take care of folks." There was no need for Lottie to remind Maggie that being a doctor had been her dream. Or that she had dreamed it for the sake of children like George.

Maggie looked around her tiny apartment and thought it had never seemed as warm as it did at that moment. Every piece of cheap furniture was loaded with charm. She looked at Catherine, sipping a glass of dark red wine as she washed up after their supper.

"Oh, Lottie," she said softly.

"Millie's young one was only thirteen," said the relentless voice on the other end of the phone.

And Maggie knew the other shoe had dropped.

Catherine said she was crazy. She said it would be the end of them. Maggie said she would come to Atlanta for weekends. She said she was a doctor and she had to go where she was needed.

"If the rednecks in that hick town knew the truth about you they wouldn't let you practice on their dogs. They'd stone you in the village square."

Maggie admitted she'd have to be careful.

"Careful?" said Catherine. "You'll be lying for the rest of your life."

The night before Maggie left, they fought again. "It's because of Lottie," Catherine stormed. "You're doing this to us because of her."

Maggie tried to explain Charles Valley to her city-bred lover.

She talked about the old pecan trees and the fruitcake recipe that had been in her family for generations. She told Catherine about the fields where her father still grew his sweet-potato crop, and the way you could smell Mama's magnolias all over the farm in spring. But the pecan trees were the ones she had climbed with Lottie, and they had read Mama's magazines together sitting under the magnolias. Catherine was no fool, and she sensed Maggie was leaving out crucial details.

She said Maggie was committing emotional suicide. Maggie tried to keep it light, but secretly she thought Catherine was right. She just didn't have any other choice. So she went home.

THE WATER IN THE SHOWER had run cold. Maggie got out and started dressing. She wanted to get to Li'l Bit's before Peggy did, and she had to run an errand first.

Chapter Nine

THE LEMONADE FOR MAGGIE was already made, so Li'l Bit brewed tea for herself. In a way she was glad it was too early to call Peggy. It would be good to have some time with Maggie alone. Peggy was soft; she gave in to her doubts and fears. But Maggie was a tough old bird, as tough as Li'l Bit herself, probably the only person in Charles Valley who was. Li'l Bit had sensed that almost from the first time they met, back when she was still a teenager and Maggie had just come home.

LI'L BIT HAD HEARD about Maggie over the years; a girl who went off to college to become a lady doctor was bound to get herself talked about in Charles Valley. But the ten-year age difference between them was big enough that their paths had not crossed.

After Maggie came home, she was busy establishing her practice, or trying to. And Li'l Bit was busy being miserable. Adolescence hit her with all its force after Harrison Banning retreated from their nightly sessions on the porch. She discovered to her horror that she was just as ridiculous as other girls her age. The only difference was, when she developed a wild unrequited crush on a boy, she had no friends to bare her broken heart to.

Dressed by her mother in fussy dresses and ruffles, with her outsized feet encased in fashionable Cuban heels, she walked through the hallways of her school alone, a large square girl whose watery blue eyes peered at the world from behind thick glasses.

She was aware, dimly, through the mists of self-absorption, that Dr. Maggie, as she was now called by everyone, was back home and wanted to start a clinic. Harrison was trying to help her. There was a time when her father would have told Li'l Bit all the details, holding forth at the dinner table until his wife declared herself ready to die of boredom. But Harrison seemed to be in retreat more and more these days. He ate his supper silently and quickly; long gone were the days of seconds on dessert and compliments to Millie. After the meal he left the parlor to his wife and his daughter and went off on aimless rambles around the property. Hitler had begun his mischief-making in Europe, and everyone talked about America getting into the war—or being sucked into it, depending on the speaker's point of view. Even Mama listened to the news on the radio. But Harrison went outside and wandered.

Every night Li'l Bit went upstairs to the attic to look out the window and watch him as he circled the lawn and threaded his way through what had once been an old pear orchard until he reached a pond at the side of the property. She watched him through the tree branches as he stood at the edge of the water, staring off into space while the sun set. Some nights he stayed there until the evening gray sky turned dark. Then he would turn and she would strain to see him as he made his way back to his house, a lonely figure whose only companion was his daughter, watching him from above. It felt like she was spying, but since he had abandoned the porch this was her only contact with him.

Then, on a hot Monday afternoon in the fall, after school had started for her senior year, she came home to find the driveway full of cars. Her first thought was that Mama's garden club was meeting at the house again, and if they stayed late Daddy would be angry and there would be a fight. But then Millie opened the back door, her eyes red from crying, and behind her in the kitchen the

counters and the table were loaded with covered dishes and platters
of food in china patterns that weren't part of any set they had ever
owned. The minister from Mama's church appeared in the doorway with a crowd of people around him. She had a brief flash of
thinking Daddy was really going to hate this party if Reverend
Davis was there. But Reverend Davis wasn't smiling like it was a
party.

The group around him parted and someone murmured "poor
child," while the minister made his way to her and took her hand
in his big sweaty one. He hadn't liked her father any more than
Harrison liked him, and she was pretty sure his feelings for her
were the same, so she knew something was very, very wrong even
before he told her that her daddy had died. It had happened early
that morning, but they hadn't known until after she went to school.
She hadn't been called all day because her mother hadn't wanted to
disturb her, Reverend Davis said, as if it were a wonderful thing
Mama had done.

She tried to tell the minister he was wrong; she'd seen her father
walking back from the pond the night before and he was fine. She
tried to say that something as big and total as death just couldn't happen so fast without any warning, and her daddy would never leave
her forever without saying good-bye. But people started swarming
around her, saying she should sit down, and she couldn't tell them
that she didn't need to, she just needed some way to make the words
they were throwing at her make sense.

Then suddenly a strong little hand was on her arm, turning
her away from everyone, and a pretty doll-like little face was inches
away from hers, and Dr. Maggie was saying in her low voice, "Miss
Banning, this is very sudden, I know, but I think your father had
been ill for some time. I told him he should make an appointment
with his doctor but I'm afraid he didn't listen to me."

The dispassionate voice was helping her organize her mind
so she could think, which was both good and bad. "What did
he . . . ?" She trailed off, unable to finish. Dr. Maggie understood.

"I wasn't his physician, but my guess would be that it was his heart. Your mama should know more after there's been an autopsy. I hope that doesn't upset you, but it's required in cases like this."

"No. I want to find out."

"Of course." There was a pause. "You should know there was no sign he was in pain. Millie found him in his bed, and she said it looked as if his end was peaceful. It's likely that it happened in his sleep and he never knew. It can be that way sometimes."

So he had been alone when he died. Her parents hadn't slept in the same bedroom for as long as she could remember. She shivered and hoped he hadn't known what was happening.

Dr. Maggie went on. "If he had lived, he probably would have been incapacitated. I think it would have been an extremely difficult life for a vigorous man like your father." Li'l Bit nodded. For her daddy to be sick and unable to work would have been impossible. Work was all he had, work and her. And she couldn't fool herself that she would have been enough.

"I'm sorry," Dr. Maggie said. "Your father was a good man. I'll miss him."

And finally, those words made it real.

In a way, that was the beginning of her friendship with Maggie. And it seemed fitting that on the day her father died she had taken the first step on the journey to what was to be her finest—or her lowest—hour; take your pick. But that was years away.

People started swirling around her again and someone said she should be with her mother, poor lamb, so Reverend Davis led her over to the couch where Mama, dressed from head to toe in black, was sitting with a hankie in her hand. But her eyes were dry.

For the next two days, while a part of Li'l Bit's heart died forever, her daddy lay in state at the funeral home used by Mama's church, the one he never set foot in. Mama's brother, a man Daddy had loathed, came down from Atlanta to be a support to her. Together they picked out hymns her father would have laughed at. Men he disliked were chosen to carry his coffin.

Li'l Bit fought with Mama. "You can't have the funeral in a church," she said.

"I'm going to do my duty by my husband."

"Daddy hated churches."

"I suppose you'd like me to have him dumped in the ground like some heathen. He will have a proper Christian burial."

"He wasn't a proper Christian."

"Well, he's gone, and I say this is how it's going to be. Your father humiliated me with his *ideas* for years. Everyone talked about him. Now I'm going to have a funeral like a normal widow."

"You can't do this to him."

"Watch me."

"I won't come."

"If you don't, you can pack your bags and leave this house right now."

For a few hours Li'l Bit considered it. She even got out the old leather suitcase with her father's initials. But in the end she was too much the logical daughter of a lawyer to go through with it. Practical considerations of food and shelter came up. She was not qualified to earn her living, and she knew it. And if she tried to leave and had to come back, Mama would make her crawl. So she put on the black dress and stockings Mama had bought for her, she got in the car with Mama and Uncle Lance, and she went to the funeral.

Standing outside the First Methodist Church of Charles Valley was one of the Negro ministers her father had represented and about thirty people from his congregation. For the first time since she had come home from school to hear that her father was gone, Li'l Bit smiled. But as Mama got out of the car she turned to her brother and muttered, "Get them away from here before the people start arriving."

"Reverend Thomas just wants to pay his respects, Mama. He doesn't expect you to ask him to come inside." Li'l Bit didn't even try to hide the contempt in her voice.

"Be quiet," said Beth.

"He was Daddy's friend—"

"I told you to close your mouth. I've been the wife of a nigger lover since I got to this town. I won't be the widow of one."

Li'l Bit drew breath to protest, but her mother turned to her with a look that was half triumphant and half defiant and said, "I'm in charge now. Start getting used to it, Margaret Elizabeth."

So she went into the church with Mama, while Uncle Lance sent away the only part of the funeral her father would have liked. As she walked into the church she saw Dr. Maggie and her parents get out of the car. And she saw the sympathy in Dr. Maggie's eyes.

HARRISON BANNING III WAS BURIED in the graveyard next to the Methodist Church where, presumably, he immediately began spinning. A week after the funeral, Judge James, who handled Harrison's affairs, called and asked Mama to come to his office for the reading of the will. At first Beth refused. She was too busy redecorating the house.

"I've been wanting to do this hateful old place over for years," she informed Li'l Bit, "but your father wouldn't let me touch it— he acted like it was some kind of shrine."

Now, dressed in black, lace hankie in hand, she was directing the upholsterers to rip the horsehair off an old love seat and re-cover it in perky chintz. Years later, Li'l Bit would learn Mama's refinishing and re-covering had cut thousands of dollars from the value of these precious old antiques.

"Can't you just come to the house, Judge?" Mama asked. "It can't be that complicated. He didn't have anyone besides me." But the judge insisted and told her to bring Li'l Bit too.

They went to his office on a Friday morning and found Millie waiting there. Mama didn't like that one bit, but Judge James was in the room so she managed a smile for Millie. Then Dr. Maggie walked in. Li'l Bit could feel how twitchy Mama was getting. This time there was no attempt at a smile.

It turned out Mama was right—Daddy's will wasn't very complicated. He gave Millie ten thousand dollars, and left Dr. Maggie fifteen thousand to start her clinic. Li'l Bit could see Mama calculating the loss of interest on investments in her head. Mama was very good with figures when she had to be. Then suddenly Li'l Bit heard her own name mentioned. "To my daughter, Margaret Elizabeth Banning, I leave the rest of my estate save one dollar, which I must by law leave to Elizabeth Banning, my wife."

The gasp from Mama seemed to echo in the suddenly silent room.

Then Li'l Bit whispered, "Oh, Daddy, no!"

"What did you just say?" Mama turned on the judge in the way that said a tantrum was coming. Judge James turned red and looked like he'd rather be anywhere else on the planet.

"Your late husband—" he began, but Mama cut him off.

"That bastard!" she said. Then she started to laugh. Out of habit, Millie started toward her to avert the oncoming hysterics, but she was too far away.

Li'l Bit got to her mother first. "Mama," she said, "please don't—" but her mother slapped her across the face.

The crack of Mama's hand on her cheek sounded sharp and loud. Out of the corner of her eye she could see Dr. Maggie flinch. Judge James had gotten, if possible, even redder. Millie had stopped moving. Mama was quiet, momentarily stunned by what she had just done.

And something cold and very calm had taken over Li'l Bit.

"Mama, we need to go home now," she said evenly.

Her mother, still in shock, nodded and started out the door.

"Maybe your mother shouldn't be driving," Dr. Maggie said. "I'll take you."

"I can drive," Li'l Bit said. "My father taught me."

They didn't say a word all the way home. When they got inside the house, her mother turned to her.

"We'll go to court. You'll turn everything over to me," she said. "There must be a way to do it."

"No, Mama," she heard herself say.

"Don't be stupid. I'm your mother. You're just a child. He can't leave his entire estate to you."

"I'm sure he could. Daddy was an excellent lawyer. He wouldn't have done anything that wasn't legal."

"I'll fight you. I'll break the will."

"You can try. But it won't look very nice. What kind of mother tries to take her daughter's inheritance away from her?"

"What kind of daughter disinherits her own mother? How will that look to people?"

"Not much better. But your problem is, I don't care what I look like. You do. Besides, a fight like that will take months, maybe even years, and we'll spend thousands and thousands of dollars. Daddy always said probate court was like fighting through a swamp. You'd know that if you'd ever listened to him."

"If you think I'm going to let you do this to me—"

"What I think you'll do if you're smart is, you'll go back to Atlanta where you belong. You never wanted to be here anyway."

"I will not leave my child—"

"You don't like me, Mama, and I don't like you. We'll both be happier without each other. Go back to Atlanta. I'll give you an allowance each month. You can rent yourself a house or live with Uncle Lance. You'll probably find yourself another husband. You're still pretty enough."

And in the end, because she did want to get out of Charles Val-

ley and the idea of being back in Atlanta with money was so entic-
ing, Beth agreed. Li'l Bit wished she had known years ago how
easy it was to manage her mama.

Beth left in a flurry of suitcases. "I'm giving you all that old
junk that was in your father's family. I wouldn't have it on a stick,"
she said, conveniently forgetting that none of it was hers to give.

At first the town was scandalized at the idea of a seventeen-year-
old girl living on her own in the big old house she had inherited
from her daddy. But slowly people got used to the idea. In spite of
her windfall, Millie elected to go on keeping house for Li'l Bit, so
people told themselves the child wasn't totally alone. And Li'l Bit
was so obviously competent that there was no way anyone could
worry about her. She drove herself to school every morning in the
DeSoto that had belonged to her father. She was always on time.
Her grades were excellent, as they always had been.

She graduated at the top of her class, with no family in the au-
dience to see her give her valedictory address. It was just as well,
because she tossed away the speech she had prepared with her English teacher and quoted liberally from Eleanor Roosevelt's column, "My Day." Since the First Lady was not well liked locally, her
performance was not a success.

Everyone assumed that Li'l Bit would go to college. After all,
people said, what else was a girl that plain and smart going to do?
Most thought she'd go to some fancy school up north like her
daddy had. But Li'l Bit had no intention of leaving the newfound
quiet in her house. Her life to that point had been dominated by
her parents. Now she was alone. No more of Mama trying to make
her *normal*. And badly as she missed him, no more of Daddy trying
to make her *special*. For the first time in her life she could listen to
her own thoughts. She didn't want to change things.

The day after her graduation she emptied her closet. The print
sundresses and little flared skirts were dumped in a heap on the
floor, along with the ruffled blouses, pastel sweaters, and silly little

hats, the gloves that were too tight, and the shoes that pinched her feet. The pile grew, so that by the time the people from the Rescue Mission came to take everything away there were ten pillowcases full, and she was left with her underwear and the clothes on her back. She went to her mother's seamstress and had plain shirtwaist dresses with gored skirts sewn up in dark colors. She bought herself several pairs of Natural Bridge oxfords.

She canceled her monthly appointment at the hairdresser's. Her bushy hair had been cut and marcelled for the last time. She bought hair nets to keep it out of her eyes while it grew long enough to be bundled up in a bun, and found she enjoyed the feeling of her hair on her neck and shoulders when she went to sleep. She purchased one tube of lipstick for dress-up, but she lost it before she had a chance to put it on and didn't bother to replace it.

When she was done, she studied herself carefully in the mirror. The name Giantess was not only accurate, it was probably kind. But at least now when she saw her reflection, she recognized the person she saw.

People in Charles Valley got used to seeing the solemn young woman going about her business in town, buying her groceries, and dropping in each morning at the post office. They stopped noticing how young her face was under the dowdy bun. Which was exactly the way she wanted it.

SUNLIGHT WAS STREAMING through the kitchen windows. Li'l Bit looked down at the black dress she had put on that morning. She seldom made mistakes anymore about what she wanted to wear, but this morning she had. Black was all wrong. She went back to her bedroom to change.

Chapter Ten

MAGGIE PULLED HER BLACK SUIT out of the back of the closet, looked at it briefly, and put it back. There was a time when the Catholic Church expected a year of mourning after a death, but that had gone the way of hats to cover the women's hair and no meat on Friday. It was just as well. She had no intention of wearing black.

It was hard to remember she was an old-timer in the church now. When she'd converted, it had seemed so monumental.

SHE'D STARTED GOING TO CHURCH with Catherine when she still lived in Atlanta. She'd been raised as a Methodist, but she'd fallen in love with the mysticism of Catholic ritual. The minor-key chants sung in ancient languages and the statues of saints brooding under high arched ceilings appealed to something in her. She'd gone every Sunday at Catherine's side until she came back home.

There was a Catholic church in Charles Valley, more like a chapel really, where a visiting priest held one mass on Sunday for the resort guests. She could have asked him about converting, but she didn't. Her affair with Catherine was a sin according to the church, and that stopped her. Catherine, the cradle Catholic, said what the priests didn't know wouldn't hurt them. But as an outsider

Maggie felt she should play by the rules. So she went to mass as Catherine's guest when she was in Atlanta, but she avoided church and saw patients on the weekends when she stayed home—which, to the delight of her elderly parents, she was doing more and more.

When she'd come back, she'd known it wasn't going to be easy to start a practice. It had been bad enough finding patients who would trust a lady doctor in Atlanta, and Charles Valley was a lot less liberal. Friends who had known her family for generations ducked their heads guiltily when she walked into Krasden's drugstore, because they were sticking with old Doc Brewster even though he was on the verge of retirement.

But soon word got out among the poor and desperate, Negro and white, that the new lady doctor was not only dirt cheap, she was smart and knew what she was doing. Maggie's practice began to grow, not just in Charles Valley but throughout the entire county. She spent most of her time on the road, usually driving from one crisis situation to another. Her clientele did not send for the doctor easily. Maggie was called in only after home remedies, the laying on of hands, prayer, and, in some cases, witchcraft had failed. Often, by the time she got to the scene, all she could do was stand by helplessly and watch her patient die, knowing the death could have been avoided.

As her workload got heavier, the weekend trek to Atlanta started to seem awfully long. Too often when she got there, Catherine was moody and difficult. Besides, people didn't stop needing their doctor simply because it was Saturday or Sunday. Babies spiked fevers on the weekends, and women went into labor. On a Friday night when she was supposed to be in Atlanta going to the theater with Catherine, Maggie was sponging down a five-year-old boy whose typhoid fever had reached the critical stage. She canceled a Saturday lunch to stay home and teach new mothers who could not read or write the basics of hygiene.

Neither Maggie nor Catherine would admit what was happening. But it was hard to ignore the relief in Catherine's voice when Maggie said she thought she'd stay home this weekend and catch up on her sleep, or the relief in Maggie's voice when she thanked Catherine for being so understanding about it. Maggie hung on to the relationship because for her Catherine was a kind of lifeline. Lord knew why Catherine hung on. Maggie never asked.

MAGGIE PULLED UP HER KNEE-HIGHS, hateful things, but pantyhose were much too hard to maneuver into, and she never went bare-legged because of the scar she'd gotten in the barn fire so many years ago. She could still remember how sad the long slow breakup with Catherine had been. There were times when it really was a blessing not to be young. And there were other times when she would have given anything to be back in the thick of even a dying romance.

HER FIRST MEETING with Harrison Banning had taken place about six months before he died. She'd told him she needed his advice, and he asked her to come to his house on Sunday morning after his wife and daughter had gone to church.

"I had three cases of smallpox last month," she told him, after he'd seated her on his front porch. "Smallpox! In this day and age!"

Harrison had smiled wearily. "I know it's hard, trying to help when there's nothing you can do."

"There's plenty I could do! But I need a place where I can do it. All I have is a desk in my mother's parlor; most of the time I work out of my car. I need an office, with equipment and a sterile environment."

"And two or three more doctors like you," Harrison had said.

"All I want is one assistant. I've worked it out in my head a million times. But I can't afford it, and I can't ask my parents. They're not getting any younger, and sending me to medical school was a big drain on them.

"My patients can't pay more than a dollar or two a visit, and usually I wind up taking barter. If I get any more chickens I'll be selling eggs as a sideline. Mama's already given me my own hen-house. Thank God we have a farm."

"Selling eggs might make some money for you."

"More than my practice! It's so frustrating. Our new drugs can work miracles. But when a mother can't afford to put food on the table, how can I convince her to spend money on an inoculation for her baby against a disease it doesn't have? Even if I do let her pay me with a chicken, the vaccine still costs money. My hands are tied." In another second she was going to start wailing like a lit-tle ninny, so she finished quickly. "I need a clinic. I need a financial plan for providing medical care."

At this point most men would have found a nice way to get rid of her. She was a woman who had chosen an impossible profession and was now complaining because she couldn't afford to open a clinic to serve poor white trash and Negroes. Most men would have suggested she find herself a nice husband and leave the doctoring to the menfolk—who understood it was a business, not a charity. But Harrison wasn't most men.

"What kind of financial plan?" he said.

"An arrangement where the people who can afford it pay a monthly fee, and those who can't, pay what they can. Many places have been experimenting with plans like that to insure against hos-pitalization costs. In Birmingham they charge sixty cents a month. And for years in Canada, in certain provinces, they've had what they call municipal doctors, who are paid by the government. I'm at a disadvantage because I'm a woman, of course. That's the real problem."

Harrison studied her for a second. "You know Dalt Garrison got married last year?"

"I don't think Dalt's daddy will be sympathetic—" she began.

"And young Dalt hasn't had an idea that wasn't his daddy's since he was born. I know. But I have a feeling his new little wife is another story. My guess is, Miss Myrtis thinks of herself as quite enlightened. I think you and she should get to know each other."

So Myrtis and Maggie had lunch. And a few days later Myrtis Garrison stood with her reluctant young husband at her side and informed her formidable father-in-law that she would be presenting him with his first grandchild. The baby would be delivered by Dr. Maggie, she announced. If it should be a boy, he would be named Grady after his granddaddy.

As Myrtis went, so went many of the young wives of Charles Valley. Maggie didn't make a major dent in Dr. Brewster's practice, but she finally had a few patients who could actually pay for her services. She began to look around for an appropriate place for her clinic.

"I have my eye on the old sweet-potato warehouse," she told Harrison. "If enough rich women get pregnant in the next six months, I may be able to make a down payment. But I'll still need money."

"We'll work out something," said Harrison.

But weeks went by and she didn't hear from him. Then, when she had finally decided he must have given up on her and her clinic, he died and left her fifteen thousand dollars.

MAGGIE LOOKED HERSELF OVER in the mirror. Her skirt came down just low enough to hide the loathed knee-highs. She checked her watch and winced at the time. She wasn't delaying the inevitable, she assured herself. It was just that getting herself together wasn't a fast process anymore, what with having to put in her dental bridge and the arthritis in her hands. Thank the Lord she didn't have to fuss with a hearing aid. But she'd had to frost the cake, and then. . . . She stopped herself. The truth was, she *had* been delaying the inevitable. Trying to, anyway. She picked up the slice of cake she'd carefully wrapped, walked out of the house, and got into her ancient Volvo.

These days she tried not to drive any more than she had to, and never after dark, unlike Li'l Bit, who was still making the roads a hazard for man and beast. But today she was going too far to walk.

She nosed the car cautiously out onto the highway, stopping to twist her body so she could look both ways before venturing onto the road. The locals knew her car and watched out for her tricky left side, but tourists could be a hazard. She compensated by driving very slowly, figuring that way they couldn't miss her. It made people wild, of course—she remembered how she used to hate little old ladies behind the wheel when she was still young enough to zip around the country roads—but she got where she was going in one piece. At least she had so far. She crept along the highway, ignoring the angry drivers starting to honk behind her, and let her mind wander.

AFTER HARRISON'S DEATH, Maggie watched in amazement as Li'l Bit transformed herself from a schoolgirl into a dowdy matron. Maggie herself would not have worn Natural Bridge oxfords if her life depended on it. At college she had developed a taste for chic, pretty clothes that would last all her life, and when she was really broke she'd been known to go without lunch to pay for her weekly manicure.

Later, she and Li'l Bit would discover common interests. They would agree on politics and a shared passion for Agatha Christie's murder mysteries. But what brought her together with Li'l Bit in the early days was the clinic. After Beth Banning left town, Li'l Bit invited Maggie to her home for lunch. They sat on the porch and ate peanut-butter-and-jelly sandwiches. Then Li'l Bit blushed bright red and got to the point.

"I'd like to work in your clinic with you," she said. "I'll help you any way you need."

Actually, Maggie had been pondering the problem of an assistant—or, more specifically, the problem of paying for one on her limited budget.

"You won't have to pay me," Li'l Bit said, reading her mind. "I don't need money."

"I need someone in the office full time. It's not a job for a volunteer."

"You can count on me."

"You'd have to take care of my books, run my schedule, that kind of thing."

"What I don't know, I'll learn. I'm quite intelligent." Li'l Bit brushed an unruly wisp of hair out of her eyes.

Maggie looked at her, with her old-lady getup and her ridiculous—no, her *atrocious*—shoes, and wondered if she really could trust this strange girl. "There might be times when I'd need you to help me with the patients," she said.

"I'm sure I could do that."

"You don't know what it's like. These are people who are terrified and in pain. They'll take it out on you, because they're too afraid to get angry at me. You'll see things that will turn your stomach, and you cannot react. You can never let anyone see you're repelled or frightened. You can never cry."

For the first time the girl looked a little unsure. Then she rallied. "I'm not a sensitive person," she said. "I'll be all right."

"The hours will be long. And erratic. I may need you to be in the office on evenings or weekends."

"I won't be going to parties and dances. I'm not pretty, so I'll never have a beau." Maggie must have looked embarrassed, because she hurried on. "Please don't feel you have to argue with me or tell me I'm handsome in my own way or any of the other euphemisms people use when they're talking to a plain girl. I can look in a mirror. I know what I see. I'd have preferred to have been beautiful, any girl in her right mind would." For a brief moment Maggie saw something wistful flicker in her eyes. "But facts are facts. And in a certain sense, once you realize you'll never be a belle, it's a relief. You can get on with the things that matter to you."

"What things matter to you?" Maggie asked faintly.

"Being important. Which means being useful. That's the standard way for women like us, isn't it?"

"Women like us? I don't—"

"Of course you want to be useful," Li'l Bit broke in impatiently. "There's no other reason for you to have come home. This is a terrible place for someone like you."

For a few irrational seconds, paranoia ruled in Maggie's brain as she wondered exactly what this strange girl knew about her.

"You're a fun-loving person, that's obvious," Li'l Bit went on. Maggie breathed a small sigh of relief. "There's not a lot of fun to be had here. Particularly not in the profession you've chosen." The blue eyes that were now studying her, she saw, had something of Harrison's shrewdness in them. "You'll make your mark on this place," she continued. "You might even be able to change things for the better. You'll be very useful. And for whatever reason, that's what you've chosen. Like me."

Maggie wanted to run. She wanted to shout that she hadn't come back for something as sad and hopeless—and loveless—as being useful. She hadn't given up on fun. Or life. Or romance.

She got herself away from Harrison's bizarre daughter as fast as she could. She called Catherine and went into Atlanta that weekend. She didn't fight with Catherine once, even when she sulked. They went to a restaurant and a movie, and Maggie spent money she didn't have. And when she came back home she told herself how much she loved Atlanta and how much she had missed it.

🌿

The clinic was built in the old sweet-potato warehouse that sat next to the railroad station. Since the train was the only means of transportation for most of her patients and it stopped at the warehouse five times a day, the location was perfect.

The night before Maggie was supposed to open her clinic, she couldn't tear herself away from it to go home. She was circling her shiny new empire, marveling at the wonder of it, when there was a knock on the door behind her.

She turned and saw Lottie standing in the doorway. It was the first time they'd seen each other, close enough to talk, since she got back home. Which could have been because they'd both been so busy. Although she doubted it.

Lottie's face was thinner; there were too many frown lines carved in it and not enough of the grooves caused by smiles and laughter. She was wearing the shapeless gray uniform Garrison Gardens foisted on all its maids, but Maggie could see that she had thickened through the middle. The long legs were still slim, and she hadn't resorted as the other maids did to the soft wide slippers that were easy on swollen feet. But there was a heaviness to the woman standing in front of her. The Lottie of today wouldn't run through fields so fast she made her own breeze, and she wouldn't climb up pecan trees so high it was like she was soaring. The loss seemed heartbreaking, but then Maggie reminded herself that she didn't soar or run much herself these days. And Lottie would hate it if anyone felt sorry for her.

"Hey, Maggie," Lottie said. Maggie felt something in her chest tighten. She was Maggie. Not "Miss Maggie" or "Dr. Maggie," just plain Maggie. All the times she'd imagined this meeting, she'd been afraid she wouldn't be.

"I'm glad to see you, Lottie," she said, in a voice that wasn't shaking much at all. "Want to come in?"

Lottie stepped inside. There was no reading her. That was new. When they were young, Charlie Mae was always on Lottie for showing too much of what she felt.

They stared at each other a little too long; then Lottie said, "I wanted to see—" at the same time Maggie said, "Would you like to see—" and Lottie smiled. It wasn't her old bright smile, it was a much more subdued one. But it was all right. Because at that moment Maggie understood they were not going to talk about what had happened all those years ago in the barn. They were not going to go back and clear the air because they were not the kind of people who did that. And that was all right too. So she said again, "Would you like to see this place?" And Lottie said yes.

"Let me give you the grand tour," Maggie said.

When it was over, Lottie smiled her new subdued smile and said, "It's fine, Maggie. It's real fine."

And Maggie asked, "Would you like some lemonade from my fancy new icebox?"

Lottie hesitated. Then she said, "Just for a minute. I got to get home. James is working and Momma's watching James Junior. You know how Momma can be when she's mad. And my young 'un can try the patience of the Lord."

Maggie pulled two wooden chairs up to her examining table and Lottie sat down.

"How have you been?" Maggie asked.

"Good." Lottie paused. Then, as she always did when she had something on her mind, she came right out with it. "We're going to leave Charles Valley, Maggie. James wants to go up north."

It took a couple of seconds, but then Maggie heard herself ask, "Where are you going?"

"To Detroit. His sister Julia went there with her husband and her kids. Now it's all James can talk about."

"Do you want to go?"

There was a pause. "Julie earns more money working for one

white lady than I do cleaning twenty rooms a day at the resort. Her husband earns more in a week than James makes in a month. But I made James take me to Detroit to see it; his brother works for the railroad and he got us a pass." Lottie stopped and rubbed her eyes. "Maggie, you never saw anything so dirty and ugly in your life. It smells. There's no yard for the kids to play. Julie can't put in a garden. Near where they live it's called Paradise Valley. It's a terrible place, pool halls and dance halls going all night. Julie's oldest boy sneaks off to go there with his friends. She's going to have trouble with that child, I know it."

Anger and relief mixed equally in Maggie. "If you feel this way, you shouldn't go."

"There are more chances there. James says that, and I guess he's right. I know he is." She paused, swallowing hard. "But you have to be strong to live in a place like that, Maggie. I'd like to wait until the children are older, then go. But James . . . he hears what he wants to hear and he sees what he wants to see. He saw streets paved with gold in Detroit."

Maggie knew she was hearing a distilled version of an argument that had been going on for months, round after weary round. Then something hit her.

"You said 'the children'?"

"I'm going to have another baby. That's why James wants to go soon. He wants his children to be Northerners." Lottie stood up. "I have to go home. Momma will be all over my child if I don't." She started for the door, but Maggie stopped her.

"Are you sure about Detroit?"

"I'll have the baby here, and I'll wait for a while. But I'll go. Not for the streets paved with gold. James says he doesn't want to raise his son where he has to be afraid to look a white lady in the face. He doesn't want the kids to grow up where we have to be afraid. That's what I'm going for." She turned and started out. At the door, she stopped and looked once more around the room. "This place is just the way it should be. I knew you'd do it right, Maggie," she said, and she left.

Maggie wasn't sure how long she sat in her new examining room, staring at nothing much.

The next weekend she broke it off with Catherine, who didn't seem too surprised or upset. Maggie started going to mass in the little chapel near the resort. After two Sundays she told the priest she wanted to become a Catholic.

She asked Li'l Bit Banning to be her assistant in the office, and they began a campaign to vaccinate every child in the county against smallpox, typhoid fever, and diphtheria. Sometimes Maggie paid for the drugs out of her own pocket, sometimes Li'l Bit underwrote the cost from her trust fund. They were starting to make a difference. Maggie knew she was very useful.

Lottie had a girl and named her Nella. By that time the world had already turned upside down because Japanese planes had bombed a military base on Hawaii called Pearl Harbor. Young men Maggie had gone to school with raced to the town hall to sign up. Their baby brothers went too. The young male doctor who was supposed to be taking over Doc Brewster's practice was in flight school somewhere up north. Overnight Maggie was the only doctor in town. Her private clientele became as big as her clinic practice. She was able to make a down payment on an X-ray machine, and she could afford to have her nails done regularly. From Atlanta she heard that Catherine had joined the Wacs.

For a while the news from James's sister in Detroit was grim; the car factories were retooling for the war effort and the Negro workers were the first to be laid off. But those stories quickly gave way to tales of a boom town, and James wanted to be in the middle of the action. Lottie finally agreed that the time had come to leave. In

June, he went north ahead of her to get a job and find a place for them to live.

At around four in the morning, as he was getting off a streetcar near the Roxy Theater on Woodward, he was caught in the race riots that rocked Detroit that summer. He was one of thirty-four people killed, twenty-five of whom were Negroes. Lottie's brother-in-law shipped the body home to be buried.

Lottie asked Maggie if she could move back into the cabin with her babies and Charlie Mae. She couldn't afford the rent where she was without James's salary. Without even waiting to ask her parents, Maggie said the cabin would always be Lottie's home.

So Lottie didn't leave Charles Valley. The lines got deeper on the sides of her mouth, and even the new subdued smile was gone. She sent her son up north to live with her brother-in-law as soon as he turned sixteen, because that had been her husband's wish. She wrote James Junior letters, reminding him to say his prayers and stay away from Paradise Valley, and she sent money every week to Julie for his keep. But she didn't send her baby girl north to join her brother. She said she was waiting for Nella to get more grown up, but Maggie thought she kept the girl with her because she'd gotten lonely by then. Whatever the reason, Nella grew up in the cabin where Lottie was raised. And then Nella's daughter, Vashti, lived there. For a while.

MAGGIE TURNED OFF THE HIGHWAY. The Nature Preserve, Garrison Gardens, the resort, and Charles Valley were behind her. Pretty subdivisions and minivans gave way to sagging farmhouses and trucks loaded with hogs on the way to slaughter. Maggie spent several minutes behind a tractor that slowed traffic until the driver finally turned off at a small feed and grocery store with a gas pump in front.

Then, like some kind of ancient fantasy city rising out of the mists, a collection of modern buildings appeared on her right. She drove through an entrance gate under a sign that read PLEASANT VILLAGE, ASSISTED CARE FACILITY and headed for the wing of the large building where Lottie now lived. The slice of cake sat on the seat next to her. She'd called ahead to let the nursing staff know she was coming, so Lottie would be waiting.

Chapter Eleven

L AUREL WAS ONLY TEN MINUTES LATE for work, but Hank was there already. He stood in the doorway of what his mama somewhat grandly referred to as *the lobby* of the *Gazette.* The building that housed the paper had been through several incarnations since it was built in the twenties. Before Hank took it over for the *Gazette* it had been a bakery. In the rainy weather a faint aroma of vanilla still lingered. Hank's mama's so-called lobby was where the display cases for the cakes had been.

The man standing in front of Laurel was not a vision of masculine beauty. When he put himself in hock to his mama for the rest of his natural life by buying the nearly moribund *Charles Valley Gazette,* Hank had decided quite rightly that the survival of his project was going to depend not on readership but on advertisers, so he had adopted a personal style designed to be reassuring to the business community. His crisp suits and sports jackets were purchased from the Brooks Brothers discount outlet in Dothan, Alabama. His knitted ties were pattern-free, and he kept his thinning hair military short. It wasn't the most flattering look for a round face with protruding eyes and a little red rosebud of a mouth.

Laurel was expected to wear skirts and hose when she was on the job, but she was exempt from the dress code on weekends.

She and Hank split all the work of the newspaper. They laid out the paper together in a weekly all-nighter. Hank did the editorials and Laurel did the editing. He covered the stories that could be called news. She did the fluff and fielded hysterical phone calls from tigress mamas who were pissed about the way the paper covered Betty Lou's engagement or the bridal picture that made Samantha Claire look like a panda bear in a wedding dress.

To give Hank his due, he was good at what he did. His editorials tended to be long on God and the collapse of moral standards in society, but that was what his readers wanted. He covered all the town news thoroughly, and most people supported his efforts to keep the *Gazette* alive. The paper had been around since the twenties, after all.

"You're late," Hank said. Laurel ignored him and went to her desk. The working area of the newspaper was partitioned into three cubicles, the largest of which served as Hank's office. Laurel's space was in the back where the daylight never reached and the air seldom stirred. In between were the computers. Laurel slid into her chair. Hank, who had followed her, parked his chubby ass on her desk.

"I hear someone had quite a night last night," he said. His tone was disapproving but his large eyes glittered. One of Hank's nastier hobbies was imagining her sex life. "That's no excuse to be late. You're lucky I'm in a good mood this morning, missy. I told you if this happened again I'd dock you."

"It's only a few minutes."

"You're supposed to be here on time, ready to do your job—"

"I'm here now. Let me do it."

"You're not supposed to be sleeping in because you spend your nights catting around with strangers."

"What I do with my time off is my business."

"You better watch your step, Laurel, or you're gonna wind up just like—" He had the good sense not to finish the thought.

"Just like my ma. Is that what you were gonna say?"

Even Hank knew when he'd gone too far. "I'm only saying it for your own good."

They stared at each other with mutual dislike. If he could have found someone else who'd work as cheap as she did and do as much, he'd have fired her long ago, in spite of his creepy fantasies about her. If she could have found another job that gave her the same pride as working for a newspaper, she'd have quit. One day one of them was going to snap and end it.

But not this morning. Hank stomped to his cubicle and came back with a sheaf of papers torn from a yellow legal pad and covered in a spiky old-fashioned longhand. He thrust them at her.

"Take a look at the column Reverend Malbry sent in for the opinion page," he said. Reverend Malbry was one of their "volunteer columnists," a rotating group of ministers who delivered three or four paragraphs of personal opinion on a variety of subjects every week. It took hours of editing to make the volunteers sound professional—or even comprehensible.

She took the sheaf of papers silently. "If anyone needs me I'll be at the sheriff's office," Hank said. "Picked up a tip on the police scanner. Vashti Johnson's body was found in Dr. Maggie's cabin. I called Ed and he confirmed it. She committed suicide."

"How the hell do they know that so fast?"

"She left a note. Seems she was sick. Cancer; she'd had it for a couple of years." He paused and she could see he was already composing a headline for the story in his head. "CHARLES VALLEY DAUGHTER COMES HOME," he intoned goopily. Hank's writing style landed somewhere between the Bible and a Mother's Day card.

"I don't see how you can say this was her home," Laurel said. "The woman hasn't been here since her mother's funeral."

Actually there had been a sighting of Vashti two years earlier, or the rumor of one. If the kid who worked at Brown's Convenience Store could be trusted, Vashti had stopped in one afternoon for gas and some vinegar-and-salt chips.

"It doesn't matter where else she lived or how often she came back, she was one of ours. And this paper is gonna do justice to her death." Hank marched out.

🦋

At her desk, Laurel picked up Reverend Malbry's manuscript and forced herself to start deciphering his illegible handwriting. But her mind was back at the cabin in the woods where Vashti had chosen to die and had chosen to have the three Miss Margarets there with her. Whatever that was about.

LOTTIE'S ROOM WAS IN THE BRIGHTEST WING of the nursing home, the one that got the most sun and overlooked the pretty garden. Maggie had seen to that. The orderlies had already pulled Lottie's chair up to the window so she could look out. Talking was difficult for her since the last stroke, so it was hard to know what she liked anymore, but the staff said the sight of the garden seemed to soothe her.

Lottie wasn't looking out the window now. The slice of cake Maggie had brought sat untouched on the plate. She was sitting upright, her stroke-ravaged face expressionless except for the eyes trained on Maggie and the tears spilling over them.

"It's over, Lottie," Maggie said gently. "We brought her back to the cabin last night. And we stayed with her to the end." She reached out to wipe away Lottie's tears and rub her cold hands. For so many years she had been afraid to touch Lottie. Now none of that mattered.

"She didn't want you to know until she'd done it, dear one. That was the only reason I didn't come and tell you. It was very quick. She was ready. She'd been through so much." The tears had stopped. Lottie nodded ever so slightly and leaned in. "Tell me," she said, working hard to make the words clear. "I want to know, Maggie."

"Vashti was diagnosed two years ago. Remember?"

Lottie nodded. "Tumor," she said. "They operated. She was better. I thought."

"It came back. She always knew it could. That's why she started working so hard for the children, and on her own research, of course. That's what we have to think about now. She never gave speeches or made public appearances before her diagnosis. In a way it spurred her on, and we have to be grateful for—"

She couldn't finish the sentence. Because at that moment she didn't feel grateful. Later they would talk about Vashti's accomplishments and the amazing way she had used the last two years. Now all they had was loss and sorrow.

"When . . . ?" Lottie asked.

"The symptoms started coming back about six months ago. That was when she called me and told me what she wanted. We did it her way this time, Lottie. It was all the way she wanted it."

There was another little nod and then no sound, as Lottie cried silently and Maggie held her.

HANK HAD FORGOTTEN to buy coffee filters again. Laurel lined the basket of the strainer with a paper napkin and dumped a pile of Maxwell House's finest into it. As the coffeemaker creaked into action, her mind went back to the tableau she'd seen the night before, the three women hugging one another on the porch of the cabin. Most people in town would think it was the most natural thing in the world for Vashti to want them with her when she died. Everyone knew how tangled up her family was with all three of them. But Laurel knew something else.

WHEN LAUREL WAS TEN years old, Nella died and Vashti came home to bury her. Ma heard about Nella's death and used it as excuse number three hundred and twenty-eight to hit the honky-tonks out on the highway. But on the day of the viewing Laurel had ridden her bike over to the black funeral home. She hadn't been quite sure what she wanted to accomplish, maybe it was just that Nella had been such a mythic figure in her life that she couldn't believe the woman was really gone. Or maybe, as usual, she was looking for some way to end her ma's misery. Those were the days when she still believed she could.

She never spoke to Vashti. When she got to the funeral parlor, the three Miss Margarets were there. They were standing with Vashti in a back hallway outside the room with the casket, and Vashti was blocking their way in. Laurel hid herself in the shadows and listened. "Get the hell out!" Vashti shouted, and Laurel had the feeling she wasn't the kind of person who shouted often. "Get away from me and my mother, I don't want you here!" There had been murmured protests Laurel didn't hear, and someone said something about *just for one minute,* but Vashti shouted again. "You've done enough! Now leave us alone." Laurel pulled away from her safe place at the wall just long enough to see Vashti's face twisted with anger and grief. She backed away as fast as she could and left.

IN HER BRIGHT ROOM at the nursing home that was now her world, Lottie's eyes searched Maggie's face. "You?" she whispered. "You and Li'l Bit? Peggy?"

"We're all right. It was hard. But she came around, Lottie. She came back to us. That meant so much to Li'l Bit and Peggy, that she came back at the end."

"And you."

"And me. She wasn't angry at us anymore. She wasn't angry at you. After all the years. . . ."

And suddenly it was Maggie who was crying and Lottie who reached out with her good hand to stroke Maggie's cheek.

LAUREL TOOK A DEEP SWALLOW of her coffee, which was nice and muddy with a hint of paper-dye flavoring. The thing she'd learned about getting through one of Reverend Malbry's journalistic efforts was, you had to keep believing there was a light at the end of the tunnel. Let yourself give up for one minute and you'd had it. She'd already figured out that what seemed to be "a doll's toes" was "adultery." She was tackling a phrase that seemed to be about hacksaws and parrots when she heard a knock at the front door.

"Door's open," she called out. She heard someone come in. "Who is it?" she yelled.

Whoever it was wasn't answering, but she could hear them in the front of the building. She tossed down her pencil and went to investigate.

Josh was standing in the lobby, looking at the ugly couch and chairs that decorated the area, courtesy of Hank's mama.

"What are you doing here?" she asked.

"I see you got to work all right."

"No thanks to you."

"Give me a break. I tried to drive you."

"Fine, you're a prince. Why are you here?"

He paused. "Vashti committed suicide. She was sick—"

"I heard."

"Oh."

"Never underestimate the power of a small-town grapevine."

"She left a note, but I never got a look at it. Your pal Billy Joe Bob wouldn't let me near it. He wouldn't let any of his minions talk to me, either; only local press at this point, I was told."

"Sounds like Ed."

"Speaking of local press, your boss should have someone covering the story besides that guy who dresses like Ken Starr without the sex appeal."

"Actually, that *is* my boss."

"Does he ever ask the right questions?"

"Josh, if you came here to make cracks—"

"No."

"Or to tell me about Vashti—"

"Not that either."

"Then what do you want?"

He paused. "Look, I know you're pissed at me and I'm sorry we got off on the wrong foot—"

"The wrong foot? Is that what you call it?"

"If you'll just—" He stopped. "Given the way things have turned out . . . I'm sorry I took you home last night, but—"

"But there I was in a bar, half naked—"

"Is that bothering you?"

"No." But it was—sort of.

"Honey, I've seen girls ten years younger than you do things that—never mind. Just trust me, you singing "Jesus Wants Me for a Sunbeam" in your underwear doesn't even register on the Richter scale."

"Is that supposed to make me feel better?"

He blew out a lot of frustrated breath.

"I'm busy, and you need to get out of here," she said, and turned to go, but he stopped her.

"I took you home because . . . because I've always been a pushover for smart angry girls who figure if they're funny enough no one will notice how unhappy they are."

"I am not unhappy."

"And in spite of many years with a very good shrink, every time I meet one, I still think I'm the man who's gonna get through to her and turn her life around." He gave her a grin. "And . . . you *were* half naked."

She didn't even give him a flicker of a smile. "And my father was part of a book you've been trying to write for years."

"Which I did not know. And I wouldn't have gone to bed with you if I had."

"Because you can have a roll in the hay with anyone, but getting dirt for your book—now, that's important."

"I'm not looking for dirt."

"I have to work."

"Okay, you want the truth? You bet I want to pump you about

your father. I've been working on this book for a year and a half, and I've got a hell of a lot invested in it. If you've got anything to say that could add to it or make it better in any way—yes, I want your story." He took a breath. "But I've also been thinking about you all morning. I wanted to find you. And I wanted to—" He drew a deep breath and let it out slowly. "You have to work," he said, and started to leave.

And because she could never ever in her life leave well enough alone, when he was almost out the door she said, "Don't go."

BY THE TIME MAGGIE LEFT, Lottie still hadn't eaten the cake. She stopped at the desk and asked them to put it away for her; then she called Li'l Bit on the public phone in the lobby.

"I'm on my way," she said. "Have you heard from Peggy yet?"

"Not a word," said Li'l Bit grimly. "I'm going to give her another half hour and then I'm going to call her."

"No, let her sleep. I'm sure she needs it."

Li'l Bit made the high little sound in the back of her throat that meant she was rolling her eyes in disapproval.

JOSH CLOSED THE DOOR and came back into the lobby. Laurel sat on the couch and waited until he sat next to her. "You already know the good parts of my family saga," she said, "if you've done your homework. My father—John Merrick—and Grady Garrison got into a fight over Nella Johnson, the mother of your heroine. Grady was so drunk he forgot to miss my daddy when he shot at him. So I wound up being a bastard, since at the time my ma had a bun in the oven, as we cute hicks say, but she and John hadn't made it down the aisle yet. Nella and Vashti left town, and Vashti became your American success story. That about sum up your knowledge?"

"Pretty much," he said carefully.

"Okay, here's the part that didn't get into the newspapers because Mr. Dalt kept it out. My daddy and Grady weren't just having a little fun sharing a pretty black woman who may or may not have been willing. That was an ugly little pastime of theirs that I'm sorry to admit most folks around here dismissed as boys being boys. No, they were so serious about Nella they killed her husband one night."

If Josh said anything, one word, she was going to throw him out. If he even showed a sign of sympathy, he was history. His face was a blank.

"Yeah," she continued. "They ran him over with a car and left him by the side of the road. He may have been dead before they took off; he certainly was by the time the highway patrol found him. The official word on Richard Johnson was he died in a hit-and-run. But everyone knew who did it. They would have gotten away with it because of Grady's daddy. But when Grady used my father for target practice . . . well, even Mr. Dalt couldn't keep the lid on that.

"So my daddy was dead, and Grady was packed off to jail, and my mother stayed here in town because, to be honest about it, she was too dumb to do anything else. Down here in those days having a baby without a daddy wasn't chic, it was just slutty, and she couldn't accept that my daddy had done her like that. She believed him when he said he loved her and she let herself get knocked up because he swore he had changed his ways. Like I said, she wasn't the sharpest tool in the shed.

"When he died it broke her heart, and I hate to offend your PC sensibilities but she was ignorant and racist enough that it made it a whole lot worse for her that she lost out to a black woman. So she probably wasn't much of a human being, and in the general scheme of things, it probably didn't matter that she became a drunk and a joke." She forced a smile that was way too bright. "That's my contribution to your great work, Josh. I'm the daughter of the redneck who killed a man and then got himself shot. Stick me in a footnote and go make a million dollars selling your book to the movies. I want Sandra Bullock to play me."

She waited for him to say something. But of course now that she wanted him to talk he didn't. He just looked at her. And then he moved to her. It was a slow move, like he was underwater, or maybe that was just the way it seemed to her. Then they were facing each other. At most they were only a foot apart. She was the one who closed the gap.

"I'm not sure I like you," she said softly.

"I know," he said, at pretty much the same decibel level.

For two people who hadn't known each other long, they seemed to have quite a repertoire of kissing. Last night it had been mostly playful. This was more about bodies pressing against each other and mouths bruising lips against teeth. When he finally let her go, her knees did a little sagging thing. He seemed to be okay, which made him really hateful. Until he said, "Shit." Which made them both laugh.

And then the thing about laughing with a man who had his arms around you was, it could really get to you, so she pulled away.

"One more thing you might like to know," she said, in a masterful change of subject, "the reason the case against Grady Garrison was so tight that even his daddy couldn't get him off? Miss Li'l Bit and Miss Peggy would have testified against him."

"I never read a word about that."

"Nothing was ever written. Grady pled guilty and there never was a trial. But Miss Li'l Bit actually saw the shooting from the ridge behind her house. And Dr. Maggie knew from old Lottie that Nella had been seeing the two men on the sly for months. The clincher was Miss Peggy. She saw Grady trying to hide the murder weapon in his daddy's gun cabinet. There was nothing even Mr. Dalt could do after the police heard that."

"She told them?"

"Oh, yeah."

"She was his stepmother."

"Yes, indeed."

"Grady died in prison."

"Uh-huh. Ran into a couple of good old boys who didn't like him."

"Peggy Garrison helped send him there."

"You betcha."

"Her husband's son."

"Right."

"Sweet Jesus."

Chapter Twelve

PEGGY WAS DREAMING ABOUT A DOG. A large starving Irish setter was clawing at the glass doors off the back patio, begging to come in. But she couldn't let him. Because in the way that you know these things in dreams, she understood the dog was really Grady. And there was no way to help him. Still, the sick look in the dog's eyes would haunt her for the rest of her life. It had been haunting her for years. The part of her mind that knew she was dreaming wanted to wake up because the dog was crying now, whimpering in pain, and if she couldn't get herself awake soon the sound would turn to a man weeping. With a huge effort she hurled herself back into consciousness and woke up to look into two brown canine eyes. Elvis had been watching her sleep. The fact that she had fallen asleep—all right, passed out—on the couch in the living room with an empty bottle of bourbon on the floor beside her instead of tucking herself into her bed was enough of a departure from routine to worry him. She reached out to ruffle his scruffy head. "I'm okay," she whispered to him. At the sound, the rest of the pack, which had been sleeping in various spots around the living room, scrambled awake and crowded around the couch, demanding to be petted or at least noticed. "It's okay, babies," she told them. "Mama just had a bit of a night." She pulled herself to her feet and made her way gingerly to the kitchen door to let them out into their pen. Nausea slopped around her insides in sickening waves. Bending over the food bowls to feed the dogs this morning was going to be a challenge. She walked a fine line as it was; excesses like last night's were a strain on organs already battered by daily infusions of alcohol, according to Maggie, who warned of diseases painful and ugly. But facing the world without the edge taken off was impossible. It had been ever since Grady was taken to jail. She sat at the kitchen table and rested her swirling head in her hands.

FOR HER IT HAD ALL BEGUN with Grady. That was the irony of it. He had made her the person she was. He'd made her weird. Or, if you were listening to Maggie and Li'l Bit, different and an outsider.

She couldn't remember a time when Grady wasn't a bigger-than-life figure in Charles Valley. He'd been sent off to private school from the day Miss Myrtis realized that the teachers in the public kindergarten were not willing to discipline the Garrison heir. A kicking and screaming Grady was delivered over his father's protests to a hard-nosed private school, where the staff understood that Miss Myrtis wanted her son to learn to sink or swim on his own. For the next eight years, until he was finally packed off to the first of three military academies, Grady Garrison had the shit kicked out of him on a daily basis. But the kids in Charles Valley, seeing the pony his daddy bought him as compensation and hearing about wonders like Grady's swimming pool, never realized what their prince was enduring.

They ran into him at Sunday school, where Grady was a fat scowling presence who never learned even the shortest Bible verse assigned to him. On the rare occasions when he was available to play with the locals, he was mean and lordly. Everyone knew one day he would step into his father's ventilated Florsheims. It would be Grady who was the county's largest employer. He would put judges on the bench and representatives in the state capitol, and no state senator he objected to would ever wind up in Washington. He would have a monthly lunch date with the governor. He would entertain presidents, if they were Republican and conservative. And Grady would be rich; all the children knew that. The Garrison money was a fact of their lives and a source of local pride. Everyone knew how the family had outfoxed the Yankees after the Civil War and kept their fortune out of the jaws of Reconstruction.

The truth was not quite as romantic as the legend. In fact, if the South had won its Glorious Cause, the Garrisons might well have been tried for treason. At the first sign of trouble in the years before the Civil War, they had taken all their money out of the South and quietly invested it in northern factories that fed the Union war machine. After the war was lost, they invested closer to home again as soon as the climate was safe. Several decades later they plowed everything into the burgeoning Georgia fabric mills. The resulting millions had been the basis of a fortune that was the stuff of folklore in Charles Valley.

People said it was a good thing that Mr. Dalt was so rich. The rumor was it had cost him a new school library to get Grady through his fancy middle school. Two of the three military academies Grady attended refused to be bought off and bounced him during his sophomore year; no one was quite sure why.

Miss Myrtis, meanwhile, was trying to plan his vacations for maximum enrichment. As a child he went to summer camps designed to foster self-reliance or cultural enlightenment. As an adolescent he was forced to volunteer on an archaeological dig in a desert somewhere in the Middle East.

From what folks at home could see, none of it did him much good. He was only in Charles Valley a few weeks out of the year, for which most people were profoundly grateful. Grady had a taste for redneck company. His most loyal follower (*friend* would have been too strong a word) was a seventh-grade dropout named John Merrick. When they hooked up the stories started to fly, about black families being paid off after drunken shooting sprees in colored town, and a trailer-park princess who was set up for life after having been subjected to the attentions of Grady and his sidekick. They said Miss Myrtis was mad enough to let Grady stew in his own juice for that one. But Mr. Dalt bought a brand-new home for the girl and her sister in a neighboring state, where the enterprising ladies soon established a successful house of ill repute.

Neither Mr. Dalt nor Miss Myrtis was dumb, so the question was, How had they managed to make such a mess of their son? Some thought it was Miss Myrtis being so tough. Some thought it was Mr. Dalt being so soft. Others suggested that maybe they spent too much time on good works and business and not enough on their child. But the majority chalked it up to Grady's nature. He was just born mean as a junkyard dog, they said.

Two who refused to believe that were Peggy and her mama.

BY THE TIME SHE WAS TWELVE, life had taught Peggy two things: Money was the most important thing on earth, and men were far more efficient at getting it than women. Like all lessons that stick, she had learned hers the hard way. When she was ten her daddy died in a car wreck while driving home from an Auburn football game on a sunny Saturday afternoon in October. Her father, who had been a lawyer and should have known better, went without leaving a will or life insurance. He never expected to die so young. Plus his sweet fluttery little wife cried whenever he brought the subject up.

It took his widow eighteen months to go through his savings—Peggy's mama had a great sense of style but no head for figures—and then mother and daughter were on their own. The beautiful old home Mama had so lovingly decorated had to go. They rented a tiny house with barely enough room for them and the stray mutt Daddy had brought home one evening. The landlord balked at having a dog living in his little cottage and only agreed after demanding an extra deposit which wiped out two weeks' worth of the food budget.

Mama went to work as a saleswoman at Sally Boots's Dress Shop, a place she had never dreamed of patronizing back in the days when she could afford new clothes. The chic stores of Atlanta had been her turf, and she was a disaster at selling the cute prints and fringed denim she could hardly bring herself to look at, much less recommend. Soft hearted Bootsie kept her out of pity but put her on a commission instead of paying her a salary. Mostly, Peggy and her mother lived on the Social Security checks the government sent because they'd lost their breadwinner and an occasional handout from Mama's family. At the end of the month before the checks came in they ate cornbread sopped in buttermilk for dinner like poor people.

There were others who had it worse, families scrabbling out a life on dirt farms in the backcountry, but Peggy's mother was not bred to poverty. She lacked the swagger and pride of redneck poor. She just became shabby and ashamed. Late at night, Peggy would hear her poor sad little mama crying and she would hold the dog tight and pray for a new father.

Instead, God sent her breasts. They popped up on her chest as if by magic one night while she was sleeping, or at least that was the way it felt. Soon after the breasts sprouted, her skinny tomboy's body turned itself into a thing of curves, with rounded hips, a tiny waist, and long elegant legs. She had been prepared for menstruation, her red-faced mother had given her a book, but these new bumps and lumps were an intrusion she hadn't asked for. At first she was angry about what had happened, but then she began to be aware of the effect she was having on the boys around her. She had a sense of possibilities. She wasn't sure exactly what they were yet, but she knew her new body was giving her a valuable power. Grown men were looking at her too, in the grocery and the drugstore; even the school principal had to work hard to keep his eyes away from her chest when she wore her white angora sweater tucked into her circle skirt and cinched with a wide elastic belt. The effect on the hapless Mr. Dean was illuminating. She began to experiment—tastefully, she was her mama's daughter after all—with cosmetics. She bought peroxide and began lightening her honey-brown hair by degrees so Mama would believe her when she said it was sun streaks. Then one night Mama brought home a push-up bra from the dress shop and handed it to her. After that she realized there was no need to hide anything. Her soft helpless little mother understood better than she did the campaign she was starting to launch.

For the next two years she honed her flirting skills and became known as a tease. It wasn't fair because she never actually promised anything, but there was something about her that *seemed* to promise. It was in the way she carried her body in clothes that were a tad too tight, while wearing lipstick that was one shade brighter than a nice girl should put on. Peggy never withdrew in shock when she was slow dancing and a hard-on suddenly materialized in the pants of her overheated partner. She never cried and declared she wasn't that kind of girl when a stray hand found its way inside her bra during a necking session. She looked the perpetrator in the eye and smiled a knowing smile she had picked up from watching Barbara Stanwyck at the Saturday movie matinee. But she always put a bit of air between herself and the afflicted dance partner, and she always removed the wandering hand. She listened unmoved to pleas of undying love, respect forever, and enraged complaints in which the term *blue balls* figured prominently.

Boys couldn't figure her out, and it made them crazy. They drove her home in cars steamy with frustration and swore they would never see her again. But they always did. Because while she was saying no, Peggy managed to suggest that she was on the verge of saying yes. And every boy she'd tormented wanted to be there when she finally gave in. What they didn't know was, she never would. Because the boys she was dating were simply a warm-up. Peggy had her eye on a much bigger prize than a high school senior with his own car and a summer job at Burger Queen. Without being sure exactly how she was going to pull it off, Peggy had set her sights on none other than Charles Valley's version of the Prince of Wales, Grady Garrison. Later, when she looked back, she realized it had been Mama who started pointing out every time Grady was back in town.

She had heard the rumors about him, the whispers about drinking and the wrong kind of girls, but the details were vague and, as Mama pointed out, people were jealous and the Garrisons were an obvious target. Whenever she and Mama drove past the resort, or the massive stone entrance to the huge log cabin Miss Myrtis had built behind a grove of towering pines, she was reminded once again of how great the Garrison family was. It didn't seem possible that anyone who had been raised in such solid, respectable splendor could be capable of the kinds of things the gossips said about Grady. And then the bills would come in again and she would hear Mama weeping, and any little doubts she had about trying to capture the Garrison money would melt away.

She had no specific game plan for accomplishing her goal. Two years of torturing the masculine population of Charles Valley High had taught her the futility of such plans. Experience had taught her you always wound up winging it, which was a special gift of hers. The problem was getting access to her target. With Grady away from home most of the year, her opportunities for catching his attention were limited.

Then, one hot June, Myrtis Garrison had her first heart attack and Grady came home for the summer.

WHEN PEGGY SAW GRADY, she was in the parking lot outside Jenson's General Store with a bunch of kids who were waiting for Miss Li'l Bit's station wagon. It was a sweltering day, and as she did every summer, Miss Li'l Bit had asked a group of young people to her house for swimming lessons. She'd started having the lessons in the pond on her property years ago, after her father died and left her the house. Miss Li'l Bit's mama was alive somewhere, and there was some sort of story attached to the reason why she didn't live with her daughter, but Peggy and her friends weren't too clear on the details. It didn't seem to matter much. The idea of Miss Li'l Bit needing a parent was ridiculous.

In fact, Li'l Bit Banning was only ten years older than Peggy, but it never would have occurred to Peggy or any of the other kids to drop the *Miss* in front of her name. There never had been anything young about Miss Li'l Bit. She was square and slow-moving. She spoke slowly too, in a flutey voice that sounded like Eleanor Roosevelt probably would have if she'd been born in Georgia. But it wasn't the way Miss Li'l Bit looked or spoke that made her seem old. It wasn't even the hair done in a knot at the back of her neck, or the old-lady shoes, or the thick glasses she peered through. It was the way she acted and the things she did. Like giving free swimming lessons to anyone who wanted them. This year she had added a Red Cross lifesaving course for her young guests. For most of them it was an excuse to cool off on a hot day, show off their bathing suits, flirt, and have a picnic lunch provided by Miss Li'l Bit. Saving lives was not high on their list of priorities. Peggy was pretty sure their benefactress was aware of their attitude. Though Miss Li'l Bit might seem hopelessly out of touch to the teenagers who were taking cheerful advantage of her hospitality, Peggy had noticed a sharpness in the blue eyes behind the thick glasses. Her take was that Miss Li'l Bit didn't miss a trick.

But on that Saturday morning, Peggy wasn't thinking about Miss Li'l Bit or anything except getting to the pond. She was wearing a new white bathing suit under her blouse and Bermuda shorts, a suit so cruelly revealing of the least figure flaws that it had been marked down twice at Boots's and Mama had been able to pick it up for a song. They both knew Peggy had nothing to fear. She'd left her blouse unbuttoned and tied the tails tightly around her waist to emphasize the point.

There were at least fifteen kids in the parking lot when Peggy's mama dropped her off. Those who had cars would drive together to Miss Li'l Bit's house, and those who didn't would wait for Miss Li'l Bit to pick them up in her station wagon. But this morning, instead of cramming themselves into the cars or running into Jenson's for a last-minute Coke, everyone was over at the far end of the parking lot. Peggy went over to investigate. The object of their attention was a cherry-red Chevy convertible with a white top and white leather seats. No one had ever seen it before. That in itself wasn't unusual in Charles Valley; the resort drew a well-heeled crowd, and expensive cars were all over the place during tourist season. But this jazzy car was a far cry from the sober sedans the guests usually drove.

Speculation about the car's owner began to fly. "Tall, dark, and handsome," one girl offered.

"Blond and built like a brick you-know-what," one of the boys said. "She's probably in Jenson's right now."

"*He* is."

Peggy wondered what a resort guest, male *or* female, could be buying in a little local store that stocked staples like Grape Nuts cereal and motor oil.

Then Grady Garrison walked out of the store carrying a carton of beer.

It had been a couple of years since she'd last seen him close up, and he'd changed. The last traces of puppy fat were gone now; he was lean and, even for an area of the country where no skin escaped the rays of the sun, he was richly tanned. There was a swagger to his walk as he made his way to his convertible.

The other kids backed off, embarrassed to be caught slobbering over Grady's property. But Peggy recognized the hand of Fate reaching down to give her a gift. She moved around the car so Grady couldn't see her, ducked down, opened her purse, and dumped the contents onto the asphalt. She'd seen a movie in which the girl did that so she could miss her train and stay with her lover who was married. She couldn't remember if it was Doris Day or Audrey Hepburn who had the lead. She hoped Grady hadn't seen the same film.

As she bent down to retrieve her belongings—not the most attractive position, but it couldn't be helped—she saw that Miss Li'l Bit had pulled up in her station wagon. She froze, scared those smart blue eyes might have caught her emptying her bag onto the ground. But she told herself not to be dumb. Miss Li'l Bit probably couldn't see that far, and even if she could it was none of her business.

Grady was getting closer. She was alone now. The stragglers who didn't have rides had climbed into the back of Miss Li'l Bit's station wagon. Peggy busied herself with picking up pennies and dimes. Grady's shadow fell over her, and she gave a little gasp as if she was startled.

"Goodness," she said, looking up at him. "You scared me." She smiled a pouty little smile and ignored her racing heart.

"Sorry." He was standing between her and the sun. When she looked up at him he was a dark figure outlined against a sky so bright it hurt her eyes. She couldn't see the expression on his face. For a moment she wanted to run to the safety of Miss Li'l Bit's car and a day spent learning to save lives in the shallow end of Miss Li'l Bit's pond. But then the sun glinted off the stone in the ring Grady wore on his right hand. It was his granddaddy's class ring from Vanderbilt. Grady was his granddaddy's namesake, and passing down the ring was a proud family tradition. She took a deep breath.

"I was admiring your car and I dropped my bag," she said, in a voice that sounded unbelievably steady.

He was looking down at her; she still couldn't see his face.

"I was going swimming over at Miss Li'l Bit's." She made a fast decision not to mention the lifesaving lessons because that sounded too young. "Your car is a dream," she added, a little desperately. He still hadn't said a word. She wasn't sure what to do next. The idea of running came back. She'd just leave her new lipstick and mascara and her house keys and all the rest of it scattered on the gravel of the parking lot and go. Then a voice called out from behind them.

"Peggy, we're ready." Miss Li'l Bit was leaning out the window of her station wagon, which was now loaded with giggling, squirming adolescents. Grady snapped his head around in the direction of the sound and she could see his profile. She thought he frowned but she couldn't be sure.

"Come along, Peggy, you don't want to keep the others waiting." Miss Li'l Bit's voice had taken on a sharp edge. Suddenly Grady squatted down and smiled. He had a big smile, lips opening wide to show white perfect teeth. She wondered if he'd ever worn braces. Mama had thanked God and the dentist when he said Peggy wouldn't need them. Braces were so expensive.

"If you want to go swimming, come to my house," Grady said softly.

It was the invitation she'd wanted. There was no reason to back off. He straightened up and pulled her to her feet. "Come on," he urged, and opened the car door. He had a funny accent, harsh and kind of flat; he must have picked it up in those northern schools.

"Peggy!" The edge in Miss Li'l Bit's voice was sharper. Peggy looked over and saw she was getting out of her station wagon.

"Hurry," Grady said, with a playful wink. "Before she comes and drags you away from the big bad wolf."

Afterward she would try to remember if he had pushed her into the car or if she had climbed in on her own. He put the carton on the seat next to her and ran around to the other side to get in. As he leaned across her to lock her door, she thought she smelled beer on his breath.

"Peggy," Miss Li'l Bit called out.

"My things—" she began, but he was already turning the key in the ignition.

"Too late," he said, and peeled out. Somewhere under his tires her lipstick and her mascara were ground into the gravel. As they raced toward the parking lot exit, Peggy turned to see Miss Li'l Bit standing next to her station wagon, staring after them.

WHEN THEY REACHED THE HIGHWAY, Grady took a beer out of the carton and opened it with a church key he had hanging from his rearview mirror. Peggy started to protest as he took his hands off the wheel to punch holes in the can; the college student who had plowed into her father's car had been driving with his knees and balancing a bottle of Wild Turkey against the steering wheel, and she never let boys drive her if they had been drinking. Besides, being seen running around town at ten o'clock in the morning with a date who was sucking beer out of a can was low rent, even if he was Grady Garrison. But instinct told her Grady wasn't just showing off like the other boys. A reprimand wouldn't stop him, it would probably make him do it even more.

He smacked his lips. "Nice and cold," he said. "Help yourself."

"No, thanks," she said, trying to keep the disapproval out of her voice. He shrugged and drove on in silence. Clearly it was up to her to start a conversation.

"I can't wait to see your pool," she said. "I've heard so much about it. Well, I guess everyone has. I mean, everybody knows Mr. Roosevelt used to go swimming in it when he was visiting your daddy."

"Roosevelt's dead," he said flatly. He took a swig of beer and floored the gas pedal. The Chevy jolted and roared down the highway at a speed that made Peggy catch her breath. He heard her and laughed.

"You're not chicken, are you?"

"You're going kinda fast," she shouted, over the wind that was whipping her hair into her face. He looked at her for the first time since they'd gotten into the car. Then he smiled and pressed down even harder on the gas pedal. They were flying now, taking curves at a sickening speed. Peggy braced her feet against the floor of the car and forced herself to keep quiet.

Finally they came to the fork in the highway, the tip of the wedge of land where his house was. The mad ride was over. Peggy allowed her legs to relax. But instead of turning up the long winding drive to his home, Grady raced past it and continued down the highway.

Peggy couldn't keep quiet anymore. "What are you doing?" she yelled, over the sound of the air roaring past them. For an answer he finished his beer, tossed the can out of the car, rammed a fresh one between his knees, and started to fumble with the church key. The car swerved toward the soft shoulder of the road. Peggy stifled a scream. He righted the car and tossed the can of beer at her.

"Open it," he commanded. With shaking hands she obeyed. It sprayed all over her blouse and her hair and the top of her new suit. Grady laughed.

On the left, Miss Li'l Bit's house was coming up. For a moment, Peggy thought he was going to let her out, that the whole nightmare ride had been some kind of cruel practical joke. Instead, tires screeching, he turned to the right, onto the dirt road that led into the Nature Preserve.

They bounced over holes and tree roots, skidding off the road more than they were on it. They passed the shack in the depths of the woods where the Merrick family still lived. A rusted pickup was parked in front. Peggy prayed that someone might see the car whizzing by and call the police, but it didn't look like anyone was home.

They went deeper into the forest until the road petered out to nothing. The car jerked to a halt. Grady reached across her and opened the door.

"Get out," he said.

"What are we doing here?"

"Do what I tell you."

"I thought—"

"You thought I was gonna take you to my mother's house?" The northern boarding-school accent was blurring into pure Georgia. "You thought I was gonna bring home trash like you?"

"I'm not trash—" she began, but he kept on going.

"My mother is sick. She's probably gonna die." He turned to look at her with eyes that were wild.

"I didn't know—" she started, but he was in his own world of hurting and not hearing her.

"They told me last night. Just like that. She's gonna die."

She tried again. "I'm sorry—"

"And you thought you were gonna flash those big titties at me, and I was gonna take you into her house."

It was close enough to the truth that she didn't know what to say. He got out of the car and came around to her side.

"I told you to get out!"

"Grady, I don't want to—"

"Don't you call me by my name! I didn't give you permission to call me by my name!" He was screaming now. He grabbed her arm and started pulling her out of the car. Instinctively she seized the steering wheel. He reached across and pried her hands loose, bending back her fingers until she cried out and let go. She tried to slide across the seat to get out on the other side. Her head was jerked back viciously. He had her by her hair and was dragging her back. She heard herself begging him to stop, but he kept pulling until she was out of the car and on the ground. She tried to get up, but he pushed her back down into the dirt. She tried to scramble away from him, but he grabbed her legs and held her. She gave up and started to cry. He watched her weeping at his feet. He had stopped screaming at her now. He pulled her up until she was standing.

"Shut up," he said quietly.

But she couldn't stop crying. "I want to go home!"

Casually, as if it were no big thing, he drew his hand back. She felt it coming at her face before she saw it; then it connected, and her cheek was alive with pain. Blood was in her mouth, her eyes blurred. The hand came back the other way, this time the stone on his ring cut open a gash above her eye. There was more blood now; it seemed to be pouring down her face and neck. Her new white bathing suit would be ruined.

"I told you to shut up," he said. She nodded as hard as she could. The pain was making her dizzy. She didn't want to fight anymore, she wanted to do whatever she had to do to keep the hand from coming at her again.

"Take off your clothes."

She wasn't sure she'd heard him.

"Don't look like that. I've heard about you. You run around like a bitch in heat until some poor fool calls you on it; then you act like your pussy's lined with gold. These hillbillies may let you get away with that shit, but not me."

The hand was moving back; it would come at her again. She wanted to be brave now, she wanted to fight, but her head was swimming with pain and the blood was still coming down from her eye and she was afraid the hand would break the bones in her face so it would be ugly forever. And then she would have nothing.

She untied the blouse she had put on so carefully that morning. Impatient, he pulled it off and yanked her shorts down. But he couldn't do the suit.

"Get this fucking thing off!" he shouted. She hesitated, and the hand pulled back to hit. The hand was all now; avoiding it was the only thing that mattered. Obediently, she reached up and pulled down her shoulder straps. Then, as if she were in a terrible unstoppable dream, she peeled her beautiful new suit down her body until it was a fat white sausage at her feet.

After that it was a blur. He pushed her down on the ground. Stones and twigs and dry grass ground into her back. Then he was on top of her. For a second she tried to keep her knees together but the hand pulled back, ready to come at her, and she opened her legs. Her mind went away. Then he pushed inside her, and the ripping and the hurting started. And then everything went black.

WHEN SHE CAME TO someone was shaking her, and there were two voices.

"Get up, you little bitch, I didn't hurt you." She recognized Grady screaming again.

"Christ Almighty, what've you done to her?" That was the new voice.

"She asked for it."

"You beat the crap outa her."

"Served her right." Grady was grabbing her, trying to make her sit up. "Stop playing games, damn you." Then his hands were on her throat.

"Grady, don't!" She heard a scuffle and the hands were gone.

"Leave me alone!" Grady was shouting at his companion now. "I know what I'm doing!"

"You're drunk as a skunk. You gotta get outa here."

"You saying I got to worry about that tramp? *Me?*"

"This ain't just catting around. She's a white girl!"

"She's trash!" But his voice sounded less sure.

"Her mama belongs to your mama's church, for Christ's sake. Let's go."

Something fell on top of her, her blouse and shorts but no bathing suit. There were sounds like they were moving away. Then a rustle of leaves and a protest from the voice she didn't know. "Grady, don't be stupid." There was a sound she had just recently learned to recognize, of a hand hitting soft flesh. She opened her eyes. Grady's back was to her. Over his shoulder she could see John Merrick rubbing his jaw.

"Don't ever call me stupid, you fucking redneck son of a bitch,"

Grady said, in a steely quiet voice. Through her pain she saw the fury in John Merrick.

"Dammit, one day I'm gonna—"

"You're gonna do nothing." He'd stopped screaming now, and the Georgia lilt was gone from his speech. He was back to his harsh northern sound. "Go on, go home to that hell hole I wouldn't make my dog live in." There was a moment when she thought John Merrick might strike out. She could feel how much he wanted to, but instead he turned on his heel and walked away. She watched Grady as he walked to his horrid red car, got in, backed around, and drove off.

IN THE KITCHEN, Peggy lifted her head, which had exchanged swimming for throbbing. She had a game she played with herself on mornings like this. The rule was: As long as she didn't vomit she hadn't been that drunk. Today she was going to lose the game. She lurched to her feet, vaguely aiming for the hall bathroom, but changed course just in time to make it to the kitchen sink.

She sat again and waited for her insides to settle. Her control was slipping, which was probably cause for alarm. On the upside, she was feeling a hell of a lot better now that she'd been sick. She got to her feet carefully and continued her mission to the bathroom. Li'l Bit would be calling any minute, and somehow it seemed necessary to brush her teeth before talking to Li'l Bit. Even on the phone. Especially on this morning.

She seemed to be destined not to reach the bathroom. The phone rang, sending sharp spikes into her already bleeding brain cells. If she planned to keep up her present lifestyle, she really should look into something a little more mellow for her telephone. Maybe some kind of soft buzzer. She picked up the receiver.

"Hey there, Li'l Bit," she said quickly, hoping to forestall a lecture. "I'll be over in about an hour. I got a late start."

"Are you all right?" Li'l Bit asked. Obviously there had been an early morning conference and Li'l Bit and Maggie had agreed to be gentle with her. Peggy hated it when they did that.

"I overdid it a little," she offered. Li'l Bit didn't take the bait. Her girlfriends really had decided to make soft paws. It was actually kind of sweet.

"Maggie isn't here yet," Li'l Bit went on. "She called from the nursing home to say she's on her way." Peggy groaned inside. The nursing home meant Maggie had told Lottie, an exercise in sorrow that would leave her looking so old and fragile she'd break Peggy's heart and scare the hell out of her. The thought of losing Maggie or Li'l Bit put her into a cold panicky sweat these days. "I wish she'd called me," she said. "I could have taken her."

"She probably didn't want to wait that long," said Li'l Bit, with just enough of her usual acid to be reassuring. "You better hurry. Ed is coming over in a little while. Someone saw us at the cabin last night."

The spikes in Peggy's head dug deeper. "Oh, God," she said.

"It'll be all right," Li'l Bit said. "We'll get through it." But there was something wrong with her voice.

"Li'l Bit, what else?"

Silence. Then, finally, "I had another phone call after I spoke to Ed. It was from a writer. He's from New York. And he says he's writing a book about Vashti."

Bile washed its bitter way up Peggy's throat, but she swallowed it back down. "Did he say what he wanted to talk about?" she asked.

"General impressions we might have about Vashti."

"We can do that."

"And any light we might be able to shed on the night John Merrick died."

"I see." Her voice stunned her, it was so calm. But her poor battered mind was sorting fast through a jumble of fears. *I always knew someone would start wondering*, she thought.

"Peggy, after all these years, even if anyone did want to go back, they'd never find anything"—Li'l Bit paused to search for the right word—"untoward."

"I wasn't worried."

"We have no reason to be."

And of course Li'l Bit was right.

Chapter Thirteen

YEARS AFTER GRADY ENDED HER CHILDHOOD FOREVER, Peggy was listening to a woman's TV talk show when the subject of rape came up. She learned that rape was something you never got over. You learned to live with it, said the authoritative lady expert, who obviously had never been through it. "No shit," Peggy had replied to the TV screen. The expert went on to say that decisions made right after the *incident* were crucial to future recovery. Peggy had thrown a small porcelain figure of a Rottweiler at the TV screen.

AFTER GRADY LEFT HER, she dressed in her torn blouse and shorts. The cut over her eye had stopped bleeding, but her cheek had started to swell and her whole head throbbed with a pain that made her want to pass out or throw up. The other, far more intense pain she was feeling, she refused to think about. She started shaking as if she were cold but she knew she wasn't. She had to get home before she passed out again. But the thought of Mama's face and the way Mama would cry was overwhelming. She felt herself start to sag toward the ground and got down on her knees. The ruined bathing suit was in a little heap where she'd taken it off. She picked it up and got to her feet, ignoring the sickening waves in her

stomach. She stumbled into the woods where the kudzu was thick
and tossed the suit as far as she could. The effort was almost too
much for her queasy stomach, but she wouldn't let Grady have the
satisfaction of making her throw up in the grass. She leaned against
the trunk of a tree and waited until the nausea passed. One thing
was clear to her, through the mists of pain and shock. She understood it without question: Mama must never know about this.
Which meant she needed help. Slowly and painfully she made her
way back to the dirt road and started back to the highway.

When she passed by the shack, she got off the dirt road and
went behind the trees just in case John Merrick might be home and
see her. But the old pickup was gone.

Finally she reached the highway. Miss Li'l Bit's house was on the
other side of the road. Cars were parked in the driveway; the other
kids were still there. She ducked into the woods and waited.

She didn't know how long she hid there. Pain made hours and
minutes melt together. Finally the kids came out. She could hear
them laughing, teasing, and flirting as they got into their cars. Miss
Li'l Bit got into her station wagon and drove off with the rest.
Peggy kept on waiting.

After what seemed like hours, Miss Li'l Bit came back from
driving everyone to the parking lot. Peggy watched until she was in
the house and then crossed the highway and rang the doorbell. It
was Millie who answered. The look on her face told Peggy everything she needed to know about how her own face must look.

"Could you get Miss Li'l Bit?" She did her best to get the words
out cleanly, but her swollen lips made them mushy. Millie understood anyway. She brought Peggy into the main parlor and disappeared. A couple of minutes later, Miss Li'l Bit rushed in. Peggy
turned to face her and Miss Li'l Bit stopped cold.

"That little bastard!" she trilled, in her high funny voice. Peggy
wanted to laugh, but she couldn't make a sound.

❧

After that things moved quickly. Millie brought her some bourbon, her first taste of alcohol. Even as a woman in her sixties she would still remember how it found its way into the cold place inside her, a place she thought would stay cold for the rest of her life, and warmed it.

Miss Li'l Bit called Dr. Maggie, who closed down her clinic and came over to clean Peggy's wounds and stitch the cut above her eye. Then Miss Li'l Bit drew a bath for her, but she was shaking too hard to undress. Dr. Maggie made her swallow a pill and lie down again, until it took effect and made everything seem far away. Then she couldn't keep herself from talking. Miss Li'l Bit seated herself in a wingback chair, and Dr. Maggie perched on an ottoman, and feeling as if she was in a dream Peggy told them all of it. She told them about the white bathing suit and what the boys said about her. She told them about Mama crying every night and Peggy being the one who had to fix it. And she told them about seeing Grady and realizing she had to make her move and the way she had dumped her new mascara on the ground. Miss Li'l Bit and Dr. Maggie sat still as stones and listened. Peggy didn't cry once, not even when she told them everything Grady had done. They started saying over and over that none of it was her fault, but their voices were too far away and they must have seen her attention was wandering, so they stopped. After that, Millie and Miss Li'l Bit took off her clothes and sponged her clean. They wrapped her in one of Miss Li'l Bit's robes that was old and soft, and she lay down on Miss Li'l Bit's old-fashioned couch and floated on the power of the pill, or it could have been the bourbon.

"Let her sleep now," she heard Dr. Maggie say through the fog around her. But Peggy couldn't. Not yet. She forced herself to sit up. Dr. Maggie and Miss Li'l Bit were at her side.

"Mama," she said. "Don't tell her."

The two older women exchanged looks.

"She has to know, dear," Dr. Maggie began, in her gentle low voice, but Peggy cut her off. "No!" she said. Tears pushed up against her eyes, and the crying finally started. "Mama can't—" she tried to say, through the sobs. But there was no way to explain that for her frightened little mother this would be too much.

The two women soothed her. They said she should go to sleep now and they would talk again later. So she let herself drift off, and while she did Miss Li'l Bit called her mother and said there had been an accident. A car and Grady Garrison were mentioned. And as Peggy could have predicted if they'd asked her, Mama had hysterics and wanted to know if Grady was hurt because she was afraid the Garrisons might blame Peggy. They told her that both Peggy and Grady were all right, although Peggy was bruised and shaken and had taken something to make her sleep. Miss Li'l Bit suggested it would probably be better if Mama didn't come to get her until later. Her mother agreed eagerly. If Miss Li'l Bit and Dr. Maggie were stunned by how easily Mama turned her daughter over to virtual strangers, they never said it.

When Peggy woke up, before her mama came to get her, Dr. Maggie tried to talk to her again. Miss Li'l Bit sat by silently.

"You've been through a terrible ordeal," Dr. Maggie said. "Your mother should know."

"No."

"She can help you." Out of the corner of her eye, Peggy saw Miss Li'l Bit shift impatiently.

"No, she can't. All she'll do is cry."

"I'm sure she'll be upset, but—"

"She won't want to hear. She'd rather I lied to her. If I tell her what happened she'll say I'm lying."

"Peggy, she wouldn't!"

"She will! Because that would be better. I'm damaged goods now."

"Child, what a terrible thing to say."

"You think everyone else won't say it?"

The Three Miss Margarets

"Your mother—"

"Mama wanted me to *marry* him! Don't you understand? I was supposed to get *married*! Now who's going to want me?"

"You're still the same person you always were."

"No, I'm not! And you know it! You know what people will say. If anyone finds out, that'll be the end for me."

"But the police—" Dr. Maggie started to say.

"I don't want to talk about it! I just want to leave it alone."

Miss Li'l Bit stepped in. "Maggie, you know what will happen to her if she tries to tell the police that Grady Garrison raped her. Dalton will have a dozen witnesses who'll say she went willingly."

"And the bruises on her face?"

"An accident with the car. Or she tripped and fell. I don't know how the lawyers will argue it."

"Don't you think this is a conversation she should be having with her mother?"

"She just told you her mother will be useless. I agree with her."

"That is not for you to say."

"You didn't hear the woman on the phone."

Dr. Maggie didn't answer. Miss Li'l Bit moved so Peggy had to look at her.

"I understand why you don't want to say anything, Peggy. But the boy shouldn't get off scot-free. Maggie and I can do something about that."

"Li'l Bit—" Dr. Maggie broke in, but Miss Li'l Bit cut her off.

"We can, Maggie," she said, and after a second Dr. Maggie seemed to understand what she meant because she nodded slightly. Then she turned to Peggy. "We can't make this right, dear," she said, "and I'm still not sure it wouldn't be better for you to go to the police and take your chances—"

"I won't," Peggy said.

"Then will you give Li'l Bit and me permission to help? It'll be better than doing nothing."

They stood in front of her, two women who were older than

she was and probably way smarter. They weren't telling her all of this would go away if she trusted them. They weren't saying they could make it all better. They were just offering to help her as much as they could. She couldn't remember the last time anyone had done that.

There were sounds of a car in the driveway. A car door slammed. Mama had come to get her. In another minute she would be ringing the doorbell. When she saw Peggy's battered face she would burst into tears. Peggy would have her hands full calming her down enough so she could drive them home. Suddenly she felt tired. Miss Li'l Bit and Dr. Maggie were still waiting for her answer. "You do what you think is right," she said. And she moved to the front door to bring in her mama, who was already sobbing loudly out on the porch.

By the time Peggy woke up the next morning, Grady had left town. He was going to work on the new resort his family was building near their lodge in Montana. The police hadn't been contacted. And according to Miss Li'l Bit, who came to visit, Mr. Dalton didn't know a thing. A few days later, a note came from Myrtis Garrison inviting Peggy to tea.

She didn't want to go. But Dr. Maggie and Miss Li'l Bit said she should.

"You made a big decision when you chose not to report what happened, Peggy," Dr. Maggie said. "It wasn't right that you had to, but now that you've done it you have to make it work for you."

"Myrtis Garrison isn't the warmest person, but she's fair," Miss Li'l Bit said. "Give her a chance to do what she can to make amends."

Mama insisted that she wait until the swelling went down and her eye was no longer black and blue. Then Peggy went to tea. She had little sandwiches with no crusts and cookies with almonds in them on the patio that surrounded the pool where Grady had said he was going to take her swimming. Miss Myrtis sat upright on a white wicker lounge chair and said she was not well and she found herself in need of someone young and energetic to run errands for her for the summer while she recuperated. And if Peggy was interested, she named a salary that was three times what Mama had ever made in her best week at Boots's. And Peggy said yes, she would like very much to work for Miss Myrtis. They never once mentioned Grady.

When she brought home her first week's pay, Mama was ecstatic. And if she suspected that the sudden windfall had anything to do with her daughter's accident, she never asked. Just the way she had never asked what happened to Peggy's new white swimsuit.

When summer was over, Peggy kept on working for Miss Myrtis, often skipping school when she was needed. Only by now they had stopped pretending that she was simply running errands. She was a paid companion to a sick woman who had not regained her strength after her heart attack because she was never going to.

Even sick, Myrtis kept to an incredible schedule. She was on the boards of more hospitals, rescue missions, children's homes, and soup kitchens than Peggy could count. It was not enough to simply give a check, she told Peggy; she believed in being involved. She spent her days going to endless teas and lunches and planning meetings. At night, especially during the season when the Lodge was full, she and Dalton entertained. Before she got ill she was up before dawn every day, she told Peggy, with something as close to pride as Myrtis Garrison would allow herself.

Dalton and Myrtis didn't have servants; their household staff was provided by the resort. Every morning Myrtis called the housekeeping department at the Lodge, and maids, gardeners, waitresses, or whoever was needed would be sent over. On the day of a party, food in steam trays and chafing dishes would show up as if by magic.

But illness was sapping Myrtis's strength. She stayed in bed later and later in the morning, and she needed naps in the afternoon.

Now it was Peggy who arranged the flowers that came over every other day from the resort's cutting gardens. If a party was planned, it was Peggy who saw to it that the maids swept the patio around the pool for the cocktail hour and Peggy who ordered the platters of spicy cheese wafers and tiny butter biscuits with country ham that Myrtis was famous for.

On the days when Myrtis was so tired she had to bow out of the dinner or the happy hour, Dalton would take the guests over to the Lodge, while Peggy and Myrtis listened to the radio or played endless games of canasta until he got home. If Peggy thought Myrtis was in pain, she learned never to ask. And when she did something extra like polish the silver because it hadn't been done in a while and she couldn't stand to see anything so beautiful get tarnished, she learned that her boss would never say thank you. Myrtis signed Peggy's generous paycheck every week, and that was it.

Peggy didn't mind. From the moment she walked into the oversized log cabin, she loved it. All the living room furniture was built to order, it was big, and it looked like it would last for eternity. The walls and floors were heart pine, the hardest local wood you could find. The rugs on the floor were old and dark, antiques that had cost a fortune because they had already lasted through other lifetimes. Money was never mentioned. Whenever something needed to be fixed or replaced, it was. There was a sense of plenty and order that felt wonderful to Peggy after years of cornbread suppers.

But there were times when something cold and black seemed to descend on her and threaten to bury her. She knew it was left over from the day in the forest, and no amount of silver polishing or flower arranging would help. Those were the days when she found an excuse to ride her bike to Miss Li'l Bit's house. She would get there in the late afternoon after Dr. Maggie had finished work, and the two women would be sitting on the porch, enjoying the first cool breezes of the day. There would be a Coke for Peggy, Miss Li'l Bit would sip her icy cold sweet tea, Dr. Maggie would have a lemonade as tart as she could stand it, and the talk would start. Names Peggy dimly recognized—Picasso, Faulkner, Welty, Marx, and Freud—flew over Peggy's head like birds migrating in autumn. Fierce debates were waged over Miss Li'l Bit's taste for murder mysteries by Dashiell Hammett and Dr. Maggie's love of Frank Sinatra. Miss Li'l Bit said opera was the greatest art form, although she had given up someone called Wagner after all the country had been through in the war with the Germans. Dr. Maggie owned a television set, but Miss Li'l Bit felt the infernal boxes were the end of civilization. Miss Li'l Bit was devoted to Reddi-wip and cake mixes, but Dr. Maggie felt they were the work of Satan and would not have them in her house. As they talked and argued, Dr. Maggie emphasized her points with manicured hands tipped with scarlet nails, while tendrils of Miss Li'l Bit's bushy hair pulled out of the knot at her neck.

They knew each other very well, having worked together for years in Dr. Maggie's clinic. Even now, when Dr. Maggie had hired a nurse and a receptionist, Miss Li'l Bit still showed up twice a week to help with the books. Listening to them was an education for Peggy, and not just because of the things they talked about. She had never heard women argue so passionately on so many subjects without at least once invoking the opinion of some man.

There were things they agreed on. They both admired Eleanor Roosevelt, although Dr. Maggie said she was the type of woman who gave being good a bad name. And they both believed passionately in more rights for Negroes.

Dr. Maggie had always treated Negro patients in her clinic, which didn't upset most people. But she always addressed them by their last names and said Mr. or Mrs. or Miss, which did bother many. Although, Peggy noticed, they weren't so bothered that they wouldn't call Dr. Maggie out of her bed in the middle of the night when they needed her.

Miss Li'l Bit gave money to an organization called the NAACP, and she was very excited because they were suing some school board in Kansas about segregation. If they won it would mean white children would have to go to school with colored children. Miss Li'l Bit said that meant there would finally be real equality. Separate but equal was a joke, she said.

When the black moods drove Peggy to the porch, she sat quietly, hoping the two older women would let her stay and listen silently to them until she felt better. But eventually they always turned to her. And a duet of high and low voices would begin.

"If you give in to depression, that monster will win. You can't let that happen." That was Miss Li'l Bit's flutey sound.

"Just remember, you didn't do anything wrong." That was Dr. Maggie's rich low cello tone.

"Think of him as a sick animal you happened to run into." High voice.

"It wasn't your fault." Low voice.

"He's evil." High voice.

"You have to fight." Both voices, almost in unison.

The voices found the place inside her that had not been damaged beyond repair. And little tiny flames of anger started to grow, which probably saved her. And no doubt led her to play a part in what came later.

PEGGY POURED HERSELF A SMALL SHOT, no more than a swallow really, from the thermos she'd filled and taken into the bedroom. Her makeup was done, no small feat this morning. She quickly flipped through the contents of her closet, rejecting anything with even a hint of black in it. Li'l Bit and Maggie might wear it, they were older than she was and sometimes they reverted to the rules they grew up with, but she couldn't bear it. She made her choice and slipped the dress gingerly over her head, which was aching less since she'd had her medicinal nip. Outside, the dogs were barking. She let them in and put down their food bowls, something she couldn't have imagined doing an hour ago. Let's hear it for the thermos, she thought.

There was still one thing left to do. She punched a private number on her quick-dial and was rewarded by a cheery voice announcing that it was housekeeping at the Garrison Gardens Main Lodge and asking how could it help Mrs. Garrison this morning. She told it to send someone over to let her dogs out in two hours and to check again if she wasn't home by five. The voice said it would be delighted and wished her a fine day. She headed for her car, realizing that, after all the years, she still felt like a kid with her very own genie in a bottle when she called the Lodge and gave her orders as Mrs. Garrison.

As Myrtis Garrison got sicker, people talked about the way Grady stayed away and about the coolness between mother and son on his brief visits home. Mr. Dalt was said to be mystified and distraught. But whatever it was that had come between mother and son, it didn't go away. Grady spent his winters in college and his summers out in Montana working for the family.

Miss Myrtis's heart was failing by degrees. Peggy often found her gasping for air, her face as white as her bedsheets. It was obvious that she hurt most of the time, and she was terrified, although she never said it. When she was really bad, Peggy read out loud to her, novels by Dickens and Jane Austen that bored Peggy to tears but seemed to distract Myrtis from the pain. And maybe from the fear she wouldn't talk about.

Meanwhile, Dalton began building Garrison Gardens.

It was a tradition that each generation of Garrisons did something to enhance the thousands of acres the family owned. Dalton's father, Grady, had built a stone chapel complete with a church organ in one of the many pine forests and named it for his long-suffering wife—probably, according to the local gossip, as a tribute to her years of ignoring his infidelities.

But it was Dalton who put the resort on the map by building the huge gardens and the beach and opening it all to the public. He was accused by his friends and family of exploiting the town for commercial gain and destroying the natural beauty of the area.

As Dalton was either enriching his heritage or destroying it, depending on your point of view, Peggy's school career was staggering to a close. She continued skipping days and sometimes weeks, in order to work for Miss Myrtis, and barely passed her courses. To her mother's dismay, she refused to try out for cheerleading or homecoming queen. She wouldn't have made it anyway. She'd lost her sparkle. She still wore makeup, when Mama reminded her, but most times when she ate off her lipstick she forgot to excuse herself and go to the ladies' room to put on more. She cut her hair short because it was easier and stopped adding the "sun streaks." And her clothes were enough to send Mama to bed in despair. Gone were the figure-hugging sweaters and cinch belts. She wore white blouses loosely tucked into dowdy pleated skirts now. "It's hanging around those two old maids, that's what's doing it!" Mama cried out in frustration.

But the truth was, Peggy was spending more and more time taking care of Miss Myrtis. And Mama wasn't going to complain about that. So she fretted, but she didn't interfere. Meanwhile, proms and parties and finally graduation itself came and went. After Peggy got through her final exams by the skin of her teeth, she didn't even consider Li'l Bit's generous offer to help her go to college.

"Wouldn't you like to be with people your own age?" Maggie asked. "You might have fun."

"I have fun right here on this porch, Maggie." She'd dropped the titles; they were plain Maggie and Li'l Bit now. She didn't have to explain to Maggie that she had nothing in common with people her own age anymore because of Grady. Maggie always knew what you were saying when you didn't say it.

"You told me I made a big decision," she said. "Now I have to make it work."

Maggie nodded unhappily.

"Besides, Miss Myrtis really needs me now. I'm going to work full time for her."

What she didn't tell Maggie and Li'l Bit was how many nights she kept Dalton company when Myrtis was too tired to come down to dinner.

She did it because Myrtis suggested it. "She's afraid I'll grab a sandwich in the kitchen and swallow it in front of the TV if I'm on my own," Dalton said, with a wink. He was the kind of man who winked when he was kidding because he wanted to make sure you got his joke.

So Peggy sat at the big dining room table and chatted with him about his all-time favorite movie, which was *Shane,* and her favorite, which was anything with Audrey Hepburn, and he said he didn't know what people saw in that stick, he liked a girl with meat on her bones like Marilyn Monroe. And while they chatted, Peggy remembered how much she used to love talking about movies and things that were silly.

Then one night the most powerful man in her small world came home grinning like a bad kid and carrying a grease-stained brown paper bag from Lenny's Barbecue. And after swearing her to secrecy he produced two drippy shredded pork and coleslaw sandwiches, which he served on TV trays in the living room with paper napkins, and they watched *Leave It to Beaver* while they ate.

After dinner he told her about the experimental new breeds of plants they were creating at the Gardens, and they laughed because she couldn't pronounce the Latin names of all the flowers and he admitted neither could he at first. He took her out to the backyard to his private flower beds behind the swimming pool, where the gardeners had planted a new kind of pink tea rose that had been bred in the greenhouses, which he couldn't name Myrtis, because his wife hated her name, and he couldn't call Beloved, because she said that was too syrupy. Then suddenly he was starting to tear up, which embarrassed him until Peggy made him laugh by mispronouncing another flower name.

One afternoon, after the Gardens had opened for the public, he asked if she had seen them, and she said she hadn't, so he insisted on taking her. There was no way to tell him that she hadn't been to the Gardens because you had to go through a pine forest to get to them and his son had made her afraid of the woods. But she knew he wanted to show off his creation, so she got in the car and prayed that there would be hundreds of people there.

Dalton didn't drive her to the greenhouse, or the beach, or any of the places where the schoolchildren played and families had picnics. He took her on one of the roads he'd put in the old forest where the live oaks and pines grew so thick that their branches blocked out the sky and the ground smelled moldy like it was damp even when it hadn't rained. And the fear that started growing inside her was so strong that when he stopped the car she couldn't breathe. But then he pointed at something ahead of them.

"Look at that," he said, in a hushed voice. So she made herself look and saw a small stone building. It was square and rustic, almost like a small cottage. But then she moved a little and she could see the spire through the trees. And on the side wall there was a stained-glass window with brilliant blues and greens and reds. A sign by the side of the road said MISS LUCY'S CHAPEL.

"Would you like to go in?" Dalton asked, but she shook her head no.

"This is Myrtis's favorite place in all of the Gardens," he said. "I think she likes it better than anything I've built. My daddy put it up after Mother died." He looked at the chapel. "My father was a great man."

"I think you're a great man," Peggy said, and then couldn't believe how pleased he seemed. Although what he said was, "Bless your heart, I'm not even smart."

"You were smart enough to build the Gardens."

"If you listen to most of the people I know, I turned a little piece of paradise into an eyesore and betrayed the family trust."

"I don't know about any of that. But a lot of people come here and have fun. And because of you a lot of people have jobs who didn't before."

Again, it was the right thing to say. "That was what I wanted," he said eagerly. "To make this town self-sufficient and give a man a chance to earn a living for his family. It was never just to make money for myself."

"I don't see what's wrong with making as much money as you can," said Peggy. "If I could, I'd make tons of it."

He stared at her for a second and then he laughed. "Haven't you ever heard that money is the root of all evil?"

"Yes, and people who think that should try being poor."

He stopped laughing. "What would you do with tons of money, Miss Peggy?"

There was a time when she could have given him a list of the pretty clothes she wanted, and the perfume and makeup. But she hadn't bought any of those things since his son taught her what fear was.

"I'd be safe," she said.

After a moment he said, "Are you sure you don't want to go inside my daddy's chapel?"

And now she knew what he wanted to hear, so she shook her head. "I'd rather see the Gardens and the beach you built."

He took her through the Gardens and the beach, and all the guests who were lined up had to stand back and wait for them to go first, and all the employees turned themselves inside out for them. And she enjoyed every minute of it.

But she decided not to tell Li'l Bit and Maggie.

🦋

Myrtis got worse, and a professional nurse was brought in to care for her. But even though she couldn't play cards anymore and she never left her bed, Myrtis still liked to have Peggy there. So Peggy stayed at her job. She read to Myrtis when she was up to it, and arranged the flowers that still came in from the cutting garden, and sometimes she just sat with the sick woman and held her hand until she fell asleep. And in the evenings she listened to Dalton Garrison tell her stories about the great accomplishments of his forebears, and she told him he was better than all of them as if she knew what she was talking about. And what they were both really doing was helping each other get through his wife's death. But she didn't tell Maggie and Li'l Bit that either.

Then finally the fight was over. There was a heart attack in the middle of the night and Myrtis went to the hospital for the last time. Grady flew home from Montana, but his mother was already in a coma and she died before he could get there.

At first Peggy tried to get out of going to the funeral. She had managed to avoid Grady through all the years she worked for his mother, and the one thing in life she knew for sure was that she wanted to go on avoiding Grady; and she couldn't very well do that at a funeral. But Dalton asked her to come to the ceremony and the private reception afterward. And when she tried to get out of it, he was so hurt she couldn't refuse. Besides, the little flames of anger inside her said she belonged at that funeral, she had earned her place there.

She was alone in the kitchen when Grady walked in. He hadn't changed much. He was still lean and tan, maybe even more tan than he had been. His hair was still sandy gold. His eyes were still bright blue, and the look in them was still evil.

"You little bitch," he said. "You lied to my mother and she believed you. And now you run around this house like you own the place. But that's over. Mama's gone and I'm coming back home.

And if you're smart you'll make sure I never set eyes on you again." Then he walked out.

Peggy looked around the shiny kitchen that was bigger than the entire ground floor of the shabby house she and her mother rented. She walked into the living room and looked at the people eating the little rolled sandwiches and tiny cakes that had been made specially in the Lodge kitchen and sent over on huge silver trays covered with starched white linen napkins. She saw people sitting on the matching custom-made couches that cost more than a year's worth of the Social Security checks she and her mother would go back to living on after her salary stopped. And she watched Grady Garrison stand at his father's side while people came up to them in an informal receiving line. She watched him accept condolences for the death of the mother who had forced him out of town. From the look of joy on Dalton's face, she knew Grady was telling everyone that he was coming back, and she watched people who were not delighted pretend they were. She picked up her purse and left the house she had come to love and think of as home.

The next day Grady flew back to Montana to wrap up his business and come home for good. For the first time in years, Peggy went to Krasden's drugstore and bought herself a light-pink lipstick and a perfume that smelled gently of flowers. She went through her closet and found the last dress her mother had bought her before she started wearing old-lady blouses that were two sizes too big. She put the dress on and draped a cardigan over her shoulders. She still looked demure, but there was a hint of the old sparkle Mama had been pining for.

She found Dalt in the bedroom at the log cabin, trying to sort through Myrtis's things. When she offered to help him, he said she was an angel of mercy.

By the time Grady was ready to come back from Montana, Dalton and Peggy had eloped.

❧

PEGGY DROVE HER CAR up Li'l Bit's driveway and stopped be-hind Maggie's elderly Volvo. She picked up her trusty thermos from the front seat of her car and started up the lawn. Then she looked at Li'l Bit and Maggie sitting on the front porch, and she started to laugh.

"Are we a sight or not?" she asked, as she climbed up the steps. "Look at us, three old biddies decked out in white after Labor Day."

Chapter Fourteen

*L*AUREL OPENED THE DOOR to the newspaper office and let herself inside. Hank was nowhere in sight, praise be. She'd been playing hooky. After Josh had taken himself off she'd closed down the office, leaving Reverend Malbry's journalistic effort unfinished, and gone off on what she planned to say, if asked, was a personal errand. Knowing full well that that wouldn't cut it with Hank, and what she had done was really stupid. Still, she had a sense of mission accomplished, brilliantly, as it turned out. And if there was a part of her mind that was a little squeamish about the fact that she had risked Hank's wrath for a total stranger who had made her talk about things she normally kept buried—well, to hell with it. She reached into her bag and pulled out a business-size envelope. On the back flap was the raised blue stamp of the sheriff's department. She put it back in her bag. She could have dropped it off at the Lodge on her way back to the *Gazette,* but she wanted to deliver it in person after she finished work.

Ten minutes later, she had her red pencil in hand and was slashing two pages of lovingly misspelled quotes from Scripture. She sensed that Josh was standing in front of her before she looked up and actually saw him. He was either excited or angry about something. His pale eyes were so alive they were practically giving off sparks.

"Look, I told myself I wasn't going to get into this, because it's none of my business—and talk about complicated!—but I just can't—"

"Josh?"

"What the hell are you doing here?"

"Excuse me?"

"Why haven't you gotten out of this dump?"

"I work here."

"I mean, this town! You said your mother stuck around because she wasn't smart. Baby, lack of smarts is not your problem. And anyplace in the world has got to be better for you than this—"

"Really? You think I should have left?" It was amazing the way he could piss her off in an instant. "Why didn't I think of that? Oh, yeah, I did think of it. I even did it. Got myself a scholarship. At Jacksonville State. It's not Harvard, but it was out of town. But the thing about being the kind of drinker my ma was, eventually your liver goes and most of the rest of you follows, and somehow it just didn't work for me to sit in my creative writing class while she was back here dying all by herself. We simple country folk are funny that way about family. And of course we never have health insurance, so when we die slow and hard the bills mount up. And another funny thing about us is we feel like we should pay them."

"Fine. Pay off your debts, but you don't have to stay here to do it."

It was what she'd told herself a hundred times. That didn't mean she wanted to hear it from someone else.

"It's not that easy."

"Anything's got to be better than staying here with all that bullshit about your father and mother. For God's sake, you're young and beautiful and smart as—"

She had to stop him, because he was getting to her again. And she hadn't let that happen since the day Denny wrecked the pickup driving them out of town. "You know, you were right before; this is none of your damn business."

He stopped. "Sorry."

Of course that made her feel even worse. "Josh, I know you meant well, it's just—"

"No, I've got to watch the crusader thing. My problem, not yours. I'll let you get back to work."

"Wait. I have something for you."

She grabbed her bag and started fishing around in it. "The thing about Ed is, he always underestimates people," she said. "For instance, when the county made him hire a woman on the force, Ed swore she'd never see the inside of a squad car, even though the woman he took on came from a long line of law enforcement types, and her daddy used to be Ed's boss. When he stuck her with all the paperwork the guys hate doing, Sherilynn was pissed. And she's a chip off the old block." She found the envelope and held it out to him. "So when I called and explained how I wanted that suicide note Ed wouldn't let you see, Sherilynn sneaked it out of the file and made a copy for me."

"You got me a copy of Vashti's suicide note?"

She nodded, and even though she had skimmed it quickly, she came around her desk and stood next to him so she could read it again with him. It was dated almost three months earlier.

Vashti's note began in tiny precise handwriting:

In the interests of efficiency, I address this document to the Sheriff's Department of Lawson County and to the office of the medical examiner of Charles Valley. You will be reading this after I have ingested a lethal dose of secobarbital sodium. It is my intention to terminate my life. The choice is mine alone.

Two years ago I was diagnosed with glioblastoma multiforme, a grade IV astrocytoma, or brain tumor. Surgery followed by radiation and chemotherapy reduced tumor bulk, restoring acceptable levels of mental function and quality of life, although not a cure, for approximately twenty months. The initial symptoms then reappeared, and subsequent examination revealed the tumor had recurred as well as seeding of cancerous cells to previously healthy tissue. After discussion it was determined that further surgery would be ineffective. Radiation and chemotherapy were continued, but symptoms became more severe, and in spite of treatment some mental deterioration has already begun. It is not my wish to continue my life under such circumstances. Today, as per my instructions, all treatments will cease.

They had come to the end of the first page. Josh looked off into space.

"It's like her," he said. "I can imagine her writing it."

"Read on."

The next page was dated two months later. The change in the handwriting was dramatic. It was a large ragged scrawl; a few words covered half the page.

Seizures now, Vashti had written. *Headaches. Can't remember.*

"She was losing her mind by inches," Josh said.

"Check out the last page."

He flipped it over. Vashti had managed to get a barely legible *Fri night* printed across the top. Underneath in large block letters, she had printed the last word she would ever write. *SORRY,* it said.

"So she did know," Josh said. "When she let me talk to her she knew. I guess that explains it."

"What do you mean?"

"There were times when I had a feeling Vashti was covering something. It never occurred to me that she was sick. I figured it had something to do with that night. . . ."

Laurel felt herself tighten. "The night my father was killed."

"Yeah. She was inches away from telling me something big in that interview. I didn't know what it was, but she'd put this town and that part of her life off limits, so I thought . . . but now I guess I know what she was hiding."

"The cancer."

"It makes sense. If you're concealing the fact that you have a brain tumor, that would tend to make you a little secretive."

The tightness inside Laurel gave way to something close to a letdown. She pushed it aside. She didn't need to go down the road of *that night*. She'd traveled it enough with Sara Jayne to last her a lifetime.

Josh was folding the copy of the note and putting it back in the envelope. "Damn, I hate this," he said.

"You liked her."

"She gave me a run for my money but . . . she was so bright . . . and she'd had to fight so hard. . . ."

"One of your angry smart girls?"

"Shit, I never thought of that." He laughed. "Maybe. Doesn't matter. I just know she was special." He leaned over and gave Laurel a peck on the check. "Thank you for getting this for me," he said.

"What are you going to do now?"

"Not much more I can do. I'll try to talk to a few people, but I don't think I'm going to have much luck. I have a meeting in a little while with Ms. Banning."

It took her a moment. "You mean Miss Li'l Bit."

"I called her earlier. She said I could come over."

"Don't be surprised if you find all three of them there."

"That would be interesting."

"Oh, yeah. In ways you can't imagine."

"I'm just going to ask a few questions," Josh said.

"Uh-huh."

"I was surprised she was willing to talk to me at all. Those three women could be in trouble if they actually helped Vashti in some way."

"Oh, no one is gonna touch the three Miss Margarets."

"Somebody will have to investigate what they were doing in the cabin. I'm not sure exactly what the legal ramifications are down here, but—"

"I'm telling you, Yankee boy, it won't happen."

"They get a free pass? Because they're the three Miss Margarets?"

"Because Dr. Maggie has probably taken care of just about everyone in the county at some point, and she still only charges fifteen bucks for an office visit. And Miss Peggy and Miss Li'l Bit pay for most of the charities. That's not counting the times when Miss Li'l Bit gives someone money for the winter's propane out of her own pocket. Or when Miss Peggy sees to it that their kid gets a scholarship to go to college. Ed would be out of office in a heartbeat if he messed with them."

"So they do get a free pass. Cozy."

"Don't tell me this is the first time you've heard of someone getting a break from the law?"

"Thugs and friends of politicians. Not little old ladies with pedigrees."

"That's how things work down here."

"And you're okay with it?"

"I didn't say that."

"But you haven't gone someplace with a more level playing field."

"Like New York City?"

"Now you're talking about God's country." She shot him a look. "Anyone who does not love my city is confused, disturbed, or a Republican."

"Not that you're biased."

"Proudly." He got serious. "I just think . . . anonymity's a great leveler. All you need is whatever you've got going for you. And whatever you're willing to put on the line."

"And you too can become a writer for *Vanity Fair*."

"If that's the goal, why not?"

She took a long pause. "I don't know why I haven't left here," she said.

He leaned over and brushed a wisp of hair out of her face. "You should figure it out." Then he left to go see the Miss Margarets.

THE WRITER FROM NEW YORK had gotten into his enormous car and crunched his way down Li'l Bit's gravel drive to the highway. Peggy decided to risk Maggie's inevitable look of reproach, Li'l Bit's inevitable grunt of disapproval, and the vagaries of her own still-dicey stomach and smoke a cigarette.

It had been a rough few hours. First Ed had shown up to tell them that Laurel McCready had seen them at the cabin. After he'd danced around, using legal terms, they read between the lines and understood that he was going to let it go—which was a relief, but the whole thing had been uncomfortable. Then, as if that wasn't bad enough, the magazine writer who had been seen all over town with Laurel had come over to ask questions about the night John Merrick died. He already seemed to have a scary amount of information.

They had gone into their act, although she doubted Maggie and Li'l Bit would ever admit that's what it was. Li'l Bit served him her terrible coffee in the antique Limoges cups that were so delicate they intimidated anyone with hands larger than those of a five-year-old. Maggie wandered off with every question he asked and told long disconnected anecdotes about her early days as a female doctor and the problems of setting up her clinic. Li'l Bit firmly directed the conversation toward old roses and camellias. Peggy herself had contributed a great deal of information about the new program she was starting at her shelter, training strays to be service and companion dogs.

To give him credit, the writer really wasn't taken in all that much. He knew exactly what they were doing; there were even times when Peggy thought she saw a gleam of something like amusement in his oddly pale eyes. But there wasn't much he could do to keep them on the subject unless he had been prepared to be very rude, which wouldn't have done him any good either. So they'd gotten rid of him. But it had been nerve-racking.

Peggy lit up. She inhaled and exhaled gingerly. No internal heaving registered: so far so good. Two voices immediately went into the duet of high and low she had listened to since she was fifteen.

"Peggy, dear," Maggie protested, in a low worried murmur to the air.

"Filthy habit," Li'l Bit announced, in outraged flute tones, waving away smoke.

After all the years they could still make her feel like the kid. "I need someone younger than me that I can beat up on," she'd told Li'l Bit once. She didn't say there were times when she felt jealous of the bond between them. Neither of them would have understood; they came from a time that didn't believe in that kind of soul baring.

"We have to think about the funeral," Li'l Bit said, by way of bringing the meeting to order.

"I worry about that girl," Maggie mused.

"Laurel?" Li'l Bit said. "I don't think there will be any problem. Ed doesn't want to follow up on what she told him."

"I'm not talking about last night. She told that writer everything she knows about the night her father died. It weighs on her, I think."

"That's not our problem."

"She's troubled, Li'l Bit."

Peggy watched as Li'l Bit's lips pulled back into a thin line. "We can't blame ourselves for that," she said stubbornly.

"Who else?" In spite of the bond, it seemed to Peggy that they got on each other's nerves more these days than they used to.

"There's nothing we can do."

"I've just been thinking, maybe it's time. . . ."

"No."

"But now that Vashti's gone. . . ."

"We have nothing to explain. Nothing to apologize for."

"Don't we?"

They were tired and grieving. That, more than anything else, was why they were getting into this. It was Peggy's cue to step in. "Maggie, what about Lottie?" she asked gently. "What would it do to her if we told?"

The mention of Lottie's name had the effect she'd known it would. Maggie bowed her head. "I don't know," she said.

Peggy breathed a sigh of relief. The crisis had been averted for the moment. But it would come back, she knew. Because their lives were drawing to a close and unspoken agendas were pulling them in opposite directions. Maggie wanted to tie up loose ends; Li'l Bit wanted to protect a legacy. And in the middle, there she was, the youngster who just wanted to keep things moving along with no changes. Dear God, don't let either of them get hurt, she prayed silently. I can't lose them yet.

"We need to talk about the funeral," she said.

Ten minutes later, after Maggie had taken charge of the whole thing, church and all things religious being her domain, Peggy stood up. Her head was aching, and both Maggie and Li'l Bit looked exhausted. It was time to go.

At the edge of the porch, Li'l Bit and Maggie gave each other the same air kisses they'd been exchanging for fifty years, no matter how cross they were with each other. And then, in the shorthand that they had developed over the same fifty years, Maggie said to Li'l Bit, "Maybe we have to trust, just a little."

Li'l Bit shook her head; her voice was begging. "No one today will ever understand how it was, Maggie. They can't!" There was a pause when Peggy thought Maggie might start the fight all over again, but then, mercifully, she left it alone.

Peggy took her arm to help her down the porch steps and over the lawn to her car. Maggie looked back at Li'l Bit watching them from the porch. "She had so little and she lost so much of it," she said softly, to herself. "She lost too much." Then she turned to Peggy, who was holding the car door open for her, and reached up to give her a hug. "Try to eat something, Doodlebug," she said gently. "You have to take care of yourself, you know. Li'l Bit and I would be lost without you." She got in her car, started it, and crept erratically down the driveway, a little old lady whose head barely reached above her steering wheel.

Chapter Fifteen

PEGGY'S FAVORITE DISC of golden oldies was playing on the car's CD player. She lit a cigarette, cracked open the window, and pushed the gas pedal to the floor. The headache was threatening to become a monster and she needed to get home, where she could pull down the blinds and put cold cloths on her forehead. That was still her treatment of choice—along with regular nips of Gentleman Jack, since she was the kind of old-fashioned girl who believed in sticking with the fellow who had brought her to the party.

Maggie said Li'l Bit's loss was too big. Ever since they'd had the final call about Vashti, Peggy had been thinking about losses. She, Li'l Bit, Maggie, Nella, and Vashti had all paid a price. And in spite of what Li'l Bit said, Laurel and her mother had paid too.

She didn't like to dwell on sad thoughts. Letting yourself get blue was as bad as letting your roots grow out or your lipstick wear off. There were certain things you owed the world around you, like a smile and looking good, and any woman over the age of twenty-two who thought she looked good fresh-faced was either an idiot or blind. But for the past few days smiling had been hard. She had regrets on the brain.

On the CD player, Doris Day was singing about the future not being ours to see. Well, old Doris didn't know the half of it.

❧

WHAT NO ONE EVER KNEW, especially Li'l Bit and Maggie, was
how much she had cared for Dalt in the beginning. What she felt
wasn't the romantic sexy love other girls her age dreamed of, but
that kind of love had never been in the cards for her, and not just
because of what Grady had done. She'd never had the luxury of
being a romantic about sex, not since the day her mama bought
that first push-up bra. Or maybe Mama didn't have anything to do
with it. Maybe there had always been something chilly at her core.
Once she had worried about that.

Now Patti Page was crooning about waltzing with her darling
the night they were playing the beautiful Tennessee waltz. Peggy
sighed and stubbed out her cigarette. There had been times, especially in the days before she had discovered the benefits of going
through life with a slight buzz on, when she had wondered what it
would feel like to be knee-knocking heart-racing hot for a man.
She'd gotten glimmers of it when she watched love scenes in
movies, and there was a book by James Michener of all people that
had made her twitchy and discontented for days. But that was years
after the rawness from the rape had healed, and by then she had
made the second big decision of her life and become Mrs. Dalton
Garrison.

WHEN SHE FIRST MARRIED DALT, when she was still just a traumatized kid, all she'd been worried about was pleasing him. For all
the flirting she'd done before Grady took her into the woods, her
knowledge of sex was sketchy. Afterward, she'd pretty much shut
down all interest in the subject. She knew Dalt liked looking at her
pretty body; that was a familiar male reaction. He didn't seem to
expect her to admire him the same way, although when she said
he was handsome in his wedding suit she could tell how much it
pleased him. But he didn't excite her in the way she knew a girl

was supposed to be excited by the man she married. And she didn't know how she was going to hide that when she was alone with him in a room with a bed and with his wedding ring on her finger.

She needn't have worried. A lot of smiles, a sigh or two, and "I'm so happy I could die," whispered to him when all the heavy breathing was over, seemed to please him just fine. He hugged her, called her his little sweetheart, and then rolled over and fell asleep. The man she had married was not one who looked beneath the surface. "I don't like trouble. I keep things simple," he told her years later, when she no longer saw it as an asset.

When she got older she wondered what he had made of the fact that she wasn't a virgin when he took her to bed that first time. Maybe he hadn't realized it, which was the best argument she'd ever heard of for a repressed Baptist upbringing.

Whatever he thought or didn't, when she told him she was happy she hadn't lied. He was going to be as easy to handle as any of the boys she had tortured in high school, and the relief made her downright giddy. After that first night she was sure she would have him eating out of her hand in six months.

She had underestimated herself. By the time they were halfway through their honeymoon he was delighted, with himself and with her, in spite of feeling guilty because they'd gotten married just two months after Myrtis died and because Peggy was young enough to be his daughter.

She figured out real fast that Dalton had a dirty little secret. He didn't really want to be the great man Myrtis had made him into. He had a gift for making money, and he liked to be generous to people he cared about as long as he was giving them things he wanted them to have. Charity in the abstract left him cold. It had been Myrtis who insisted on the good works that made the Garrison name famous throughout the state. Dalton wrote the checks and let her fill in the amounts.

He had appreciated Myrtis's goodness. Actually, he'd been in

awe of it. But something about the way he laughed when he described her "fussing" at him to support her pet causes made Peggy
decide she would never fuss at him about anything. He was the
son of a domineering man who had married a good woman, and
though he loved them both they had made him feel inadequate.
Peggy would not repeat the pattern.

When they were deciding where to go for their honeymoon,
he offered her a choice of genteel locations in Charleston and Sa-
vannah. But then, almost as an afterthought, he suggested Miami
Beach, and the look in his eyes told her that was what he really
wanted. They stayed at the Fontainebleau Hotel in the most expensive suite they could book on short notice. The first night there, he
looked out the window at their endless views of water and man-
made beach and said, "Myrtis would say this is so tacky." And Peggy
knew she had done the right thing.

So her honeymoon was a breeze. She ate the thick steak dinners
he loved to order, and she squealed over the presents he bought
her. She went with him to nightclubs where the showgirls' cos-
tumes were just this side of vulgar and giggled at comedians who
were just raunchy enough to shock but not really offend. Tennis
was Dalt's game, but she didn't know how to play, so she encouraged him to find other partners and sat on the sidelines cheering
him on. But mostly she listened to him and agreed with him.
When he said something she knew Maggie and Li'l Bit would not
approve of, usually about colored people keeping their place, she
let it go. And if that made her less of a person, so be it. Dalt was
good to her, and generous beyond anything she had ever imagined.
He had fallen in love with her in spite of the fact that she was
maimed on the inside, and he had solved the problem of what she
was going to do with the rest of her life by marrying her. She owed
him.

On her last night in Florida she had a glimpse of something else, a
kind of love she felt she could have with Dalt. She sat across the

table from him in a hotel dining room that was so expensive that after two weeks it still gave her goose bumps to swallow the food. She'd spent the afternoon buying the luggage she needed to carry the pretty new clothes she'd bought in the hotel shop without once looking at the price tag. Around her neck she was wearing Dalt's most recent present, a heavy gold necklace with a big diamond in the center that Mama would say was not appropriate for a girl her age, but who cared? Through a haze of well-being she studied her husband. His short gray hair was thinning, and he was getting ready to lose the fight to keep his waistline. But the squint lines that creased his tanned face spoke of an outdoorsman who was still vigorous and full of life. And when he looked at her, his eyes had a way of shining that made him seem younger than any boy she had ever known.

As if he had read her mind, he suddenly put down his knife and fork and took her hand.

"Sweetheart," he began, then stopped and turned red under his tan. He looked off at a silver-haired couple doing intricate footwork on the dance floor. "When Myrtis died, I never thought I—" He stopped again. Then he turned back to face her squarely. "I love you, sweetheart," he said. "And if I ever forget to show it, even for a couple of days, you remind me. Hear?"

She said, "Oh, Dalt," and started to laugh it away, but he held her hand tighter.

"Just don't let me forget. Ever," he said. Then he quickly went back to cutting his meat. And for a moment a window opened inside her heart and she saw how possible love could be.

Two nights later, when they got back home, Grady had already moved in.

PEGGY DROVE THROUGH THE STONE GATES and started down the driveway, home at last. It felt like she'd been gone a million days. On the CD player, Eddie Fisher began singing "Oh, My

Papa," and how in the world that fresh-faced young man had turned into the desiccated old fool she saw on her television screen she'd never know. Liz and Debbie were both in far better shape, even with Liz's brain surgery. It was clearly one more demonstration of the superiority of the female sex.

She drove around to the side of the log cabin and let herself in through the kitchen entrance. The dogs danced around her, barking and jumping, thrilled out of their sweet canine minds to see her again. And, as sometimes happened when God was in a really good mood, she could feel the headache start to retreat. Figuring she should follow doctor's orders and help a good thing along, she checked out the fridge. Loving hands from the resort kept it stocked with a variety of cheeses and cold cuts as well as fruits and vegetables. She decided to risk a couple of slices of ham and an apple; then, to be on the safe side, she poured herself a medicinal dollop of Jack, settled back on one of the kitchen chairs, and closed her eyes. The dogs swirled about for a few seconds and then flopped down around her.

DALTON WAS BESIDE HIMSELF with joy at having Grady back. Peggy made herself smile and swallowed back her terror. She managed to say if Dalt was happy, she was too. Grady didn't even try to hide his hostility. It seemed to ooze out of him, until finally even Dalt couldn't ignore it any longer.

"We're gonna have to be patient, sweetheart," he said to Peggy, as they got ready for bed on their first night home. "That boy has been through so much. His mama turning on him like she did and dying before he had a chance to say good-bye." He paused. "I used to ask her all the time what he did. I thought if she'd just tell me I could make it right, but she would never say. Just told me she didn't want him home. Her own son."

"I'm sure Miss Myrtis had her reasons," Peggy heard her voice saying, from a long way off.

He shook his head. "She was always too hard on him. She was a good woman, but she never understood. Some people need things a little . . . light. We can't all be perfect. . . ." He stopped. "The boy was hurt by what she did. He doesn't show it, he acts so hard, but I know after she died he was torn up inside. And then I went and got married . . . you know that didn't help. And now . . . I want to make him feel this is his home again, sweetheart. For as long as he wants to stay. Do you understand?"

She nodded, in spite of wanting to scream. And she got into bed next to him. And when he bent down and kissed her breasts she made herself give a little sigh of pleasure.

The next morning she waited until Dalt was up and out of the house before she got out of bed. She dressed herself carefully in a dark-green silk dress with a high neckline that had cost so much it made her gasp, and pulled her hair back into a bun at the nape of her neck. She put on the emerald ring that Myrtis had kept in a safety deposit box because she thought it was too big to wear. She called the resort and told Housekeeping she needed some people to come over and help get the house back in order because they'd been away. Two of the maids and a gardener showed up twenty minutes later. She set the women to work in the pantry next to the kitchen and told the gardener to prune the shrubs outside the kitchen window. Suddenly she was freezing. She went to the cabinet in the living room where Dalt kept his liquor and poured herself a shot glass of bourbon, like the one Li'l Bit had given her the day she came out of the woods beaten and bruised. It got inside her bones and warmed her the way she remembered. Then she went into the kitchen and sat at the table with a cup of coffee in her hands to give her something to hang on to. And she waited.

Grady rose a little before noon and came into the kitchen. He stood still and stared at her, and she clutched the coffee cup so hard she thought it would break in her hands. But when she spoke, her voice was steady.

"Before you say anything to me," she said quietly, "there are two women working in the next room and there's a man right outside that window."

"You think I give a shit?"

"You should."

"What do you think they're gonna do? They work for my father."

"They work for my husband." She could see that stop him. "The women are named Molly and Etta Mae; the man is Frank. They work here a lot. They know me." She could see him try to take in what she was saying. Unwelcome facts were registering for the first time. "You have to get out of this house," she continued. "I want you gone before Dalt gets home." He moved across the kitchen fast and loomed over her, and for a moment she thought he was going to hit her. She made herself stay put and looked him in the eye. "If you touch me, I will scream and Molly and Etta Mae and Frank will come running, and you'll have to explain to your father. Dalt already knows how angry you are. We talked about it last night after we went to bed."

The suggestion of intimacy got to him. He hadn't thought about this new reversal in their positions. He backed up, just enough to put the table between them.

"This is my home, and I'm not going anywhere, you little bitch," he said, but she noticed he was keeping his voice low.

"If you don't go, I'm going to tell Dalt what you did to me," she said evenly.

"He'll never believe you."

"I'll take my chances." If the coffee cup had been one of the thin ones from the good china she would have broken it by now, she was holding it so hard, but she went on. "Dalt's always wondered why Miss Myrtis turned you out. When I tell him, a lot of pieces are going to fall into place."

"I'll tell him you wanted it. That you were begging for it."

"Did you ever wonder what happened to me that day? Who

saw me?" He hadn't, of course, so she paused to let the thought sink in. "I went to Miss Li'l Bit's house. Dr. Maggie stitched me up where you cut my forehead." She said "Doctor" and "Miss" deliberately, to remind him that they'd be impressive witnesses. "I still have the scar; it's right up by my hairline." She thought about lifting her hair and showing it to him, but she wasn't sure what her hands would do if she took them off the coffee cup. "Dr. Maggie and Miss Li'l Bit will be glad to tell Dalt what I looked like."

"You were swishing your tail around. . . ."

"They've been wanting to tell him for years."

"You were asking for it. . . ."

"That's all three of them: Dr. Maggie, Miss Li'l Bit, and Miss Myrtis. Do you really want to go up against them?"

He wanted to hurt her so badly she could feel it. But there was something else in his eyes too. The beginning of fear.

"I don't care who you get to lie to him!" he burst out, but then he quickly lowered his voice. "He won't believe it because he won't want to. That's how it works. Dalton Garrison doesn't believe what he doesn't want to believe. I'm his son, and he won't want to believe that about me."

Suddenly she didn't need the coffee cup anymore. She let it go and stood up. "But he *will* want to believe anything I say, because I make him feel young. And he doesn't want that to stop. If I'm lying, he'll have to go back to feeling old and alone. I'm ready to see which one of us he'll believe. What about you?"

He looked at her, and she had to work to keep standing. But in the end he wasn't quite stupid enough to do anything to her. He turned and walked out. She sat back down and held the coffee cup for dear life.

Dalt was devastated when he got home and found out Grady was gone.

"I wanted to make it up to him," he repeated over and over during the next few days. "I didn't want him to feel like he was run out of his home again." Since Grady had moved in to one of the most expensive villas the resort had to offer, he hadn't gone very far, but Peggy didn't point that out. Dalt was disappointed, and she was learning fast that when Dalt was disappointed it had to be some-one's fault.

"Did you have words with Grady?" he asked.

She shook her head and looked as tragic as she could. "It was as much of a surprise to me as it was to you," she said.

"I shouldn't have gotten married so fast. I'm not blaming you, sweetheart, I know it's not your fault." While he might have thought he meant that, she knew she'd lost some of her luster for him.

Chapter Sixteen

MAGGIE LET HERSELF INTO THE KITCHEN and then locked the door. This was totally unnecessary, but it gave her enormous satisfaction. It felt like she was locking out the world, especially Li'l Bit and Peggy. She loved them both, but right now they were making her weary.

Laverne was snoozing on her bed, not having heard her come in. Maggie walked past her quietly. The dog took her duties very seriously, she'd be upset if she knew she'd slipped up on one of the basics of her job, the ecstatic greeting of the mistress.

"All that bouncing around and barking has to make you feel like an idiot at your age," she said to the top of the dog's head. "I wouldn't do it for love or money. Stay right where you are and sleep."

She was worried about Li'l Bit and Peggy. Li'l Bit was carrying such a load of anger, Maggie couldn't imagine what it felt like to lug around that kind of burden. Peggy carried a burden too, a wad of guilt she lightened with her Gentleman Jack. How much longer could she keep that up? For that matter, how much longer before Li'l Bit's blood pressure went straight off the charts? Medication could only do so much.

The hard part was, they went back so far. It was hard to trace who was where when. Friendships that had been around for a while

had an ebb and flow, times when you were in one another's pock-
ets, and times when you were all involved in your own lives. You
kept in touch, but you weren't as close as you had been. That was
what had happened to them after Peggy married Dalton. Not necessarily because she married him, although that played a part. Both
Peggy and Li'l Bit had been going through a lot at that time, but
neither seemed to want to talk. And the one immutable rule of
their friendship was *Thou shalt not push.*

FOR MAGGIE, those years could best be summed up by the word
contented. She discovered there was an unexpected bonus to the
role she'd taken for herself, the one she privately thought of as
Nun Without the Habit. She was at peace. Not wildly, mindlessly
blissful—she'd given up on that; she worked hard, didn't expect
anything, and was surprised at how pleased she was with her life.
Even when both her parents died within months of each other, she
managed to say—and meant it—that she was glad neither one of
them had had to live too long without the other.

Lottie continued to live in the cabin behind Maggie's house with
Nella, and that was a big factor in Maggie's new sense of satisfaction. Lottie was back in her life, although the walls were up. Maggie accepted that they always would be, and kept her own up too.
    Lottie's children brought about the new connection. Charlie
Mae had died and there was no one to commiserate with Lottie as
her babies were growing up and growing away from her.
    James Junior had finished high school in Detroit, but any hopes
Lottie might have had for college died quickly. His uncle got him
a job on the railroad, and he married a girl he described as "peppy."
Lottie said she had hard eyes and smoked cigarettes. Her name was
Dora, and on her first visit to Georgia she announced that being
south of the Mason-Dixon Line gave her the heebie-jeebies. She
made it clear that she considered her mother-in-law hopelessly

countryish. Lottie had to face it that James Junior had become a stranger who talked through his nose and dutifully showed up once a year on his momma's birthday, without his reluctant wife and children. "He's James's child," Lottie said to Maggie. And Maggie could see it; the boy had all the ambition and lack of sensitivity of his father.

But Nella was hers, Lottie said. Privately, Maggie thought Lottie was wrong; if there was anyone Nella took after it was Charlie Mae. From the beginning the child was practical as dirt, competent in ways Lottie would never be, without a drop of Lottie's imagination or intellectual curiosity. She stayed in school only because Lottie insisted on it.

"She's smart, I know she is. But she isn't. . . ." Lottie searched for the words.

She isn't hungry the way you were, Maggie wanted to say, but didn't. Your baby girl is not you, dear one. Nella would never cry because she couldn't learn to read fast enough. Or because her best friend went to a better school and was getting ahead of her.

However, Nella was lovely, although she didn't have the fierce beauty Lottie had had when she was young. Nella was soft and pillowy, with big eyes and no sharp angles to her personality. At least, that was the way most men saw her, and they found her very attractive. It scared Lottie to death. The clashes between them started early.

"Mama doesn't understand why I like him," said Nella at age fourteen, of her first boyfriend. "I think he'll be a good daddy."

"That's no way for a child your age to be thinking," Lottie decreed.

"I don't like school," said Nella, age fifteen.

"I've got money saved up for your tuition and the list of colleges Miss Monross gave me," said Lottie.

"I want to have eight babies," said Nella, age sixteen.

"After you have a diploma, you can go anywhere in the world," said Lottie.

"I don't want to leave home," said Nella, age seventeen.

"At least apply to Spelman!" Lottie yelled.

"They'd never take me," Nella cried.

"There's a place in North Carolina—"

"I'd be homesick."

"Do it for me. Please," Lottie begged.

But for once in her placid, docile life, Nella dug in her heels. By the end of her senior year, she announced she was going to get married. He had left school two years ahead of her. His name was Richard.

"He's talking about moving to Atlanta—that's something. She'll have a better chance to make something of herself there," Lottie said to Maggie, clutching at straws.

The day after Nella graduated, they announced they'd be staying in Charles Valley.

"Nella begged me," Richard said with a laugh. "She said, 'Do it for me, baby. Please.' And I just couldn't say no."

Maggie couldn't look Lottie in the eye.

So while Peggy figured out the ups and downs of being the wife of Dalton Garrison and Li'l Bit went on her own emotional roller coaster, Nella and Richard moved in with Lottie. And that was where they lived when Vashti was born.

Chapter Seventeen

*L*I'L BIT LOOKED DOWN AT HER HANDS. They were big, almost big enough to be a man's, with rough skin and sinews so pronounced they looked like bones. The arthritis that was nibbling away at her knees had not touched them. Because of her gardens. Sometimes she thought most of what was good in her life had come from her gardens. She walked to the back porch and looked out.

They'd had the first frost of the winter two days ago, and it was time to mulch. Her tulip bulbs were already in the ground, and she'd harvested her sunflower seeds, making sure she left some seed heads on the plants for the birds. She still had to finish cutting back her perennials, and she hadn't yet prepared the bed for her early spring peas. She looked up at the sky. The winter sun was at its warmest of the day, and she could still get in a few hours of work. It would feel so good to get her hands dirty just for a little while. She went to her bedroom to change into her ancient overalls.

WHEN SHE STARTED OUT she barely knew a shovel from a hoe. There were no gardens on the property. At least, they weren't visible to her untutored eye. Later she would learn to spot the bones of old beds buried in forests and meadows.

For all that he loved his home, landscaping wasn't one of her father's passions. He had inherited a house with shallow lawns, surrounded by forest. He kept his grass mowed, he pruned the holly in front of his porch, and he made sure there was a path cut through the forest so he could go for his nightly strolls to the pond. Beyond that he wasn't interested.

But he did have an oil painting of the back of the house, done in the days when the gardens around the old mansion had been the pride and joy of the Justine Plantation. The painting, in all its glory, hung over his desk in his study. When she was a child, it fascinated Li'l Bit.

"Oh, yes, the old pleasure grounds, as they were called," Harrison said, when she asked about it. "Impossible to keep them up today, much too time-consuming. And extravagant. I wouldn't waste my money on such nonsense."

His wife rolled her eyes heavenward, but Li'l Bit understood. Her father lived uneasily in the skin of a rich man. He had achieved a fragile truce with his conscience by working for the public good and living simply—at least as simply as a man could in a house with five bedrooms and two parlors. Harrison's sense of right and wrong could produce some fairly tortured loops of logic. So Li'l Bit dropped the subject of the gardens—until years later, when her father had died, the house was hers, and she had time on her hands. Lots of time.

It was a period when her two friends were both busy. Peggy had just married Dalt and was busy trying to make a go of what had to be one of the most difficult unions ever. Maggie was working long hours at the clinic and seemed absorbed with Lottie and Nella. She and Maggie and Peggy still tried to get together on her porch at the end of the day, but it was difficult. And often Peggy or Maggie would have to cut the time short. It seemed to Li'l Bit that everyone's life was full but hers.

She knew she had a lot to give, but no one seemed to want it. For the first time in many years she found herself thinking about men. It hit her at odd times during days that had suddenly gotten too long and nights that were even longer, a vague stirring that stopped being vague and became embarrassing. She had stupid dreams of kisses and arms holding her that she knew came from bad movies and worse music. She saw beauty in men she had known all her life; her lawyer, the trust officer who handled her money, the postmaster, and even Mr. Lawless, who worked in the grocery store—all would have been stunned if they knew what she was thinking. Of course, she had money and a wealthy woman didn't have to be alone, if she was willing to make certain bargains. But that kind of barter wasn't her style. So she paid the price for having been born both proud and homely as a mud fence.

She had trouble sleeping and took to wandering the house at night, often winding up in her father's den. One night the old oil painting caught her eye again. As she looked at the colors, the pinks, greens, yellows, purples, blues, and reds rioting over the canvas, she knew what she wanted to do. She might be plain herself, but she would make something beautiful.

She started in without knowing what the hell she was doing. She had no plan and had not asked anyone for advice. There was a long curved hump in the backyard that seemed to correspond to the terrace garden in the oil painting. Closer inspection of the hump revealed that it was actually a low stone wall buried under earth and grass. On a fine Monday morning, right after her breakfast, she began digging it out, armed with an ancient shovel she'd found in the barn.

Noon found her in Jenson's General Store, buying a new shovel, gardening gloves, a spade, a variety of gardening forks, overalls, a straw hat, and boots.

She went back to the wall and dug until it was time for Peggy and Maggie to come sit on the porch. She was so engrossed in her project, she barely had time to cram her hair back into its net and change out of her overalls before they arrived. There was an impressive collection of blood blisters on both of her hands, and her back ached. She was very happy.

It took her a month to clear the wall. Then she started digging a flower bed next to it. And she began reading books about gardening. But the advice in them was technical, and she was after romance and history. She dreamed of heirloom roses and pass-along camellias in old gardens reborn. She went into Atlanta to hunt for out-of-print books on landscaping and came back with a moldy tome written by Andrew Jackson Downing.

"He was a nineteenth-century landscape artist," she told Peggy and Maggie as she showed off her musty treasure. "He revolutionized gardening in America before the Civil War." She read sections of his *Treatise on the Theory and Practice of Landscape Gardening* to them.

"Fascinating," said dutiful Maggie.

"Honey, do you ever think about going out on a date?" asked Peggy.

And she kept on digging her long curved flower bed—without, as Peggy pointed out, having put one seed in the ground.

The truth was, she didn't know what to plant. It was as though she was waiting for direction, either from the earth or from the books, she wasn't sure which. She just knew she had to wait. And dig.

Peggy said she was getting strange. Li'l Bit argued that she always had been considered eccentric so it was nothing new. Peggy said this was different, and not quite healthy. Maggie said somewhat dubiously that she hoped Li'l Bit was having fun with her new hobby.

She finally finished the bed early one afternoon in April. It spread out in front of her, a perfect semicircle of raw earth, waiting for her to make beauty happen.

"What are you going to do with it?" a voice behind her asked.

She whirled around to see a man standing in her backyard.

"Didn't mean to startle you," he said. He had thick black hair that fell over one eye so he had to brush it back. "Name's Walter Bee." He stuck out his hand to shake hers. His hands had the same kind of calluses she had recently acquired, and they were big, so her own big hand was engulfed. He was tall enough that she had to look up a little to see into his eyes. "I'm the new head gardener at the resort. Mrs. Garrison said to come over because you need help."

"You sure dug yourself one hell of a hole," Walter Bee said. "What're you putting into it?"

"Roses," she said, to say something.

He looked up at the sky and down at the bed. "Well, your sun is right for them," he said. He bent down and picked up a handful of the dirt and rubbed it between his fingers. She watched and wished she knew what he was feeling for.

"Gonna have to do some work on your soil," he said. "Roses aren't gonna like this." His hair fell into his eyes again as he talked. His eyes were very deep-set, a shade of brown so dark it was almost black. He could probably shut you out fast with those black eyes. "Got to get enough peat moss and compost mixed in here, might could try Epsom salts too; that should make them happier. And you'll have to raise the bed so they'll have the drainage they like." He was wearing a work shirt and blue jeans. He was waiting for her to say something.

"That sounds very . . . complicated. Maybe I should start with something easier than roses."

"They're not that hard. Just fussy, that's all. They want what they want, and they get it 'cause they're worth it." He smiled. "Like the way you spoil a pretty girl."

She nodded solemnly. One thing she'd always understood was the power of being pretty.

"What else do you want to plant?" he asked.

"I thought, old-fashioned flowers. The kind that might have been there when the place was built." She had spent the last few months compiling lists of flowers, but now here in the sunshine with this man looking down at her ever so slightly, it felt like every name had flown out of her head. She grabbed a few back. "Lilies, and . . . violets, daisies, camellias, gardenias, daffodils—not all together, of course. I have some books—"

"Don't need them. Walk me through the bed and show me what you want."

So she started. And the flower names came back to her as she took him on a tour of her fantasy garden. Sometimes he stopped her because she used a Latin name he didn't know. And once in a while he'd say she shouldn't plant this shrub in front of that one because it would grow too tall, or she was putting in too many perennials that would bloom and die at the same time, and he would suggest something else instead.

"Should we write some of this down?" she asked once.

"I've got it all in my head," he said.

Afterward, she brought out a pitcher of iced tea and a piece of paper and they sketched out a plan for the garden, and he was right; he did remember everything she'd said.

"That's a lot of planting for one person," he said. "You could hire the work out. I could find some men for you."

"I want to do it myself," she said, "so it's mine." And from the way he nodded she knew he understood. So it was a surprise when he drove up to the house the next morning in an elderly pickup and rolled a wheelbarrow full of mulch off the back end of the truck.

"I have Wednesdays off at the Gardens," he said. "I'll start at one end of the bed and you start at the other, and we'll get the job done twice as fast as you will on your own."

And before she could say anything he was pushing the wheelbarrow to the far end of the garden.

They worked silently as the sun rose and burned off the morning mist. He was faster than she was, but she watched him and picked up pointers. When the sun was directly overhead they stopped and washed their hands at the outdoor faucet. He used a pocketknife for his nails. She used a scrub brush. She liked it that they were both fanatics about keeping their big strong hands clean.

She served him one of the two egg-salad sandwiches Millie had made for her lunch, and found some pickles and potato chips. He liked his iced tea super-sweet the way she did.

"Mrs. Garrison called you Li'l Bit," he said. "What's your real name?" She told him. He nodded as if he approved. "Margaret is real pretty," he said. They went back outside into the hot sunshine and continued to work.

As the sun started to fade, she worried about Maggie and Peggy showing up; she wasn't quite sure what she'd do if he was still there. But he stopped working, pretty much the way he'd started, with no explanation, and began packing up. He left without saying anything about coming back.

"Did Walter Bee come over to help you?" Peggy asked, when they were sitting on the porch.

"Yes," said Li'l Bit, and added casually, "he seems very knowledgeable."

"Dalt says he's amazing. He knows as much as any of the horticulturists, and more than a couple of them, about grafting and breeding and all that. But he doesn't have a degree. Dalt's pretty sure he never even went to high school."

"How did Dalt find him?"

"He just wandered in one day looking for work. He's from somewhere in Alabama, that's Dalt's guess. Someplace in the backwoods. Probably dirt poor."

"How did Dalt manage to deduce all that?" Li'l Bit asked, with more of an edge than she intended.

"The man had to sleep in the back of his truck when he started working. He couldn't afford to rent a place until he got his first paycheck. But when Dalt offered him an advance he turned it down. Got real stiff-necked about it. You know the way country people can get."

Li'l Bit thought about Walter's sunburned neck, and every instinct told her Peggy was right; it could get stiff in a second if he even suspected he was being looked down on. Any friendships he had would be on his terms. Not that it would make any difference to her. She knew better than to expect him again. She wondered if Peggy had made Dalt pay him extra for working on his day off. She decided not to ask.

The next day, working in the garden seemed much harder than it had before. For the first time Li'l Bit noticed how the bugs bit. The red clay was heavier to shovel than she remembered it, and the humid air was heavier than the clay. The sweat poured down, her eyes hurt from squinting in the sunlight, and her back was sore. Since she took pride in being honest with herself, she knew why. But there wasn't anything to do except keep working and wait for the time when she would stop listening for his truck coming up the drive. She never mentioned any of it to Peggy and Maggie.

At night, she scrubbed her hands clean and looked in the mirror, which was something she hadn't done in forever, not more than the occasional glance. Because there was no reason; her mother had driven that point home years ago. But now she looked.

The years hadn't improved her. On the other hand they hadn't made her any worse, which was probably the bright side to being homely; you were fairly timeless. For a brief moment she thought about going to the drugstore and buying a lipstick, but she discarded the notion. If you looked like a horse the last thing you needed to do was make yourself look like a ridiculous horse. Better to keep your dignity. No amount of lipstick would give her a chin that balanced her nose. She would never have cheekbones that were visible to the human eye. She wasn't fat, but her six-foot frame had filled out to what would charitably be called solid. The mass of frizz that was her hair would never be sleek, and it was still "the color of mouse," as her mother had once said. Those who loved her would have to do so for her sterling character and fine mind. In her experience, that group did not include men young enough to be interesting.

She lay on her bed fully clothed and did not sleep. It might be admirable to see yourself clearly, and there was great pride in knowing you had never made a fool of yourself by imagining that you were what you were not. But just once she would have liked, with all her heart, to know what it felt like to be a woman men wanted to spoil.

The next morning was Saturday. She got up early, determined to stop wallowing. She showered, changed into fresh work clothes, and, using the sketch she'd drawn with Walter Bee, began making a list of plants she wanted to buy. She'd found a nursery about fifteen miles outside Macon that advertised itself as the Old Garden Center and claimed it sold "antique blooms." It sounded like as good a place as any to start. She packed her lunch for the drive and was heading toward the garage when Walter's truck pulled up.

"Found some old rosebushes," he said. "Thought we might try to moss them off before you go buying any."

The brown paper bag full of her lunch fell out of her hands to the ground. She left it there and forced herself not to run like a wild thing to get into his truck.

He drove her through the backcountry where the houses were old and many miles apart and the fields were laid out in neat blocks around them. Cotton tufts from the last crop had caught in the daisies and weeds that grew on the side of the road.

Then, abruptly, the tidy fields gave way to land that had gone back to wilderness. Wild vines and kudzu choked the trees that surrounded the property. The outlines of what had once been fields were barely visible in grass that was high enough to come to her waist. Walter pulled off the road onto what had once been the beginning of a gravel drive. In front of them they could see a blackened chimney rising above the broken remains of a huge fireplace and the stone foundation of a house. Climbing up the side of the chimney was a mass of pale-pink rambling roses.

"Don't know how long that thing has been burnt down," Walter said, "but I went up and took a look at those roses. Seemed like the ones you were reading about. Sal—something."

"Salet," she said. "They're old Noisettes." But she didn't even see them. She was still too busy looking at him.

He grabbed a bucket of water with peat moss soaking in it from the back of his truck, along with his gun, in case there were snakes, and gave her a roll of aluminum foil and a bag of a powdery substance he called "root tone," and they started beating their way through the brush to the old ruin. As they got close, the scent of roses came at them like a wall of perfume in the hot, still air.

Judging from the stone foundations, the house dated back to the time when kitchens were built separately from the main house. Charred beams and lumber lay almost buried in the ground; pieces of window glass embedded in the dirt caught the sunlight. The fireplace attached to the chimney had probably been a bake oven. A portion of rusted tin roof rested against it, weighed down with mud.

"Wonder what happened here," Walter said, in a hushed voice. She wanted to tell him she was thinking the same thing, but she just murmured, "Yes," and watched him standing there in the hot sunshine.

They started working. "Mossing off" was a technique for rooting new plants from already existing ones. "I've done it with crotons when I worked down in Florida. Don't know how it'll take with roses, but it's worth a try," he said.

He showed her how to find a likely stem and then strip away the outer layer in a band that was about an inch wide, "wounding," he called it. He spread a handful of wet peat moss out on the foil, sprinkled it with the root tone, and packed it over the band of bare stem, twisting the foil like the ends of a baked potato. "It's late in the season, but we'll come back in three weeks and see if we have roots," he said.

She nodded, as if she cared as much about the roses as she did about the fact that he was going to be around for another three weeks.

When it was time to go, he clipped long stems of roses, dozens of them, and gave them to her when she sat next to him in the truck. Her lap was full of color, more shades of pink than she had ever known existed. She thought she'd never be happier than she was right then and told herself to remember it.

Walter came to her house every Wednesday and Saturday. Sometimes they got into his truck and drove to nurseries, where she spent money like a greedy kid let loose in a toy store. Sometimes they went hunting in old graveyards and abandoned houses for heirloom plants—mostly roses. Once they saw a tiny house that was almost completely blocked from the road by Betty Sheffield Supreme camellias. With Walter betting her she wouldn't do it, Li'l Bit went up to the front door and rang the bell.

They spent two hours drinking terrible homemade wine and wandering through the garden while the woman who owned it regaled them with stories of the great-aunt many times back who came from Virginia holding precious camellia cuttings in her lap the whole way. They left with cuttings of their own wrapped in a damp tea towel that Li'l Bit mailed back.

After six weeks, the roses they had mossed off took root. Li'l Bit still viewed Walter's presence in her life as a miracle. Every time he drove up in his truck, it was almost enough to make her believe in God.

She didn't know where he came from, or who his people were, or if he even had any. When they had lunch he told her about the goings-on at the Gardens, and she told him about her volunteer work. She knew sometimes if a woman wanted a man to see her as more than a friend, she had to give him a little encouragement, and she would have risked it if she'd known how. But she didn't have an inkling.

Then one day when he was getting ready to leave, he walked around the house to the back door. "We should put in a gardenia bush right next to the kitchen window," he said. "Every woman should have a gardenia outside her kitchen so she can smell it while she's cooking."

She laughed. "It would be wasted on me, I can't boil water. Millie does all my cooking." She meant to be self-deprecating, and maybe a little funny, but once the words were out she wanted to kill herself. Because she could see him remember all at once that she was rich and that his boss's wife was one of her best friends.

"That's right," he said. "You don't have to do for yourself. I forgot." Then he got into his truck and drove off.

When he didn't come the following week she told herself he was busy. The week after that she told herself it was just as well he was gone before she'd had a chance to make a complete fool of herself. She made herself stop the nightly replaying of the fatal moment, when she had ruined everything, and got into bed.

In the middle of the night she was awakened by a sound like someone scraping the ground outside her bedroom window. She always opened the windows when the weather was warm and never thought twice about it. But now, suddenly, she was aware of just how alone she was in her big empty house.

She lay in bed trying to decide whether to get her baseball bat or make a run for Maggie's place. Then a breeze blew in the window, ruffling the curtain, and the heady scent of gardenia floated in on the air. She got up quietly.

Walter was just finishing tapping down the soil around the roots of the gardenia bush he had planted when she came up behind him. He sat back on his heels to admire his handiwork and she watched him for a moment. Then he sensed her presence and turned his head.

"There you are," he said, his voice soft in the night. "I saw you walking around in your room and figured you'd heard me."

All she had on was her white cotton nightgown; she hadn't even put on her robe and slippers. Her hair was out of the net the way it always was when she slept. She sat down next to him on the ground.

"I knew your hair'd be beautiful when it wasn't all tied up," he said, before he kissed her.

Later on, when they were in her bed, she only stopped him once. "I've never—" she started to say, but he put his finger to her lips.

"That's fine, Margaret," he whispered.

So she made love for the first time in her life. She wasn't young and she wasn't beautiful, and she had no idea if the man would be staying. But she had the perfume from her new gardenia bush floating in through her window.

Walter came to her house four nights a week and stayed with her. But he never moved in. And she never asked him to. He needed his own place for his pride, and if there was one thing she understood it was pride.

Over time she learned little tidbits about him that she hoarded like precious stolen things. He had been one of ten kids. They were tenant farmers who had to move a lot. He told her the first thing his mother did when they were in a new place was plant a gardenia bush outside her kitchen window.

They discovered the remains of two more terraces in her back lawn and dug them up. They rescued wisteria and honeysuckle from the ridge behind the house and old daffodils from the edge of the pond and put them in the restored beds.

It was all going so well, and then she decided she wanted to put in a garden outside her bedroom.

LI'L BIT BALLED UP HER MASS OF HAIR under a scarf—it hadn't gotten any tamer now that it was gray—and walked to the window to look out at the perfectly manicured, enclosed garden outside. It was built on a semicircle against the side of the house, encompassing her old gardenia bush. In the center of the garden was a small circle of lavender and eight gravel paths that ran from the hub to the perimeter like spokes of a wheel. Formal, and much stiffer than the big beds they had already put in, it was the most ambitious project she and Walter had tried. If she had known then . . . but she hadn't.

WHEN SHE FIRST BROUGHT IT UP, Walter was as excited about the project as she was. She had read about a parterre garden in one of her books by the ever-helpful Mr. Jackson Downing. It was a circular garden cut by pathways into equal pieces like a pie. At the center there was usually some focal point like a statue or a fountain. Li'l Bit proposed to make her garden a semicircle against the side of the house next to her bedroom. Her gardenia would be at the center, and she would put a small door in her bedroom so that she could have direct access. Her new garden would be a bastardization of a true parterre, but she wanted to maintain as much of the historical flavor as she could.

"We'll put in a low boxwood hedge around the outside," she said, when they started making the sketches.

"Have a tall one," Walter urged. "The garden's outside your bedroom, and it'll give you privacy."

"I think the correct way is to keep it low so you can see the flowers inside." She was busy filling out an order form for some plants she was buying from a nursery in Connecticut, so she added, "Look it up in the book."

There was a pause. Then he said, "We'll do it your way."

"I'm not sure I'm right. Look it up and read me what it says."

If she hadn't been so busy she might have seen the expression on his face. If she hadn't gotten so comfortable with him, the silence would have put her on guard. But she was busy and she had gotten comfortable, so she said, "Try the big book on the shelf over the desk, the one by Downing."

Then she finally looked up and saw that his face was scarlet under his tan, and his black eyes had closed down. And all the times he had refused to write anything down because he had it "in my head" came back to her. She tried to remember if she'd ever seen him going through a brochure or a book or a magazine or a catalog. And without thinking, she blurted out, "My God, you can't read."

He just stood in front of her getting redder and redder and not saying a word while the silence roared around them. And because she wanted to make it seem unimportant, and because she was her father's daughter, she said, "That's nothing. I could teach you in no time." And of course he walked out.

She waited three long nights for him to come back; then she got in her car and drove to Garrison Gardens. She found him in the greenhouse grafting azaleas.

"I think we should plant herbs in the bedroom garden," she said, as if they had been talking about it earlier that morning. She wanted to be casual but nerves made her clip words so they came out snooty. "I've called that nursery outside Marietta, and they still have some lavender. Should we plan to drive there this weekend?" There was no response. She wasn't sure what she was going to do if he turned her down.

"I really think this is something we should discuss. Neither of us should have the final say." He was just looking at her, not saying a word.

Suddenly she was furious. After all the years of teaching her-self to accept being alone, she had suddenly been given happiness. And now this bull-headed man standing in front of her with his stiff neck and his closed-off black eyes was about to take it away. "What you are doing is wrong," she said, stumbling over her words. "It's selfish . . . no, it's criminal to throw away something that is so good, and . . . and you have no damn right! If you like being mis-erable, find another way. Don't do it to me, because I don't want any part of it."

She thought he was going to tell her to go to hell and she wouldn't know how to turn and walk away. But instead he said, "We're throwing away a whole lot of rosemary here at the Gardens. I'll bring some over tonight after work." And she nodded and said, "Good." And when she got outside the greenhouse door, she took her first real breath in three days.

They never mentioned reading or teaching him to read again. When they put in the parterre garden, they let the boxwood hedge around it get as high as a man's shoulder, so it enclosed the garden outside her bedroom window and made it into a magical little world.

She had ten more years with him, years when her gardens were beautiful and she was not lonely. She assumed Peggy and Maggie knew what was going on, although she never told them, because they stopped staying late on the afternoons when they knew Walter would be coming over.

For more than a decade she had a life that was as good as anyone's life could be. Until that night at the cabin.

LI'L BIT PULLED ON HER WORK BOOTS and went outside. The flowers in the three terraces were all brown now, but the ridge that led to Lottie's cabin would stay green all winter because of the pines. When her terrace gardens were in bloom there would be hundreds of flowers in the beds: dahlias, mignonettes, hyacinths, primroses, scarlet trumpet honeysuckle, azaleas, lily of the valley, cape cowslips, snowdrops, daffodils, tulips, camellias, and gardenias, all spread out in lush swatches of color. And scattered along the stone walls were the trees: purple beech, mountain ash, weeping poplar. Most of all there would be roses, pale heirlooms with names like Gloire de Dijon, Ro Souvinere de la Malmaison, and Salet.

There was not one plant on the entire property, from the Johnny-jump-ups to the Judas tree, that she didn't know. Even though she might have to give in someday and hire someone to help her, she would be in command of every inch until she died.

She started for the shed where she kept her supplies and then stopped. She turned and headed in the opposite direction, to the edge of the woods. Since she seemed to be stuck in the past today, she decided she might as well be totally maudlin about it.

Li'l Bit made her way through the woods until she reached a small clearing surrounded by a low rock wall. The old graveyard of the Justines and the Bannings hadn't been used in generations when she and Walter discovered it; the forest had all but reclaimed it. They had cleared away the trees to give the few remaining bushes and plantings a better chance in the sunlight. She walked to the headstone she had put up only ten years ago.

When Walter died, it had been years since she'd talked to him. She'd seen him from time to time; it was a small town, after all. He had stayed on to work at the resort. Peggy was the one who told her he had died and didn't have any family to bury him.

So even though it caused much whispering, Li'l Bit took over. Walter was cremated, and she took the ashes back to bury them in the old cemetery they had discovered in her woods. She would be buried next to him, she decided. "So if any of that afterlife lunacy is real, start working now on getting used to the idea," she told him.

Now she stood in front of his headstone. "I'm sorry if you were angry," she said. "But I did the right thing. I didn't have any other choice." She leaned over and pinched a few yellow leaves off the gardenia bush she'd planted next to his grave. "It's just . . . sometimes it's hard to believe it was worth it."

Chapter Eighteen

PEGGY GOT UP, PUSHED THE kitchen chair back from the table, and started walking; it was the only thing to do when the ghosts were hovering. She made her way upstairs to the mezzanine. She almost never went there anymore. After Dalt died she had moved out of the bedroom they had shared; now she slept in a small guest room on the first floor. She could have moved out of the house altogether after Dalt was gone. But she felt she had paid for the place.

On the mezzanine she passed the big master suite and headed for a small room next to it. On the other side of the room was the door to another suite, the playroom, bedroom, and bathroom that had been Grady's when he was a child. If you were into symbolism, which she never had been until lately, you might say it was symbolic that this little room was squeezed between the two big chunks of Garrison-dominated space. Because a million years ago, in another lifetime, this was the room she had planned to use as a nursery.

WHEN SHE WAS FIRST MARRIED she hadn't even thought about having a child. She was still too wary. But as time passed she realized her incredible good luck was not going to vanish. She really *was* Mrs. Dalton Garrison. She had all the shoes and dresses and hats and jewelry she could ever want. She had a house for her mama. She had a car with a driver. She had china and linens and silverware and glasses and rugs and sofas. She had long dinner parties with people old enough to be her parents, hours of time on her hands during the day when Dalt was working, and lonely nights when Dalt was out of town. She didn't have any friends of her own except for Maggie and Li'l Bit.

And they were disappointed in her. They had expected her to pick up Miss Myrtis's causes where she left off. There was no way to explain to them that Dalt might be fond of her, and he might enjoy showing her off, but he didn't want her to have causes, or any thoughts that weren't his.

Most nights when he was home, they swam in the pool after dinner, Dalt doing laps to keep in shape, she clowning around next to him trying to distract him. But there was the night when he came up behind her and whispered in her ear, "Pull down your suit," and when the words brought back horrors and she froze, he started to pull it down for her. She was afraid she would start screaming, but the hands peeling down the suit were gentle, not mean, and when he turned her around to look at him, it was sweet kind Dalt smiling his young-boy smile, not the twisted red face of his son, and the scream stopped in her throat. Then the water was stroking her body, along with his hands, and when he pressed against her they floated together. Above them, the summer moon was so bright it was practically like sunshine coming through the trees. Dalt started to laugh from sheer pleasure, and she thought someday he could wash away forever what his son had done.

So when he led her out of the pool and back toward the house, she stopped him. "No, here," she whispered. She lay down on one of the long wicker chaises and tried to pull him down next to her. "I have to go in the house and get something, sweetheart," he said.

But that wasn't what she wanted. She reached up and kissed him and heard the little shudder his breath did when he was excited. "Not tonight. Please," she said.

"We can't take a chance."

"I'm an old married lady, I'm not taking any chances." She reached for him again.

"I can't," he said. "Not yet, sweetheart."

That was her cue to leave it be, but for once she didn't pick up on it.

"Why?"

He was getting irritated with her. "I couldn't do that to Grady. Not now." He turned away to indicate that the conversation was over.

"Don't you want to have a baby with me, Dalt?"

He went and got them two towels to wrap up in. In the bright moonlight she could see the belly he was starting to grow in spite of how hard he worked not to have it. It made him look old.

"We have plenty of time to think about all of that," he said. "Right now, I have to get that boy back on track." Then he added, a little more softly, "I know he's not a child, but he's so lost right now, sweetheart. I have to help him."

That was it. He left her there in the moonlight and went off to bed.

And that was when she knew she might get Grady out of her house, but she would never get him out of her life. And maybe it was the beginning of everything that happened later.

Dalt continued to fret over Grady. And he continued to blame his remarriage for Grady's endless screwups. Grady started working at the resort full time. He was given a fancy title and a big salary and an office next to his father's, and Dalt told everyone how proud he was to have his son at his side. There were regular complaints from employees who had to work for Grady. There were the schemes

Grady came up with, like the nightclub in the lobby, which cost a small fortune and had to be closed because no one used it. And there was the accusation, never proved because the accountant who made it was fired, that Grady had been skimming money from the Gardens' nonprofit funds—funds that allowed them to maintain their tax-exempt status.

"He's just learning," Dalt said, the first time Grady messed up.

"He's having a hard time adjusting," he said the second time.

Finally, he said, "He made a mistake; everyone makes mistakes."

But Peggy noticed he scaled back Grady's duties until there was nothing left really but the title and the salary. And because he felt guilty about doing it, he wouldn't even consider anything—like having a baby—that might upset "the boy."

But a need had opened up inside Peggy. She looked around her big safe house, and she saw a little girl in it. A child who raced through the halls, yelling and laughing, who made messes finger painting, had the run of the whole place, and never once felt grateful for it. A girl who took it for granted because it was hers and she belonged there. Peggy would teach her daughter to be as smart and strong as Maggie and Li'l Bit. Her little girl would never worry about pleasing anyone. She would never be afraid.

So Peggy took measurements in the little room she'd chosen to be the nursery. She picked out wallpaper with dancing bears on it. She picked the name Amanda for her dream baby and promised herself that no one would ever call her Mandy.

And then Dalt said no. Finally and forever. He didn't want to have any more children. He explained it to her as if he were talking to a slow-witted child herself. "There's more involved than you've thought of, sweetheart. Grady grew up thinking he was going to inherit everything. That may seem cold-blooded to you, but there's a lot of money at stake. He has a right to know his inheritance is secure. And I'm not sure I want to divide up the pot too many ways. I don't believe in doing that." Then he smiled at her, as if that would make it better, and said, "Besides, you don't want to give any young 'un an old coot like me for a daddy."

And when she cried and said this was something they should decide between them, he said, in the cold voice he used when he was firing unsatisfactory employees, "Don't make me choose between my son and you, Peggy."

So the little room she thought would be a good nursery became a walk-in closet with moving racks for her dresses and a wall of shelves for her shoes.

"I probably would have been a terrible mother," she told Li'l Bit and Maggie, when she could finally say it lightly. "Would have raised ax murderers." Neither of them smiled.

"I know it isn't easy to stand up for yourself when you feel grateful," said Li'l Bit, "but sometimes you have to." Which seemed to suggest that the rumors were true that she had hunted down Walter Bee at the Gardens and given him what for about something. Obviously, whatever it was about, she'd won, because after a brief hiatus he'd been back at her house four nights a week. "Dalt is wrong not to let you have children," Li'l Bit said emphatically.

And Maggie added, "No one should be cheated of that."

And then, because they were Maggie and Li'l Bit, they changed the subject.

But years later when Dalton was so sick and Li'l Bit and Maggie were taking turns spelling her when she nursed him, Peggy remembered what they'd said. She wondered whether, if any of them had had children of their own, it all might have been different.

PEGGY TURNED AWAY from the little room, which still held the bulk of her wardrobe in mothballs. The upshot of the room's not becoming a nursery was that she never did fall in love with Dalt the way she could have. She hated Grady for that, too. That was the dark little fear that never went away: She could never be sure of her motives. She was always afraid she'd done what she did, at least in part, to get back at Grady.

Chapter Nineteen

*L*AUREL WALKED TO THE PLACE in the lobby where the cake showcases had stood, back when the *Gazette* was Krausner's bakery. She sniffed. It was true; the vanilla smell did linger. Suddenly she was nine years old again and standing in that very spot, ordering the biggest birthday cake Krausner's would sell her for six dollars and twenty-nine cents. It was not a memory she wanted to go back to. But that was what made the past such a bitch. Once you started remembering, like she had with Josh, you didn't get to choose what came back to you.

SHE'D HAD TO HITCH A RIDE from her house to town so she could order the cake. Then she proudly counted out her money while Mr. Krausner wrote down her instructions in his spiral notebook. She could still remember what she'd told him she wanted: a cake covered with white icing with three big pink roses right smack in the center and around them, written in chocolate, *Happy Birthday Sara Jayne McCready*. After some debate with herself, she had decided against the less formal *Ma*. The grandeur of the event she was planning called for her mother's full name spelled out in the swirling cursive that was the mark of Krausner's best.

The cake had to be from Krausner's. Everyone knew you couldn't have a real birthday party without one. The Krausner's cake was as important as the balloons and singing "Happy Birthday."

Laurel herself had never had a birthday party. When she was real little she hadn't known exactly when her birthday was, the day she was born not being something her ma wanted to dwell on.

She'd been invited to a few parties by kids in her class at school. Denny's mama always saw to it that she got an invitation with Snoopy on the front wearing a happy-birthday hat and holding a balloon with lines on it that had the time and place written in. And there were a couple of other tenderhearted mothers who tried to include her. Sara Jayne never let her go. "We can't invite them, so you're not gonna go and make us look pitiful because you can't pay them back." Laurel understood. Most of her mother's belief system was up for grabs at any point in time, but the one constant mantra in the chaos was, No-one-is-ever-gonna-feel-sorry-for-us.

Which was all the more reason for them to have a party. Laurel knew instinctively that in spite of the men who came out of her mother's bedroom in the mornings, Sara Jayne was alone and friendless, even more than Laurel herself. That was why her mother was so unhappy that nothing Laurel did ever helped. Not the plaster of paris ashtray with her handprint in it that she made in school, or the times she cleaned the house until everything was shiny like on television commercials.

Her mother needed friends, nice friends. If she had some, it would change her life and, by proxy, Laurel's. So Laurel was going to have a surprise party for Sara Jayne. In one masterful stroke she would establish them as people who issued invitations and had the right to accept them. They would belong. It would make her ma happy. Because who could resist a party where people sang your name and gave you presents just for being born? At age nine, Laurel Selene was not troubled by self-doubt. That had developed slowly over the years.

❧

One thing was clear, she would need cash. Cakes and balloons cost money. But certain enterprises are blessed from the start. Or maybe it was the Lord helping those who helped themselves. Laurel had two semiregular sources of income. Three afternoons a week she stayed after school and worked for the school librarian; on weekends she did chores around the Methodist Church for the preacher's wife, even though Sara Jayne was technically a Baptist.

By dropping hints to her two benefactresses, Laurel managed to wangle another day of work a week out of each of them and started making her party plans. She knew the right date, because her mother's birthday, unlike hers, did not go totally unnoticed. Every year her ma got a birthday card with two five-dollar bills tucked inside it from her own mother, a person Laurel was never to refer to as her grandmother. She'd met this mystery relative once when she was barely old enough to grasp the significance of the event, and she had a vague recollection of a tiny woman with skin pulled tight over little bones, who immediately got into a fight with her ma and left without even coming into their house for a glass of water.

But the birthday cards still came every year. And every year Ma took the money to her favorite bar—which Laurel could have told her grandmother was what would happen if the lady had ever wanted to know. But thanks to the cards, Laurel knew the date was November fifteenth. She set the time at five o'clock, which seemed right for a gathering of grown-ups.

But which grown-ups? She couldn't just set up a table outside the SuperSave and give out invitations like they were raffle tickets for a pancake supper. For the first time, little doubts started in the back of her mind, but she pushed them away.

Finally she settled on four women: Denny's mother; Mrs. Peters, the preacher's wife; Miss Hudson, the school librarian; and her beloved English teacher, Miss Norton. With such a small guest list it wouldn't be the grand event she had envisioned, but if Denny's father came, and Reverend Peters, and if Miss Hudson would bring along the aged mother she lived with, there would be enough people to make a good sound if they all sang "Happy Birthday" really loud.

After getting the balloons and the candles and paying in advance for the cake, her money was running low and she had to wait to buy the invitations. By the time she got them, it was too late to put them in the mail, so on the day before the big event, she delivered them by hand.

Neither Miss Norton nor Miss Hudson were at their desks, so she left the invitations for them. After school she biked to Denny's house and stuffed his mama's invitation in the mailbox, and then she headed for the church. Mrs. Peters was in the vestry, sorting through clothing that had been donated for the poor, and she insisted on reading the invitation right there and then. When she finished she looked a little stunned. Laurel realized there was a potential disaster she hadn't thought of. People might not show up. She began talking fast.

"It's a party for my ma, it's her birthday. I have a cake and balloons and candles—"

"That sounds lovely, dear," Mrs. Peters said, in the tone kind adults used when they didn't mean it. "Does your mama know about this?"

"No, ma'am. It's a surprise."

The word *no* was hovering on Mrs. Peters's lips; Laurel could see it. Desperation made her smart. Although she was pretty sure lying to a preacher's wife damned you to hell, she blurted out, "I didn't do it by myself. I had help from . . . from my grandma."

For a moment she thought Mrs. Peters was going to ask her what her grandma's name was, and she would have to die right there in the vestry. But instead Mrs. Peters smiled wearily. "Of course I'll come, dear. Thank you so much for inviting me."

"You'll have a good time," Laurel assured her. "I bought the cake from Krausner's." She ran off, leaving Mrs. Peters to watch after her.

When she looked back on it now, she figured the poor woman was probably remembering the old saying that no good deed goes unpunished.

ON THE DAY OF THE PARTY, Laurel woke up with a knot in her stomach. The enormity of what she was planning hit her, and she thought briefly of bailing out on the whole thing. But she'd given out the invitations, and Mr. Krausner was probably putting the roses on the cake at that very minute. There was no turning back. She checked to see that her ma was still safely sleeping, then got dressed, strapped her basket on her bike, and took off. She never rode her bike to town, it was too far and there was no way to get there without going on the highway. But this morning she didn't have any choice.

Even though it was still early, cars and pickups whizzed past her, threatening to push her into the ditch at the side of the road. Eighteen-wheelers sprayed her with dirt and pebbles; diesel fumes made her eyes burn. A flatbed truck full of chickens on their way to the slaughterhouse pulled up next to her for a while; she was so close to it she could smell the stench and see the doomed birds flapping their wings. She promised God she would never ride her bike on the highway again if He would just let her get to Krausner's. God was listening. She got there as the shop was opening.

The birthday cake was beautiful beyond her wildest dreams; it made her mouth water just to look at it, with pink roses so big they could have been real, and her ma's name looking grand in chocolate swirls. She carefully lowered it into the bike basket and started the return trip.

By the time she reached the driveway to her house, her arms and neck were aching from the effort of keeping the basket steady.

There was a small porch on the back of the house where she was planning to hide the cake. She had started walking her bike over the bumpy grass when a familiar voice called out, "Where the hell have you been?"

It never occurred to her that Sara Jayne would get up so early. She tried to cut around fast to the back, but she was too late.

"What's that?" Her mother came out into the yard and indicated the bike basket with her cigarette. It seemed to be one of her more alert mornings; she was even dressed. Laurel stood rooted to the ground. All her plans and work would be for nothing if she didn't think of something to say. But she just couldn't.

"I asked you a question." Ma looked in the bike basket and saw the name on the cake box. "What are you doing with a cake from Krausner's? Answer me."

It dawned on Laurel that everything didn't have to be over. There wouldn't be a surprise anymore, which was disappointing, but it also might be for the best, because now at least she could be sure Ma would put on a skirt and blouse for the party, which was something that had been worrying her. She pushed down her kickstand so the bike wouldn't fall over.

"It's for your birthday," she said.

"You wasted good money on that?" Ma gave a short laugh and turned to go back to the house.

"It's for your party," Laurel said.

Sara Jayne whirled around. "My what?"

"I'm having a birthday party for you."

Her mother was coming toward her. "What the hell are you talking about, girl?"

"I invited some people—"

"You did what?"

"We're gonna sing 'Happy Birthday'—"

"You asked people to come here? To this pigsty?"

"I got a cake. It's so pretty—"

"Who did you ask?"

"Just some people."

"Who?"

"Mrs. Peters. She said she was real glad—"

"You invited the preacher's wife?"

"She wanted to come." Her mother grabbed her arm so hard it made her eyes water.

"Ma, please. I wanted you to have something nice. . . ." But her mother was dragging her across the yard to the house. "Ma, it'll be all right."

"All right?" Sara Jayne was screaming. "All right?" She pushed Laurel through the door of the house. "Look!" She grabbed Laurel's head, twisting it back and forth. "Look at this! You asked people to come to this?"

Laurel was sobbing now, in big painful gulps. "I'll clean it—" she started.

"You can't get this clean enough for decent people! Don't you know that? Don't you know how decent people live?"

"Ma, I'm sorry—"

"Stop crying, damn you! I'm the one who should be crying. I'm the one who's stuck with you!"

And that was when Laurel Selene McCready, age nine, learned that there were times in life when there was no way you could cry enough for the hurt you felt, so she stopped.

"Who else did you ask?" Sara Jayne demanded. Past caring, Laurel told her. Ma dragged her into the kitchen. "You come in here," she said.

"What are you gonna do?"

"You're gonna do it. You're gonna call every one of those ladies you asked to come here, and you're gonna tell them you're a little liar. You're gonna tell them there is no party." Laurel had a picture of telling Miss Norton, whom she loved, and Miss Hudson, who was kind to her, and Denny's mother—and most of all, Mrs. Peters.

"I don't know the phone numbers."

"I'll look them up for you."

"I can't. . . ."

"Tell them it was a joke."

"Please, Ma, don't make me."

"You got me into this, you're gonna get me out of it."

"I won't."

The belt was out of her mother's blue jeans so fast she almost didn't see it. But she felt it as it landed on the back of her legs.

"You do this to me and then you say you won't?" Ma was screaming so high it was almost funny. The belt started falling in a pattern. "You took away everything!" *Whap!* "I've got nothing because of you!" *Whap!* "Nothing!" *Whap!*

The belt was hitting her on the shoulders and the back, but she didn't make a sound. She could feel Ma was tiring. Soon it would be over.

Sara Jayne dropped the belt on the floor, and stared at her, panting to catch her breath. Painfully, Laurel started for the phone. Her mother stopped her.

"No. Go outside," she said. Laurel went out to the front yard.

After what felt like hours her mother came out, got into the car without a word, and drove off.

SARA JAYNE DIDN'T COME BACK for the rest of the day. Laurel sat in the house and waited, not knowing what to do but not caring much either. Five o'clock came and no one showed up at the door looking for a party, so she knew it had been taken care of. At eight o'clock she made herself a sandwich. At ten she filled the tub and, in spite of the welts on her back and her legs, scrubbed herself carefully. She spread the sheets neatly on the sofa that served as her bed and went to sleep.

Toward morning, a familiar sound woke her. Ma was fumbling with the front door. She closed her eyes as Sara Jayne made her unsteady way into the kitchen. Then there were more sounds, of drawers opening and her mother bumping into things. Once she muttered "shit." Laurel kept her eyes closed.

Sara Jayne came out of the kitchen and moved to the sofa. "Hey," she said in a loud whisper, as she leaned over her. Laurel could smell booze breath. "Come on, I know you're not asleep. You heard me crashing around in there." She sat on the sofa near Laurel's feet and put something on the floor in front of her. Laurel didn't look to see what it was.

Sara Jayne started to laugh. "Want to hear a joke? Not a one of them was going to come." She took a drink from the glass she'd brought with her from the kitchen. "Your skinny little school-teacher started saying something about dinner plans before I even got a word out. That old bitch that runs the library nearly slammed the receiver in my ear; your pal's mother acted like she'd never heard of any party. And your Mrs. Peters was so happy when I said it was off, I thought she was gonna start crying." She laughed again, more quietly. "I embarrassed myself for nothing." She reached over and shook Laurel. "Come on, sit up. I've got something for you."

It was the only way she'd go away. Laurel sat up. Her mother leaned down to the floor, brought up a plate, and handed it to her. It was a hunk of cake. Her ma had hacked it out so there was a whole rose on it. None of the little ridges that made the petals had gotten squashed on the bike ride home the way she'd been afraid they would. It sat there, big and pink and perfect.

"Eat it," said her mother. "No point in letting it go to waste."

Laurel put it down on the floor and curled up in a ball on the corner of the sofa as far away from her mother as she could get.

Sara Jayne shrugged. "Be that way. I'm gonna have me a party." She found her guitar, which was leaning against the wall, and went out on the porch.

At first she was just strumming, not playing anything, just weaving together snatches of music she knew. Then the music worked itself into "Happy Birthday." She played it through and then started messing around with it, making it sad and lonely like an old country song. Then everything was quiet. And then, the way Laurel knew it would be, the next sound she heard was her ma crying. She lay in the darkness until the crying finally stopped and she was sure there were no more sounds coming from the porch. Then she went into the bedroom and took the pillow and blanket off her mother's bed and went outside.

Sara Jayne was asleep, lying stretched out on the porch swing. As Laurel wedged the pillow under her head, her mother murmured, "It wouldn't be like this if he was here. He loved us, baby." Laurel put the blanket over her and went back inside.

Chapter Twenty

*L*AUREL WALKED BACK to her desk, looked down at the sheaf of yellow legal-pad pages covered with Reverend Malbry's spindly handwriting, and admitted defeat. There was no way she could do any more work on the loopy article. She'd have to come in on Sunday to finish it. She put it away and left the office.

THE SPORTSMAN'S GRILL WAS CLOSED, but Denny's truck was parked outside. Laurel turned into the shopping center parking lot, pulled up next to the truck, and looked in the front window of the bar. Denny was inside, washing the floor. He hurried to the front when she started banging on the door.

"A second pair of hands," he said. "Get you a mop. I'm doing the ladies' room next."

"Don't you have someone to do this kind of thing?" she asked, as they swished soap and water over the bathroom floor.

"He quit. Good help is hard to find these days. Daddy's always going on about it."

"No one out there willing to do demeaning work for starvation wages?"

"You're not being fair. Daddy saves the demeaning work for blood relatives."

She mopped in silence for a while. Then she said, "Did I ever tell you about the time my Grandma McCready came to see Ma and me?" she asked.

She could see him shift gears into his supportive mode. "No, I don't believe you have."

She powdered the sink with Ajax and began to scrub, keeping her eyes on the buildup around the faucet. "Ma's father threw her out when she told him she was knocked up and the daddy had gotten himself killed before making it right with the Lord. My grandfather was a deacon in his church, and the way he read the Bible the right thing to do was to cut off his seventeen-year-old daughter to fend for herself without a penny and a baby on the way. Then one day the old man got the word from God that he was wrong about the cutting-off thing, and in fact it was his Christian duty to forgive. So he sent his wife to give Ma the good news. The only hitch was Ma had to say she was—well, they wouldn't use the word *raped;* they said *forced.* So she wasn't a whore, after all, just a victim. Guess they figured, what with my daddy being dead and all, there wouldn't be an opposing point of view. She told them to go to hell."

"Good for her."

"It must have been hard to do that, you know? She must have wanted to go home so much. She was just a kid herself, waiting tables, trying to keep care of me. . . ." She took a long pause. "I'm just saying, my ma—she wasn't all bad, you know?"

"No one ever said she was."

"I do. All the time."

"She wasn't exactly mother of the year either."

"She was weak."

"She was a drunk, Laurel."

"Maybe she wouldn't have been, if he had lived."

"Drunks always have an excuse—"

"You don't know what it did to her, when he died the way he did."

"—and the children of drunks always have an excuse for them."

"I'm honest about her."

"As much as you can be."

"I know what she was, Denny. But she didn't start out that way."

"There's a statute of limitations on how long you can feel sorry for yourself."

"She couldn't get past what happened. I think it was because she could never be sure. She'd go on and on about how that man loved her and he had gotten a big new job to support us and he never would have done what they said. But she had to twist her mind into knots to keep believing it. Maybe if she could have accepted it—" She stopped and threw the scrub brush into the sink.

"—she wouldn't have been a mean drunk who treated you like shit. Is that what you were gonna say?" Denny asked.

She walked out of the ladies' room with him behind her. He sat her on a stool at the bar and poured her a soda. She wanted a beer, but it went against Denny's religion to give anyone a drink when they were upset. "Why are you going back over all this stuff?" he asked.

She took a swig of the soda. He'd given her RC, and she wished it were a Coke. "Josh, the writer, said when he interviewed Vashti he thought she was holding something back. Now he figures it was about her being sick. But when he said it, do you know the first damn thing that came into my head? *Maybe Ma was right. Maybe the night my father died it didn't go like everyone said.* Can you believe I started up with that crap again, after all this time?"

"Unfinished business, sugar."

"I don't want to be crazy, Denny. I spent my life with a crazy lady."

"Maybe you're still not sure it's all that crazy."

"I know what happened that night. Everyone within a two-hundred-mile radius around here knows."

"Okay." But he was waiting for more.

"When I was little I used to believe her. I bought all of it: He did love us, he didn't kill Richard, he wasn't there with Nella for his nightly piece of ass, and the three Miss Margarets lied. I believed he wasn't really dead, he was just waiting somewhere, and someday he'd come back and marry Ma. He was gonna bring us presents: mine was a Barbie doll, and she was gonna get M&M's with peanuts. She loved those." She paused. "Say something."

"What do you want, Laurel?"

The question caught her off guard. "I don't know . . ." she started, then the words spilled out. "I want to stop being stuck. I want to stop caring about things that happened before I was born. I want someone to swear to me that I'm not like my mother."

He watched her for a moment. Then he said, "I think it's time you took the box home."

It took Laurel a second to register what he'd said. "Where the hell did that come from?"

"It's something I've been thinking for a while."

"I don't want the damn thing right now."

"I can't keep it in my daddy's storeroom forever."

"I didn't realize it was crowding you."

"You gotta look at it. Or don't. Throw it in the trash. But do something. She's been gone a long time."

"I'll take it. Just not today. Okay?" He waited for a minute; then he nodded and went back to the ladies' room to clean the commode. She finished the soda and left.

WHEN LAUREL ARRIVED AT HER HOUSE, the SUV was already there and Josh Wolf Eyes was sitting on the porch steps.

"Is that a real outhouse in the back?" he asked.

"Not only is it the genuine article, it is a historic landmark. An honest-to-God cement one-holer as put up by the CCC boys during the Depression. Did you get a look at the workmanship on the inside?"

"Actually, that didn't occur to me."

"Well, it was the deluxe model. I'm very uppity about having one."

"I'm sure." He was silent, working his way up to something. "I saw a whole lot of deer about fifteen minutes ago."

"That'll happen when you're in the woods."

He got up and started pacing around her front yard. "I had my talk with the three Miss Margarets."

"And it was like trying to kick your way through a couple of miles of wet chiffon."

"Nice image. They gave me some of the worst coffee I've ever had in my life and then—well, if there's anything you want to know about what it was like for a young female doctor to establish a practice here in the thirties, just ask me."

"I see."

"I'm also up on old roses and camellias."

"Bet there isn't too much you don't know about the Charles Valley Animal Rescue either. Did the subject of Vashti come up at all?"

"I tried. They let me know that they didn't feel inclined to talk about anything other than her many accomplishments. They were very polite about it."

"Oh, always."

"After that, I went to see Vashti's grandmother at her nursing home. They wouldn't let me near her. The supervisor seemed to know I was writing a story."

"News travels in small towns. Maybe when everyone's calmed down in a couple of weeks you can try again."

"No, I can't." He stopped pacing and sat back down on the steps. "I had a call from my agent yesterday. Vashti's obituary was in *The New York Times*. He wanted to know when I'm planning to let him see some pages, since obviously I'm not going to be talking to her. And I do have a first draft finished." He sighed. "He's a nice boy, my agent. He's only twelve, but he's smart. I gave him a song-and-dance about wanting to get some more background down here before I do my final edit. He said I was stalling."

"Why? Are you scared?"

"That's the theory laid out by the wunderkind."

"After all the writing you've done? Come on."

"I write pieces for magazines—they run five thousand words, tops. This is a book. And not a book the world is panting for. I have been working on it for a year and a half. That's a hell of a long time to be out of commission in my business. Especially if you're carrying my alimony payments." He paused. "And I'm an old guy in a kid's game. Do you know how young most of the writers are who do what I do?"

"What difference does that make? You're not a movie star."

"I want to get out before they throw me out, Laurel." He took a deep breath. "It's not just that I want the fucking book to be good, I *need* it to be good. I'm scared shitless."

"When are you going back?"

"Tomorrow."

"That soon?"

"I want to do one final edit. Then I've got to send the manuscript to my agent and see what happens." The sun was starting to set; the trees were black against a glowing orange sky. He watched for a moment. She could tell he didn't want to look at her. "Speaking of which," he said, "what you told me, the story about your father and Grady killing Richard. I want to use that. I'll say it was just a rumor, nothing substantiated. Will you be all right with that?"

A few days ago she would have been angry. But she'd told Denny she wanted to let go.

"Go ahead," she said. "It's time I stopped trying to protect a dead man I never met."

They sat in silence and watched the sky do its thing.

"It *is* beautiful here," he said.

"It has its moments."

They were silent again. "You could call me sometime," he said finally. He turned to her, and his eyes were soft in the fading light. "Or you could come see me."

"You want me to come to New York City?"

"We don't have any historic outhouses. But the sunsets are spectacular because the pollution from New Jersey refracts the rays." He looked away again. "Just a thought."

"I may take you up on it," she said.

"Really?" He sounded downright eager.

"I'll think about it." The idea of being in New York City with Josh showing her around was so appealing it was frightening. "Have you ever had grits?" she asked.

"That would be the white paste they put on the plate with my breakfast eggs at the resort until I told them not to, right?"

"I fix mine with cheese. If you're game, I was planning to have them for supper."

"I'd like that." But he didn't move. She leaned up against him. For a moment she thought of trying to explain to him that he'd not seen the best of her, because the things he brought up were hurtful and she really could be a lot nicer. She also thought of telling him she was sorry he was leaving. But then he put his arm around her, so she decided, for once, that she would leave well enough alone.

He wasn't crazy about the grits, she could tell. But he loved the fried fish she fixed to go with them. And after he helped her wash the dishes, they didn't have any discussion about him going back to his hotel.

The next morning she was up and dressed when he came into her kitchen. She poured him a cup of coffee and placed a manila folder full of papers in front of him.

"What's this?" he asked.

She made herself busy spreading butter on some toast. "Those are some things I've written. I want to know what you think."

He groaned. "Please don't do this."

"You're a professional writer. You have to know what's good."

"I don't, I know what I like. I'm not a judge."

"Just be honest. That's all I want."

"Shit."

But he took the folder and started to read. For a while she stayed in the kitchen with him, but he said, without looking up, "I can feel you staring—get lost." So she went outside with her coffee and tried to tell herself she hadn't made a pathetic fool of herself. Just when she was about to run inside, grab the papers from him, and throw them in the trash, he came out.

"When did you write this?" he asked.

"The short story about the kid throwing the birthday party was when I was in college. The other pieces were for the newspaper, human-interest stuff. Hank never published any of it."

"He's as stupid as he looks."

"Really? You're not just saying that? You really liked them?"

"Yeah, I did."

"Because I can take it if you didn't. I can take criticism—you haven't seen that side of me—but I can."

"Laurel, I think you can write. You've got a nice way with language. You're funny. What can I say? I liked what I read, but it's just an opinion. And don't you dare cry on me. Not after being such a hard-ass all this time."

After he left, she drove herself over to McGee's. Denny was sitting in his usual booth, eating an order of raisin biscuits.

"I want the box," she told him.

Chapter Twenty-one

ACTUALLY, THERE WAS A BOX and her ma's guitar. The box was a large cardboard carton Sara Jayne had kept under her bed. The guitar was probably quite valuable. It had once belonged to the great Bill Monroe, who handed it down from the stage into the arms of a giddy teenaged Sara Jayne after a tent concert in Vidalia, Georgia.

When Laurel got the box home, she put it in the middle of the living room floor with the guitar next to it and eyed them warily, like a house pet circling a nest of snakes. Sara Jayne hadn't left much in the way of personal effects. In addition to the guitar, there had been a heavily studded denim jacket, some jeans, half a dozen T-shirts, and the box. It contained what her mother referred to as "my case against those old bitches."

Laurel had never looked inside it, but when she was small she believed it held magical artifacts that would prove John Merrick's devotion and the perfidy of the three Miss Margarets. After that happened, she and her ma would make everyone who had ever put them down eat dirt. It was a belief that got her through many a bad day.

Her ma never opened the thing in Laurel's presence, but when

she was having an attack of the blue devils, Sara Jayne would haul
it out from under the bed, crying and cussing. Gradually the battered old carton changed character in Laurel's mind. She associated it not with miracles but with Sara Jayne being mean. Then it
stopped appearing altogether, and Laurel figured it was gone. Until
she was cleaning up Sara Jayne's bedroom after she died, and there
it was, crammed into a corner of the closet behind a broken ceil-
ing fan and a stack of old telephone directories. She couldn't bring
herself to throw it away, so she gave it to Denny with the guitar.
And now it was back.

Laurel picked up the old guitar and did a couple of strums.
It needed new strings, but old Bill's name was still written on
the neck in shiny gold paint that hadn't chipped. She took it to a
corner of the room and set it upright against the wall. Then, unable to delay any longer, she took a deep breath and opened the
box.

At first she wanted to throw the whole damn thing against the
wall. Then she started to laugh. Because she should have known. It
was full of junk. No miracles or horrors, just junk. There were
three dead flowers tied together with a crumpled silver ribbon and
impaled on a rusted corsage pin. There was a blue button that said
THE BEACH AT PANAMA CITY, a pink satin ribbon that was too wide
for a hair bow, a plastic champagne glass with ancient residue still
in the bottom, an envelope with a birthday card in it, another envelope full of movie theater stubs, and a bright red dress with a hal-
ter top and a skirt so short it was basically a wide ruffle, made out
of some kind of fake silk.

She lined the stuff up on the coffee table. This was her ma's big
proof, a box full of a teenager's souvenirs. She didn't know who to
feel sorrier for, herself or Sara Jayne. Probably both of them. She
opened the birthday card. Inside was a note written in the familiar
childlike handwriting that was on the front page of the books on
her wall.

Baby—

This is my present to you. I got the job for us. They will put the story in the newspaper. I'm not much for writing, but I want you to know, like it says in the song, I love you so much it hurts me. Happy Birthday.

Love, John.

Laurel turned over the envelope and looked at the postmark. The card had been sent the November before she was born, three weeks before her father died. So Sara Jayne was right about one thing. John Merrick had gotten himself a new job. One that was splashy enough to warrant coverage in the newspaper.

Laurel scooped up the whole mess and dumped it back into the box. A pack of pictures held together with a dried-up rubber band fell out of the skirt of the dress.

The pictures had been taken sometime in the late sixties. They showed her mother and father, young and having the time of their lives at some kind of fair or amusement park.

Given what a monumental figure he had been in her life, she'd seen relatively few pictures of her father. Sara Jayne had had a snapshot in her wallet that featured a guy with puffy sideburns and a grin that, even as a kid, Laurel had felt carried an awful lot of "screw you."

The young man looking out at her from these pictures was laughing. His hair was slicked back, and he wore a white short-sleeved shirt and brown pants with bell-bottoms. He was good looking, in an ordinary sort of way.

But young Sara Jayne was a revelation. She was wearing the red dress from the box. With impossibly long and glamorous legs stretching out from under a short skirt, a mass of auburn hair, and big hazel eyes, she was a knockout.

In a couple of shots her parents mugged for the camera together. Then, Laurel decided, they must have lost whatever stranger they had asked to help them, and John took pictures of Sara Jayne alone. She was wonderful: fresh-faced and eager, smiling the sweet smile Laurel had always known was there but could never get for herself. The last picture was of the two of them again. His arms were around her and she was leaning back against him, her head tilted up so she could smile dreamily at him; he looked down at her tenderly.

Which didn't matter a damn, Laurel reminded herself. Because while he was looking tenderly at Sara Jayne, he was getting some on the side. And killing a man and ultimately getting killed in the process. She tossed the pictures into the box and started for the garbage pail with it, but she couldn't make herself throw it in. Telling herself she was a damn fool, she took it into the bedroom and stuck it in the closet. But with the box in the closet and the guitar in the corner of the living room, Sara Jayne was suddenly back in the house, taking up all the oxygen again. Laurel had an old familiar desire to run.

She went to the bookshelves, pulled out a book at random, turned to the front, and stared at the names written in her father's handwriting and her own. An image of the radiant girl who had been her mother and the young man looking down at her with love in his eyes floated across the page. She put the book down and went out.

LAUREL HAD HER CHOICE OF SPOTS in the police station parking lot when she pulled in. The Sabbath was a light day for crime in Charles Valley, and the place was deserted except for the pickup with a GUNS, GUTS, AND GOD bumper sticker that belonged to Sherilynn. On top of all the other indignities she endured, Ed made his token female work on Sundays. Laurel parked next to the truck and went inside.

Sherilynn was seated behind the counter in front. She was a good ol' girl with all the heavy eye makeup and big hair normally associated with her type. She was definitely not what one would picture behind the wheel of a squad car—which didn't dampen Sherilynn's ambition for highway patrol in any way. Her daddy had been on the force for twenty-two years, his daddy had been there for twenty-six. Sherilynn was determined to carry on the family tradition.

"Hey, Laurel," she yodeled cheerfully. "What're you doing here on the Lord's Day? I'd've thought your butt would be in church, praying for your sins. I know that's where mine should be." She laughed heartily at her own wit and Laurel forced a smile. She and Sherilynn had never been pals. If she was honest about it, that had been Laurel's choice. Throughout the years of her affair with Ed she'd clocked in a lot of hours at the station house, and she'd often seen the sympathy—and sisterhood—in Sherilynn's Maybelline-fringed eyes. But she never picked up on it. Because she was too humiliated, she'd told herself. But she knew that wasn't it. Sheri-lynn's neck was a tad too red for that free-thinking egalitarian Laurel Selene McCready. Laurel might get high and sing in a bar, but she worked for the newspaper and had gone to college for almost a year. Her daddy might have been trailer trash, but her ma's people, although bastards, were pillars of their community in the next county over.

"You give that note to your Yankee boy?" Sherilynn asked casually, but her shrewd eyes were watching Laurel hard.

Laurel nodded. "And the boy was grateful."

"Well, good. Always glad to help the course of true love."

"Actually, the Yankee took off for New York."

Sherilynn sighed. "Short but sweet—ain't it the way with visitors? From what I heard he wasn't bad looking. And he tipped real good over at the Lodge." Through a vast network of family relationships and friendships, Sherilynn was on top of all major gossip in Charles Valley. Laurel wondered how many people she'd told about smuggling out the suicide note for Josh.

"In case you're wondering, I never mentioned you getting that note for him to anyone," Sherilynn said, reading her mind.

"Thanks."

"Honey, I'd be up the old creek without a paddle myself if Ed knew."

"Right." Laurel took a beat, then started testing the waters. "Isn't it something, Vashti coming back here to die after all these years?"

Sherilynn shrugged. "It was still her home, I guess."

"I wonder how she got herself here. The way that note looked, she was real far gone at the end."

"That was all planned out. When Vashti got sick for the last time, she came east to Atlanta to stay with a woman: Catherine something or other, an Italian name. She's a nurse, works in a hospice up there. And get this: She's the niece of some roommate Dr. Maggie had a million years ago."

"How did it work? How did Vashti get here?"

"She decided when she was—well, when it was time to . . . you know. . . ." Sherilynn paused delicately. Laurel nodded. "Then this nurse called the three Miss Margarets, and Miss Peggy and Dr. Maggie flew to Atlanta, rented a car, and drove Vashti back here. They took her to the cabin, and she did what she had to do. If you want, I can print out a copy of that report for you," she added.

"That's okay."

"I just thought maybe you were asking all these questions 'cause you wanted to try writing a story about this yourself instead of Hank. I always liked to read what you wrote in the school newspaper when we were in high school."

Slightly dazed by support from such an unexpected source, Laurel murmured, "Thank you."

"Sure."

"Hank would eat glass before he'd let me do any real writing. Well, you know how that is."

"Tell me about it," Sherilynn said grimly.

Feeling that a bond had been established, Laurel plunged ahead.

"The three Miss Margarets have always been real close with Vashti's family, haven't they."

"That's the way I always heard it."

"Wasn't your granddaddy on the force back when—" it took a bit of work to get it out—"back when Grady killed my father?"

Sherilynn threw her a startled look and nodded.

"Did he ever say anything about it?"

Sherilynn eyed her warily. "The case was pretty much open and shut."

"Pretty much?"

"There were some questions. . . ."

"What kind of questions?"

"No police questions. Nothing official like that."

Laurel felt herself go very still. "But?"

"It was just . . . my mama knew your . . . she knew John Merrick. They came up together. And a lotta people who did know him thought—" She stopped short. "Look, Laurel, are sure you want to talk about this?"

"That's why I asked. People thought what?"

"It just didn't seem right. What they said about how he died."

The stillness could become a problem. Laurel made herself move a little.

"Don't get me wrong," Sherilynn went on. "The way I heard it, John got into fights all the time. Him and Grady would beat the shit outa each other if they'd been drinking. And when it came to women, well. . . ." She paused awkwardly.

Laurel managed a smile.

Encouraged, Sherilynn plunged ahead. "Daddy used to say, 'You get John Merrick partying hard enough, he'd fuck a snake if someone would hold it down.' But he wouldn't fight Grady for a woman. More like, they'd both, you know—"

"Take turns." Laurel finished the thought for her.

Sherilynn shrugged assent. "And there'd be no way either one of them would pick up a gun over a black girl. Just wouldn't happen. So the whole story didn't sit right with a lot of folks."

"And no one ever thought to mention that to me or my mother because . . . ?"

"It wasn't an easy thing to bring up. You used to beat the snot out of any kid in school that said your daddy's name. This is the first time you've ever asked anybody about it that I know of. And your mama, when she was alive . . . well, she pretty much turned up her nose at the folks who knew John before she was around, you know? Not that you could blame her, my mama always said."

"If there were all those questions, why wasn't there a police investigation into my father's death?"

"Honey, what I told you was just folks talking. What with Dr. Maggie backing up Nella, and Lottie and Miss Li'l Bit saying Miss Li'l Bit saw it happen, and even Miss Peggy ready to testify, who was gonna listen to a bunch of rednecks John hung out with in bars? It's not like anyone had any evidence. And then Grady pled guilty." She paused. "According to Daddy, everyone was just glad to see the whole thing go away."

"I'm sure they were." Laurel stood up. "Thanks." She started out, but Sherilynn called after her.

"For what it's worth, my mama always said that after John heard about you, he changed. Talked about going back to church and getting right with God. He meant to be a real good daddy to you. Least that's what Mama thought."

When Laurel's teeth got ready to start chattering, she knew she was scared. They didn't even have to start doing it; just the cold shaky feeling that they were about to was enough. It had been that way ever since she was a kid. She'd come home from school, Ma would be gone, she'd fix supper for herself, clean up, and get herself into bed, proud of how grown up she was, and the teeth would begin going so hard they sounded like castanets.

It probably shouldn't have been a surprise that they started up when she thought about talking to the three Miss Margarets—even though there was nothing wrong with asking them a few questions about things that had been bugging her over the years. They'd understand a daughter's curiosity, she told herself. Maybe they wondered why she'd never come to them before. She was a grown woman and there was nothing to be afraid of.

So when she drove home from the police station, she slowed down as she reached Miss Li'l Bit's driveway. Then she speeded up and passed it. Miss Li'l Bit was too tough to tackle on her first try. She headed for Dr. Maggie's place. Her teeth were doing the castanet thing in double time.

Chapter Twenty-two

MAGGIE SAT AT HER KITCHEN TABLE checking off items on her list for the funeral. She had chosen the hymns and the scripture readings with Lottie's minister. There would be no viewing of the body and no announcement of the event in the papers. Time and place would be spread by word of mouth only. These were Vashti's orders, typed on her computer when she first got her diagnosis two years ago, back when she still wasn't in touch with any of them. When Maggie, Peggy, Li'l Bit, and Lottie still thought Vashti hated them and were heartbroken about it.

But then, of course, they did hear from Vashti, and she told them what she needed from them and their hearts were broken again. But they were happy too, because Vashti was back. Vashti had that effect on all of them. It had been that way from the beginning.

FOR LOTTIE IT WAS love at first sight. And it was clear the feeling was mutual. From the moment they laid eyes on each other, grandmother and granddaughter shared something special.

"She's so smart, Maggie," Lottie said. "Look at the way she watches what's going on." And it did seem as if the bright eyes in

Vashti's round baby face took in everything that happened around her.

Before Vashti could walk, Lottie brought her to the clinic. Riding high in her grandmother's arms she would point an imperious pudgy finger at an object and Lottie would carry her over to inspect whatever it was that had caught her attention, telling her what it was clearly and slowly. Sometimes Maggie would be pressed into service when Lottie didn't know the correct technical name for a piece of medical equipment. On Lottie's orders, no one ever spoke baby talk to the child.

As soon as Vashti could toddle, Lottie walked hand in hand with her through the fields where Lottie and Maggie used to run, teaching the child the names of trees and plants. By the time she was three, Lottie had taught her to read. By the time she was four, Vashti was sitting under the old magnolia tree with her books.

For Maggie, it was like seeing Lottie all over again. Actually, it was like seeing the carefree creature Lottie could have been if she'd had gentle Nella for a mother.

Nella turned out to be full of surprises. One day she showed up at the clinic with Vashti right before Maggie was about to close up. Vashti was wearing her best dress with matching hair bows.

"Would you take her to Miss Li'l Bit's when you go today?" Nella asked.

"You want me to take the baby?"

"I want Miss Peggy and Miss Li'l Bit to get to know her like you do." Nella bent down to fluff the ruffled skirt of Vashti's dress. "Momma thinks because I'm not smart I don't see how smart Vashti is. But I see. And I know this baby is gonna need the best of everything. Miss Peggy and Miss Li'l Bit and you, you can do things for Vashti that I can't. So I want you all to love her."

It was like Nella to plot and admit it. "What does Richard think?" Maggie asked. Nella's husband was a proud man who had let it be known that he was not thrilled about his mother-in-law's white lady friends. He had a good job on the new Garrison Gardens security force, and his dream was that one day he'd make enough money so Nella could stop working there as a maid. He wanted his own house. It embarrassed him to live in the place that Lottie's former employers had given her. He bragged that neither he nor Nella had ever worked as servants for a private family.

"Richard's mad at me," Nella said. "He says we don't need any help from white people. Vashti's going to grow up with black pride, and that's enough."

"I suppose that's understandable," Maggie said carefully.

"The man's a fool. Vashti will have all the black pride she needs. But she's going to have everything a little white child has too—as much as I can get for her, anyway. So would you take her with you? I'll come get her after half an hour. She'll be good."

And before she knew it, Nella was gone and Maggie was alone with Vashti. It was, she realized, the first time she'd ever been responsible for a young child who wasn't a patient.

"Uh . . . we're going to meet some friends of mine," she told the child, who nodded solemnly and slid her hand into Maggie's.

"Yes, ma'am," Vashti said.

Peggy and Li'l Bit seemed as overwhelmed as Maggie was by the addition to their little group. After Maggie made the introductions and Vashti had said, "How do you do, ma'am" twice, all four of them stood on the porch staring at one another. Finally Peggy was inspired to say, "What a pretty little girl you are."

Obviously this was familiar territory for Vashti. "Yes, ma'am," she said. "I'm smart too."

This hooked Li'l Bit, who squatted down to be at eye level with her. Not to be outdone, Vashti squatted down too. This made Li'l Bit and Peggy and Maggie giggle, which seemed to tickle the child, who let out a surprisingly big laugh for such a little person. Then Li'l Bit brought Vashti a Coke and a sandwich. And the little girl chatted with them. Her mother showed up to take her away before any of them had a chance to get bored, and the three childless women fell in love with Nella's baby.

Nella was masterful in the way she handled her campaign. Knowing she was dealing with women who were not used to small children, she never let Vashti overstay her welcome. The child was always polite, funny, and bright—and whisked away before she or her hostess of the afternoon could get tired of each other.

"We're being courted," Peggy told the others once, when they were on the porch by themselves. And they agreed. But they didn't care. Vashti filled a need for all of them. And Nella knew it.

Each gave to the child in her own way. Maggie bought her pretty dresses with matching hats, and Peggy gave her a mountain of toys, including a bright blue tricycle that she insisted Vashti ride around the mezzanine of her house one afternoon when Dalt was out of town. Li'l Bit bought books for her and told her stories about W.E.B. Du Bois, Brown *v.* Board of Education of Topeka, Thurgood Marshall, and Rosa Parks. And when Richard protested that he didn't need a white lady teaching his daughter black history, Nella told him to hush.

When Vashti was old enough for school, Nella asked for help for the first time.

"Vashti's way ahead of the other children, but you know they're not going to let a black child skip a grade," she told Maggie. "I want her to go to the Catholic school."

She was right. The recently integrated public school system was in chaos, and white teachers forced to teach black children discriminated in hundreds of ways. A parochial school was Vashti's best hope for a decent education.

So Maggie spoke to her priest, Li'l Bit picked up the cost of the

tuition, and Peggy saw to it that Vashti had pocket money for ex-
tras. Richard said she didn't need them, but Nella told him to hush
again.

At the end of Vashti's first year at Sacred Heart Academy, Peggy,
Maggie, and Li'l Bit sat between Nella and Lottie with Richard in
the auditorium and applauded like their lives depended on it while
Vashti, who was one of five black kids in the school, walked away
with more awards than anyone else.

And Lottie's face shone with a happiness it hadn't had since the
days when she and Maggie planned to go to college together and
Lottie was going to save the world.

Vashti was clearly destined to be a star. Maggie, Peggy, and Li'l
Bit were all grateful to be a part of the child's life. Which made it
even harder during the bad years when she hated them.

THE FRONT DOORBELL WAS RINGING. Puzzled, Maggie went to
answer it. No one who knew her used her front door. Even Jeho-
vah's Witnesses came to the kitchen. Some stranger must have gotten lost, she thought. She opened the door to Laurel McCready.

IT HAD TAKEN LAUREL three trips around the pie-shaped piece of
land to get up the nerve to drive up to Dr. Maggie's house, get out
of her car, and knock on the door. And having done this, it was
taking all the nerve she had left to keep herself from running back
to the car and hauling ass out of there. But then the door opened.
And the enemy was standing in front of her. When did she get so
small? Laurel wondered. And weary looking?

The last time Laurel had been face-to-face with Dr. Maggie had
been at the hospital when Sara Jayne lay dying. All three of the
Miss Margarets had tried to help Laurel during that time. Dr. Maggie had offered to monitor Sara Jayne's treatment for a fraction of

what Laurel's doctor was charging. Naturally, Laurel turned her down. Let's hear it again for loyalty, Ma.

Dr. Maggie pulled herself up to her full height of five feet. "Laurel, what a pleasant surprise," she said, in a voice that had an old-lady quiver in it. "Please come in."

Laurel nodded and followed her into a living room filled with family photographs in silver frames. A large dog was sleeping on a brightly colored mat by an old wingback chair. "Can I offer you something?" Dr. Maggie asked. Laurel shook her head silently. Soon she was going to have to start making some sounds.

"Dr. Maggie, I—" she cleared her throat—"I know what a loss it must be to you. Vashti Johnson's death."

Dr. Maggie's low voice corrected her. "It's a loss to the entire country."

"Right. But it's a very personal loss to you and Miss Peggy and Miss Li'l Bit."

This time it was Dr. Maggie who nodded, and Laurel could tell that she didn't trust herself to speak.

"You must be very touched. I mean, it said a lot, the way she came back here . . . to be in the cabin. For the end."

She got another silent, painful nod.

Feeling like a total shit, she continued. "I was kind of surprised. I guess she made it up with you—"

Suddenly Dr. Maggie found her voice. "What are you talking about, Laurel?"

Talking fast, Laurel told her what she'd overheard at the funeral parlor when Vashti came home to bury her momma and threw the three Miss Margarets out.

"I don't remember that ever happening," Dr. Maggie said firmly without even a hint of old-lady quiver in her voice.

"I do."

"Laurel, dear, whatever you thought you overheard when you

were eavesdropping that day, obviously you misunderstood. It was a very hard time for all of us, and I'm sure things were said that could be open to misinterpretation. Now we're in the middle of another difficult time, and I'm afraid it's made me very tired. If you'll excuse me. . . ."

Laurel knew she hadn't misinterpreted anything. But Dr. Maggie started out, leaving her with no option but to follow or try a flying tackle on a little old lady.

At the front door, Dr. Maggie turned to her. "The past belongs to old fuddy-duddies like me, Laurel. Please don't let it drag you down." There was something urgent about the way she said it.

Laurel hadn't even started on the questions she wanted to ask about the night her father died. But the fragile little creature who was practically fainting from fatigue had her on the run. "Yes, ma'am, I'll let you get some rest," she said, in a respectful tone she hadn't used since high school,

In the car she kicked herself for being a wimp.

IN THE HOUSE, Maggie sat and waited for her pulse to stop racing. Part of her had wanted to break down and tell the girl what she had every right to know, but she couldn't do that without Peggy and Li'l Bit agreeing. They were joined at the hip on this. It was worse than a legal contract or shaking hands on a spit pact when you were a child.

Finally she went to the phone and dialed. "Peggy darling," she said, "you need to know what just happened."

Chapter Twenty-three

*I*N SPITE OF THE FACT that there was no formal announcement of Vashti's funeral in the *Gazette,* Laurel had talked Hank into letting her go just in case they wanted to cover it after the fact.

The church was filled with white flowers. White roses and camellias decorated the altar and the pews. White wicker baskets full of white lilies lined the walls. According to the woman who sat next to Laurel, the Funeral Dinner Committee had set up a reception in the Fellowship Hall for folks to go to after the burial. Vashti hadn't wanted a big funeral, but the church ladies had done themselves proud on the buffet out of respect for Miss Lottie.

Laurel listened to this recital and nodded knowingly, trying to act as if she was a regular churchgoer and not a sinner who hadn't set foot inside a house of worship since her mother died.

The local black community had turned out in force to say goodbye to Lottie's granddaughter, and the church was packed. There was a good showing of white faces too. A few of them who were old enough to have worked with Nella or Lottie were wearing Garrison Gardens uniforms. In one corner a group of men and women huddled together looking lost. All of them wore dark suits made of heavy fabrics that did not figure in a Georgia wardrobe. "They worked with Vashti," said Laurel's informant. "They called the police to find out where the funeral was and flew all night long from the West Coast."

Lottie was in her wheelchair in the position of honor at the front of the church. She sat there silently receiving condolences, never once shedding a tear. A young nurse from the home hovered over her protectively. People stopped by her briefly, saying a few words, to which she responded with a nod; sometimes she reached out to take a hand in her good one. The nurse seemed to have assigned herself the job of timekeeper, so no one lingered too long.

And in the back of the church, in the very last pew, Miss Peggy, Miss Li'l Bit, and Dr. Maggie sat together. Everyone in town knew they had planned and paid for everything.

The service began with the choir singing, and the church was filled with the sound of celebration and sorrow. Then the minister came down front and started preaching Vashti Johnson home.

Though she tried to fight it, Laurel couldn't help comparing this funeral with another one. At that funeral there had been no choir singing their hearts out. The minister had not known the woman who died and had not liked what he had heard of her. Only Denny and his mama sat with Laurel in the front pew.

The choir launched into "Peace in the Valley," and Laurel's eyes filled. There was no way to stop it. At the front of the church, the nurse had angled Lottie's wheelchair so she could see the congregation. As Laurel wiped her eyes, she thought she saw Lottie watching her.

Finally the church part of the service was over. People began filing out to go to the graveyard.

Laurel held back, waiting to follow the others, and found herself alone in the doorway with Lottie and her caretaker. They seemed to be stuck. Someone had put an afghan over Lottie's lap, and the fringe had caught in one of the chair's wheels.

"Let me help," Laurel said to the nurse. She knelt down to extricate the fringe. When she looked up, her eyes met those of the silent woman sitting in the chair. "I'm Laurel Selene McCready," she said. "Do you remember me?"

She didn't expect an answer, certainly not more than the little nod of the head everyone else had been getting, but Lottie said, "Y . . . es, Laurel." She reached out her hand, and Laurel took it without thinking.

"I'm so sorry," she said, "about your granddaughter." And then, for reasons she would never understand, she blurted out, "I want to thank you—for all those times . . . the food . . . years ago. I never did thank you—" But Lottie was shaking her head.

"No," she said. "No . . . thanks."

"Miss Lottie, they'll be waiting for you," said the nurse behind them. The hand holding Laurel's gave it a gentle squeeze, and then Laurel stood up and followed Lottie to the cemetery.

The minister invited everyone at the graveside to come to the reception. Laurel started to go inside with the rest, but then she stopped. A tall bulky figure had broken away from the crowd and headed toward the graveyard. Miss Li'l Bit was going back to say good-bye again.

Good manners, decency, and common sense said it was a lousy time to try to question the woman. On the other hand, she just might be off guard. Laurel started after Miss Li'l Bit, only to have her arm grasped firmly from behind and to feel herself being forced to turn around. The scent of bourbon was in the air. She found herself face-to-face with Miss Peggy.

"Laurel, how nice," said Miss Peggy, as if they'd just bumped into each other casually—and as if her hand wasn't doing a remarkably good imitation of a tourniquet on Laurel's arm. "I've been wanting to talk to you."

Years of dealing with a drunk had taught Laurel to read the signs. Miss Peggy had had more than a few. However, her blue eyes were sharp.

"I'm sure you know how close I am to Li'l Bit and Maggie," Miss Peggy said, in a chatty voice. "We've gotten in the habit of taking care of one another. You'll understand how protective you can be about your friends when you get older, dear, and they're all you have." She paused. "Li'l Bit and Maggie are kind of frail now, and all of this is very hard on them. They loved Vashti a great deal, and they've gotten to the age where they don't take loss as well as they did when they were young. I'd hate for either of them to be fussed at, Laurel. Especially today."

"I have a few questions I want to ask Miss Li'l Bit."

"I'm sure you understand this isn't the time to ask them."

"When would be a good time?"

"Laurel, dear, perhaps you didn't understand me. I don't want Maggie and Li'l Bit to be hurt. Ever. Now, I'm sure Hank would have a hard time replacing you, because you really do keep his newspaper going, but he wouldn't want to lose all the advertising money he gets from Garrison Gardens resort either. And I do have influence with the board." She paused to let the threat sink in.

Laurel was torn between admiration at her balls-out honesty and wanting to smack her. Miss Peggy seemed to understand, because she smiled sympathetically.

"I'm too old to be afraid of anyone anymore, Laurel," she said. "And I will take care of my own." She turned and walked to her car as Laurel watched.

As soon as Miss Peggy's car had pulled out of the church parking lot, Laurel got into her own. She opened the car window to get some air, and in the side mirror she saw that she and Miss Peggy had not been alone. Lottie, minus her faithful caretaker, was sitting on the porch of the church in her wheelchair, looking in Laurel's direction. Laurel wondered how long she'd been there. She started her car and drove out of the parking lot. In her rearview mirror she saw that Lottie was watching her go.

❧

MAGGIE HAD STAYED AFTER the funeral to help with the cleanup, but it was clear the Funeral Dinner Committee had everything in hand. She was starting out the door when the nurse who was attending Lottie came up to her.

"Miss Lottie wants to see you," the girl said. She took Maggie out to the parking lot, where Lottie's chair was next to the nursing-home van.

"Have to talk . . . Maggie," Lottie said.

"Of course. I'll come see you tomorrow."

"No. Now." Lottie looked up at the nurse standing behind her chair and indicated the church cemetery. "Over . . . there," she said.

"Yes, Miss Lottie."

"I'm not sure—" Maggie began, but the girl had already started pushing the chair.

They stopped at Vashti's grave. The little nurse murmured something about Miss Lottie not tiring herself by staying too long and melted away. Lottie and Maggie were alone.

Maggie forced herself to look down. Vashti's new grave was a red clay wound in the green lawn. White flowers from the church covered it like a massive bandage. It's too soon to come here, Lottie, she wanted to say. The ground is too raw and so are we. Give me a few days to get it prettier in my mind. Then I'll come with you and look. But Lottie wasn't looking down at the ground. Her eyes were raised up to Maggie's face. The hand in Maggie's tightened its grip. "It's time . . . Maggie," Lottie said.

BY THE TIME SHE GOT HOME from work on Monday, Laurel had spent the better part of the day beating up on herself. She had gone to a funeral where she had no business being and harassed two old ladies, just because Sherilynn had a conspiracy theory. She told herself it had to stop.

She fixed dinner, taking much longer than usual to eat and to clean up the kitchen. She washed her hair and dried it. She made a halfhearted attempt to do her toenails.

Finally, she gave in. She went to the closet, got the snapshots and the birthday card out of the box, and spread them out on the coffee table. Young John Merrick stared at her from the pictures, looking eager and sincere. I wasn't as bad as they said I was, he seemed to be saying. She couldn't ignore him.

So what if Sara Jayne was right? What if something else did happen the night Grady shot her father, and the three Miss Margarets were lying about it? Why would they do that? She wondered vaguely if there might be some point in asking Sherilynn for her daddy's phone number and calling him. He was retired and living on his boat in Florida. But what could she say? "Did you guys get it all wrong on the biggest case that ever hit this town?" seemed a bit tactless.

She opened the birthday card and read the inside again. Then she reread it. John had mentioned some kind of job, one that was important enough to warrant a story in the *Gazette*. How long would it take to go through the newspaper morgue and see if there was any mention of a job for John Merrick? Laurel had a key to the building.

She looked at her watch. It was after nine. She should stay home, watch a little television, and go to bed. She got her purse and headed out.

LI'L BIT HUNG UP THE PHONE wearily. For the past two hours she and Peggy and Maggie had been making marathon calls, arguing back and forth until all three of them were exhausted. At first she and Peggy had stood together, solidly opposed to what Maggie wanted to do. Then Peggy began to waver, worn down by the force of Maggie's hoarse tired voice repeating the same arguments, the lateness of the hour, and possibly the refills of Gentleman Jack that Li'l Bit heard splashing over ice cubes on the phone. Finally Peggy capitulated and Li'l Bit was left alone, still insisting that she would never go along with them.

AT A LITTLE AFTER THREE IN THE MORNING, Laurel rubbed her burning eyes and looked around the windowless basement room that was the *Charles Valley Gazette*'s morgue. She couldn't remember the last time she'd stayed up this late when sex and/or music hadn't been involved.

The morgue consisted of floor-to-ceiling filing cabinets filled with old newspapers in oak-tag folders—no microfiche or computer files here. Some of the papers were spotted and smelled of mold; others were crumbly dry and brownish yellow. She had already worked her way through the month her father was killed, the three months preceding his death, and the two months following it.

The reporting on the story was terse, which was to be expected in a newspaper that could have been shut down with a snap of Mr. Dalt's fingers. In late November there was an announcement of John Merrick's death from a gunshot wound in a brief column placed on the front page below the fold. No space had been wasted on journalistic frills like who, what, where, why, or when. There was no mention of Grady Garrison or Nella Johnson, no mention of witnesses. The bulk of the piece was devoted to the history of the deceased's checkered past and previous problems with the law.

Two weeks later another story appeared—this one buried on the back page of the paper—that informed the reader that Grady Garrison had admitted to second-degree murder in the accidental shooting of John Merrick during an altercation. Sentencing would follow.

That was it. No mention at all of a job. Frustrated, Laurel bundled the papers into their folders, put them back into the file cabinets, and left.

By the time she got home she was past frustration and into depression.

She walked into her cramped living room and turned slowly, taking in every corner and article of furniture. "This is my life," she said out loud. "I live in a house I hate with the sofa I used to sleep on as a kid because Ma never got around to buying me a bed. I've got a wall full of old books from my dead daddy, the murderer. I live with ghosts."

She ran to the closet in the bedroom, pulled out the carton of junk, took it into the kitchen, and threw it in the trash. Then, just for good measure, she dumped the remains of the grits on it.

Which accomplished exactly nothing. She knew that. Because even if she locked the door on this place and ran to New York to be with Josh, a part of her would still be trying to make things right for her ma. And she'd still be hoping her daddy wasn't a mindless animal who killed a man so he could screw the widow.

She sat on the sofa and looked at the wall of books. "I'm trapped," she said.

That was when she noticed she had a message on her answering machine.

Chapter Twenty-four

THE NIGHT BEFORE, when they finally made their decision and left the message for Laurel, they hadn't discussed where they would sit when they talked to her. But when Li'l Bit walked out to the porch, Maggie and Peggy automatically followed, even though the afternoon sun was starting to fade and it was getting chilly. Maggie pulled a heavy cardigan around her shoulders and sat on her swing. Peggy took her place in the rocker and put her thermos on the porch floor next to it. Li'l Bit had already brought out a straight-back chair from the kitchen. As Maggie and Peggy settled in, she set the kitchen chair so it would be opposite the big wooden one she used.

No one spoke. Peggy and Maggie seemed to be waiting for her to go first, but she wasn't about to say anything. This meeting was their idea. She went inside and brought out Maggie's lemonade, her own iced tea, and a glass for Peggy, who was thoroughly capable of sipping straight from her thermos if she didn't. It had been many years since she'd given up bringing out a Coke for Peggy, but she had one in the fridge, along with a Dr Pepper and some apple juice. She had no idea what Laurel McCready drank.

She had given in to them because she was tired, not just of fighting but of the whole business. And besides, they had nothing to be ashamed of. So why was she ready to jump out of her skin? And why did Peggy look so grim? And why was Maggie sitting up in that ramrod-straight way that said she was holding herself together with spit and Scotch tape?

"We did what was right," she said, to no one in particular.

"We did what we thought was right," Maggie amended.

"We did what we had to do," said Peggy.

Then they all stiffened and didn't say anything more because a car was coming down the driveway. It stopped by the boxwood hedge at the side of the house and Laurel got out. They watched her come toward them.

LAUREL GOT OUT OF THE CAR and saw the three women on the porch. They sat in a row, watching her walk toward them and, for no reason she could put her finger on, scaring the hell out of her. She walked slowly, hoping that something, a rogue tornado twisting out of the sky or a once-in-a-lifetime Georgia earthquake, would keep her from reaching them.

THAT GIRL COULDN'T MOVE any slower if she was trying to make us all crazy, Peggy thought. One more minute, and I'm going to drag her up here by her hair.

She looks frightened, Maggie thought. As frightened as we are.

There's nothing to be afraid of, Li'l Bit thought. We did the right thing.

LAUREL REACHED THE STEPS to the porch. She started up as Miss Li'l Bit pushed herself out of her chair and Dr. Maggie let herself off her swing, and they both came to her. Miss Peggy also rose, but she stood in the background.

"Laurel, thank you for coming," said Dr. Maggie.

"May I get you something to drink?" asked Miss Li'l Bit.

"No, thank you," she said. She stood awkwardly in front of them. They didn't seem to know what to do about her either. Finally Miss Peggy moved in. "Take that chair, Laurel," she said, "and let's get started."

"Peggy—" Dr. Maggie said.

But Miss Peggy cut her off. "We need to get this over with," she said. "If you stay out here too long you'll get one of your chest colds. And if we don't start soon, we'll lose Li'l Bit to apoplexy." She turned to Laurel as if the other two weren't there. "Please sit," she said. "This is going to be a strain on them, so the sooner we get going the better."

Laurel sat. So did Miss Li'l Bit and Dr. Maggie. Laurel turned to Miss Peggy, but it was Dr. Maggie who spoke. "We want to tell you how your father died, Laurel," she said. "We want you to know what really happened."

Having gotten the ball rolling, Peggy sat back to let Li'l Bit and Maggie take over.

"You have to understand what it was like thirty years ago," Li'l Bit began, her elegant voice getting flutier and more elegant as it always did when she was under stress.

"Laurel will be fair," Maggie murmured.

"She has to understand the context."

"She wants to know about her father, not politics."

"This is about right and wrong."

Peggy closed her eyes and let herself smile. The familiar old duet was going again, the mix of high voice and low that had been the only constant source of support in her life. If only this young woman sitting in front of them with the suspicious eyes could understand how dear it was.

"Dr. Maggie, you said you were going to tell me what happened the night my father died." Laurel's voice cut through the cool air. Peggy opened her eyes.

"Yes, we did," said Maggie. "It all began with Vashti's father,

Richard." She paused for a moment; then she looked to Li'l Bit, giving her the floor. This part of the story was Li'l Bit's to tell.

LI'L BIT THOUGHT ABOUT DISAGREEING with Maggie, because it began much further back than Richard. It began with injustice and inhumanity and evil, with concepts of right and wrong a lonely man taught his young daughter on this very porch. But Peggy and Maggie would say she was complicating things if she went into all that, and maybe they were right. So she folded her hands in her lap and began telling the story Maggie's way.

"In the late sixties the Gardens became so popular the board decided they needed guards at the resort. No one liked the idea much, but the time had come. They put up gates and fences, and they hired men to patrol the grounds and guard the entrances to the various attractions. You have to understand the way the workforce was set up at the Gardens in those days. Menial jobs were done by African Americans; they were the maids and waiters and gardeners. Whites were the housekeepers and head gardeners. The new job of security guard carried more authority than the work usually done by African Americans, but since it was rough outdoor work, African Americans were hired. One of them was Richard Johnson.

"Then they found they needed a security staff working indoors, and they hired whites for those positions. One of them was your father. Grady Garrison got him the job.

"Sometimes the guards would be asked to cover for one another, if they needed more men for a big event or if someone was out sick. Without anyone realizing it was happening, the security staff became integrated. It was the only staff at the resort that was. I'm sure that doesn't sound like much to you today, but it was monumental back then.

"The security staff grew until they needed someone to oversee it. The job title would be Chief of Security, and it would be an executive-level position. Some of us thought an African American should fill it. There had never been an African American in charge of a department at the Gardens before, and we felt this was a golden opportunity. Again, I wish I could make you understand what a revolutionary idea that was. We suggested it to the board."

PEGGY CLOSED HER EYES again, and let Li'l Bit's voice chirp over her. A group headed by Li'l Bit and Maggie had indeed gone to the Garrison Gardens board to suggest Richard Johnson for the new position. But in those days the board did what Dalton wanted. Which Li'l Bit and Maggie and Lottie and Nella knew very well. So they wanted Peggy to take it up with Dalton. Garrison Gardens was no little local resort, it was known all over the world, Li'l Bit argued. They couldn't keep acting like a bunch of backwater big-ots forever. Richard had worked as a guard for five years at the Gardens; he was smart, dependable, and well liked.

And he was Vashti's father, which trumped all the other reasons as far as Peggy was concerned. Peggy would have walked over hot coals for Vashti. They all would have.

Vashti was eleven by then, confident, affectionate, and smart as a whip. Nella wanted the honor of the new job as much for her as for Richard. "I want Vashti to see her daddy go to work in a suit," she said. In addition to working in a suit, if Richard got the new job he would get a big hike in salary. Nella also wanted that for Vashti.

So even though she never talked to Dalt about business, Peggy went to him about Richard. Dalt was torn.

"I'm not saying you're wrong, sweetheart," he said. "I'd like to give it to Richard; he's a good worker. But it's too late. Grady already promised the job to John Merrick."

"Dalt says he doesn't want to undermine Grady's authority," Peggy reported back to Li'l Bit and Maggie. "He says Grady's really trying hard now, and he has to stand by him."

Normally they would have let Peggy off the hook, particularly

Maggie, who seemed to have a pretty clear idea of just how things were with Dalt. But not this time.

"You can't go on being afraid forever, Peggy," she said. "You're not the child he married anymore."

"You have a right to speak your mind," Li'l Bit said. And the duet began.

"You have an opportunity to do something important."

"You have the responsibility."

"If you stand up to Dalton, he may surprise you."

"It might be good for him."

"It will be good for you."

And then Maggie brought out the heavy artillery. "This is all Grady's doing. Once again Dalton is going to give in to him. Don't you give in, Peggy. Not this time."

She went home and tried again with Dalt.

"This is the perfect job for Richard."

"Grady promised the job to John."

Memories of John in the forest with Grady on the worst day of her life crowded her mind.

"Grady had no business making promises before he talked to you. Richard deserves that job. And it'll look good for the resort. It's the right thing to do, Dalt."

"Next time. Richard will get the next job."

"As what? Chief of the Horticulture Department? Head of Sales? You wouldn't dare put a black man in charge of any other staff, even if he did have the education for it. This is Richard's one chance."

"Sweetheart, don't do this. You're making me choose." He repeated the warning that had always stopped her before.

"Yes," she said. "This time I'm asking you to choose."

There was a silence, as both of them tried to absorb what she had just done.

"He's my son—" Dalt began.

"And I'm your wife."

She saw him hesitate and felt if she couldn't win this time it would be the end of her. Just once he had to be on her side. "I'm asking you to do this for me."

"Peggy—"

"If you don't—" she was afraid of pushing him too far, but there was no turning back "—I may know some things you'd rather not hear. About Grady."

"What could you possibly—" he started to say, but then he stopped. She could see his mind clicking. He was remembering all the hours she had spent with Miss Myrtis, and all his own unanswered questions, and as he stood in front of her, she watched the fear grow. And maybe because of that, or maybe because it really was the right thing to do, or maybe a little of both, he gave in to her.

"SO RICHARD WAS OFFERED the job Grady promised your father." Peggy came back to the present in time to hear Li'l Bit winding up.

Maggie took up the story. "When Grady heard what had happened, he was furious."

Peggy leaned back. She could remember Grady's fury. It was not something she could ever forget. And since he was no fool, he knew exactly where to lay the blame.

"YOU DID THIS," GRADY SAID. His face was tight with rage, but she saw something else in it too: confusion. And the beginnings of panic. For the first time in Grady's life, Dalton wasn't siding with him, and he'd never thought that could happen. "I know it was you who put Daddy up to this. Because of that little brat you're always slobbering over."

"I suggested Richard for the job. That's all."

"You did something to make Daddy change his mind."

"He's getting older. Maybe he's tired of you."

Being Dalton's son was the only ground Grady had to stand on, and Peggy could see how much that thought scared him. At the time, it pleased her enormously. Which was really stupid. Because there was an old rule that said the only thing more dangerous than an angry animal was a scared one.

LAUREL TRIED TO CLENCH HER JAW. If ever there was a time when she wanted control over her chattering teeth this was it. She forced her mouth open enough to form words. "So Richard was going to get my father's job," she prompted the three women in front of her.

Dr. Maggie responded. "Yes," she said.

"What happened?" Laurel asked.

"Grady tried to persuade his father to change his mind," Dr. Maggie said.

Peggy felt herself smile again. *Persuade* was such a Maggie way of putting it.

"YOU'RE GIVING A WHITE MAN'S JOB to a nigger!" Grady shouted at Dalt. "What do you think the men will do when they hear that?"

It was stupid of Grady. Opposition always made Dalton dig in harder, and once he had announced his decision, even though originally he'd fought against it, he expected his wishes to be carried out. "What I think is, I think I'm gonna run my business my way," he said. "And anyone who doesn't like it can stop collecting his paycheck. Including you."

He didn't mean it. He never would have followed through. But Grady and Dalt were both seeing a side of each other they had never seen before. For Dalton it meant having to face what he'd always known but managed to avoid, that his son was weak and petty and cruel. For Grady, his new hard-nosed father was a total shock. He ranted and raved, but Peggy could see Grady was frantic.

PEGGY PICKED UP HER GLASS and poured a little whiskey into it, not too much, because she had to make her store last. It seemed like they'd been talking forever, and they'd barely scratched the surface of what they had to tell this girl. It was going to be a long night.

"YOU MUST UNDERSTAND, none of us saw what happened the night Richard died, Laurel," Maggie was saying. "What we're telling you is what we pieced together from what we heard later.

"After Grady realized he wasn't going to be able to change Dalton's mind, he went to find your father at his house. Your mother didn't live there, of course. She and your father weren't married."

Maggie smiled at Laurel the way she did when she wanted to make bad news easier for a patient. From what Peggy could see of the girl's face, it wasn't helping.

Maggie went on. "Lottie and Nella were working late at the Lodge. Richard was home with Vashti. He was due to start his new job in a week, but there hadn't been an announcement yet." Maggie paused. "I try to put myself in John Merrick's shoes sometimes. To imagine what it must have felt like to have gotten that opportunity and then have it taken away."

In the darkness, Peggy watched Laurel strain to get every word as Maggie continued.

"Grady went to John's house, and he and your father had a few drinks. It was Grady's idea for them to go to Lottie's cabin and scare Richard off, run him out of town. John went along with it. They got into John's car."

Maggie leaned back wearily and Li'l Bit sat up straighter, ready to take over. It was as if they were handing off the story like a runner's baton. Li'l Bit began the next leg of the race.

"I want to reiterate what Maggie said," Li'l Bit began. "Everything you're about to hear was pieced together after the fact. Some of it was from Vashti, and some was what Grady and John confessed to Dalton."

"Just tell me," Laurel said.

Li'l Bit nodded. "Richard saw John's car coming down the road. He knew about John and the job so he probably suspected what was coming next. All we know for sure is, he told Vashti to stay away from the window and started out. When she tried to go with him he pushed her down on the floor so hard her teeth cut her lip. Then he ran outside. Vashti got to her knees and looked out the window to see a white man get out of the car and come toward her father. For a moment they talked; then the white man hit her father. She saw her father hit back. She tried to scream, but she couldn't get any sound out. Then a second white man got out of the car. Richard saw the second man and started to run. The first man got back in the car and started it; Richard was trying to get to the woods. We think he didn't go back inside the house because Vashti was there. So he ran toward the ridge behind the cabin. The car started after him. The white man on the ground ran to the side of the car shouting, but Vashti couldn't hear what he was saying. He reached in and tried to grab at the man who was driving, but he fell and the car went on.

"Richard was starting up the ridge, but he tripped and fell. As he tried to get up, the car went forward and ran over him. Then it backed away. Richard was on the ground. And the car ran over him again. Then it stopped. The first white man got out of the car and the second ran over to her father. He bent over Richard and put his head on Richard's chest. He looked up, and Vashti saw him shake his head. Then everything went blank for her. It was days before she could remember any of it."

Laurel felt her voice come through her throat like something made out of sandpaper. "Richard was dead?"

"Yes. John and Grady got him—the body—into the backseat of the car and drove to the county line. They left him on the side of the highway. But then Grady lost his nerve and they told Dalton."

"Which one did it—killed Richard?" the sandpaper voice rasped. "Was it my father?"

"No," said Miss Li'l Bit.

"Are you sure?"

"I'm sure," Peggy said. It was her turn with the damn baton.

Peggy lit a cigarette and began. "That night after Grady left, I went to bed early, but Dalt stayed downstairs. I woke up when I heard someone banging on the front door. Dalt answered it, and I heard the door slam, but no one came in. I went around to the front of the house and looked out. Grady and John were with Dalt, but the windows were closed, so I couldn't hear what was going on. Grady and John seemed to be arguing about something. Dalt stopped them. I started to open the window, but it made too much noise. Then Grady said something, and Dalt pulled back and hit him hard with the back of his hand. Grady just stood there. Then Dalt came into the house and Grady and John drove off. I went back to the bedroom. Dalt came upstairs a few minutes later and I pretended to be asleep. I thought if he was finally angry enough to cut Grady loose I wasn't going to say anything that might put his back up."

Peggy paused and tried to smile, but she could feel it come out twisted. "I was so glad Dalt was finally seeing the light.

"Dalt didn't stay upstairs; he went back down and I heard him go into his study. Twenty minutes later the sheriff came over." Peggy stopped again, and looked at Laurel. "It was ten o'clock at night, and the sheriff was coming to our house. I still didn't realize what kind of mess that had to mean. All I could think was that Grady was in trouble and I was glad.

"It must have been a couple of hours later that Maggie called. Lottie and Nella were frantic. They'd gotten home from work at about midnight. Richard was gone, and Vashti was on the floor with her lip cut. She couldn't tell them what had happened; Maggie said she was in a state of shock. Maggie had checked her over but they were going to take her to the hospital to be sure she was all right. And they were going to call the police.

"I knew whatever had happened, Grady and John had a part in it. I went downstairs to Dalt." Her cigarette must have burnt down. In the darkness she saw Li'l Bit lean over to take it from her and stub it out in the ashtray at her feet. Peggy turned to Laurel. "I don't know if I can make you understand—" She stopped.

"Just tell her what happened," said Li'l Bit.

Peggy took a fresh cigarette out of her case and lit it. She had said practically the same thing that night: *Just tell me what happened, Dalt.*

DALT DIDN'T EVEN TRY to explain. He just looked out the window into the dark night and said, "I was hoping you slept through all that."

"No," she said. "I saw Grady and John, and I heard the sheriff come. And now Richard is missing. I want to know what those two did."

She figured he'd give her a fight. She was ready for him to be mad that she was questioning him. Or he'd say she was imagining things, that she didn't know what she was talking about.

"I never should have given Richard that job," he said. "I knew Grady wouldn't stand for it."

"What did they do?"

"It wasn't supposed to go so far. I believe he was telling the truth about that. They just wanted to scare him."

"Dalton, what happened?"

"They went to Lottie's cabin and Richard was there. Richard

and Grady fought, and from what John said, Richard was winning." Dalt let out a deep sigh. "That was why it happened: Grady can't stand to lose; he couldn't even when he was little." He saw the way she was looking at him and went on quickly. "John finally went to help him, but that made it worse. Grady got into the car and started after Richard. Richard couldn't get away."

"Grady ran him down?"

"He loses control. He gets mad and he doesn't know what he's doing—"

"He ran Richard down with the car?"

"He didn't mean—"

"Don't! Don't even try to make excuses for him!" But then a chilling thought hit her. "You told the sheriff all this, didn't you?"

He felt ashamed, she could see that. But he had closed down in that cold tough way he had that said not to get in his way.

"It's been taken care of."

"You're going to cover for him?" He looked away. "He killed a man, Dalt. He ran him down like a dog in the road."

"He's my son!"

"You can't do this."

"He's *mine*, Peggy. I have to protect him."

"You may have to. I don't." She started for the phone, but he stopped her.

"The sheriff's going to investigate personally," he said. "It'll be a killing that never gets solved. That's how it's going to happen. There's nothing you can do."

"I can tell everyone who will listen. I'll find a newspaper or a reporter on television—"

"I'll stop you. I can do that. Please don't make me."

"You can't let him get away with this."

"I can't let him go to jail. He'll die there."

"Like Richard died?"

"This is the last time I'll help him. I promise you. It is."

"Dalt—"

"I'm asking you to leave it alone. Pretend you were asleep to-night."

He wasn't a bad man. He hated what he was doing, she knew that.

"That's all you have to do. Just pretend you don't know."

He'd loved her in his way, probably more than she'd ever loved him. And in spite of everything, he'd been the best husband he'd known how to be. Everything she had she owed him. This was the first time he'd ever asked her for anything.

ON THE PORCH it was still again. Three pairs of eyes were on Peggy, waiting for her to go on. She knew that even after all this time, Li'l Bit and Maggie were still hoping she could explain what she'd done next so that they could finally understand it. But of course they never would.

"Dalton asked me to help him cover for Grady," she said, "and I did. I went to the cabin. Maggie and Nella were at the hospital with Vashti. I sat with Li'l Bit and Lottie, and we waited for Richard to come home. I knew he was dead, but I sat there and waited as if I thought he was going to come walking through the door. I stayed until Maggie and Nella came back. I don't think I could have kept it up if I'd seen Vashti, that would have been too much for me, but she stayed at the hospital overnight.

"I kept on sitting and waiting with Nella. I said I'd been asleep all evening. And all I could think was, Please, God, let me get out of here before someone calls to say they've discovered Richard's body. But the sheriff did his job very well. He managed to avoid finding it until the next morning, and I'd gone home by then. After that, the lying was easier. That night was the worst."

Laurel grabbed her hand. "Miss Peggy, I don't care what lies you told. I don't give a damn about that. I need to know about my fa-ther."

"Your father didn't kill Richard. Grady did it. Dalton told me that."

"And my father tried to reach into the car and stop him—"

"Your father went to a man's house to beat him—" Miss Li'l Bit said, but Laurel broke in.

"Then he tried to stop it."

"Yes, dear," said Dr. Maggie. "Your father tried to stop it."

"And it was all over a job. It never had anything to do with Nella."

"No."

"Then what the hell happened? Where did the story about Nella come from? Why did Grady kill my father?"

Chapter Twenty-five

THE THREE MISS MARGARETS looked at one another, and Laurel could see the energy pass between them, the unspoken bargains and agreements.

"I've always thought if I hadn't lied—" Miss Peggy began.

"It would have happened anyway," Miss Li'l Bit said.

What would have happened? Laurel wanted to yell. But they were going to do this at their own pace and in their own way. Dr. Maggie seemed to be up again.

"People in town knew something was wrong," she said. "The sheriff was too sloppy handling the investigation. Lottie and Nella were insisting that Richard would never have left Vashti alone. And it was clear that the child had seen something that traumatized her. But the sheriff only went to the cabin once, and he went alone."

Miss Li'l Bit picked it up again. "People started saying there was something else going on. But it didn't make any sense that the sheriff would cover for John Merrick. He wasn't. . . ."

"Important enough?" Laurel said.

"Yes," said Miss Li'l Bit, without flinching. "The only family in town with that kind of power were the Garrisons. And everyone knew Grady got himself into messes all the time. People started speculating.

"Then all of a sudden a rumor started that Nella had another man—a black man, of course—who got into a fight with Richard and ran him down by the side of the road."

"It wasn't anything concrete." Dr. Maggie took over. "But the gossip stopped people from talking about Grady and John. Which was what it was meant to do, of course."

"There were many white people in town who were happy to believe it," said Li'l Bit. "It was more comfortable for them to think that two black men got into a fight over a woman instead of having to ask questions about the Garrisons from whom all blessings flowed. Besides, there were people who had thought for years that Lottie and her whole family didn't know their place. And Richard had gotten a white man's job. So some people were glad to see them get their comeuppance."

"No one knew who started the story. But Dalton was a man people listened to," said Dr. Maggie.

Laurel nodded.

Maggie watched Laurel. She wished they could write out the rest of the story and hand it to her to read when they weren't around. Or maybe make a videocassette, with all of them taking turns talking. She thought she'd heard of wills being done that way, or had she seen it on TV?

She didn't want to live through it again. She was too old. But if anyone had suggested sparing her, she would have been spitting mad, she knew that. So she had to get on with it.

"When the stories about Nella started, I couldn't take it anymore," she said. "It was too cruel. Nella had lost her husband, and her little girl was in shock. Vashti couldn't remember anything about that night. She could barely talk.

"Li'l Bit and I were convinced Grady and John had killed Richard. And we were convinced Peggy knew it."

🌿

SHE AND PEGGY HAD IT OUT after Richard's funeral, when Peggy couldn't look any of them in the eye and Maggie smelled liquor on her breath.

"I know that man is your husband, but you have to stop lying for him," Maggie said. "Forget what it's doing to Nella and Lottie, they'll get past this. Even Vashti will survive. But you won't."

"I don't—"

"Don't try to tell me you don't know what I mean. You're betraying people you care about. You're letting a horrible miscarriage of justice be done, all so Dalton Garrison can tell himself his son is just a troubled boy."

"You don't understand—"

"Grady raped you. Are you going to let him get away with murder now?"

"Whatever I do, it's not for Grady—"

"It's for Dalton. I understand that."

"No, you don't. You and Li'l Bit will never understand what Dalt's done for me. Where do you think I'd be now if he hadn't married me?"

"You don't have to be grateful—"

"Yes, I do. You two don't know. Li'l Bit has been rich her whole life. You're smart and educated and you can earn your keep. You've never been afraid. You've had it easy."

The memory flashed through Maggie's mind of two little girls watching in horror as the barn floor beneath them burst into flames. She thought of the days following the fire when she thought the shame would crush her, and the years afterward when she hid in Atlanta. Until she finally gave in and gave up on a chunk of life that most people considered a birthright.

She had turned and walked out. If she hadn't been so angry, maybe she would have stayed. And maybe she would have talked Peggy into telling the truth. And maybe the rest of it wouldn't have happened. There were so many maybes.

🌿

IN THE DARKNESS, Peggy said, "I've always wondered if I could have stopped it."

Li'l Bit said, "I've always wondered if I started it." She turned to Laurel. "We were all angry about what was being done to Nella. Then we heard about John Merrick getting the job at the resort."

LI'L BIT LEANED BACK IN HER CHAIR. She remembered when she heard about John getting Richard's job. It made her so mad she couldn't sleep. Walter found her in the middle of the night pacing in the garden outside the bedroom. "This is about John Merrick, isn't it?" he'd said.

She'd told Walter about Richard getting the job away from John. It was one of the rare times when she talked to him about anything that even skirted close to race. He hadn't said anything, but she was afraid he might sympathize with the plight of a white man who had a job taken away from him so a black man could have it. If he did think that way, she didn't want to know it.

"I'm fine," she said. "Go back to sleep."

But Walter wasn't going to let the subject go. "You think John Merrick killed that man to get his job back. That's why you're out here wearing holes in your bedroom slippers. You're judging that man, and you don't know for sure what happened."

"Oh, yes, I do."

"Because he's poor white trash—"

"Because it's how he and Grady operate. Because Dalton covers up for Grady, and they think they can get away with anything, and they're right."

"Margaret, you're not being fair. You don't know Merrick. You've never even talked to the man."

Walter didn't mean she should actually confront John. She knew that. It was just one of the nastier ironies of the whole nightmare that he was the one who planted the idea in her head.

"I FOUND YOUR FATHER working at the Gardens," Li'l Bit said to Laurel, "and I started talking to him about Richard and the accident. He tried to be casual, as if it had nothing to do with him, but I didn't believe him. I said Maggie and I were convinced that the sheriff was lying. And I said Nella and Lottie weren't going to let it drop. Then I lied and I said Vashti's memory was starting to come back, and I was sure it was just a matter of time before she could tell us what had really happened. I'm not sure what I thought I was doing. I wanted to get through to him, to frighten him. It was one of the worst mistakes I've ever made."

THEY WERE COMING TO THE END, Laurel could feel it. And for a second she wasn't sure she wanted them to go on. She'd lived with questions all her life, and believed that everything would be better if she had answers. But what if it wasn't?

"The night it happened, Dalton was out of town," said Miss Peggy. "He'd been finding excuses to be away ever since Richard was killed. I think he was waiting for things to die down. I was alone in the house."

"I was in my bedroom," said Miss Li'l Bit.

"I was at Lottie's cabin," said Dr. Maggie. "I'd been going over there every evening to check up on Vashti." The three women exchanged another one of their looks. Then Dr. Maggie went on.

"Nella and Lottie and I were in the main room. We saw headlights coming down the drive. It was still light out, but just barely. All three of us rushed out onto the porch. I'm not sure why we did that. You'd think after what happened to Richard we'd have stayed inside. But we went out. John Merrick drove up in that red car of his. He stopped the car, slammed the door, and started for the cabin. I remember hearing the cabin door behind me open. I thought it was Nella or Lottie opening it for some reason. I never even turned to look.

"John called out, 'I want to talk to you!' And for one ridiculous moment I thought, Oh, it's all right. If that's all he wants, it's fine. And the truth is, we don't know if that's all he did want. But he was walking toward the house so fast, and he was so angry. . . . I turned to Lottie to say maybe we should go back inside. Then I heard a sound coming from my left. At first I thought something had exploded. Then I realized it was a gun going off. John screamed, and in the half-light I could see his hand go to his chest, just above the heart. I turned and Vashti was standing between Lottie and me on the porch. She had her father's hunting gun in her hands. Richard took her hunting with him sometimes. He always said she was a good shot.

"Someone yelled 'Vashti!' I think it was Nella. But the child wasn't hearing. There was the sound of another shot. And John was on the ground. Lottie made a move toward Vashti. So did I. But she was already off the porch. And I was so stunned. We all were. All we could do was watch.

"John was lying on the ground, I believe he was dead by then. I think I remember the coroner said the second bullet was probably the one that killed him. Vashti kept on moving until she was standing over him. She looked at him for what seemed like a long time. God knows what was going through her mind. Then she dropped the gun.

It was silent on the porch. "But my father didn't kill Richard," Laurel whispered. "He wasn't the one."

"It was dark out. She saw him come out of the same car. And he was a white man," said Miss Li'l Bit.

"But he didn't kill anyone," Laurel repeated. Because it was so important to keep saying it out loud.

"No," said Dr. Maggie. "And Grady didn't kill him."

❧

MAGGIE SIGHED. If only it weren't all still so clear in her mind. Her memory was failing her in so many ways these days, why couldn't a little fortuitous senility wipe out that night? It seemed only fair. But she could still see it as if it were happening all over again.

VASHTI DROPPED THE GUN and Nella ran to her.

"Momma?" Vashti said. Nella tried to lead her away from the gun and the dead man on the ground, but Vashti wouldn't move. She stared at the man she had killed, and in a voice that didn't have any feeling she told them what had happened the night her daddy died. When she was through, Nella still couldn't move her.

Next to Maggie on the porch, Lottie said softly, "No. Please, no."

But it had happened. And there was nothing to be done. Through the shock Maggie could see it start to sink in for all of them. Numbed brains were putting it together quickly. In one minute, a man had died and Vashti's life had ended. The wonderful future they'd all envisioned was gone. Now they had to start thinking in terms of consequences and how to save her from the worst of them.

"She's only a child," Maggie said.

"She killed a white man," said Lottie.

"She had a mental breakdown because she saw her father murdered," Maggie said. "We can prove that. We'll get her the best lawyers."

Lottie turned to her and Maggie knew what she was going to see in her face, the defeat and the despair. But the Lottie who looked at her came from years ago, before so many losses had taken their toll. This was the Lottie who climbed pecan trees to the highest branches and talked her into stealing fruitcake batter from Charlie Mae's big ceramic bowl.

"We can't let this happen, Maggie," Lottie said.

🌿

ON THE PORCH, Peggy watched Maggie. She looked weary, but not as bad as Peggy had been afraid she'd be. Maggie said in a ragged voice, "We decided we couldn't let Vashti take the blame. So I called Li'l Bit and Peggy."

It was a call Peggy would never forget.

MAGGIE'S VOICE HAD BEEN CALM on the phone. She just gave Peggy the bare bones of what had happened. By the time Peggy got to the cabin, Li'l Bit was already there.

"I'm going to drive Lottie and Vashti into Atlanta to stay with a friend of mine," said Maggie. "We have to get Vashti away from here. So I won't be here to corroborate what Nella and Li'l Bit are going to tell the police."

"What are you going to say?" Peggy had asked, dread making her mouth dry.

They were going to say Grady did it. That he and John got into a fight over Nella—and Grady shot John. Li'l Bit was going to say she was a witness. Then, when she got back, Maggie would back up the story by saying she'd seen Grady at the cabin since Richard died, and John had come too, at different times. Which would play on the rumors that were already circulating. And of all the things they were throwing at Peggy, that was the one that stuck in her brain.

"No," she said. "You can't do that to Nella."

But Nella was standing next to Lottie, holding her mother's hand so tight it had to be stopping the circulation and saying it was what she wanted. "We have to have a way to explain it," she said.

"We need you too, Peggy," Maggie said.

"No."

"You have to help," said Li'l Bit.

"I can't. Please don't ask me."

And the duet had begun in earnest.

"It's justice," said Li'l Bit.

"It's for Vashti," said Maggie.

"Grady deserves to be punished."

"Vashti doesn't."

And then Lottie, who had never begged for anything in her life, was begging. And Nella was still holding Lottie's hand as she begged too. And sitting there, silently watching her with haunted eyes no child should have, was Vashti.

It all came at her so fast and hard there wasn't time to think. Later, she couldn't actually remember saying yes.

IT WAS NOW PITCH BLACK on the porch, but Laurel could see Miss Peggy rub her hands together for warmth.

"It won't be much longer," she said. "We're almost at the end.

"We had to report the shooting. Maggie left for Atlanta with Lottie and Vashti. We were going to say they'd left late that afternoon to take Vashti there for a doctor's appointment the next day. Then I drove past Grady's villa to see if the lights were on. I'm not sure what we would have done if he wasn't home. But we were lucky. I guess you could call it luck. I went back to the cabin, we wiped the fingerprints off the gun Vashti had used, and I took it home. I put it in Dalt's gun cabinet. Then I waited."

"I was the one who called the police," Miss Li'l Bit said. "I told them I'd been in my bedroom, and I'd seen John's car drive by, and since I'd seen Grady go by earlier I ran out to the top of the ridge to see what was going on. I told them Richard's death had made me nervous, and I was afraid something else might happen." She paused. "I said I got there in time to see John get out of the car, and Grady come out of the cabin, and then I saw Grady shoot John.

I described it exactly the way Maggie said it happened. But I said it was Grady. I said he had the gun with him when he got into his car and drove away."

Miss Peggy went on. "Later, when the police showed up to question me, I said I'd seen Grady sneak into the house and put the gun in the cabinet. When they tested it, of course it matched the bullets from John's body." She paused. "Things were going so fast I thought sure they'd catch us up on something we'd forgotten or didn't know."

Dr. Maggie said, "All I could think was, we had to protect Vashti."

"We didn't trust the sheriff or Dalton or the town to be fair," said Miss Li'l Bit. "We had to take care of it ourselves."

"I think what made it seem reasonable was, it fit with the other rumors," said Dr. Maggie. "It explained what had happened earlier. The story was, Grady and John killed Richard, and then Grady killed John. And that was the story that stuck."

It seemed at last that they were through. In the darkness they turned to Laurel.

"Grady had never paid for anything he'd done and he never would have if we hadn't done what we did," said Miss Li'l Bit.

"Lottie and Nella had been through so much, they didn't deserve to lose Vashti too," said Maggie.

"And Vashti didn't deserve to have her life destroyed before it started," said Miss Peggy.

"But my mother deserved what happened to her?" Laurel's voice cracked through the night air. She'd stopped shivering. She hadn't noticed when she started getting warm. "Is that what you're saying?"

"No," said Dr. Maggie. "But Vashti's need was so urgent."

"And my ma's wasn't? What about me? What about my needs?"

"What we did was the lesser of two evils," said Miss Li'l Bit.

"And you were the ones who got to decide that?"

"We didn't know your mother was going to have a baby," Dr. Maggie said.

"But the truth is," said Miss Peggy, "we weren't thinking about Sara Jayne. We were faced with a little girl who was in trouble—"

"I was a little girl. I spent most of my life in trouble."

"We all tried to help your mother and you," said Dr. Maggie. "Each of us tried."

"Charity. When all my ma wanted was the truth."

"We couldn't," said Dr. Maggie.

"She had a right to know, damn it! I had a right to know my father didn't kill anyone."

"Yes, you did," Miss Peggy started to say, but Miss Li'l Bit interrupted. "Your father didn't kill Richard," she said, "but he went to the cabin to beat him into giving up his job. And he went back later to scare Richard's family after I stupidly let him know we were suspicious of him. I'm sorry if it hurts you to hear this, but John Merrick was not a man for you to be proud of. I wish he hadn't died, for all our sakes. I'm sorry it was so hard on your mother. But she didn't have to let it ruin her life, and she didn't have to do what she did to you. That was her choice. My choice was to save a little girl and punish a murderer. I'll take full responsibility for that."

She spoke with the authority Laurel had longed to hear from Sara Jayne when she was small, and that made her hate Miss Li'l Bit even more.

"Grady Garrison was killed in jail," she said.

"Yes," said Miss Li'l Bit. "He got into a fight and he was killed."

Laurel turned to Peggy. "He was your stepson," she said. "You sent a rich white boy to the state prison. You had to know what was going to happen."

"He was a rich white *man*, not a boy," said Dr. Maggie. "And he was guilty of murder. He killed Richard."

"He belonged in jail," said Miss Li'l Bit.

"And you got to judge that?" Laurel knew she was shouting, but she couldn't stop. "You got to play judge and jury? No. You played God."

"We took responsibility—" said Li'l Bit.

"You played God! You old—" But she stopped herself. And forced herself to look at them. They were sitting facing her, three tired women who had just admitted to more crimes than Laurel could count, and they still looked virtuous and respectable and . . . so goddamn *right*.

"Well, you sure have been busy," she said, more calmly. "Running around deciding who gets to live and who gets to go to jail and get their brains beat out. Maybe now it's my turn. Maybe I'll decide to make *you* pay." And before she really lost it, she got herself off the porch and into her car and drove as fast as she could down Miss Li'l Bit's perfect driveway.

On the porch, Peggy finally broke the silence. "That went well," she said dryly.

"You shouldn't have said that about her mother and father, Li'l Bit," said Maggie.

"Her father was a coward and a bully. It's not our fault her mother fell apart. Every one of us tried to help."

Peggy poured the last drop out of her thermos. "How hard did we really try? I hate to say it, but I was glad when she turned me down. I just wanted her to go away."

"That's ridiculous," said Li'l Bit.

"No, it's not," said Maggie, "and we all know it." She started to get up, wobbling a little from so many hours of sitting still. Peggy jumped up to help and found she had to steady herself. It wasn't just the effects of Gentleman Jack; she was stiff too. Laurel had called them old. She wasn't sure she was ready for that.

"What do you think she'll do?" she asked.

"I don't know," Maggie said. "I can't begin to imagine what

she's thinking." She smiled sadly. "I wonder if that girl knows how vulnerable we are now."

As she said it, Peggy felt herself shiver a little and she saw Li'l Bit do the same.

"I'll give you a lift home, Maggie," she said. And for once Maggie just nodded. There were no arguments about walking home.

Chapter Twenty-six

L I'L BIT WATCHED PEGGY AND MAGGIE go down the drive-way until Peggy's taillights disappeared. Then she picked up the flashlight she kept by the front door for emergencies and walked around to the side of the house to the garden off her bedroom. In the middle of the high hedge that protected the bedroom from the side road to Lottie's cabin was an empty space, a break in the thick boxwood that allowed an entrance into the garden from the out-side. At least, that was what it looked like.

Li'l Bit bent as low as she could over the empty space in the hedge and scraped away the pine needles that were mounded at the base of the bushes. It took several minutes and she finally had to get down on her knees, but she found what she was looking for buried under years of mulch and dirt: the remains of two old boxwood stumps.

"Still there," she said out loud.

She went into the garden and sat on the stone bench she'd re-cently purchased from a catalog that did medieval replicas. This night felt as endless as that night so long ago.

AFTER PEGGY LEFT WITH THE GUN, Maggie took Lottie and Vashti to Atlanta. Li'l Bit and Nella told their story to the police, who left with the body of the dead man. After that there was noth-ing left for Li'l Bit to do except pray to a God in whom she did not believe that they would get away with it. One thing they were all clear on: No one else must know. No family or friends. Before she left for Atlanta, Maggie, who seemed to have developed a brilliant criminal side, had insisted that everyone promise. Li'l Bit, Nella, Lottie, and Peggy had all agreed.

Nella swore she would be all right alone, and Li'l Bit went home to try to get some sleep. But every time she started to drift off, the memory of standing in front of the sheriff and telling her pack of lies pulled her back. Eventually she went into the living room, took *A Tale of Two Cities* down from the shelf, and read until she dozed off sitting upright in her chair. That was where Walter found her when he came over early the next morning.

"Heard there was a problem at old Lottie's cabin last night," he said. "You all right?" Anticipation of this moment had been one of the many things that had kept her awake. She had to lie to Walter, because she had promised the others. And because she didn't know if she could trust him.

She looked at him standing in front of her, a worried frown on his sun-dark face. She worked with him and made love to him and after all the years she still couldn't believe how lucky she was to have found him. He made her feel beautiful. She knew no one else would ever do that again.

But there were things she had never discussed with him because he was illiterate and poor and she had her own prejudices about the class he came from and she didn't want to find out if she was right. Now she had no way of knowing how he would react if she told him what she'd done. Plus, she'd given her word. So she told him the lie she had told the police. After she finished, he gave her a strange look.

"You told the sheriff you were in the bedroom when you saw Merrick's car drive by the house?" he asked.

"Yes, I was going to get ready for bed—"

He pulled her to her feet. "Has anyone from the sheriff's office been back down that road since you said that?"

"I don't think so. No one has come to the house."

"We'll have to take a chance," he said, more to himself than to her.

"Walter, I don't—" but she stopped because he was already heading out the door.

"Get into your car and park it crossways at the end of the road. Flood the engine or run it partway into the ditch on the side so you get the wheels stuck, do whatever you have to, but don't let anyone drive up that road until I tell you." He was racing to his truck. He got out an ax and headed for the hedge. And to her horror, she understood. There was no way she could have seen John's car if she had been in her bedroom, because long ago it had seemed romantic to close in the garden outside her window by letting the box-wood grow high as a man's shoulder. Too high to see a passing car on the other side of it.

"Go now, Margaret," he said. And as she drove off she could hear the sound of an ax cutting wood. Seconds later the sound was drowned in music from the kitchen radio.

Mercifully, no one came to the house. When Walter finally brought her back to see the hedge, there was a break in the middle of it where he had cut down two bushes. "I couldn't prune the boxwood back enough so you could have seen over them. The in-sides of the bushes would be too woody; any gardener would know you just did it," he said. She nodded mutely. "This way you could have seen the car through the break. It looks like it's an entrance to the garden. And with the pine-needle mulch I spread over the stumps, only someone who's looking for them will find them." She nodded again. The enormity of her near miss was just starting to hit her.

Walter was staring at her. He was waiting for her to tell him why she had suddenly started lying to the authorities. He wanted the truth. He had earned it; he had just put himself on the line for her. She wanted to tell him.

But images flashed in her mind. She saw the shame and agony on Nella's face as she sat in front of the police and choked out the story of sleeping with two men while her husband was still alive. She saw Peggy take the hunting rifle after it had been wiped off and put it on the front seat of her car so she could take it home and betray her husband. She saw Lottie looking like she had just gotten a reprieve from a life sentence. She heard Maggie making them promise to keep the secret. And she saw Vashti's face as they bundled her into the car and sent her away.

"Thank you," she said to Walter.

It was like she'd slapped him. For a moment he was hurt and just looked at her. Then the anger started. He walked out without a word.

For the second time in her life she lost a man she loved. But Walter did it fast, in one night. Not like her father, slowly withdrawing. She never could decide which way was better.

But it took her a while to accept. At first she waited for him. She went back out to her gardens and worked and listened for the sound of his truck pulling up next to her house. But he never came. Her gardens were brown, dying in the cold of late fall. The chores she had to do, the mulching and the pruning, would not give her any rewards until spring. The gaping hole in the hedge outside her bedroom window was a constant reminder of everything she wanted to forget. She closed her little door to the garden and put a curtain over the glass so she couldn't see it.

Finally she admitted that Walter was gone. She got up one morning, dressed herself, and started out. Then she stopped, turned around, and went back to her bedroom. She stayed there all day, fully dressed, lying on her bed in the dark.

She wasn't sure how many days she did that. Millie came and

went, leaving sandwich fixings on plates and in covered bowls. After she was gone, in the middle of the night, Li'l Bit got out of her bed and ate the food out of the containers in the kitchen by the light from the refrigerator.

Then one morning she was awakened by the sound of curtains being yanked back. Her bed covers were pulled off.

"Get up, or I'll throw you on the floor!" a voice said. She opened her eyes to see Peggy leaning over her. "If I can get myself out of bed every morning and face another goddamn day, so can you!"

"You've been drinking," Li'l Bit said.

"Yes," said Peggy, "and I'm gonna keep on. Because it gets the makeup on my face and the clothes on my body and it gets me through breakfast, where I sit and watch Dalt want to die and know I caused it." She looked years older than she had a few short weeks ago. "I don't care what it takes to get you out of this damn bed and into some clean clothes. If you think a drink will help, just name your poison and I'll bring you a bottle. But you don't get to give up, damn it; you don't!"

So Li'l Bit got out of bed and got dressed in her work clothes and gave Peggy a drink while she had her coffee. But when she had to go out to the garden, she hesitated. Until Peggy walked out ahead of her.

Peggy stayed all morning, watching while she cut back her roses. At noon they had lunch. Not in the kitchen, on the porch.

Three weeks went by. The sheriff never did send anyone to check out her hedge. Then Grady pled guilty, because Dalt threatened to stop paying for his lawyers if he kept on saying he was innocent. Dalt had finally given up on him, and without his father Grady's resistance quickly collapsed. So Grady went to prison, even though right up to the day they took him away he was still telling his daddy he was innocent. And because there was no trial, no one had to lie in court. Nella left town to be with Vashti in Atlanta, and Lottie came back to Charles Valley alone. Nella and Vashti would not be coming home again. But the women had gotten away with their lie. They had won.

Li'l Bit saw Walter in the town every once in a while, although he knew her schedule and usually managed to avoid her. Once she saw him at the post office, and she had to keep herself from running to tell him about the new rose cuttings she'd mossed off and the new fruit trees she'd put in. She wanted to tell him how long it had taken her to go into the gardens again. And she wanted to tell him how the perfume from her gardenia still came into her room at night. Most of all she wanted to say she missed him. But she still couldn't tell him why she had lied. So she let him go by without stopping him. And eventually she got used to passing by without speaking when she saw him. And she got used to being alone again.

For a while Peggy and Maggie tried to keep her company when she worked in her gardens. But Maggie had to work in the clinic and Peggy hated being in the sun, so that didn't last very long. They took to staying later in the afternoons on the porch, the way they had before Walter started spending the nights with her. She never told them why he stopped coming, although she told them about the near escape with the boxwood hedge. They were smart, so she was pretty sure they put two and two together.

Chapter Twenty-seven

P EGGY MOVED WITH HER DOG PACK into the living room, sat on the couch, and picked up the TV remote control. But the late-night offerings on the tube couldn't compete with her memories.

PEGGY WAS THE ONE WHO CALLED DALTON and told him about John Merrick. But she waited just long enough so that it was too late for him to help Grady. By the time he was back, the police knew about the gun in Dalton's case. She braced herself for arguments and yelling, but he just bowed his head and she watched the energy drain out of him. Or maybe it was his spirit.

"Why?" he asked no one in particular. "Why would he do this?"

She couldn't talk. He didn't seem to notice.

"It was all for that woman? He said it was about the job. He says he never even went near her."

"He's lied before," she managed.

"He says *you're* lying."

From somewhere she got the strength to look into his eyes. "Which one of us do you believe?" she asked him.

In the end, he believed her.

✴

The high-priced Atlanta legal team Dalton hired said there was nothing for Grady to do but plead guilty. The local good ol' boy Dalt hired to cover their bases on the home front agreed. Although the testimony from Li'l Bit and Maggie was damaging, they might have had a hope of shaking it. But the gun was too much to fight. So Dalt issued his ultimatum. And Grady capitulated. Dalton went by himself and sat in the court to listen while his son was sentenced and taken away.

When he came back home, Peggy was waiting for him.

"I'll leave, if you want me to," she said

He poured himself a drink. "No, I don't want you to go," he said. "You're all I have now." She had a drink with him, and he didn't say a word about it. It was the first time she drank before noon.

He quit working and turned over the running of the resort and the Gardens to the trust. He stopped walking the grounds of his home and never even noticed when the gardeners let several of his favorite pink tea roses die. He stayed up late after she had gone to bed and fell asleep watching television. Eventually, he took to sleeping in the guest bedroom down the hall. They stopped entertaining, leaving that to the energetic young man from Vanderbilt who was hired to run the resort in his place. Dalton dropped all his political interests. Except for Peggy's daily two hours on Li'l Bit's porch, neither of them went out much.

They lived together in a silence that screamed through the house, bouncing off walls and getting caught in the corners, and the only thing that ever seemed to quiet it was the tinkle of ice in glasses. They lived like that and waited for something to deliver them.

Then Dalton had his first heart attack. In a way it was a gift. Now they had an excuse for the silence. Peggy took over his physical therapy and his diet, devoting herself to him completely. And if he never thanked her, at least he leaned on her arm when they went on their daily walk. And if she missed the vital man who had brought her little presents for no reason except she was so cute, she kept it to herself. Because by then she understood the bargain she had made. And she understood how utterly useless it was to look back.

The only time Dalton left Charles Valley was to go visit Grady in prison. A driver from the Lodge picked him up and returned him. He never suggested that Peggy might want to go with him.

After one of those trips he brought home a stray dog his driver hadn't been able to miss when she ran out into the road. Her leg was broken and her mange was so bad the vet said it would be a kindness to put her down. But she was about to give birth to a litter, so Dalt kept her alive. When the pups were born, the mother was too sick to nurse. Peggy and Dalton fed them every three hours, wrapping their tiny bodies in blankets and resting them on their chests so the little guys could feel their hearts beat. Three pups and the mother died, but two survived. And when the vet said they were out of danger, Dalton looked genuinely happy for a moment.

The puppies had the run of the house. The screaming silence ended. And every once in a while, as they scrambled and barked around him, Peggy could hear Dalton laughing. She let herself hope that things would get better.

Then the call came from prison that Grady had been killed. And there was the funeral, where she didn't even try to stop Dalt from drinking; she just did her best to keep up with him. The puppies were banished to the yard and the house was still again. And she and Dalton went back to waiting.

They waited for one more year. Dalt's second heart attack was a massive coronary that killed him instantly. Li'l Bit and Maggie planned the funeral she could never remember, and Li'l Bit stayed with her for a week afterward. The night before Li'l Bit left to go home, she came into Peggy's room with the two young dogs on leashes.

"They've been neglected," she said, as the dogs shied and tried to run. "It'll take some doing to make them civilized. But you have to find something to take care of. It's the only way."

That night Peggy started working with the dogs. Dalt had called them Hunt and Whitey. She renamed them Ricky and Lucy.

Chapter Twenty-eight

SOMEHOW IN THE PROCESS of telling Laurel the story they'd lost the core of it, Maggie thought, as she settled into her big wingback chair. They hadn't made Laurel understand. And while Maggie wasn't about to apologize any more than Li'l Bit was, she did want to be understood. She wanted Laurel to realize the cost.

Poor proud Li'l Bit had lost the man who had made her happy for many years. Peggy had watched Dalton die by degrees and lived with the guilt of knowing she had helped cause it.

And what had she lost? Maggie asked herself. Vashti, of course. But then, they'd all lost the child for a long time. No, what Maggie had lost was an innocence about herself. She had never known she could be ruthless.

SHE HAD TAKEN Vashti and Lottie to Catherine in Atlanta. They had to keep the child away from Charles Valley, for her sake and theirs. So Vashti and Lottie stayed with Catherine until Grady pled guilty and Nella could leave Charles Valley. They decided Vashti would finish out her school year in a private academy in Atlanta. After that, they were going to send her north to a prep school in New England. Given her test scores and grades and all the new suddenly fashionable outreach programs for southern black students, it seemed like a pretty sure thing that she would get in somewhere. They all agreed the child had to have a fresh start.

It wasn't that they were unaware that what they were doing might be bad for Vashti emotionally. They were worried about that. The little girl had been through a major trauma, and to take her away from everything she knew at such a time was not the best way to help her heal. But it was too dangerous to let her stay at home. So they sent her off and held their breath.

Vashti seemed to adjust. Her grades were good and she never complained. Nella fussed sometimes because she was too quiet, but all in all it could have been a lot worse, and they breathed a collective sigh of relief when, after the year in Atlanta, Vashti was accepted at Phillips Academy in Andover, Massachusetts.

When Maggie and Lottie went to Atlanta to see Vashti and Nella off, it was a shock to see how much Vashti had changed. The bright little girl was gone. In her place was a tight, controlled child who never laughed.

"We can't expect her to be like she was before," Lottie said sadly.

"She's got so much bottled up inside," Nella told them.

So Maggie took Vashti aside and said, "If you feel troubled, you need to talk about what's bothering you to your momma. Or you can call your gran or me. Don't let it stay inside, dear one. Talk about it." That was all she said. Then Vashti and Nella left for Massachusetts.

Again, Vashti seemed to do well. Her teachers were pleased with her, though Nella was still fretting that she didn't seem to be making any friends. The worried women back home told one another she was just adapting to a new place. And, above all, as Lottie said, they couldn't expect her to be the same child she had been. There had to be scars.

❧

Then one Saturday morning Nella woke up in their apartment in Massachusetts to find that Vashti was gone. She'd left a note saying she was going home. Nella called Charles Valley, and Lottie hurried to Atlanta to try to intercept Vashti at the bus station. But while Lottie was gone, there was a knock at Maggie's kitchen door. She opened it to see Vashti standing on her back porch.

The child looked thin, and of course she was tired. But she had lost the tightness; there was a light in her eyes.

"Hello, Dr. Maggie," she said.

The scolding she'd planned to deliver vanished. Maggie hugged her and brought her into the house. "You scared us half to death, child," she said. "Are you all right?"

"I hitchhiked from Atlanta. I had to see you, Dr. Maggie."

She had never said *doctor* before. It had always been just plain Maggie.

It took a matter of minutes to call the bus station and have Lottie paged. But Vashti didn't want to speak to her grandmother. "I have to talk to you," she said.

Maggie settled her in a chair at her big kitchen table, put a pile of cookies and a glass of milk in front of her, and waited.

"I want to tell Mr. Dalton what I did," Vashti said. She hurried on as Maggie started to protest. "I can't keep it a secret anymore. I think about it all the time. I dream about it at night. You said I should talk about it—"

"To your mother, or your grandmother, or me."

"And I know what you'll tell me. That I wasn't to blame. That I'm a good girl and I didn't deserve to have this happen to me. Momma says it every time I wake up crying. But it doesn't help."

"Going to Dalton won't help either."

"It will if I can make him understand. That's what the priest said."

And then it all came out. Because of what Maggie had said about talking to someone, she'd gone to a Catholic church in Andover and asked to speak to the priest.

"I didn't tell him what happened that night, I just said I committed a crime. He said I should make amends to the person I'd injured. That's Mr. Dalton." The man probably thought she'd been shoplifting. Maggie loved her church, but it wasn't the first time she wished the clergy would stick to praying.

"That priest couldn't have known how complicated this is."

"If Mr. Dalt just understands—"

"Darling child, he won't. We all lied, and now his son is in prison. There is no way Dalton will ever understand that. You can't tell him. For your sake, and your mother's sake, and your grandmother's sake."

She watched the reality dawn on the little girl. "And for you and Miss Peggy and Miss Li'l Bit," she added.

I am a coward, Maggie thought. I should tell her not to worry about us. To just do what is best for her. But instead she nodded her head. "Yes," she said. "We'd all be in trouble."

The light in Vashti's eyes went out. "I'm afraid," she said softly. "I was so mad, Dr. Maggie. I remember how mad I was."

Maggie took a moment. "When you get back to school, I think we should try to find a psychotherapist for you to talk to."

Vashti shook her head. "You just said I can't tell anyone. It might hurt Gran and Momma and you."

"Talking to a doctor is different. They can't tell anyone what you say."

But it was too late to argue with Vashti; she'd already seen the possible repercussions. "I can't take the chance," she said. And as much as she hated herself for it, Maggie breathed a sigh of relief.

"Come outside with me," she said.

Her intentions were good, that was some comfort later. All she was trying to do that night was pass along the source of her own strength. She took Vashti out to the pecan tree and told her about young Lottie climbing up high like a queen over all she surveyed. She told the girl about Lottie's dream of being a doctor and the school that closed so she couldn't finish high school. She left out the night in the barn, but she told the rest—about Lottie's husband, who died trying to move his family to a better place, and her son who became a stranger. She told Lottie's story with all the love she had. And then she said, "You have the chance to make all the dreams come true, for all those people. You can get an education and you can do something wonderful. You can't throw this chance away. Too many people paid too much for it."

Vashti looked at her. "I'm so unhappy," she said.

"I'm not sure I know what happiness is," Maggie said. "It seems to come when you're not looking for it. It's not something you can control. But you can control how well you do your work. And working well can bring you joy."

She never meant it to be emotional blackmail. At least, that was what she told herself.

Whatever it was, it seemed to do the trick. Vashti went back to school, and once again her teachers were delighted even if her classmates found her aloof. She excelled in math and science, with an emphasis on biology. But Nella continued to fret. "She doesn't seem happy," she said. "All she does is work."

Then, when Vashti was sixteen, Grady was killed. And Maggie got a phone call. "You never should have covered for me!" Vashti's voice screamed into her ear. "You should have told the truth about what I did!"

"Vashti, darling, we talked about this—"

"Nothing would have happened to me if you had told the truth."

"You don't know that."

"Bullshit! I was a little girl. They wouldn't have done anything to me." She had a clipped northern way of talking. Maggie wondered what she looked like now.

"Dear one, you haven't been down here in a long time. You've forgotten how it is."

"Oh, yes, I know. You and Miss Peggy and Miss Li'l Bit had to take care of the poor little colored child."

"That isn't fair. Your granma and your momma wanted to protect you. We were all afraid for you."

"So you lied. And now another man is dead. And my momma and my granma are in it, so I can't say anything. I just have to live with this for the rest of my life."

"Grady Garrison killed your father."

"He should have gone to jail for *that,* not for what I did."

"It wasn't that simple."

"Go to hell, Dr. Maggie. You and Miss Peggy and Miss Li'l Bit and my gran can all rot in hell," she said, and slammed down the receiver.

The next time Maggie saw her was at Nella's funeral. When Vashti threw her out and young Laurel McCready overheard it.

Vashti stayed away from them for years after Nella's funeral. Even after Lottie's second stroke, she only came back for one day to see her grandmother installed in the nursing home and then she left. Maggie, Peggy, and Li'l Bit got used to the idea that she was gone from their lives. At least they tried to. Then one evening two years ago as Maggie was getting ready for bed, she heard a car come up the drive. By the time she got herself to the kitchen, Vashti was at the back door.

"Hi," she said. For a moment Maggie thought her mind was playing tricks on her, because Lottie was standing in front of her: Lottie at her prime, young and strong and beautiful. Except that Lottie had never worn a severe black suit. Or had her hair cropped and styled. "May I come in?" Vashti asked. She had a bag of potato chips.

Wordlessly, Maggie opened the door.

"I'm sorry if I startled you," Vashti said.

"No. I'm just so . . . I never expected . . ."

"I know. I'm sorry about that too. So sorry, Dr. Maggie."

"Don't. There's nothing to apologize for."

"Oh, I have a lot to apologize for." Then she grinned Lottie's grin when she stole the fruitcake batter. "But I'm counting on you to forgive me." The grin vanished. "I had to blame someone, Dr. Maggie. That was the only way I could live with it."

"I know. We all knew."

She started to say something; then she stopped. "Could we go outside?" she asked.

They went out and she walked to the pecan tree, with Maggie following. Vashti handed Maggie the potato-chip bag, reached for the lowest branch, and tried to pull herself up on it, but she couldn't get high enough. "How the hell did Gran ever climb that?" she asked.

"She wasn't wearing that skirt or those shoes," Maggie said.

"I wish I could get up there, just to know how it felt."

"Come with me," said Maggie.

They got the ladder out of the shed and Vashti carried it to the tree. She climbed up and perched herself on the lowest branch. "Is this cheating?" she asked.

"Only a little."

"Can you come up here? I think this branch will hold both of us."

Maggie climbed up and forced herself not to look down as she sat on the branch. If I break my neck it will be worth it, she thought.

"I don't feel very queenly," Vashti said.

"We have to climb higher for that," Maggie said.

"We should probably quit while we're ahead." Vashti began swinging her legs like a child. Maggie let hers swing a little too and waited for the girl who was now no longer a girl to say whatever it was she'd come so far to say. Vashti opened the bag and offered it to her.

"I guess the way normal people think of it, my life hasn't been all that hot," Vashti said at last. "No kids, no man. For a long time, not even a lot of friends. But when I add it up, it's been pretty amazing. Because of the work and the political stuff. You were right about that. It gave me joy."

"You sound like an old lady taking stock. You have years ahead of you."

"Well, actually, that's what I wanted to talk to you about."

And they sat in the pecan tree together while Vashti told her she was going to die.

And after she had choked back the tears that wouldn't do any good, and asked the questions that Vashti answered with scientific precision, Maggie listened while Vashti told her what she'd come for. "I want all three of the Miss Margarets there with me when I go," she said.

"You haven't wanted to see us for years."

"And now I'm coming back to lay this on you. It's a bitch, I know."

"That wasn't what I meant."

"I need you. I won't be afraid if you're there. I want three tough broads to see me out."

It wasn't a special night. There was no thunder or lighting, not even a full moon. Just still summer air and crickets making their dry music. She was sitting on a tree branch next to Vashti, who would be coming home to die. And the two of them were swinging their legs like little girls. And eating potato chips.

MAGGIE GOT TO HER FEET and went outside. She walked to the pecan tree and looked up to the top branches. When they'd talked to Laurel, she realized, what had gotten lost was the reason they did it all. They hadn't made Laurel understand about Vashti. Laurel should have heard more about her. Not just the things she accomplished, the circle she made in her life. I wish I'd told Laurel about Vashti coming back to Lottie's pecan tree, Maggie thought.

Chapter Twenty-nine

*L*AUREL WAS LYING ON A PIECE OF FURNITURE that wasn't her bed, fully clothed and covered with what appeared to be an itchy white wool blanket. She made herself focus and recognized the couch she was on.

"Denny?" she mumbled.

"She *is* alive after all." Denny loomed over her. "Coffee?" he asked.

She nodded.

"Lord, I don't know how you can do that after the night you had." He headed off to the kitchen of his tiny immaculate apartment.

"Do what?"

"Move your head around like that. I'd have been puking my guts out. There's a fresh toothbrush in the medicine cabinet," he called out, as she made her way to the bathroom.

When she came out he had a steaming cup of coffee and two white pills on the saucer waiting for her.

"Caffeine tablets?" she asked hopefully.

"Aspirin. You need me to fill you in on the gory details of your activities last night?"

"Nah. I was pissed off. I came to the bar, had a few beers, you wrestled me for my car keys in the parking lot, and I wound up on your ugly couch with your daddy's old navy blanket over me. Which itches."

"You are talking about a proud heirloom."

"I think it gave me a rash."

He eyed her in silence for a moment. "So what are you going to do about it, sugar?"

She couldn't remember if she'd told him about what she'd heard on Miss Li'l Bit's porch or not. "Do about what?" she asked.

"Whatever pissed you off so bad," he said.

She hadn't told him. "They lied, Denny," she said. "Ma was right."

"The three Miss Margarets?"

"All those years I spent thinking she was crazy. And being ashamed every time anyone said my daddy's name." She swallowed. Denny was staring at her, his face blank. "And then those old ladies sat there on their damn porch last night and told me they were right to do it. 'We're terribly sorry, dear Laurel, if we fucked up your life, but we had to do what we thought was best.' Can you believe that?"

"I can believe they'd do what they thought was right," he said.

"Do you want to hear what they told me?"

"All right."

But suddenly she wasn't sure she wanted to tell him. Because she didn't want to hear a lecture about seeing it from their point of view. More important, she didn't want to be told that there was nothing she could do about it. Which was what he was going to say, and he'd be right. She could go to the police, but she couldn't prove any of what she'd heard unless the three Miss Margarets were willing to repeat it. There was no way Hank would print the story, and even if he did, how many people would believe it? All she'd accomplish would be to rake up the old scandals about her father. And she could wait for Josh's book to come out for that— she stopped herself mid-thought. She knew what she wanted to do.

Denny was watching her. "You want to tell me about it, sugar?"

"No," she said. "I want you to drive me to the airport."

She got her ticket through the travel desk at the resort. They booked her on standby so it wouldn't cost more than three weeks' worth of groceries.

"Tell Hank I had to leave town," she said to Denny as they hit I-85. "Say . . . I don't know what. Make up some excuse."

"I'll tell him you had a death in the family," Denny said. He probably meant to be funny, but neither of them laughed. Then he said, "Laurel Selene, do me a favor. Do whatever you need to do in New York. Just get all this behind you."

PEGGY, MAGGIE, AND LI'L BIT were on the porch. Behind them the sun was setting. Peggy said, "Laurel is taking a trip to New York City. She left this evening. The girls at the travel desk down at the resort were talking about it."

Li'l Bit said, "Wasn't she friendly with that writer who was here from New York? The one who was writing a book about Vashti?"

"The way I heard it, she got to know him quite well," said Maggie.

The breezes that swirled through Li'l Bit's fruit trees were lovely on warm summer evenings. But in late autumn they were too chilly for comfort. Maggie cuddled deep into the pretty new jacket she'd just gotten from the Land's End catalog. Li'l Bit pulled a thick old sweater around her, and Peggy poured herself a drink.

LAUREL HAD CARRIED HER SUITCASE on board with her, so she walked off the plane straight to the waiting area where Josh was standing and beaming at her. He did a funny little shrug when he saw her and opened his arms wide.

Josh's apartment was about the same square footage as her house in the woods—without the land around it, of course. By way of compensation, there were two doormen in the lobby of his building who wore uniforms that looked vaguely military and screened all strangers who tried to enter. They also collected packages and messages and what seemed like mountains of dry cleaning for the people who lived there. Josh had purchased all this magnificence for over half a million dollars, and he paid another twelve hundred dollars a month in something called maintenance fees. He felt lucky that he had gotten it all so cheaply.

His kitchen was small but equipped with shiny professional-looking appliances, none of which were ever used. On one pristine counter next to the phone was a basket full of menus from restaurants that delivered. Josh's idea of eating at home, she learned, was to order his meals from these places. The rest of the time he went out. Every once in a while he picked up something already prepared at his supermarket and heated it. He called this cooking.

On her first night there he ordered something from a Chinese restaurant, but they went to bed and let the food get cold.

IT WAS THREE DAYS since Laurel left Charles Valley. At the meeting of Habitat for Humanity, Peggy finished signing a check for four thousand dollars to cover the cost of the roof on a home the group was building for a family.

"Will you be working on the house this weekend?" the president of the work committee asked her, as the meeting broke up and they headed out the door.

"I've got my hammer and nails."

"By the way, my son found a puppy at the dump this morning. The poor little thing was trying to run, but one paw was pretty badly torn up. Buckshot would be my guess. I called over at the shelter but they said they're full up."

"Where's the dog now?"

"I told Tommy he could put it on the back porch until I had a chance to talk to you. There's no way Big Tommy's going to let us keep it."

"I'll follow you home and pick it up," said Peggy.

And as she got into her car she thought how life kept on going. Houses needed roofs and stray dogs needed homes. The world didn't stop because she was waiting to hear what Laurel McCready was going to do next.

"WE HAVE A PROBLEM," said the nun who ran the interdenominational outreach program for all the churches in the area. She'd come into the thrift shop where Li'l Bit worked two afternoons a week. "We need drivers to take the Faranelli child to her chemo treatments in Macon. The other children are home from school for the week, and, frankly, the mother is overwhelmed."

"I'll take her," said Li'l Bit. It would be good to have more to do. It would keep her from thinking about Laurel in New York.

"I'LL CLEAN UP THIS BURN for now, but you have to get this child to the hospital. I'll call ahead for you," said Maggie, to her last patient of the day. It had been unusually busy, which was all to the good. Otherwise she would have spent the day fussing about what Laurel McCready was doing all this time in New York.

JOSH'S BUILDING HAD A GARDEN on the roof that was called a common space. He told her he liked to go up there in the evenings sometimes for a little peace and quiet. Given the fact that there were four other couples up there, peace and quiet seemed to be a relative term. Still it was one of the few places she'd found in Manhattan where you couldn't hear any noise from the street. Not a lot anyway. She huddled deep into the coat Josh had lent her and looked up at the sky. He said you almost never saw the stars because of the city lights—but the moon was full.

"Well?" he said. He was standing next to her; she saw the little puffs of his frozen breath out of the corner of her eye. She turned to look at him. The bright sky of the city was behind him; his face was shining with the cold. He'd just asked her—again—if she wanted to stay in New York with him.

"I don't know," she said.

"Stay until you do."

"I can't do that."

"Anything I can do to help you make up your mind?"

He was probably the nicest man she'd ever find. He was sexy and he was already halfway to being in love with her. If she stayed in New York he would see to it that she didn't have to struggle. She would live in his half-million-dollar apartment. He would even find her a job; he'd already told her that. Josh was the hero her ma had been waiting for, the man who would take care of them. Laurel wondered what it felt like to have someone take care of you.

Down below her on the street a car alarm went off. Dogs started barking. She looked up again and thought it probably wouldn't be too long before you never even missed seeing the stars.

"You really love this city, don't you?" she said.

"It's my home."

"I know."

"You don't have to make up your mind right now."

But she did. She had to make up her mind about a couple of things. "May I read your book about Vashti?" she asked.

"It's a rough draft."

"I know. May I?"

"Yes."

By the time she finished it, he had ordered in some pasta from a Tuscan restaurant.

"Well?" he asked.

"It's going to be a great book, Josh."

"Yeah?"

"Yeah. Makes me wish I'd known her."

"She was an amazing woman."

She nodded. "I got that. I liked the way you wrote the end. About her going full circle."

PEGGY WONDERED IF SHE SHOULD GO INSIDE and get an afghan for Maggie. Even though the sun was still shining, it was too cold to stay out on the porch. But none of them wanted to go inside yet. Because Laurel had been gone for four days, and somehow it was easier not to be cooped up indoors. Although they weren't admitting it.

Whatever happens, I can handle it, Peggy thought. But Li'l Bit and Maggie are too old for the humiliation.

I'll be all right, Maggie thought. At my age, what can they do to me? But Li'l Bit and Peggy are still young enough that they could be hurt.

I'm tough, Li'l Bit thought. But Peggy and Maggie are so breakable.

There was the sound of a car coming down the gravel driveway. Li'l Bit and Peggy got up and moved to the edge of the porch. Maggie made herself take a deep breath.

Laurel got out of her car and started walking across the lawn to the porch. She was carrying a brown paper bag. "I've been away for a few days," she said.

"To New York—we know," said Li'l Bit.

"Did you have a good time?" asked Peggy.

"I thought there was something I wanted to do there—but there wasn't."

"Oh," said Maggie.

"Can I offer you something to drink?" asked Li'l Bit.

"Actually I brought some beer, if that's okay."

"Beer. Why didn't I think of that?" said Li'l Bit. "Would you like a glass?"

"I can drink it like this," Laurel said.

She sat on the front step. Li'l Bit sat back in her father's chair, and Peggy returned to her rocker. Maggie swung gently on her swing.

"Laurel, have you ever thought of adopting a dog?" Peggy asked.

"Tomorrow I'll get in a supply of beer," Li'l Bit said, to no one in particular.

ABOUT THE AUTHOR

LOUISE SHAFFER, a graduate of Yale Drama School, has written for television and has appeared on Broadway, in TV movies, and in daytime dramas, earning an Emmy for her work on *Ryan's Hope*. Shaffer and her husband live in the Lower Hudson Valley.

Visit her website at www.threemissmargarets.com. Shaffer can be reached at www.contactshaffer.com.

ABOUT THE TYPE

This book was set in Bembo, a typeface based on an old-style Roman face that was used for Cardinal Bembo's tract *De Aetna* in 1495. Bembo was cut by Francisco Griffo in the early sixteenth century. The Lanston Monotype Machine Company of Philadelphia brought the well-proportioned letter forms of Bembo to the United States in the 1930s.

12